almost there

Dani Deane Series #2

Laurel Garver

Copyright © 2016 Laurel W. Garver

Paperback edition
ISBN 978-1530836918

Cover photo by Oleander Schatzki

For my mother,
keeper of the family stories
who taught me to look
for grace in dark places.

Also by Laurel Garver

Never Gone
Dani Deane Series #1

Muddy-Fingered Midnights

Emotions in the Wild:
A Writer's Observation Journal

Chapter 1

In Paris, art seeps into your feet and drips from your fingertips. Dark-eyed buskers in berets squeeze out sweet accordion songs, and the birds trill along. The air tastes like *crème brûlée*; the light is melted butter. Or so I've heard. In two weeks, I'll find out for myself.

I can see it all now: In the golden mornings, Mum and I will set up matching easels on the banks of the Seine and paint side-by-side. She'll be too excited to sleep till noon, too inspired to stare blankly at the wall. Her sadness will fall away like a too-heavy coat, and she'll once again fill canvas after canvas with works of aching beauty.

We'll while away the hot afternoons in the Louvre, communing with the masters. Finally meet some of her long-lost French relatives. Wear goofy hats and stuff ourselves with pastries and laugh like we haven't in ages. Every day will be a chick-flick montage of *joie de vivre*.

Or is it *joyeux de vivre*? Theo would know.

"Theo? Thebes?" I shake my boyfriend, who snoozes beside me on the couch with his school tie loosely askew and notebook open in his lap. When he doesn't react, I stroke his left forearm. He swats at me with an oar-calloused hand, mutters, "Stalin... Churchill...Roosevelt."

He must be in bad shape if he's dreaming history notes. "Never mind. Just rest."

I'm not exactly the most diligent study buddy either. It's hard to focus when I'm two finals from freedom. Two finals till I can shop for my France wardrobe, till I can dedicate maximum brain space to *merci, s'il vous plaît,* and three thousand other phrases that will keep me from looking like a lazy *américaine.*

I pull out my highlighter and mark my top three café picks near Notre Dame Cathedral in *Paris, Summer 2009*, just published in March. I wonder if these places serve iced decaf lattes. Or is iced coffee a gauche American concoction? Yet another thing to ask Theo.

His sleeping face pinches. I reach to touch his cheek, then stop. Facing finals right after two weekend crew regattas in a row has already made him totally stressed and exhausted. I'm probably stressing him more by talking nonstop about my trip. For him, it means five long weeks apart. We'll Skype every day and muddle through somehow. The painful separation will be totally worth it when Paris works its magic and Mum's back to normal.

The kitchen phone jangles and I guiltily stuff my Paris guidebook under a couch cushion. Theo stirs, but doesn't shift enough to free my hair from under his sleep-heavy head.

Why isn't Mum answering? Is she napping again?

With a swift tug, I free my hair. The hefty textbook I'm supposed to be studying slides off my lap and thuds to the floor. I sprint to the kitchen, reaching the phone on the tenth ring.

"Mrs. Deane? Mrs. Grace Tilman Deane?" A woman asks.

"Just a sec. I'll get her."

I carry the handset through the apartment to the spare bedroom we use as a studio and gingerly knock on the door. No answer. Is Mum hiding or deep in another epic zone-out? Since she left her stressful Madison Avenue advertising job for art school, thanks to a foundation started in my late father's memory, Mum should be having the time of her life. Art was the passion she couldn't pursue when she was young for a lot of stupid reasons. But now that she's actually living her lost dream, paint seems to dry on her palettes more than her canvases.

I press my ear to the door and hear only the low hum of the air conditioning. When I peek inside, our husky-mix Rhys raises his head, perks his ears, gives a fangy yawn. On the easel above him sits a white canvas with a single red stripe down the center. Beside the easel is an empty stool. What the heck? Did she go back to bed?

I stare at the phone a moment. Chances are it's just some stupid survey or courtesy call. Nothing worth waking Mum for.

I clear my throat and mimic Mum's smoky alto. "Hello?"

"Mrs. Deane? This is Nurse Lowman from North Penn Health System. In Wilkes-Barre, Pennsylvania? It's about your father. Daniel Tilman?"

Good Lord, now what? Poppa hasn't gone berserk on another doctor, has he? You'd think the time he got hauled off by security would have shamed him into changing his ways. Mum should let them press charges this time. Poppa might finally get a clue about how big a jerk he is.

I deliver the standard Mum line: "My apologies. How can I assist?"

"There's been an accident, Mrs. Deane. Your father...his condition is needing surgery and we have to get your approval to proceed."

My guts drop seven stories. I wouldn't be surprised to find them out on Columbus, pancake-flattened and dimpled with taxi tire marks. "Poppa's had an accident?" I squeak.

"This isn't Mrs. Deane, is it?" Her tone is so cold, my wet tongue would stick to it.

"Sorry, it's...Danielle, the daughter, I mean Mr. Tilman's granddaughter. I'm sorry about pretending to be my mother. I thought you were a telemarketer and Mum's not feeling well. Since I'm family, too, it wouldn't be against HIPAA regulations for you to tell me what happened, and I can let her know, right?"

"I'm afraid not, Danielle. I have to speak to your actual mother."

Crap. It must be bad. Really bad.

"Um, okay. I'll, ah, go find her." I cover the mouthpiece and head to the master bedroom.

In the phone, I can distantly hear the nurse crack up and tell her medical cronies, "Get a load of this: I've got some kid from New York on the phone who knows about HIPAA regulations! City kids! Gawd. She's probably been playing the stock market since kindergarten."

I'd love to give this bumpkin nurse chick a piece of my mind. Tell her that the adult world finds some of us young and makes us grow up fast, whether we're ready or not.

But I don't say this, because my persistent knocks are getting no response from Mum at all. As I step into her dark bedroom, I'm surprised by a strange, sour smell. I pat her bed, expecting to feel the warm hump of a leg. Instead, I touch something thick and sticky. Blood? I bring my hand to my nose. Ugh. Spoiled milk.

I switch on the bedside lamp and find a toppled Stonyfield ice cream tub that's left a gooey puddle on her silk bedspread. Okay, it's organic, but still. The woman's a gym addict. Grabbing a tissue to clean the goo off my fingers, I see a worse sign: Mum's cell phone is on the dresser. But Mum is gone.

I take a deep breath, then uncover the mouthpiece of the phone. "Um…" I tell the nurse, "I think we might need to call you back."

* * *

Seeing the empty key hook by the front door sucks the air right out of me. Dear God, no. I crush the paper scrap with the hospital's number in a trembling fist. For all I know, Poppa will be dead in minutes if they don't operate. But without Mum's approval, they legally can't.

I cannot believe Mum left Theo and me alone in the apartment. She usually checks on us every ten minutes like clockwork, bugging us with questions or roping Theo into chores like opening jars or pulling things off high shelves. It's like she has this bizarre fear that we're going to rip each other's clothes off at any moment and make me the next teen pregnancy statistic.

Well, she can't have gone far — probably just to the little market on Columbus to pick up dinner ingredients. Surely she'll be back any minute. I should call the front desk and ask the doorman if he saw her go out. Theo could hold down the fort while I look for her.

Gosh, I can just picture her standing in line at Rico's, looking for all the world like a bohemian free spirit in her snug t-shirt, paint-spattered jeans, strappy sandals, gobs of gypsy jewelry, hair in long, loose layers. She'll glance up from her basket of Thai basil and coconut milk, see my face and just know. Know that I'm about to hurl a bomb at her. Know that trouble's found her yet again, like it always does.

How can I tell her? How? It's only been a year and a half since Dad's car crash and the month of ICU agony before he was snatched from us. How can she possibly cope with Poppa right now? He's as fatherly to her as a lion is to a gazelle.

I just wish I could make this all go away.

I look at the hospital number in my hand again, and my mouth goes as dry as a day-old croissant. What if Poppa and his car—? There's no ice on the roads, but a couch could tumble off a truck, or a rogue deer leap out of the woods and straight through his windshield. Poppa could have massive bleeding on the brain right now — pressure building like floodwaters behind a levee, flattening everything. Cells, synapses, ganglion crushed, dying, dead. I've seen it before.

My grand Paris dream starts to pull away, a face in a taxi window. Off toward Midtown. Off to find a more worthy recipient.

Who can help me stop this taxi from driving away with my dream?

A homeless drug addict steps in front of the taxi in my mind and it stops. The coked-up guy stands there, fists on hips, chin jutted out, dark eyes flashing, as if daring the driver to flatten him in his frayed cords and Nietzsche T-shirt. Uncle David?

He winks at me, then in a blink transforms from his old stoner self into the bald, flannel-shirted craftsman I now know and love. Of course. If there's anyone who can help me sort out what to do about Poppa, it's Mum's younger brother, the prodigal son.

I carry the phone to my bedroom, hit four on speed dial.

Chapter 2

"Ah-yup," Uncle David says, another weird Maine expression that's crept into his speech. A table saw whines in the background. The tone changes as the blade tastes wood, gearing up to a horrific shriek like someone being tortured. A woman with serious lung capacity. A shot-putter. One of those beefy opera singers.

I close my bedroom door, shout, "Hey! It's Dani. Could you go to your office maybe?"

"Hey niece o'mine, what'd ya say? Keegan's ripping boards and I can't hear squat. I better go to my office." He shouts something to his assistant and gradually the heinous squealing fades. "A'right. Office. Shoot."

"I need your help right away. Some hospital called saying Poppa's been in an accident and they want to operate immediately and they need approval from Mum, but she's not here and I don't know where she went or exactly how long she'll be gone or anything, and the nurse lady who called wouldn't give me any details at all but it must be pretty bad if they have to operate. I'm seriously freaking out. Could you please, please, please call the hospital and see if you can find out what the heck is going on and give them the okay to operate?"

"Whoa. Accident? What kind of accident? Car accident?"

Images of crumpled fenders, broken glass, thick smoke, and charred car remains click through my mind in rapid succession. *Not again, Lord. Please, not again.* I wobble, sink onto my bed. "I—. I don't *know*," I choke.

"Sorry, I'm just in shock. I mean, after your dad..." he gives a low whistle. "Gracie's been through this kind of hell one too many times. Give me that number. I'll see what I can do."

"Thanks," I wipe my eyes and give him the nurse's name and number. "What should I do now? Mum could be back any time. She's gonna just curl up and die when she finds out."

"Well..." he drawls, "I reckon there might be, you know, divine providence in her missing that call. It's about time I had a go at being the responsible kid. Don't you worry, and don't say nothing. Got it?"

"You want me to lie to Mum?"

"I'd like to spare Sis some grief for a change, so let's keep this between us for now. No guarantees it'll work, but it's worth a shot. Go back to what you were doing and just be normal."

I snort. "This should be good. I've got two finals tomorrow."

"I'm real sorry, Dani. Go study and try not to worry too much. God's watching over you and Gracie. He won't let you be tested beyond what you can bear, as the Good Book says."

* * *

Just be normal, Uncle David said. Right. I've got exams, a dying grandparent, a missing mother. My dream summer hanging in the balance. Well, not so much a dream as a nightmare-chaser. An antidote to the poison that's been building inside of Mum.

I plod back to the living room. My throat aches even more when I see Theo's face tipped onto a couch cushion, muscles slack in peaceful sleep. If Mum and I don't get to Paris, then what? Mum becomes even more sad, more sick? Breaks down? Goes to the hospital and I go where? To freaking Maine with Uncle David? I'd rather sleep on park benches.

I kneel at Theo's feet and shovel papers back into my history binder. My face's reflection in his polished school shoes is stretched like a limp, useless noodle.

How could Uncle David say we're not being tested beyond what we can bear? Jeez. Mum and I are still trying to recover from losing Dad. Do we never get to settle into normal? Real normal, not pretend normal. Not resigned normal.

Church words flood my mind and push back the rising tide of self-pity. What Uncle David said is only half-true. Part of the story. There's more to that passage — a promise: "When you are tested, he will provide a way out, so that you can bear up under it."

Right. There *is* a way out. My uncle will handle this. He'll get Poppa the care he needs and everything will be fine. Mum can stay at a safe distance and just…send him a get well card. We'll head to Paris as planned and leave our worries behind.

I pile my binder and textbook on the far end of the couch, untuck my shirt again, twist my pleated skirt askew, and sink into the cushions beside my boyfriend. Theo registers my return by dropping his head back on my shoulder and draping his warm arm across me.

I pull *History: Modern to Contemporary* onto my lap and pretend to be engrossed in the Soviet takeover of Eastern Europe, the Iron Curtain falling, the Cold War blowing in. But I can't stop my hands from trembling as I turn the pages. I practice French phrases in my head, but *quelle heure est-il?* sounds vaguely like "kill or steal" and I picture Parisian police descending on me for asking the time. I open my mental sketch book and let strokes flow over the whiteness, but the virtual charcoal stick crumbles in my inner grasp.

All right, God, I want to trust you here, but what the heck are you doing? How will Mum ever believe you aren't out to get her? She needs to be healed, not drawn into Poppa's world and his hateful words: she's "uppity," "useless," "a waste of space" with "no use for a soul."

I know you expect me to be still, Lord, and believe you're going to fix this. Can't you give me something to hold onto before I tear out my own hair?

Theo grunts in his sleep, nuzzles against my collarbone, his whiskers scritching across cotton. I rest my cheek on the back of his head and breathe in the familiar scent of his scalp, his musky vanilla cologne. My anxious mind stops flailing and I sink into memories of our last rooftop picnic.

We nestled on a tattered afghan, my spine curled against Theo's chest, blanketed from the chilly spring air by his toasty arms. The sun sank behind the buildings and distant windows lit up, one by one. In awed silence we sat, listening to whirring HVAC units and the distant hum and honk of traffic below. I could not imagine a more perfect peace than this.

But soon the roof access door banged open. Mum appeared in her paint-spattered smock, bringing us a bag of Chinese takeout. Theo jumped to his feet to make space for her on the blanket, but she backed away, shaking her head. She stared at the sparkling Manhattan skyline for a moment and her shoulders sagged under some invisible weight. Then, without a word, she turned and disappeared down the stairs.

In her overworked fog — or whatever was making her so droopy — Mum had forgotten to send up normal silverware. So Theo and I cracked apart the cheap chopsticks from the bottom of the bag and fed each other sloppy clumps of Chinese chicken and shrimp. Between bites, we talked about the years to come — him studying psychology, me, art. Living with our families and commuting to college here in the city to save money.

"I'll save as much of my inheritance as I can," I said, "so we can get a place of our own."

Theo prodded his Lo-mein, his ears turning pink. "I take it you plan a wedding in there somewhere," he said, more to the noodles than to me. "Shacking up doesn't seem your style."

"Yours either."

"I think my family would be more supportive of that than me getting married at twenty."

I swallowed hard. "That's just two years from now. You think...."

"Can we pull it off? I don't know, Dee. We're just day-dreaming here, right?"

Were we? It felt so tantalizingly possible. I could picture us brushing our teeth at a dinky apartment sink, barefoot and sleep rumpled.

"We'd have my trust fund and I could learn Web design. Mum has tons of business contacts — plenty to keep us fed and housed while you do med school and then your psychiatry residency."

"Web design? Uh-uh. These hands?" He grasped my wrists and lifted my palms to eye level. "They're meant to make masterpieces, not code HTML."

"I can still draw and paint on the side. Heck, I'd rather be a janitor and be with you, than have gallery shows without you."

"I don't deserve you." He pulled me close and kissed me. Soy sauce and spice.

WOOF! WO-WOOF! WOOF!

Rhys's barking snaps me out of my reverie. As he nudges open the studio and bolts for the front door, my heart becomes a thumping drum again. It's Mum. She's back.

I get my nose out of Theo's sweet-smelling hair and rivet my attention on the textbook in my lap. Theo rolls away from me, onto his other side, but he doesn't wake.

Here goes. Act One of *Just Be Normal.* Places everyone. Aaand, action!

Mum shuffles in, sorting a pile of mail, while Rhys runs circles around her. Instead of her usual strappy sandals, she's wearing ratty slippers, the once-white chenille now gray and frayed. Her hair is tangled and there's a coffee ring on the leg of her jeans. Yikes.

"Hey." Her voice is limp and breathy. "How's the studying going?"

"Great. Super stimulating. Right, Theo?"

Mum thumbs through a magazine and absently pats Rhys's head. She still hasn't noticed snooze boy.

"Yeah, definitely," I say in a pitiful imitation of Theo's bass voice. "Once we dropped some acid, the '60s came alive for us."

"What?" Mum's gaze drifts up and she takes in the scene. "He's asleep *again*?"

"Of course. He's used to crew practice at dawn. When four p.m. comes, he's out. I swear you could set clocks by it."

"Another early bird." Mum's chin puckers beneath her downturned mouth — her missing Dad expression. He woke at six every day, annoyingly chipper.

Her eyes roam. I turn to see what's caught her attention. On the wall behind me is a snapshot from my parents' engagement day, shot by a Japanese tourist Dad pressed into service, so the story goes. Dad's on one knee at Mum's feet in a grassy spot among English castle ruins. She cradles his face in her hands as if it were pure gold.

Gold turned to dust.

Don't go there. Don't let Mum go there, either.

"I suppose you told Sleeping Beauty where you went?" I say.

"He said you were in the bathroom, and I thought I'd be right back. But the condo association president cornered me in the mailroom. What an exhausting motor mouth. I could use a nap."

Another nap? No, no, no. Come on, brain. Think upbeat. Think perky.

"So!" I chirp, "What came in the mail? Anything good?"

Mum flips through the pile again. She frowns and waves a lime-green postcard at me — an RSVP card for my seventeenth birthday bash, held weeks ago. "This came from Poppa Tilman. I don't know why he bothered after all this time."

All the blood in my head drops to my toes. If I weren't already sitting, I'd swoon. Why did that have to come today, of all days?

I stuff my shaking hands under my thighs. "M-maybe it, uh, got lost in the mail."

"I don't think so. There's a note on the back: 'Sorry I missed your party, pumpkin. I'm not coping well with paper at the moment. Those infernal women your mother keeps sending can't work with my system or stay out of my business. But don't worry your pretty head none. I ordered something special that's due to ship any day now.' I should have known his silence about the invitation wasn't something so simple as rudeness."

"You think he fired *another* maid?"

"Obviously. Not that he'd bother telling me about it. In my memory, Pop's jealously guarded system is to keep every last thing and make piles to the ceiling. I'm surprised the contents of his house haven't spontaneously combusted, they're packed in so tight."

The cordless phone rings from the far end table, just out of reach. Mum picks it up and checks the caller ID. "Ah, it's David. I'll take this in the studio. Why don't you ask Theo to stay for dinner? I'm sure he'll perk up with a little food."

I say "okay" to Mum's departing back and reach to Rhys for comfort. Stroking his fluffy neck slows my galloping heart. "Oh, Rhysie, I hope Uncle David's just making small talk and he'll ask for me soon, that he won't tell her anything. For now, I guess we need to play normal. Lay down, boy." He settles at my feet with a grunt of protest.

I reach for Theo's shoulder and give him a little shake. Then a harder one. "Thebes?"

He lifts his heavy head off of me. His hazel eyes flutter open, more gold than green in the afternoon light. He groans. "Oh, Dani, I did it again, didn't I? Jeez, I'm sorry. I'm just so tired all the time. Maybe I need to start drinking coffee like you do."

I smile. "It would stunt your growth."

"Little late for that, don't you think?" He leans back, stretching, and his firm stomach peeks between his shirt hem and the waistband of his khakis. I look away and sit on my hands again before my hormones get the better of me.

"Mum wants to know if you can stay for supper."

"Yeah?" he says, poking me in the ribs. "What about you?" Poke. "Do you want me?" Poke, poke, poke. "To stay?"

"Not if you're gonna be a bully."

"*Moi?*" He strikes a Miss Piggy pose.

"*Non, ta jument méchante, qui ronfle comme un os endormi.*"

Theo roars with laughter. "My evil what? Mare? Who snores like a sleepy bone?"

"I meant twin. Ju-something…else."

"Ah. *Jumeau méchant.* Evil twin. And I do not snore. Especially not like a bone."

I roll my eyes. "Bear. I wanted to say bear."

"*Ours*, not *os. Bien? Dis-le et répète*, Danielle."

You say it. Repeat. Oh, brother.

I tip my head side to side as I chant, "*Ours, ours, ours, ours, ours.* Happy?"

"Come on, babe, cheer up. Your grammar's quite good. You used the feminine adjective with *jument*, which was great, even if it wasn't the noun you wanted."

"I'm never gonna get this. Parisians will bludgeon me with baguettes for crimes against the mother tongue."

18

"You are getting it. You're brave enough to try making jokes in another language, which is pretty complicated. Honestly, you've picked up in six months what it took me three years to learn. Of course, I didn't have a patient instructor completely dedicated to my success."

"Come on, Thebes. You've got to be bored out of your mind teaching a dunce like me."

"You are way too hard on yourself. So you made a mistake. Big deal. Who doesn't? Heck, I'm learning here, too. Remember the flashcard fiasco?"

"I'd rather not." Theo pounding the wall, purple-faced; me hunkered in a distant corner, utterly stunned by his rare flare of temper — not a scene I care to replay. Ever.

"Well, me neither. That was totally my bad. But I learned from it, right? I've had quite the adventure developing my cutting-edge teaching techniques."

I snort.

"Yeah? You doubt me? I'm deeply insulted."

"What's so cutting edge about, 'Dis-le et répète'?"

"How do you think you learned to draw? Practice. Years of filling sketch pads until your scribbles became art. Anyone who thinks they can get some new skill without practice is an idiot. So once we get through finals, we will répèter, en français every day, until you go. Très bien?"

Mum strides into the living room clenching the phone. I can almost smell the fury pulsing out of her like fumes from a hot engine.

Pas bien. Mal. Très, très mal.

"There's been a change of plans," she says.

Chapter 3

"Dinner's off," Mum says. "I need to leave for Pennsylvania right now."

Theo and I leap to our feet, saying in chorus, "What's going on?"

This is a new wrinkle. Poppa's prognosis must be really bad. But, hey, at least I didn't have to fake being surprised.

"Your grandfather." She slaps her palm with the phone. "He collapsed at the hardware store and broke his hip from the fall. A neighbor took him to the hospital. He'll be heading into surgery sometime this evening."

"What do you mean 'collapsed'? Did he have a heart attack or something?"

She runs a hand through her hair and it stays mussed like it's been gelled. Or not washed in days. "They're not sure. Could be a vascular problem. Maybe a TIA."

"What's that?"

"It's a kind of mild stroke," Theo says.

"A stroke!" My body feels like someone poured lead into it. Did I do this, wishing the Poppa problem would just go away so Mum and I can jet off to Paris? "Could he die?"

She throws up her hands. "How should I know? These medical people never tell you anything useful. He's stable. They're running tests."

Stable. One of those vague, happy-sounding hospital words. Dad was "stable" in a coma for weeks after his car accident. Until he wasn't. And then he was dead. Stable means they don't have a freaking clue if a person will pull through or not.

"I need..." Mum counts off a list on her fingers, mumbling. I can make out only her last few words. *Oh, Graham.*

Dad.

She needs him. I need him. Somehow we have to keep muddling through without him. All I know for sure is that he'd want me to do everything in my power to help her now.

"What can I do, Mum? Should I pack for us? Gather Rhys's gear?"

"You want me to walk him before you guys head out?" Theo offers.

"Quiet!" Mum barks. "I need a moment to think." She bows her head and scratches her scalp like she's got an intense itch — or she's trying to silence voices only she can hear.

I look to Theo, who's studying her with brow-furrowed concern. His gaze drifts down to her slippers, then his eyes snap up and meet mine. I nod. *I know. She's getting worse.*

I touch her shoulder. "Mum, I think you should let Uncle David take care of this."

"He's seven hours away, and I'm only three."

"What about the neighbor who took him to the hospital?" Theo suggests.

Mum shakes her head. "Family needs to be there soon, or we'll have social workers snooping around, making serious trouble when they see the conditions he's living in." She loudly exhales, straightens, and pats her hair into a tidier arrangement. "Call Heather, darling, and see if you can stay with her tonight. I'll arrange...something for you tomorrow."

"No way. I'm coming with you."

"Absolutely not, Dani. You'll take your exams as scheduled."

I exchange a look with Theo. *Help me out here, Thebes.*

He dips his chin. Message received. "She could do make-ups. It is a family emergency."

Mum frowns. "Stop ganging up on me. There won't be anything to do tonight but paperwork. It's not worth missing your finals to watch me fill in forms. If you honestly want to help, stop stalling."

"Okay, fine." I gather my school stuff, separating my notes from Theo's color-coded index cards. For now, I bide my time until I can come up with another plan.

"How 'bout me, Mrs. D?" Theo asks. "Should I pack you some dinner?"

Mum looks up from the phone. "Sure. That would be lovely." She wanders off, scrolling through the contacts list.

I hand Theo his flashcards. "Mum's thermal lunch bag is—"

"Hanging inside the pantry. I know, Dani," he huffs. "I'm here almost every day. I wish you wouldn't treat me like I'm a stranger."

"I didn't mean—. I'm just…trying to help," I choke.

"Sorry." He wraps me in a hug. "You're totally freaked out, and here I am snapping at you."

"This wasn't supposed to happen. My uncle promised he'd take care of Poppa this time. He promised! Mum's cleaned up a thousand and one of David's messes. He owes her!"

Theo pulls back, grasps my shoulders. "Wait a minute. Are you telling me you knew about this already?"

"Well, kind of. About a half hour ago the hospital called saying Poppa had an accident, but they wouldn't give any details. There was no one here but me to deal with it, so I called my uncle. He said he'd take care of everything, keep Mum out of the problem entirely."

His arms go slack. "No one here? I was here. You couldn't wake me up?"

I shrug, like "no big deal," but my face flares with shame. I turn away and fiddle with my shirt buttons.

Theo hunkers down, tries to make eye contact. "Come, *ma chérie*, do tell."

I rub my forehead to avoid his gaze. "You seemed incredibly tired. I guess I didn't want to, um…bother you."

"Your problems are my problems and they don't bother me. But this," he indicates the space between us, "*This* bothers me. Hiding stuff, pushing me away."

"Sorry, Thebes. I don't always think straight under pressure."

He frowns, then motions me to follow. "Come on. You can tell me what's going on while I pack your mom's dinner."

In the kitchen, he gathers sandwich ingredients while I wash and cut up strawberries.

"So there I was, being the idiot narcoleptic," Theo says, slathering Dijon on rye, "and you get this phone call about your grandfather. What was going through your head?"

I set down my knife. "This is gonna sound terrible, but… Paris. I was thinking about how badly Mum needs this trip. Her depression gets deeper every day. How could she possibly deal with a major crisis? Especially one with her father." I shudder.

"What's so bad about him, other than being a slob?" Theo piles on lettuce so high, Mum won't be able to get her mouth around this crazy sandwich.

"He tells Mum he wished she'd been aborted, like all the time."

"Whoa. Why?"

"Long story. She's spent her life trying to please him. Appease him. Like he's an angry Assyrian deity that curses you until you make the proper sacrifice. Anyway, when I couldn't find Mum earlier, I got totally paralyzed. Then the solution just came to me. Call my uncle. I mean, it's his father, too."

"And he told you to lie about the whole thing?"

"No. He just said he'd handle it and he asked me to not say anything. But I didn't lie."

"It's kind of a thin line, isn't it?"

"Not when you're protecting someone. Abraham let the Egyptians think his wife was his sister to keep her safe, and three religions call him a hero."

When I hand him a yogurt for Mum's bag, he gives me a hard look, but says nothing.

"It seems so wrong to let Mum face this mess alone. And how am I supposed to study? I feel like I've got a panicked hamster scampering through my brain. I wish I knew what we're really dealing with. How serious is a TIA? A broken hip is really bad, too, isn't it?"

"I'm not sure, but...I could see what the Internet has to say while you call Heather. Don't count Paris out yet, okay?"

I nod.

"And, Dani?" He zips and unzips Mum's thermal bag. "Don't count me out, either."

* * *

"Hey," my best friend Heather gasps at the other end of the line. "This Mr. Barnum or Mr. Bailey? I got some new recruits. Y'all just come on down 'n get 'em." Even after five years living up north, her Georgia twang persists.

"Heather? Is everything okay?"

"Could be better. Daddy won't be back from Dallas till six and Mama went to pick up a couple more kids for the pox party. I've gotta hold down the fort."

"A *what* party?"

"Pox. Paulie got chickenpox. His friends who haven't had it yet are coming over to get exposed. About half the first grade will be here tonight."

Her brother must look like a spotted freak with pox blisters on top of all those freckles. "Wait, kids are trying to get chicken-pox on purpose?"

She grunts. "Some parents are scared that vaccines cause autism. Crazy, right?"

"I don't know. I've heard Mum say—"

"NO!" Heather suddenly yells, "No licking!"

Good Lord, please let that be about popsicles that shouldn't be shared. An apocalyptic image of oozing sores and spit pops into my head. I fan away the wave of nausea. No way can I stay at Heather's house of plague tonight. I'm pretty sure I haven't been immunized either.

"Man alive," Heather continues. "I am *this close* to duct taping some mouths shut. As soon as Mama gets back, I'm outta here. I've got big plans for tonight."

"You do? What about our art final?"

"My presentation is all ready and it will blow your mind. I got some technical help after the English final. You wouldn't believe who, but it was so unexpected, so fantastic. We work together amazingly well. That's something worth celebrating, right? Hang on a minute, Dani. I've got a situation." There's a rustling sound, then she yells, "Nico, sit down! Paulie, pants on! I'm gonna tell Daddy! You know he'll tan your spotted hide!"

"Halt, citizens! Gather round," a guy says with a voice too deep to be one of Heather's three brothers, who are all under twelve. If her dad is out of town, who was that?

"Listen up, midgets," Heather says. "We're playing a game, okay?"

"Simon Says," the guy continues. "Heather's up first."

Heather giggles like a derpy cheerleader. "Ready? Simon says, 'Freeze!' Good. Simon says, 'Touch your nose!' Nice. Hop on one foot! Sorry, Paulie, I didn't say 'Simon says.' You're out. Go sit on the couch. Your turn to be Simon, Brady."

The phone rustles and Heather heaves a big sigh. "All right, that's under control."

"Who's playing 'Simon Says'?" I ask. "I distinctly heard a male voice that's not a kid."

"Is there something in *particular* you need?" she says, her voice flaring. "'Cause I kind of have my hands full here."

Oh-kay. Something weird is going on if Heather's keeping secrets. She normally over-shares about everything, from her test grades to her hormonal food cravings.

How could I be so stupid? Her "technical help" must be there right now, in earshot. A guy, of course. And if she's being this coy about it, someone she really, really likes.

I can't tell her about Poppa. Not when she finally has a date. I've been praying for this since her high-drama relationship with Theo's best friend Fletcher ended on Valentine's day — their third ugly breakup. Talk about awkward. I know she'd come stay with me in a heartbeat, but she really needs a new guy.

"It's nothing important," I say. "Have fun celebrating. See ya tomorrow."

Now what? Thursdays Amy is at her dad's place, which is so small, I'd have to sleep in the tub. And no way would her dad let his princess sleep over here with no parents present.

Wait a minute. This wrinkle could be the miracle I need most.

If I play it right, Mum will stop obsessing about my finals and see sense. I've got nowhere to stay and I know she won't leave me alone in our apartment overnight. Not after I had that insanely vivid sleepwalking nightmare about Dad's photos flying off the walls and attacking me. His old cricket bat couldn't protect me. Not from all that glass. So much glass. And blood. When Mum hauled me to the ER for stitches, I was lucky the doctor referred me back to my grief counselor instead of taking me straight to the psych ward.

Mum has to let me come with her.

Rhys trots into my room, his blue eyes expectant. His expression weirdly reminds me of Dad, always so eager to press me for details about my track meets or youth group events.

Theo's close on Rhys's heels. "Hey. Check this out." He plops down beside me and scrolls through images of blood vessels and clots, pelvises, femurs, and artificial joints. Rhys licks his chops like he's thinking, "bones, yum!" I try not to freak out as I read brutal-sounding descriptions of hip surgery and grim lists of problems caused by strokes. If Poppa doesn't have another, more serious stroke in the next few days, he'll still need six weeks of rehabilitation and physical therapy, minimum. Since Mum doesn't currently have a real job, it will be us, not David, stuck schlepping him to appointments. Ugh.

"That's it. My grand summer plan is officially over."

"No, it's not. You might have to postpone Paris, but it's not gone."

Mum stops in the doorway. "You all set to go to Heather's?"

"I don't want chickenpox," I say.

She and Theo exchange a glance.

I sigh. "Stop looking like I need to be committed. Jeez. Heather's brother Paul has chickenpox. I really don't want to stay with her and risk catching it. Amy's staying at her dad's closet in Soho, where I'd have to sleep standing up."

Mum grasps her forehead. "Well, I need to get on the road and I'm a little low on ideas."

"You could let me come with you," I say.

"Out of the question."

"Fine. I'll have to stay here on my own tonight."

"NO!" Mum and Theo shout in unison.

They eye each other a moment. Then Theo blurts, "She could stay with me."

Chapter 4

Each time we turn a corner on the drive to Theo's place, Mum's GPS chirps "recalculating."

Tell me about it. While we were packing, Theo's constant refrain was "it's only one night." Right. One night in which Mum's too dazed to pack her own suitcase, or even tell me which jeans are her favorites, yet she'll miraculously navigate Manhattan rush hour. One night that she'll have to drive nearly two hundred miles with a hyper dog for company. Will she remember to walk him? Will she give him chew toys so he doesn't gnaw through the German-engineered upholstery? This stupid car is too comfortable. She could zone out and collide with a semi or careen off a hillside, just like Dad did.

How do I convince her to let me come along? What reason will she listen to?

Theo insists on sitting practically on top of me. I shift away and tug the collar of Dad's old chambray shirt off of my sweaty neck. The fact that I threw it on before we left should've been a pretty obvious clue to Theo that I'm beyond not okay with this arrangement. But he only scoots closer. He takes my hand, stroking my thumb with his, and murmurs reassurances. I will my hand to stay limp, though I want to punch him. He just had to be oh-so-helpful, offering his big sister Cat's empty bedroom and his honor-roll study skill prowess. He'd carried every heavy thing and packed our car's trunk with ridiculous ease, like a Boy Scout on speed.

Can't he see that nothing good will come from keeping me in town? Mum's in no condition to drive all the way to Wilkes-Barre. No way can she cope alone in the minefield of stress waiting for her out there. She'll implode. I'll be left with no parents, no home, no future, nothing. Heck, Mum's so far gone she didn't even ask about chaperones. Did she forget that Theo's mom and stepdad work twelve-hour days?

Theo releases my hand and skims my forearm with his fingertips. "You still have a bump here, where you broke your wrist. Remember when I signed your cast?" He gives me such a sweet smile, my brain puddles somewhere south of my belly.

"Uh huh," I rasp, unable to stop staring at his lips. Is he hoping for a re-enactment of our first kiss, that electric welcome home in the limo?

Or is this a foretaste of what the evening will hold? Just us. No adults.

My gosh, is that why he's so happy, so snuggly? I might not wear a purity ring, but he knows where I stand on the whole sex issue. We talk about it enough at youth group.

"What are you thinking about?" Theo whispers. His lips against my ear make me feel even more squiggly, overheated, and ten kinds of terrified.

"Hot," I mutter and peel away my collar again.

He backs off. "Sorry. Should we close Rhys's window?"

Rhys's smiling snout sticks out the open front passenger window as he luxuriates in city scents of fry oil and hot exhaust.

Rhys. Of course. My young, playful pooch. He's too much for Mum to handle alone and I can prove it.

"Do you mind?" I ask Theo. "The food-truck smell is making me kind of nauseated, too."

"No problem." He leans forward, pulls Rhys's head inside the car, and presses the window up button. As I hoped, Rhys takes this as an invitation to play. He scrambles between the front seats and leaps into Theo's lap, repeatedly whapping Mum with his tail.

She shrieks, the car swerves.

"Rhys, no!" I shout. "Down boy!"

Mum stomps the breaks and we lurch to a halt. In typical New York fashion, drivers behind us begin a chorus of honking. Theo grapples Rhys's back end out of Mum's face while she shakily opens her window and waves on the other drivers.

"Are you okay, Mum? Man, Rhys is such a handful. I don't think driving alone with him is such a great idea. If we hadn't been here...."

Lost in thought, she stares straight ahead and absently keeps waving on other cars.

"Mum?"

"He'll have to go in his crate. We can get it from the trunk when we reach Theo's place."

"Then he'll whine the whole way and be very distracting, won't you, boy?" I scratch him between the ears, then pat my lap.

Rhys climbs off of Theo, who looks from the passenger seat to Rhys to me, frowning.

"I can't lose another parent in a car accident, Mum. Please let me come with you. I can at least help with Rhys. Why can't you see this is the right thing?"

"Why can't you see that your missing finals will only add stress to my life?"

I look to Theo for help, but he turns away, arms crossed over his chest.

* * *

None of us talks the last four stop-and-go blocks to Theo's place. Only Rhys smiles, his tongue lolling happily, glad to be out and about. Glad to be with his three favorite people.

I wish Rhys and I could do a brain-body swap, like *Freaky Friday* meets *The Shaggy Dog*. I'd have a fighting chance of keeping Mum safe. Some woof-woof answers on my history exam wouldn't be much worse than my normal capabilities. And as long as Rhys didn't drool on my artwork, I'd still get an A in Art III. The final portfolio review is just a formality.

Mum pulls up near Theo's gracious old building on Central Park West. "Enjoy the luxury accommodations, darling. And please thank your hosts for me."

"Hop out, babe," Theo says, giving a gentle backhand tap.

I swat away his hand, and go on begging. "Don't leave me here, Mum. Please!"

Theo huffs with annoyance and climbs out. Mum simply shakes her head, then bends to pop the trunk latch by her feet.

My door opens. Theo takes my arm, pulls me to my feet. "Traffic's getting heavier by the minute. Come on. It'll be okay." He locks the door behind me and goes to unload the trunk.

I hug Mum through her open window and whisper, "Please don't leave us alone. I'm not ready for this."

"Don't be silly, darling. You won't be alone. Study hard and do your best, all right?"

"Rhys's crate is assembled," Theo announces. "You want me to get him situated?"

"Yes, please," Mum calls over my shoulder.

I hug her tighter yet. "I love you, Mummy. So, so much. Please be careful on the road, and when you get there, don't listen to a word Poppa says. You're strong and brave and good."

"You can be too, Doodlebug. Starting right now." She kisses my cheeks, Parisian-style, and promises to let me know when she gets to Poppa's.

When I don't let go, she calls Theo, who pries me off of her. With a screech of tires, Mum jets off into the afternoon traffic. I watch her blue Audi get smaller and smaller as sweat prickles down my back.

"This is so wrong. I should be with her. Why is she being like this?"

"Because she's the adult and you're not." Theo tugs my suitcase out of my grip and stalks off to his building. What's he so mad about? I'm the one being pointlessly ditched.

"Come back here!" I call, waving my arms at him as if he had rearview mirrors.

A cab halts beside me and honks insistently. With a hum, the passenger-side window opens. "Where to, chica?"

I tear my eyes from Theo's back, blink at the cabbie, and drop my arms to my sides. "Uh. Sorry. I, um, forgot something back in my apartment."

The cabbie peels away, hissing obscenities.

"Love you too, honeycakes!" I holler after him.

At that, Theo stops and turns, a smile quirking the corner of his mouth. "If that guy knew he just lost a four-hundred-dollar fare, he might come back and run you over."

"I was waving for you, not him. I'm not crazy."

"Says the girl who almost got us killed with that stupid stunt with the dog."

"What are you talking about?"

"I've been trying to help and you act like you're desperate to get away from me."

His words are a slap in the face. I raise my hand to my cheek where the sting flares in my skin. "I'm so scared of what...might happen."

"What might—?" He tips his head, puzzled. Then a look of horror sweeps his features. With a panicked jerk, he steps back, knocking over my suitcase.

As I bend down to right it, he babbles at me. "You don't

think I brought you here to—? Oh my gosh. No. Not that I wouldn't like to someday, but jeez, Dani. You know me better than that, don't you? Nothing will happen. I swear on a stack of Bibles. It's not like we're gonna be completely alone, anyhow. My sister's around."

I stand up so fast, I see spots. "What? Since when?"

"Were you totally zoned out when your mom and I talked about this? Oh, right, you were packing your art. My oldest sister Beth is home. The one who's a hygienist in the practice with Mom and Jeff? You met her at our Christmas party."

The fondue was more memorable than most of the people at that party. All those expensive clothes and brilliant white teeth. It was like I'd stumbled into a commercial for designer toothpaste. Despite my paralyzing shyness that night, Theo's sisters worked hard to put me at ease. Cat, the willowy musician with a blue-streaked pixie cut, invented crazy nicknames for their parents' boring friends. Beth force-fed me appetizers and hardly let me out of her sight.

"Right. She gushed nonstop about her roommates and all their 'adventures,' like she was living in a sit-com."

"Yeah. Pretty ironic that she's home again. Her wedding's coming up, so she wants to 'simplify life' while she plans. In other words, freeload off my parents and our housekeeper while she micromanages her wedding planner."

"Lovely. A night with Bridezilla. I'm sure we'll get loads of studying done."

He snorts. Curling his hands into claws, he stomps in a circle around me. "Must have FLAAA-WERS! Me want CAAAAKE! Beeeg cake!"

I laugh. "Has it been weird having her home again?"

"A little. She left for college when I was ten, so we're figuring each other out right now. But she's mostly pretty cool.

That is, once you get past the enormous teeth, green skin, and habit of stomping around Japan in search of the perfect dress."

I cover my face with my hands. "Please don't tell her about the Bridezilla thing."

"Lighten up. She'd think it's funny. Come on, let's get out of this heat."

As we enter the heavy, brass-trimmed glass door of his building, the thick scent of lemon oil and old wood wafts toward me. His place feels a little like the Brooklyn brownstone where I grew up, with high ceilings and wainscoting and fireplaces. Except here they have a snooty Québécois doorman who sounds like the smarmy talking candlestick from *Beauty and the Beast*.

Theo waves to Bertrand and rattles off words that sound like a snake with hay fever. Something about the weather being *agréablement chaud*. Pleasantly warm. I got it! Sweet.

While Theo signs me in on the guest log, Bertrand sniffs suspiciously at my suitcase. He looks me scornfully up and down in my flip flops, cut-offs, frayed men's button-up layered over a tank top, like I'm something Theo scraped off the bottom of his shoe. I wish I'd stayed in my school uniform, no matter how sweaty it was. Put on saddle shoes and a tie and you're suddenly human to pretentious dorks like Bertrand.

He hands Theo another log to sign, then passes him a fat UPS envelope. Theo whoops "Falcon's Nest! The camp near the lake house. Yes!" and tears it open. As he reads the cover page, his brows draw together. Then he smacks the packet onto the desk. "So much for that job. I've been waitlisted."

"But they sent you a huge packet, like…you're an understudy. Maybe they'd bump you up the list if you sent a letter, got some people to talk you up. You do tutor freshman rowers and help with the kids at church."

"Oh, yeah. Elementary Sunday school. Lemme text a couple people."

While he taps out messages, I wheel my bag in circles and whistle *"La Vie en Rose."*

Bertrand's eyes narrow, like I'm somehow tainting the French tune.

"Done!" Theo chirps. "Once we get you settled in, can you help me with my letter?"

"Sure. I'm a champ at begging."

He kisses my temple. "Isn't she the best, Bert?"

"Quite." Bertrand's lip curls like he caught wind of a nasty odor.

While we wait for the elevator, Theo shuffles nervously from foot to foot and keeps looking behind him. The doors open and he yanks me on. When they whoosh shut behind us, he gasps, "Man. That was unbelievable. I'm surprised you didn't go up in flames with the evil looks Bert was shooting at you."

"Great. I think I'll go find a rock to crawl under."

"It's nothing personal against you. It just bugs him that I've grown up. He's known me since my Linus days, when I was dragging Tuggie with me everywhere."

"Your blanket had a name? That's just…I have no words."

"So watching me waltz in with a hot girl and her luggage is hard for Bert to take."

"What?"

He touches the seam of Dad's chambray near my collarbone. "You must be melting in this heavy shirt. Is this the one you carried around England with you?"

"No. That one's plaid."

"I hope it's not because of me that you're —" he makes a swirling motion with his finger— "wrapping yourself in your dad's aura or protection or whatever his clothes mean to you. I hope you'll feel welcome here, not anxious. Beth's totally excited to have you over."

We exit the elevator and I follow Theo toward his apartment, the cushy carpet swallowing my flip-flops.

His sister peeks out their door cradling a thick bridal magazine to her chest. "Dani!" she squeals. "This is so cool. Sleeping over. You're not nervous, are you? Don't worry, I'm meeting Aaron for dinner soon and you'll have the place to yourselves."

"She's staying in Cat's room," Theo says flatly.

"Ohh. Okay, bro. If that's how you want to play it." She winks at me.

"Argh!" he growls, shoving past her.

Beth turns to me, gaping. "What? What did I say?"

Chapter 5

I stand in the doorway to Theo's apartment, stunned. After all his elaborate assurances — *Nothing will happen. I swear on a stack of Bibles* — he finds a "chaperone" who's head recruiter for the Happy Hook-Up Club. I back away, hugging Dad's shirt against me.

"Please come in, Dee. It's okay." Theo gently pulls me into the foyer. "Just ignore my stupid sister. She can't resist an opportunity to embarrass me."

"Oh. Heh." My laugh sounds like I'm gagging.

He leads me past the dim living room with stiffly elegant furniture, barren landscape paintings, carefully coordinated antique knickknacks in china and cut crystal. All it needs is a velvet rope across the doorway and a uniformed guard slumped on a stool looking bored.

"Oh, come on, Linus," Beth says as she trails behind us. "Don't be like that. I can help. Tell you what — I'll change my dinner reservations and invite Mom and Jeff to join us. We need to make a guest list and that could take millennia to figure out."

Theo continues down the wide hallway hung with nineteenth-century botanical prints, saying nothing. When he stops at the third doorway, Beth stands between us and the door.

"Where are you going?" she asks.

"Our guest is staying in Cat's room. She's here to have a restful, no-pressure evening to study, eat, and sleep. Got it?"

"Please." Beth rolls her eyes. "You don't have to keep up the ruse for my sake. It's cool."

Theo shakes his head. "You are quite the piece of work, Sis." He nudges her aside and steps into a high-ceilinged room with bizarre décor — French-country-meets-biker-chick. The tall windows and bed are swathed in a black and cream toile patterned with peasants playing lutes and pan pipes. A blood-colored rug lies across the beige carpet and tattoo-design throw pillows line the bed. The walls are plastered with posters of backlit castles, surrealist art, musicians of every stripe — The Beatles, Allison Krauss, The Clash, Yoyo Ma.

My cell rings the frantic notes of the Kyrie from Mozart's Requiem. I fumble it out of my backpack and see Uncle David's number on the screen. Thank God. I head to a far corner, away from Theo and his insinuating sister.

"Uncle David, what the heck happened? You promised you'd keep Mum out of this."

"I tried, kiddo, I tried," he says. "I don't have medical thingamabob."

"Medical power of attorney?"

"Yup. Dang. How do you know 'bout that?"

"I spent a month in an ICU waiting room, remember? People talk. You pick up the lingo." I turn to see Beth with a hand clapped over her mouth as Theo whispers to her.

"Anyhow," my uncle continues, "they gave me the lowdown on Pop and said they'd keep him stable while they found Gracie to okay his treatment. That's all squared away, right?"

"Yeah."

"I hit the road as quick as I could, though I 'spect I won't hit Dunn Creek till eleven or so. How soon'll you two be there?"

"I'm still in New York. Mum wouldn't let me come because of my stupid exams. I totally could've done makeups later. I hate this. I hate the thought of her coping alone with this stress."

"I'll be there for her, and Pop's got a nice neighbor. Lord's with Gracie, too." A truck horn bellows from his end. "Whoa. I better get off the line and focus on gettin' there safe."

"Okay. See you tomorrow."

When I hang up, Beth is standing alone in the doorway, gnawing on her thumbnail.

"Linus went to get clean sheets. He told me all about your grandfather. I'm really sorry how I misread everything. I thought he was making it all up. It's just…you guys have been together a year and half and—" she throws up her hands — "I have a Freudian psychoanalyst for a father. I can't eat a hot dog or go horseback riding without it somehow being about sex."

"Your brother is trying to, um, not be like that."

"This is one of those church and God things, isn't it?"

"Yeah. Partly."

She twirls a strand of her auburn-tinted hair. "Interesting way to rebel against Dad. Huh. Anyway, I can stick around to chaperone if that's what you two need."

"Thanks. That would be great."

Theo returns, wearing shorts and a polo and carrying a stack of clean sheets. "Hey, babe, can you help me strip?"

"What?" Beth squawks.

"The bed, gutterbrain. Jeez."

My face, I'm sure, is a lovely shade of maroon.

* * *

I pace a rut in Theo's navy bedroom carpet, notebook clenched in my fists as I fire history questions at him. Worries about Mum and Poppa careen inside my head.

"You need your sketchbook?" he asks. "Or maybe a turn on our rowing machine? You'd better take a break or you'll walk right through the floor into the Kandinskys' place downstairs."

"I'm fine. Stop stalling. The original members of NATO are?"

He hops off his denim futon and stands directly in my path.

"You need a break."

I dodge left and his arm shoots out to stop me. I feint right and he knocks my notebook out of my hands and kicks it across the room.

"You bloody bully!" I scuttle after my notebook and dust it off. "Just because this all comes so easy to you! Gah! I can barely concentrate."

"I know." He gently takes the notebook from me and lays it on his bed. "I've let you interrogate me for almost an hour. I don't think this is helping you learn the material."

"Has it been that long? I should check in with Mum."

"Perfect." He steers me to the futon. "I'm gonna see what we've got to eat around here."

I dial Mum. The line rings and rings. Did she let her phone battery die? What if she picked up a hitchhiker? Someone who looked like a harmless geezer, but has a backpack full of hunting knives. He'd slice Rhys to bloody bits, then carve pictures in Mum's face while he—

"Hello?"

"Mum? Where were you?"

"Um...Route 80 somewhere. Lots of grass. Farms."

Has she been smoking something? "I meant why'd it take so long to answer?"

"Oh. Sorry. David was...on the phone. With me. Keeping me...company."

"You sound" — Stoned? Can I say that? — "awfully tired, Mum. If you start to nod off, you'll pull over and rest, right? Somewhere populated?"

"I'm fine, Dani. It's still...sun. Er, daylight. Just fifty miles to go. By the time I get there, Pop should be in whatchamacallit. Uh...Pre-op."

"Pre-op? You won't get to talk to him before his operation?"

"They said, uh...they don't want to delay that long. He could, um..."

"Bleed too much? Go into shock? What?"

"Shock. Yes, that's what they're worried about."

"How soon will you get to see him?"

"Well, he'll be in surgery a few hours. And then the, uh, after room. Post-op. Recovery."

"So, what's the plan for tomorrow?"

"Plan?"

"Yeah. How am I supposed to get out to Poppa's?"

"Right. Um...David will sort that out. We'll, ah, talk in the morning, all right?"

She hangs up before I can say more.

She doesn't have a plan. This woman who used to keep a calendar scheduled in fifteen minute increments has no plan. How many times did she say "uh" or "ah" or "um"? A dozen? For all I know, she'll keep driving west until she runs out of gas somewhere in Ohio.

Theo returns, rubbing his hands together. "I'm thinking stir fry. That work for you? Your grandfather okay? How about your mom?"

"No news. Mum's still on the road. And I have no idea how I'm supposed to get out there." The tears I'd been fighting all afternoon leak out of my eyes.

"Hey, none of that. We'll figure out a ride." He sits and puts an arm around me. "Your mom's still alive, right? Zombies haven't eaten her."

"Not funny." I glare at him. "You're enjoying this, aren't you? You love being the strong one, the helper."

He shakes his head and looks at the distant wall, frowning. "I think I need to show you something. Something I've never shown anyone."

His sister's insinuating words echo in my head. "I don't think that's a good idea, Theo."

"It's nothing like Beth was implying, okay? I need you to trust me more, so I'm going to trust you with something pretty major, because I think it will help you."

"Okay," I whisper.

He leads me to his closet. "Promise you won't laugh."

I just nod, because I'm sure my voice would shake if I said anything.

He pulls me inside and shuts the door behind us. It's a fairly standard walk-in closet with neat racks of clothes, a shoe tree, and shelves stacked with sweaters.

"What, no feather boas or ball gowns? Oh, wait, we're coming *into* the closet, not out of it." I snort at my own stupid joke.

"You promised you wouldn't laugh."

"Sorry. Defense mechanism. You're scaring the crap out of me, frankly."

"This should be the opposite of scary." He pushes aside his collection of school shirts and crested blazers, then pulls a panel off the wall. We duck into a crawl space with a water heater, and a cozy nook with a fluffy rug, beanbag chair, and chenille throw. One wall is plastered with photos of Theo and his smiling sisters rowing a canoe, squinting on a sunny dock, lying in the stretched shadows on their Pocono lake house lawn.

"Have a seat."

The beanbag chair crunches under my weight. Theo hunkers down and curls himself around me.

"Wow. Is this your secret hideout?"

His head nods against my shoulder. "Cat calls it Linus Land."

"But she's never seen it?"

"No," he says hoarsely, like he's withering up with embarrassment.

I twist in his grasp to face him. His eyes are squeezed shut, cringing. I don't know how to put into words all I feel, held in the warm, curved wall of his heart, so I just touch his cheek.

He slowly opens his eyes and watches me, expectant. Then he licks his lips and says, "You're wondering why all this stuff is here, aren't you?"

"I guess. What were you hiding from, Thebes?"

"Where do I even start?" He scratches his eyebrow. "Okay. You know we didn't always live here, in this huge, fancy apartment, right? It was my grandparents' place."

I nod. "You were in a two-bedroom in Kipp's Bay near Bellevue, where your dad worked. Then your mom inherited this place from her parents."

"Well, kind of. Mom's father died when I was six, and Gram asked us to live with her here. You'd think having amazing, free housing on the park would make life perfect. It was the opposite. Everything just...fell apart." He takes in a ragged breath.

"You don't have to tell me anything you don't want to."

"I do." His voice trembles. "Want to tell you. Everything." He swallows hard and continues. "Mom and Gramps were really close, like you and your dad, so his death hit her really hard. Gram babied her like some kind of tragic empress. Dad resented it — Mom's grief, my grandparents' wealth, competing with Gram for Mom's attention. He always had to be Number One. The next few years, he fought constantly with both Mom and Gram. He'd invite 'work friends' over — always women — and flirt with them, right in front of us. Like he had to prove he was Number One to somebody. I was too little to understand much. But I could tell that bringing those other women around wasn't right. He hurt Mom. He...*humiliated* her."

Theo gets too choked up to talk. I stroke his arm until his breathing steadies.

During those awful years, Theo tells me, his sisters confided in each other, but he had only his blanket Tuggie for comfort. He discovered this crawl space when his parent's yelling got especially loud, and the word "divorce" entered his world. Every day after, he'd hide for hours, dreaming of better times. Gram alone understood. Soon she was leaving him special things for his safe place: a chenille throw, a music box that had belonged to Gramps, a card that said "love is a sure shelter." He points to the card, pinned low on the wall.

My heart squeezes in my chest. I trace the fancy lettering with a fingernail, trying to keep my emotions under control. I want to take his pain and cry it away for him. Carve a piece from me and use it to fill the hole inside him. Even more, I want to give his wretched father forty lashes, then set him on fire.

"I— I'm sorry your dad's such a jerk. He should know better, being a shrink and all."

Theo grunts.

"It's complicated, right?" I ask.

He pulls a photo off the wall and hands it to me. It's a yellowed image of a much younger Theo with his sisters at Rockefeller Center. A voluptuous brunette I've never seen before — definitely not his mom — stands behind them, her taloned hand on Cat's shoulder. Beside the woman is a tall man with his arm snaked around her waist. If I didn't know Theo was the sad little boy up front, I'd swear this guy was him. Same deep-set eyes, slender nose, determined jaw.

"Oh. My. Gosh."

"Don't say it. Just don't." He tucks the photo behind another to blot out the cheater who looks just like him.

"You really hate him, don't you?"

"I don't know what I feel, honestly. Hate seems like the wrong word. Here's the thing: before I knew you, I had almost no relationship with my dad for years. Sure, he'd send birthday cards and some out-of-the-blue presents; twice a year he'd take me on a totally awkward outing. When your father died and you kept seeing him, I wanted to help but didn't know how, so I took a chance and called my dad for his professional opinion. Some of his theories were goofy, but whatever, it was cool to have an actual conversation with him. Everything changed for me after that. For the first time, I had hope that things could turn around, that God really could fix what's broken and make things new. I didn't want to be stuck in here wallowing any longer, I wanted to be something more. For you. Because of you."

I swivel around to face him. "You like to be the hero."

He shakes his head. "It's not a competition to be 'the strong one.' That's what I'm trying to show you. Alone, I'm just a scared kid who cowers in the dark bawling into his blankie. But you help me and I help you. Together we're both stronger. More. That's how this works, Dani." He says my name so gently, like a caress.

I'm intensely aware of his breathing, his body heat, the soapy scent of his shirt. I lean in and kiss him, just a little west of his lips. Then the tip of his nose. His chin.

He cradles my face in his hands and his mouth finds mine. He rolls me onto my back and kisses me long and slow, twirling the end of my ponytail around his fingers.

My hands slip under the hem of his polo, and I feel his warm skin, the firm muscles that line his spine. He makes a little noise in the back of his throat and kisses me deeper.

"LINUS!" Beth hollers. "Are you coming back to help with dinner or what?"

Theo pulls away, groaning. He crawls to the door, opens it a crack and calls, "Just a minute!"

He crawls back and collapses on the floor next to me. "So much for keeping my promise that nothing would happen."

"I kissed you first," I remind him.

"I don't want to be the kind of guy who says one thing and does something else."

"Like your father."

He leans on one elbow and squints at me.

"I can make deductions, too. Just because you look like him and have an interest in psychology, it doesn't mean you're doomed to be his clone."

"I'm named after him, too."

"Okay, maybe you are doomed, Teddy."

He grabs the chenille throw and swats me with it. "Don't. Ever. Call. Me. Teddy!"

I roll away from him, giggling. "Does my snuggly bear not like that nickname? Maybe he shouldn't lure girls into his love nest and make romantic speeches."

He sits back on his heels, stunned. "My gosh, I did do that, didn't I?"

"Thebes, I was only teasing. Thanks for telling me your story. It helped. Really."

"Linus! NOW!" Beth hollers.

At that, we both scramble to our feet, laughing.

Chapter 6

While Theo and Beth clown around making dinner, I sit at the kitchen island and research transportation options on my laptop. A taxi would eat up most of my Paris money in one shot. The train is cheap, but would only get me halfway there. There's only one bus to Scranton that leaves after my finals tomorrow — and it would get me there at one thirty in the morning.

I drop my head on my folded arms and groan. How am I supposed to take care of Mum and help her with Poppa if I'm stuck in New York? *Please help me, Lord. Please.*

"You okay?" Beth asks. I hear her tap at my laptop, then suck breath through her teeth. "Are you insane? Buses are full of perverts, meth-heads, and psychotic hobos. No, no, no."

"Unless you happen to have some Floo Powder, a transporter, or a TARDIS, I don't know what other option I have."

"Well, duh, why didn't you ask me?"

She calls her fiancé Aaron and tells him about my "desperate situation." Even though her Fridays off are supposed to be dedicated to wedding planning, she says, "my whole being longs for a mental vacation" that a few hours on the open road would give. For the sake of their marriage, he must let her use his car. Soon she gushes with gratitude and I know she's pulled off a wonderful feat. She rings off, her face lit with a broad grin that's strikingly like Theo's.

"Epic road trip, girl!" she crows. "So, is Linus coming with us? He and I could crash at the lake house tomorrow night. It's only ten, twenty minutes away."

The thought of Theo seeing Poppa's disgusting mess makes my stomach churn.

Fortunately, he shakes his head and says, "Sorry, I can't. I'm ushering in a wedding this weekend — Fletch's cousin, our rowing coach. I'm supposed to spy for you, Beth. Remember?"

She hurls a wet towel at him. "Research, squirt. Fact-finding."

* * *

Dinner is strangely celebratory, considering I'm still on a knife's edge about my grandfather. But having my travel plans resolved gives me a shred of hope. I dig into the velvety chicken and crisp, perfectly seasoned vegetables while Theo and Beth tell me about their craziest misadventures at the lake house — canoe-stealing bears, the local streaker, their attempt to tame a skunk. My stiff neck muscles relax and I shed Dad's shirt like snakeskin.

Theo and Beth are busy clearing the table when the intercom buzzes, so I jog off to answer it. The unit squeals, then Bertrand's voice blares, "A Fletcher Reid to see you?"

"Send him up," Theo calls. "He has the tie I'm supposed to wear in the wedding."

I give Bertrand the okay and try to think of an excuse to disappear. I'd rather not have to explain my situation to Theo's politics-obsessed best friend. He loves to turn anyone's crisis into an opportunity to act like he's a "man of the people" on the campaign trail — hand on your shoulder, earnest "listening" face, gently crooned inspirational sound bite. Heather was always swooning over his leadership qualities, his brains, his Bible knowledge — when she wasn't in a screaming match with him about these very traits, that is.

He's one of those big geeks who happen to be annoyingly good at running things, from student government to our church youth group council. Theo tends to follow his lead more than I'd like. But whenever I say so, he reminds me that Fletcher got him to not only darken the door of a church, but find faith himself.

And there's the rub. As irritating as Fletcher can be, as much as I hate how he and Heather fight, I'm forever in his debt. He helped Theo find God, and through finding God, Theo helped me survive a dark time. When I was three thousand miles away in England, falling apart about Dad's death, Theo pursued, listened, showed me true friendship. Real love.

Okay, Lord. Fine. I'll answer the freaking door and try to be pleasant.

When the expected knock comes, I find a stunning blond guy standing there holding a piece of orange silk. Big shoulders, great hair, dazzling green eyes.

"Can I help you?" I ask. I peer into the hall to see if Fletcher's out there waiting his turn in his thick-lensed glasses, hair plastered to his skull, Oxford shirt buttoned up to his throat.

"Hey, Dani. Where's Theo?" the guy says, brushing a hand over his soft, golden waves. His voice seems vaguely familiar.

"Do I know you?"

"Fletch!" Theo calls out behind me.

"No way," I gasp. His open-necked mandarin-collar polo is actually stylish and what happened to his nerdy wire-rims? I must say, Heather's ex cleans up pretty well. I sure hope she doesn't know about this. She'll be a total goner.

"You got my tie?" Theo asks.

"Forsooth, my lord." Fletcher tosses a coil of tangerine fabric to Theo, and it unrolls like a party streamer. "'Tis an ill color for thee, thou artless, plume-plucked skainsmate."

Well, he hasn't lost the geeky personality.

"Oho! Dost thou bite thy thumb at me, knave?" Theo grabs umbrellas from an urn by the door, tosses one to Fletcher and makes a jab at his friend. "*En garde*, thou motley-minded clotpole! Wherefore art thy pribbling, rough-hewn spectacles?"

Fletcher parries with his gray paisley "sword." "I need them no longer, surly canker-blossom. The good doctor hath set lenses upon mine eyes."

"Your contacts look great!" I call over the thwacking umbrellas. New, hottie Fletcher geeking out Shakespeare-style is loads better than his old, buttoned-up politician act. I suddenly picture him in tights and feel heat rise in my cheeks.

"I thank thee, milady, for thy kind ministrations," Fletcher says. "What brings thee to the den of this craven, crook-pated scullion on the eve of thy historic examination?"

"Family emergency. My grandfather fell and needs hip surgery. Mum's driving to Pennsylvania to be with him. Theo and Beth offered to put me up."

"WHAT?" Heather strides in wearing a cute sundress, her red hair pinned up 1940s style.

My mouth falls open. *I have big plans for tonight,* she'd said. *A date* she meant. With her three-times ex.

Theo whispers, "Well, this complicates things."

"Danielle Renee," Heather says, "why on earth didn't you tell me you were having a crisis? You poor thing." She wraps me in a tight hug, but I just stand there like a pole.

"I don't want chickenpox."

"Oh, honey, I should be germ-free. I Purelled up to my shoulders and changed clothes. If you'd let me know, I could've stayed with you."

Theo looks at me askance. "You didn't even *tell* her?"

"She— You—." I look from my boyfriend to best friend helplessly, then finally turn to Fletcher. "Big, secret plans, huh? All along it was *you.* Here I thought I was being a good friend keeping my drama to myself so Heather could have a chance with someone new. *Actually* new, not just an exterior remodeling. She totally lied to me. I can't believe it."

"I did not lie," Heather interjects. "I just didn't tell you everything. Jiminy Cricket. I knew you'd take it badly."

Theo cackles. "This is priceless. Now you know how it feels to be on the receiving end of your slippery ideas about truth."

I scowl at him, and at Heather and Fletcher, who now have their arms around each other.

"Dani," Theo says, "we can only help you if you stop pretending you don't need it."

"Yea and verily," Fletcher says. "I could teach you some of my best tricks to ace the history exam. That is, if my exterior remodeling doesn't repulse you too much."

I shake my head. "You could be in GQ, Fletch. And I'd be an idiot to say no to study help; I'm hopeless at history. But I don't want to wreck your night. If you two are capable of forgiving each other after that last fight, nothing on earth's going to keep you apart. Especially not me. Please go have your date."

"There's no way I can enjoy myself if it means leaving you in the lurch," Heather says. "How about we take a half hour, forty minutes to study with you, then we'll go?"

"That would be…fabulous. Thank—" My ringtone interrupts. "It's Mum."

Theo nods and leads our friends back to his room.

Mum tells me she's now at the hospital after dropping Rhys at Poppa's "house." Her voice drips with sarcastic scare quotes, which must mean his hoarding has reached nightmare proportions. He's in surgery now, she says with a weary sigh. It's a tricky one because of the mini-stroke that preceded it. According to the neighbor lady, he was talking nonsense at the garden hose display, wobbled a bit, and collapsed. He came to in a matter of minutes, crying with pain, but back in his right mind. His blood pressure stabilized once he was admitted to the hospital, but they're not taking chances with general anesthesia. He'll be numbed from the waist down but awake while doctors screw his upper thigh bone back together. Shudder. Even if Poppa's a jerk sometimes, I feel sick about him having to hear all the gruesome things they'll be doing.

Mum describes the sparkling, new hospital building, so different from the mildewing wreck where her mother battled cancer. When I try to probe deeper, her voice gets quieter and quieter. I tell her I'm praying (I have been, kind of) and promise to call again soon.

A vague sense of dread sits like an ice ball in my stomach. On the way back to Theo's room, I grab Dad's shirt from the kitchen. I snuggle into it, pull the cuffs over my hands, and rub the fabric between my fingers. Pages of my mental sketchbook flutter in my mind like a kid's flipbook: Mum's lovely face morphs into a haggard crone.

An explosion of laughter from my friends stops me in my tracks. If I show up in Dad's shirt, someone will make a big deal about it. No thank you. I can be brave and good.

As I peel off Dad's shirt in the hallway, I'm suddenly grappled in a citrus-scented hug.

"I'm so sorry about your grandpa. For not telling you about Fletch. Do you hate me?"

"Of course not. I just want you to be happy." I motion for her to follow me to Cat's room. "Obviously you've done some major work to get him looking so good, but are you sure it's enough? He can be so—." I want to say cruel, but bite it back. "Combative. About everything."

"I push him out of his book-smart comfort zone, and it's scary new territory for him. But the makeover? That was all him."

"Seriously?"

She nods. "I almost fell outta my chair when he walked into the English final looking like that. I don't rightly remember what I wrote on my exam."

"I can't believe I missed it. I wish I'd stayed on campus after my chem final."

"I tried to hide in the art room afterwards, but he followed me. Next thing I know, he's helping me turn my portfolio into this cool PowerPoint show. It was so easy between us. Like he figured out how to use his brains to build me up. And when we were finished...."

"He kissed you," I guess.

"No. He apologized. Said he was trying to become the guy I deserve. Then I, well...kissed him. Probably longer than I should have." She fans herself at the memory. "Anyway, I was gonna tell you after he and I had a chance to talk through our problems a little more."

"Wow. That's...wild. How are you feeling?"

"Confused. We have so much to work through. You sure you don't mind if we go out?"

"Whatever you need, Heather. Theo's got this. Beth, too. Okay?"

She smiles timidly. "Before we rejoin the guys, you think we could pray?" She points at the chambray shirt still clutched in my fist. "I haven't seen that since the anniversary of when your daddy passed. You're scared. Real scared."

I bite my lip. "It could be worse. Poppa only had a mini-stroke. And they're just pinning his leg bone, not replacing his whole hip."

"I don't imagine he's a good patient, and your mom's been pretty low lately. She seems muddled up about life and kinda sad all the time, doesn't she?"

I nod, eyes burning.

She bows her head. "Hey, God? You said when we're worried we're supposed to give those worries to you. You're our refuge in times of trouble. Be with Dani in her exams and on her trip tomorrow. Heal her grandpa's body and his angry heart, and give her mom strength to be kind when he's a jerk. We know you can make all things new, even grouchy old people and broken-down families. Make this mess into something beautiful. And Lord, give me wisdom to know how to—. Uuuh!" She sucks in a breath. "Of course! Thank you, sweet Jesus. Amen."

I peer at her, curious. "What was that about?"

"When I pray, sometimes I see what I'm supposed to do. Just now, I saw a car rushing down the highway. You and Beth were up front, and, well…I was in the back seat."

Chapter 7

My footsteps echo down a parquet-floored corridor lined with Renaissance art that's naturally lit by the curved skylights soaring above. I pause to study a Rubens when other footsteps join mine. A cluster of men in white coats rush past, arguing, their surgical masks flapping loose around their necks. Women in scrubs and clogs scurry to and fro. A parade of people in wheelchairs or on gurneys rolls past me. Families carry flowers or balloons and whisper worriedly among themselves.

I step in the path of a nurse and ask, "What are these sick people doing in the Louvre?"

"*Quoi?*" Her look of contempt makes Bertrand seem sweet in comparison.

I try again, in French, but she shoves me aside and strides away, railing about my stupidity in weird idioms I can't translate.

I follow the gurney parade into a side gallery, where the usual center benches have been replaced with a line of hospital beds. There are no plump, frolicking nudes on the walls here. Nothing but images of desolation: Blitzed landscapes, skeletal bodies heaped into piles. The room smells of institutional ziti, antiseptic, and pee.

Over the chattering doctors and groaning patients, I hear high-pitched squawks, like a hawk's cry coming from the far end of the room. I follow the sound out a low door into a small, circular room with a tile floor patterned like a maze. In the center of the room is another hospital bed. Mum stands beside it, her hands covered in gore. She slices a chunk of muscle off her own thigh with a hunting knife and feeds it to the creature lying there. It has an old man's body, but above the tuft of gray chest hair, its head is dark-feathered, with a sharp beak and fleshy, black waddle. It greedily gobbles up Mum's flesh, and then hisses, "More, more!"

"All right, Pop, all right," Mum says, her face wet with bloody tears. "Anything for you. Just please don't die. Not you, too."

"NO!" I yell. "I'll feed you, Poppa. Not her. Me!"

Two minotaurs in hospital scrubs appear at my side. One pins me to the wall, while the other fires up a hand-held circular saw.

"Left leg or right?" the creature grunts over the whine of the saw.

The blade rips into my flesh, and pain flames through me. I scream in agony until my air is spent and my throat aches.

Someone shakes me by my shoulders and calls my name. I feel denim upholstery against my bare arms and legs and the bump of my phone in my shorts pocket. This place smells like boy and vanilla. I open my eyes to see Theo standing over me, frowning, as I lie on his futon.

Beth sprints into the room. "What's going on?"

"She dozed off, and must've had a nightmare." Theo studies me a moment. "I think she could use a cup of tea, and that big shirt she had on earlier."

Beth scurries away, pausing to reassure their mom and stepdad that I'm not hurt.

I slowly sit up. Scattered on the floor beside me are calculus flashcards I'd used to quiz Theo for his other exam. Studying feels like a pale, grade-school memory compared to those snorting, bull-headed minotaurs and the hellacious burn of their saw.

"Man, you've got some lungs on you," Theo says. "I think you scared the last half hour of calc right out of my head."

I circle my fist over my heart, and mouth *sorry*, but he looks puzzled. Right. It was Dad who used sign language so we could "talk" when Mum was video conferencing with a client.

"Thank God you were here and not home alone. That must have been some nightmare."

I nod and make a drawing motion with my hands. I need to get these awful images out of me like poison from a snakebite.

He passes me a pencil and paper from his desk. Images roar from my brain, jangle down my arms and ravage the pages. I draw the medical staff racing through the Louvre, the gallery of macabre art, the minotaurs, and finally, my mutated grandfather.

Fabric settles onto my shoulders and there's a sharp intake of breath. "Yikes, what's *that*?" Beth points to my sketch of vulture-headed Poppa.

I write *Poppa, in the dream.*

"No wonder you screamed your head off." She offers me a cup of herbal tea.

My phone chimes. I pull it out, see that it's Uncle David, and pass it to Beth in exchange for the tea, whispering, "can't talk. Throat hurts."

She shrugs and takes the call. After explaining why she's answering, she tells my uncle about her plan to drive me out there. Finally, she asks after my grandfather and mother.

"Uh huh, uh huh," she says, her forehead smoothing out. "Okay. Great. Look forward to meeting you tomorrow, Mr. Tilman." She clicks the end-call button. "The surgery went fine, but they're keeping your grandfather in the ICU tonight. And you should pray for your mom. Your uncle sent her to the house when he caught her 'making snow.' What does that mean?"

"When most people would cry, Mum shreds Kleenex."

You could have filled rooms with her "snow" after Dad died. And just like that, my relief about Poppa's good news floats away, a scrap in the wind.

* * *

In the morning, I sprint for the shower, half dreading I'll run into Theo. After David's call last night, he patted my arm, then dove back into his calculus like I wasn't even there. Beth walked me to Cat's room and hugged me, which was nice, but not the good night I hoped for.

But why would Theo want to kiss a lunatic who screams herself hoarse? Or say "I love you" to someone whose mind is full of such freakish evil?

My nerve-addled fingers misalign button holes and I have to rebutton my school shirt twice. I leave the steamy bathroom, awkwardly tugging up my knee socks that stick to my still-damp calves. Theo's bare feet appear before me, toe-to-toe with my saddle shoes. My eyes drift from the curled hair on his calves to his navy striped bathrobe, up to the bulging pockets, where he's shoved his balled fists. Oh my. Is he wearing anything at all under that?

"Guh— g'morning," I say to the knotted belt of his robe. One little tug...

"You sleep okay?" he asks.

I swallow and pull my collar away from my sticky neck. "Yeah. No more bad dreams."

"Cool. Well, I need to grab a shower and get ready." Theo's hands come out of his pockets and he pulls the belt knot tighter, which only reveals more of his chest.

"Oh. Okay." I wipe away the sweat that's beading on my upper lip.

"Babe? My eyes are up here."

My cheeks flare so hot, I swear they're going to melt right off my skull.

When I look into Theo's face, a smile twitches across his lips. "Planning some nudes for your mental sketchbook, were you?"

"No, I was, uh…. I need to p- pack my stuff." I swivel away, but he clasps my arm.

"Dani, wait. Sorry for teasing. I know it's hard."

My eyebrows fly up. He didn't just say that.

He slaps a hand over his mouth and blushes furiously. "Oh, man. I mean, um, it isn't the easiest, having to wait and be careful. We've got to be able to laugh about it sometimes, right? Otherwise, well…."

"We're screwed? In a manner of speaking?"

He blinks at me, then chuckles. "That's the spirit."

* * *

On the walk to school, Theo shares the bagels and fruit his stepdad packed for us. Our hands brush, and I feel a happy tingle from his touch. I'm proud of us and grateful he's my ally. When the food's gone, we volley history questions back and forth. I try to concentrate on names, events, and dates, rather than let my thoughts wander west, to my sad mother, my stitched-together grandfather. Mum's early-morning text about Poppa's impatience to go home only worried me more. Will Uncle David be able to keep him calm? Or will he be as useless at containing Poppa's nastiness as Neville Chamberlin was Hitler's?

Exam time comes, and I use my mental sketchbook, as Fletcher had suggested. The History Channel images we reviewed last night click, click, click into place. Then I do the hard work of translating my mental pictures into words.

I turn in my exam, feeling wrung out, but weirdly exuberant. One last hoop to jump and junior year is over! Theo gives me a hug for luck before heading to his calculus final.

I skip off to the arts wing, swinging my portfolio. Following my purple-haired friend Toshio into the art room, I playfully swat his backside with my leatherette case.

"Yowza, Deane. Attack of the retro."

Retro? An eerie feeling prickles up my neck as I scan the room. Not one portfolio. Is this the wrong section, wrong time? No, the usual nine are all here: the Goth triplets, Hugo from Brisbane, and me and my gang — Heather, Amy, Mark, and Toshio.

I watch with horror as each classmate gives a PowerPoint or video presentation on their work and how it relates to an art career — like Amy's set design, Mark's architecture, and Toshio's animation. And Heather's presentation? Whoa. I had no idea PowerPoint could do all the wicked cool fades and text effects Fletcher added. The music perfectly matches each historic period she captured in her costume-oriented paintings, drawings, and sculpture projects. At the end, our classmates give her a standing ovation.

When Ms. Quinlan calls my name, I'm in a blind panic. I stumble to the front of the room, open my portfolio case and hastily pull out all my literature-inspired pieces. I silently pray *Help!* and imagine I'm at one of Mum's grad school parties. I blather what I know about balance, composition, and color theory, holding up examples as I talk. I reach the bottom of the pile with minutes more to fill. My classmates shift in their seats. Mark starts a brief patter of applause, the kind we give the headmaster at really boring assemblies. I am so dead.

As I pack up my portfolio, Ms. Quinlan dismisses the class and wishes everyone a nice summer. Chairs squeak, banter begins. I can feel my teacher's gaze on my scalp. When I look up, her lips are pressed together and brows drawn sharply down.

"I'm sorry," I say. "My grandfather had surgery yesterday; I ran out of time to prepare."

"Yesterday? You've had the assignment for weeks, Danielle. Weeks!" She sits on her desk, folds and unfolds her reading glasses.

"It kills me to see bad work habits get the better of you. Your drawing technique is head and shoulders above your classmates, but the beauty got lost when all we could see was poor preparation, the fruits of procrastination. Certainly not worthy of a passing grade. Do you honestly think you have the temperament for a career in illustration? It's nothing but meeting deadlines."

"I'll do the whole final over if you want, or another big project. Just please don't fail me. It will send my mother right over the edge. She's stressed enough with her father in the hospital."

Heather peeks in. "Sorry to interrupt, but our ride to your grandfather's place is here, Dani."

"There's genuinely a sick grandparent? This isn't a 'dog ate my homework' scenario?"

Heather looks horrified. "Dani's grandpa is sitting in an ICU right now. You can call Dani's mom if you don't believe us."

"My apologies. Give us a moment?" Once Heather goes, she continues. "Under the circumstances, you should have asked for an extension. But because you've been an A student all year, I'll arrange a make-up assignment. Just keep in mind, if you hope for anything higher than a C this semester, you need to submit a complete project on time. Are we clear?"

I nod, my mind racing. How will I manage this on top of everything else? But if I don't, goodbye, art school.

"Excellent. I'll e-mail the new assignment to both you and your mother."

"Could you wait until Monday? She has a lot on her plate."

Ms. Quinlan rubs her chin. "If my daughter thought half this much about my feelings, we might live on the same coast today. Very well, Danielle, Monday. Do have a good summer, and no procrastinating. Hard work beats talent nine times out of ten."

* * *

"I'm such an idiot!" I cry to Beth and Heather over a Beach Boys' song blaring from the car speakers. "I assumed Ms. Q wanted the same thing as last year. If I fail, Mum will flip. She's made insane sacrifices to get me the best art instruction since birth, practically."

"I'll ride you so hard about the new deadline," Heather says, "you won't have a squirrel's chance at a peanut festival of missing it. And I'm sure Theo will do the same."

My stomach plummets even lower. "I never said goodbye to him! What kind of heartless girlfriend disappears without saying goodbye?"

From the back seat, Heather reaches to squeeze my shoulder. "Just text him. He knows you're dealing with a lot."

When I power up my phone, silenced for the exams, there are four frantic text messages from Theo. I send him an equally frantic apology, then bang my head on the dashboard, groaning, "Stupid, stupid, stupid."

Beth passes me a bulging canvas shopping bag. "I was saving this till we hit the highway, but I think you need it now. Promise you won't tell *my* mother. She just might fire me."

I peek in the bag, then burst out laughing. It's crammed with every kind of candy imaginable. "Is this your evil plot to get new patients for your dental practice?"

Heather leans over the seat and snatches the bag from me. "Yes! The fluoride queen has gone to the dark side!"

We dive into the treats like it's Easter morning. Heather gobbles through a bag of mini peanut butter cups and tells us all about her date with "the new Fletcher." He said they were "just going out for coffee," but he took her to a funky cafe where a poetry slam was in progress. The next thing Heather knew,

62

Fletch was at a microphone, mesmerizing the room with an impassioned reading of his poem "One Hundred Hues of Heather" — a quirky cross between Song of Songs and Eminem, full of art allusions. Who knew that Fletcher Reid, the guy who watches C-Span for fun, could be so romantic?

"You're so lucky to be young and free and just dating," Beth says, merging onto the freeway. "Everything gets so much more complicated when you're engaged." She tells us about all the problems she and Aaron have had planning their wedding. She hates the venue they booked, everything costs a fortune. The bridesmaids and Aaron's mother are feuding over dress styles. She can't even decide whether to wear her hair up or down.

I offer to do sketches with sample hair styles, and Beth tears up with gratitude.

Heather beans her in the ear with a peanut butter cup. "No soggy raccoon eyes! Think happy thoughts and we'll give you a dozen virtual makeovers in no time."

I grab my pencils and Heather, her pastels. Beth cues up her road trip playlist, and we all sing along to "Life is a Highway." Miles flash by as I fill pages with sample hairstyles. The city and suburbs give way to lush evergreen forests. I take another cream-centered caramel, and as its sweetness fills my mouth, I wish I'd given Theo a kiss goodbye he'd never forget.

When will I see him again? Why won't he text me back?

Beth guffaws beside me. I snap out of my reverie and see that in my anxious longing, I've drawn her with such an enormous up-do she could be lady-in-waiting to Marie Antoinette.

Sun splashes across the page as we come around the mountain. My phone chimes.

"See," Beth says, "it was just bad reception. I knew he'd call you."

But the number on the screen is Mum's.

"Dani, darling? How were your exams?"

Something in her tone tells me this is not the time to mention my art fiasco. "Oh, you know, tough."

"Are you on your way? David said Beth Wescott was giving you a ride."

"Yeah. Heather's with me, too. I hope that's okay."

"David mentioned that plan. That's why I thought I should call to warn you before you got here with your friend. I have some rather bad news. Poppa's blood pressure spiked, and, well...it seems he's had another stroke."

Chapter 8

We're within sight of the hospital when a *kuh-doomp* beneath the car makes the three of us yelp.

"What was that?" I cry.

Grimacing, Beth slows the car to a crawl, and it rolls forward with a stuttering thump. "One of the tires, I think. Aaron's going to kill me!"

We crawl bumpingly toward the next red light, drawing stares from the motley group of nurses in scrubs, elderly people, and harried parents waiting at a bus shelter.

A man in a gray suit and sunglasses raps on my window, making me jump. He smiles and motions for me to open the window. I shoot Beth a frightened glance, but she's already working the master window control. Humid air scented with spicy cologne pours into the car.

"Havin' a bit of trouble, are ye, ladies?" His accent reminds me of Bono or Gabriel Byrne. "Roll on into the hospital car park and I'll give ye a hand puttin' on a spare, a'right?"

"Very good of you, sir. Thank you," Beth says.

"Are you sure this is safe?" I murmur as she steers the limping car into the lot. "That guy did not sound like he's from around here."

"We're on top of a busy bus and ambulance route in the middle of the day," Beth says. "Besides, I have no idea how to change a tire."

The moment she cuts the engine, he's at her window. "Could ye open the boot?"

"He means the trunk," I tell Beth. "My dad called it that, too. The spare tire's back there."

"Under all our luggage," Heather adds.

We three climb out of the car and help unload all the bags. The man soon has the trunk floor removed and is extracting a small wheel.

Heather lurches forward. "Your suit! Let me get that."

He chuckles at her concern. "Don't worry yer pretty head, miss. Had me job interview already. Let me be yer angel and the good Lord can take care of the dirt."

The man proceeds to carry the spare and tools to the front passenger side, waving away all our attempts to help him. His bus arrives at the stop, but he won't hear of leaving until the car is road-worthy again. The three of us stand by, feeling hot and useless as he jacks up the car and wrestles hardware off the front wheel with a tire iron, sweat beading on his lip and dripping down his temples.

My offer of drinks for everyone is the first suggestion he accepts, so I plod across the street to a mini-mart that time forgot. Past half-empty shelves of dusty canned goods, I find a cold case with sodas and check expiration dates before collecting some Cokes and iced teas. When I return to the car, Beth and Heather are sitting on a concrete parking bumper and chatting animatedly with our angel as he tightens bolts on the spare tire.

They gratefully take the drinks I offer, and conversation turns to Beth's wedding. Another bus arrives while our angel is lowering the jack. Though we girls insist we can stow away the tools and damaged tire ourselves, he won't hear of it, saying he can call his son for a lift. He twice refuses the money Beth offers him, relenting only when she insists on covering his dry cleaning bill and brazenly tucks cash in the handkerchief pocket of his suit.

Once we pile back into the car, he pauses at my window, hand resting on the frame. A sinuous-patterned tattoo peeps from under his cuff. "If ye need a hand with yer grandpappy who's had the stroke, give me a call, a'right?" He passes me a business card that says simply "Ronan" with a phone number underneath, surrounded by a Celtic knotwork border that I realize must match his tattoo.

As he retreats to the bus stop, I look from him to the card and back again. "Who was that guy? How does he know about Poppa?"

"He was very curious about our story," Beth says, "and asked a lot of attentive questions, so concerned and kind. A total sweetheart. Not hard on the eyes either. Well, for an older guy."

"That," Heather proclaims, "was most definitely a guardian angel."

* * *

When we step off the hospital elevator at Poppa's floor, I pause for a moment and sniff hard for the scents from my dream. Instead of cafeteria ziti, antiseptic, and pee, I smell paint and new carpet. Everything here is gleaming-new, from the stylish ceiling tiles to the textured wallpaper. Heather, Beth, and I navigate the corridor that zigs and zags among rooms where balloon-bearing visitors chat with patients and nurses check temperatures and blood pressure. Not one of them has a bull's head or a hand saw.

In the hallway leading to Poppa's room, a sallow, unshaven Uncle David greets us. He shakes hands with Heather and Beth and thanks them for coming to my rescue. He hugs me, then returns to nervously scratching his bald head that's already welted with fingernail marks. I have a brief flash of memory — how he used to yank at his hair when he was feeling anxious. Well, back when he had hair. Of course, in those days, his blood was so thick with illegal substances it was a miracle his heart didn't burst. But was it really drugs that made him so twitchy, or did they only enhance what was naturally there?

The shadows under my uncle's eyes fill my head with a hundred questions about what has happened at the hospital in the past twenty-four hours. "How's Poppa? Can I see him?"

"He's…well, how do I put this?" he drawls.

"Paralyzed on one side, droopy and weak?" Beth guesses.

"No, that's the weird bit. He seems like himself, 'cept when he talks; it's all nonsense. The stroke hit the language-making part of his brain. He can understand everything we say, but his responses are, well, what you imagine it'd sound like in a Dali painting."

"But he's out of the ICU. That's good, isn't it?" I ask.

"I guess. He was up and walking this morning and charming the socks off the nurses, so they decided to move him. As we were settling him into his new room, he got to hollering at Grace about something or other she wasn't doing to his satisfaction, then boom. Stroke."

"Did you leave her *alone* with him? Let me guess, he was being all sweet until the moment you left the room."

"Dani!" Heather gasps, appalled that I'd ever talk back to an adult.

Beth becomes very interested in the contents of her purse.

"You're right," David says. "I'm so sorry. Your dad worked really hard to set up strict boundaries so Grace wouldn't get pulled back into Pop's power. My boundaries with him are, as your dad would've said, 'total rubbish.'"

His mention of Dad sends a zing of pain through me, like I whacked my funny bone. I uselessly cradle my elbow and rub away the phantom twinge.

The door to Poppa's room swings open and we all go

guiltily quiet. Mum steps into the hall, still wearing the stained jeans from yesterday.

She's like a rag doll when I hug her. A slightly rancid one. "Hey, Mum. How are you?"

"Me? I'm...managing." Her mouth curves, a wry grimace. "Go say hello to your Poppa. He'll be glad to see you. Then we can all go get lunch? Dinner? You lose track of time in here."

"Never fear, we're here to help," Heather says. She gives Mum a heartier hug than I did, managing to squeeze a genuine smile out of her.

Beth refuses Mum's offer of gas money because I'm "practically family," which makes me blush. She excuses herself to call her fiancé about our mishap with the flat tire.

Heather propels me into Poppa's room. I brace myself to face the agony of Dad's last days all over again: tubes, monitors, and the vicious hiss of a respirator. A shattered man in a bed. The crinkles around his eyes that won't ever open, no matter how much I pray. The red-gold curls on his arm. The hundred inside jokes he won't share in his stretched-vowel, swallowed-consonant British accent.

My legs go wobbly, but Heather steadies me. "I'm with ya, honey. You can do this."

"Maggie?" croaks a man in the bed by the window. He's small and bald, with a band of gray hair circling the back of his head. A tube-type thing is taped to his fingertip, and a monitor blips cheerfully from a wall station behind his headboard.

No respirator. Not bruised and broken. Not ginger-blond. Not Dad.

Poppa.

He smiles and reaches to grasp our hands. "Kittens! Jeeps to help ya."

"Well, thank God he's calling you Maggie, too," Mum says, as we eat surprisingly tasty lasagna in the hospital cafeteria. She digs into hers with gusto, like she hasn't eaten all day.

"I reckon Mama's name is one of the few he can remember," Uncle David says. "He's called me Blue, waiter, and once, Appomattox."

"Appomattox!" Beth snickers. "That's so much simpler than David."

"The things he says are all so…completely random," Mum says as she butters a second roll. "Like having a conversation with a snowglobe. You never know which word will float by and he'll grab it. What surface most are memories of Mama and teaching history."

She's so matter-of-fact about it. But I have to wonder what other words Poppa has called her. Parasite? Poison? Or has he mercifully forgotten the things he usually blames her for?

David tells us that before this stroke, the plan was to transfer Poppa to a rehabilitation hospital in Elmerton on Monday. Because he's lost language rather than mobility, it's possible his doctors will stick with that plan. They could send him home after two weeks of intensive rehab, or they might recommend moving him to a nursing home. So much depends on how he does in therapy.

When Mum asks after Heather's family and the pox party, I slip off to the bathroom to check my phone. It's not like Theo to totally blow me off. No, that's my area of expertise. I sink into one of the cushy chairs meant for nursing moms and scroll through my text messages again.

12:31 Where are you? Art room is dark.

12:34 Fletch said he helped Heather empty your locker. You at the Irving entrance?

12:36 Where is everyone? Three cabs here, but not Beth.

12:49 Beth texted to say you headed out already. Rats. Can't believe I missed you. I feel like punching something.

I read the messages a second and third time, and see nothing but his growing frustration. The fourth time, I bump the down arrow instead of the up.

Stupid calc. I got extra time, but I doubt I pulled higher than a C. Social work looks a lot better than psychiatry, at least today. I don't know if I'll ever be good enough in math to get into med school. You'd probably tell me that I will. That God will help me. Man. I miss you already.

I'm leaving soon for this wedding in Long Island. You can text me back if you want, but I'd rather hear your voice. Call when you get a chance. <3 U, T.

He's not mad. He's sad. I can almost feel his knotted shoulder muscles against my palms and hear a sigh rattle his chest. There's no question what I should do.

Theo's deep "Hello?" from my phone feels like someone reversed gravity. My secret depths soar up and out, scattering across the miles like a sparkling river flowing from me to him.

I gasp his name, he whispers mine. Our stories jumble-tumble out. We talk about our difficult finals and our worries about reaching our dreams.

Theo's glad that Beth and I hit it off. If only he knew just how much. He'd likely blush to hear Beth call me "like family." The virtual makeovers strike him as especially funny, but he's thankful we cheered her up. Wedding planning has been such a drag for her that he and Cat have been cooking up schemes to help her elope. So far, Beth has shot down all their ideas.

Finally, I tell him about Poppa's sudden stroke and how his nonsensical speech seems to hurt Mum as much as fog would — an annoying path blocker, nothing more. With Poppa no longer able to boss her around, surely we'll be able to go to Paris like we planned.

"I hope so for your sake," he says. "Why exactly is he so mean to your mom?"

"It's kind of a long story. And weird."

"Weirder than being best friends with a blanket? Come on, Dee."

"I know...trust you more." I take a cleansing breath. "All right. My Nana Tilman, Mum's mother, had cancer a long time. They first found a brain tumor when she was pregnant with Mum, so they waited until after Mum was born to start treatment. Poppa believes that's why Nana's cancer came back over and over and killed her at fifty-three. That it's all Mum's fault Nana's gone."

"That is seriously messed up. You know that, right?"

"Yeah, but Poppa won't let it go. Mum just puts up with it."

"She shouldn't. I totally get why you want to keep her away from him."

"Do you think there's any hope that Mum can ever be okay?"

"There has to be," he says, "because God gave her you."

"Aha!" Heather crows, suddenly standing over me. "Beth owes me ten bucks. I knew you'd never go wandering off to a hospital floor by yourself."

It's awkward saying goodbye to Theo, somehow pulling back the sparkling river of feelings when my best friend is pacing the room, her gum snapping. His last, low, "Bye, babe" gives me such a shiver, I have to sit for a moment after hanging up.

It's going to be a horridly endless summer away from him.

* * *

Out in the parking lot, Heather and I retrieve our luggage from Beth's car and squash her in a group hug. She thanks us for helping her out of her wedding funk. She says that seeing what I'm going through made her realize how insignificant her troubles are.

As Beth drives away, Mum and David help us haul our stuff over to my uncle's truck. Mum promises she'll meet us at the house in a few hours. She wants to have a chat with the night nurses before she'll be comfortable leaving Poppa overnight.

Seriously? Even when Poppa can't talk, he's guilting her into putting him first.

"You should come with us and get some rest," I say. "It's what Dad would have wanted."

Mum's eyes widen. "If he could see how Pop is suffering, he'd understand."

I beg to stay with her, but Mum shakes her head, "If you three could get Pop's house in better shape, that would help me most, all right?"

"You bet, Mrs. D," Heather chirps agreeably. Traitor.

Mum walks away, but I trot after her. She gives me a stern look and says, "Enough, Danielle. I did this to him, so I've somehow got to make it right. Please just go with your uncle."

I slink back to the truck, defeated.

"Let it go," David says. "She can't hear you. I've asked Sarah from next door to swing by tonight to talk some sense into her. She's a nurse, so she oughta be able to set Grace straight about what causes strokes."

He loads our suitcases into the back of his pickup, wedging them in among his carpentry tools and some unfinished projects.

Heather gasps. She grabs my arm and points at a huge box with lots of shiny hardware around its sides. "Is that a *coffin*?" she whispers.

"Of course not," I murmur back. "It's a storage chest."

"But those long poles rigged up on the side — those are for pallbearers."

Pallbearers. Like at a funeral. I shudder.

"Is that…for Poppa?" I ask my uncle, pointing at the suspicious box.

Uncle David squints at me like I just spoke Hungarian.

"Oh, right," I say. "You always haul around a coffin, because people up and die on you every day, huh? Or are you bringing around your vampire girlfriend to finally meet the family?"

"Commission," he says and climbs into the driver's seat.

Heather gives a glint-eyed grin, then knocks five times on the casket.

"What are you *doing*?" I hiss as Uncle David guns the engine.

"Checking for the vampire girlfriend. No answer. She must be a heavy sleeper."

* * *

David turns onto my grandfather's driveway. We pass through towering brick gateposts and a grove of imposing oaks, then come into a clearing. Poppa's ranch house sits on a small knoll like a beached warship with its gunmetal-gray siding and front porch sticking out like a prow. A cluster of cannons sits in the shorn grass and oversized toy soldiers guard the front door. Tall shrubs hunker around the house like evergreen sentinels.

"Welcome to the fortress, girls," David says. "You impressed? You're supposed to be."

Heather gives me a sideways look.

"I didn't know about the cannons. Holidays are always on our turf. Dad's rules."

As we park beside the equally imposing garage at the far curve of the driveway, Rhys runs alongside the truck, barking.

"How the heck did he get loose?" my uncle says. "I had him tied up out back. He must've jiggered the latch, little devil."

We pile out of the truck into the muggy evening air, thick with the scent of grass clippings and musky, sticky-sweet flowers. A billion crickets chirp a threatening cacophony, reminding me that this is their crawly, leggy, wingy territory. I shudder.

David unloads our bags and we follow him up to the house and into the air-conditioned foyer. The cool air smells stale and attic-like. At first glimpse, I can't tell why Mum was worried about social workers freaking about "the conditions he's living in." If anything, Poppa's living room looks like a museum. Banks of shelves hold all kinds of trophies, medals, and ribbons. The walls are lined with framed newspaper clippings and photographs. Rhys sniffs around the white leather sectional sofa that faces a pale brick fireplace and a huge painted portrait hung over the mantel — Poppa in the dress uniform of a Navy officer.

"Wow," Heather whispers in awe. "Your grandfather must have been quite the heroic guy back in the day."

"Nope," my uncle says. "He never served, just pretended

with a re-enactment group. Bought that uniform at an estate sale and had Mama paint him in it."

My stomach twists. What else in this room is a lie?

The shelves, I notice, hold awards not only for breaststroke — Mum's best swim team event — but also baseball, field hockey, track, wrestling. "Where'd all these come from?"

"Some are your mom's for swimming and art. A few are mine from debate. You might say they started his passion for collecting."

"You mean he *bought* them?"

David shrugs. "He likes flea markets. He likes success."

"Could be worse," Heather assures me. "My great uncle Vance collects taxidermy birds. Feels like you're in that Hitchcock movie at his house."

"Why'd Mum send us to 'get the house in better shape'? It's a little cluttered. Big deal."

David shakes his head. "This is the company room. Take a gander down either of those halls and you'll see another story." He points to two doorways, each closed off by a velvet drape.

I peek behind the first. The dining room is a whole city of paper towers stretching from the hall to the picture window. Teetering stacks of magazines and mail-stuffed plastic baskets cover the sideboard and dining table. All six chairs are piled high with books or newspapers. Towers of yet more junk mail choke most of the walking paths around the furniture.

"The kitchen and master suite are only marginally better," David says. "I know your folks hired cleaners many times since Mama passed, but Pop just refills the space. All I can figure is that empty rooms scare him. There's a kind of logic to which collection fills which room."

David pulls aside the second drape and leads us into "the kids' wing," where he and Mum each had bedrooms, plus a shared bathroom and rec room. The hallway is so choked with stacks of books and magazines we have to shuffle by sideways.

Rhys snuffles into the rec room, searching for crumbs on rust-red carpet that's worn down to the backing in places. Mum seems to have cleared off the daybed by piling stuff onto the existing heaps, now chest-high. Her suitcase sits beside a hulking, blond-wood console TV with a dusty VCR perched on the water-ringed top. Deeper in the room, an unfinished jigsaw puzzle sits on a card table we couldn't get near if we wanted to — puzzle boxes by the hundreds block the way.

David deposits his laptop in the bedroom across the hall. It has new carpet and sleek, masculine furniture, including glass-doored bookcases fit for a professor's study. On the bedside table is a reproduction statue of some bearded dude in a toga looking pensive.

"Nice place," Heather says.

Uncle David reddens. "Pop believes that any day now I'll give up 'this woodworking nonsense,' actually finish college, get a PhD, and live in the Ivory Tower writing about metaphysics. It seems to make him happy, so I don't argue."

Clearly no one ever does argue with Poppa, whether he's being unfairly cruel or kind.

There's a clatter of falling objects in the hall. Rhys yips, then whines. We rush out to find him trapped between two toppled piles. Quickly we remove books and stack them in an empty corner of my uncle's room.

"I'll keep working on the hall," David says. "You girls oughta try Grace's old room next door. It has a big bed you could share."

Heather and I pick our way to the back bedroom. Shifting boxes to open the door, I discover that the periwinkle carpet was once a deep purple. Weird. Mum has never owned *anything* purple as far as I can remember. Unlike David's room, there's hardly room to move, so much stuff is piled in here — mostly presents we gave Poppa over the years. A tower of gift boxes hold new dress shirts still swathed in cellophane. My childhood clay creations are mixed with museum finds from London, still in their original packaging. What a waste to have schlepped all this stuff through customs. Why didn't Mum warn us about his gift graveyard?

"If you want to leave tomorrow, I would totally understand," I tell Heather as we dig a path toward the queen-sized bed. "We'll figure out some way to get you home."

She pulls a build-your-own Big Ben kit off a pile. "Are you kidding? This place gets more interesting by the minute. It beats the chickenpox brigade any day."

"Interesting? It's a complete nightmare. The living room alone gives me chills."

"Your grandpop's a mite egotistical, I guess."

"Ya think?" I retort. I reach for another pile of stuff to move, and something sharp jabs my hand. I yelp, pull away, and suck on my bleeding finger.

"What is it?" Heather clambers over and dislodges the broken picture frame from the stack. She stares at the image, frowning, then shows it to me. "Is this you and your mom?"

The dark-haired, doe eyed woman could be my mother, except her nose is larger than Mum's. She gazes lovingly at a bundle in her arms, but the glass over the baby has been chipped away with a blunt tool and there are deep gouges in the baby's face underneath.

"It's Nana. Holding Mum. I need to get her out of here as soon as possible."

Chapter 9

A thunderstorm rumbles in overnight. Wind-tossed trees become a thousand snakes that hiss through my dreams. Overgrown shrubs screech across the siding like zombies' fingernails. I watch brightness flash across the ceiling and ponder Mum's defaced baby photo.

Heather had said, "Your nana looks so happy, so love-struck with her baby girl."

"I wish I could've known her." I traced the curve of Nana's face, so full of joy and hope.

"I know you think the cancer stuff turned your grandpop against your mom, but looking at this, I'd say he was mostly jealous."

"What do you mean?"

"Well, all signs around here point to him having a pretty high opinion of himself. I think he'd resent it if anyone besides him got so much attention from his wife."

Theo's closet story about his dad comes to mind: *He always had to be Number One.*

Thunder booms so loudly the windows rattle. Rhys's whining pulls me out of bed, and I stumble off in search of my scared dog.

As I pass the rec room, Mum peeks out, her hair hanging in wet waves. "You can send Rhys in with me, if you can find him."

"He's with me, Gracie!" Uncle David calls from inside his room.

"Thanks!" she calls back. "See? Nothing to worry about. Back to bed."

"Wait." I grasp the doorknob so she can't shut me out.

"When did you get back? You look like you got rained on."

She pats her head. "Oh, this? I showered when I got in. Thanks for clearing all the junk out of the tub." Her gaze drifts down to my hand, still gripping the doorknob. She bites her lip. "Did you want to come in, Doodlebug? To, um, talk?"

"Yeah." I curl up at the end of the daybed, hug my knees, and just stare at her, the classic French beauty. It's hard to believe we share DNA. She's a gazelle, while I'm a galumphing giraffe. I tower over her by seven inches and have bland British coloring from Dad's side — grey eyes, caramel hair.

"How did it go at the hospital tonight?" I ask.

Mum watches the storm-tossed trees outside. "Pop was very...restless. I think it's starting to sink in that no one can understand him."

"His stroke isn't your fault. He flips out because he has anger issues. If anything, you're too nice to him. Besides, aren't strokes caused by problems with blood vessels and clots?"

"My brother's old flame stopped by to give me a biology lesson. But even she admitted that anything raising his blood pressure puts him at risk."

I file away this juicy tidbit about the neighbor being my uncle's "old flame," and try another approach.

"Fault and blame are just gonna get us stuck. The real question is what do we do now?"

"Well, this place is unsafe for someone as frail as he is. So I'd say the priority is making the house accessible for him and possibly a live-in nurse."

Her serene martyr voice makes my blood pressure rise. "But it's a mess!" I wail. "And we have plane tickets and a flat rental coming up *really soon*."

"How could you possibly think of going on vacation at a time like this?"

"Vacation? This is an art trip for you to prepare for your solo show. Jeez, Mum. You need time away to focus. September isn't that far away."

"Oh, Dani, it doesn't matter."

"Who says? Poppa? He never wants anything good for you. He only wants what's good for him. When are you going to stand up for what you want, what you need?"

"Well, I certainly don't need you pressuring me about grad school. I can't possibly give it any attention until Pop's house is clean and he's settled."

My heart leaps at this little glimmer of hope. "Really? If we get the house cleaned and arrangements made, we'll go?"

She shakes her head. "Two weeks isn't nearly enough time."

"Let me worry about that. Whaddaya say? Do we have a deal?"

"I don't know. I'll have to talk to David about it. Could you please go back to bed? I'm awfully tired."

I press on. "We'll talk in the morning? We'll make a plan?"

"Good night, Danielle."

I kiss her cheek, relieved that at least she didn't say no.

* * *

I wake with a start, feeling trapped under some strange weight. My legs are pinned down, not by a pile of Poppa's crap but by Heather, who's sprawled weirdly across the bed. Even after I shove her off, the crushed sensation doesn't go away.

My late-night conversation with Mum comes flooding back: the only way to Paris is through a task so huge I hardly know where to start.

Well, laying here freaking out certainly isn't going to get me to my goal. Might as well get on with things. I tiptoe to David's room and try to silently coax Rhys to come for his morning walk, but he leaps up, yodeling with joy at the sight of me.

My uncle stirs. In a sleep-blurred voice he says, "Hey niece o'mine. Everything okay with you and Grace? I heard raised voices last night."

I shake my head. "I need help with her. Maybe we can talk after I walk Rhys."

"I'll come with you. Lemme throw on some clothes and I'll meet you out front."

Rhys is christening one of the cannons when my uncle appears in jeans, flip-flops and the Nietzsche T-shirt from my taxi daydream, when I first thought to call him. It must be a sign. Dear God, let it be a sign. He must be our way out, because Mum is clearly being tested beyond what she can bear. She's ready to throw her life away for a father who hates her.

David scratches Rhys behind the ears. "Guess I should show you where your pooch is allowed and where he ain't. You can tell me what's up."

As we walk the boundaries of Poppa's land, from a pond and cornfields on one side to a creek running through the woods on the other, I tell my uncle about our travel plans for July, and Mum's insistence that we can't take the trip we'd been planning for months. Not until Poppa's house is "ready," whatever that means, and he's "settled," another vague goal. I describe Mum's recent low spirits and how unprepared she is for her September art show. He nods along to the story, interrupting from time to time to point out places where he and Mum used to play as kids.

"So you reckon she'll have a nervous breakdown if she doesn't get some time away?"

"I know that sounds dramatic, but she's had a really rough spring. Dad's birthday came and he was still gone and all the light went out of her eyes. She stares more than paints, but when she does, her work give me chills, and not in a good way. It's so dark — full of mud and crows and broken fence posts. You'd swear she crawled out of a First World War trench in Flanders."

"I wanna do all I can to help her." Frowning, he stoops to untangle the leash from Rhys's front leg. "But two weeks is a mighty tight deadline. I've got client projects to finish as it is. I don't rightly know how long I can be away from my shop, either."

"Can't Keegan and the new guy run it for you?"

"Well...they're both Narc-Anon guys. You catch my drift?"

"You want them to rebuild their lives, but you don't trust them to run your business."

"Keegan's been clean two years, but Chip, only seven months."

"You have church friends who'd keep an eye on them, don't you?"

"You're a very stubborn girl, aren't ya?" He playfully punches my shoulder.

I grind my teeth in frustration. "I happen to be concerned about my mother's mental health and what will happen to me if she has a breakdown. Apparently *you* aren't. So just forget it! I'll refurbish Poppa's whole freaking house by myself!"

I yank Rhys's leash and storm off, blindly galloping toward the pond. David promised to keep Mum out of this but has he? Heck, no. He talks a good game — *It's about time I had a go at being the responsible one* — but when push comes to shove, he's back to being the coddled baby who expects Mum to take care of everything.

It's the first I've run since track season ended, and soon I have to stop to catch my breath. Rhys plops in the grass beside me, smiling. He always loves a hearty sprint, Theo's specialty.

Poppa's house is still a good ways off, but I notice a strange outbuilding on this side of a grove of pine trees. From the house, it's not visible. I head toward it as my breathing slows.

If this place were a garage, you might fit a few cars in it. Three of the sides have picture windows that are papered over from the inside. Rhys sniffs around the perimeter, leading me to a door that's not only dead-bolted, but also chained and padlocked. What's with the high security? There has to be something very valuable or very dangerous in there. Possibly both.

My uncle huffs and puffs up behind me. "Would you please," *pant*, "let me have," *pant*, "half a minute," *pant*, "to respond?"

"What is this place?" I demand.

He holds up a finger, the "one moment" sign, and continues breathing hard.

Rhys scratches at the bottom of the door, like he smells a treat inside. My uncle says, "No," and "Stop," between rasping inhalations.

I lead Rhys in a circle around my uncle. His skin is pasty and his bald head shines with perspiration. Decades of drug use have probably done a number on his body, yet he's willing to pursue me and my runaway emotions.

"You okay, Uncle David? Is it your heart?"

He shakes his head.

"Your lungs? Because of all the pot you used to smoke?"

"I don't happen to be young," *pant*, "or an athlete," he retorts.

"I'm the slowest runner on our team, but you don't need speed for high jump."

"You know just how to cheer up an old guy, don't ya?" He pulls his sweaty shirt away from his stomach in a fanning motion. "I never meant to say I wouldn't help ya, kiddo. You just sprang this deadline on me and I had to think it through."

"Sorry for flipping out. Mum's done nothing but throw up roadblocks. I guess I heard you doing it, too."

"She's got a certain comfort level with being Pop's servant.

Don't expect her to start sticking up for herself anytime soon. Seems to me that's another battle entirely."

"So we fight for her."

"I reckon we do. Let's go see what wonders we can work today." He gives a decisive clap and heads towards the house.

"What about the—?" I call, pointing at the mysterious, locked building.

But my uncle is already out of earshot.

* * *

When I get back to the house, Mum and Heather are having a standoff in the kitchen. Mum's in the midst of a freak out because my friend had the audacity to bag up the towering piles of clean, plastic containers from years' worth of margarine, rice pudding, and cold cuts.

Mum paces from bag to bag, peering inside. "My father's very fragile. We can't take things away willy-nilly!" Her voice is strangely shrill, and she keeps looking over her shoulder, like she expects Poppa to storm in and go berserk.

Poor Heather stands there shaking. "Recycling is good for the earth, Mrs. D. I didn't mean any harm."

"Calm down, Gracie." David strokes Mum's arm. "You're scaring the girls over nothing but trash."

"It's okay, Mum," I pipe up. "Two of each size should be plenty for one guy."

"We're not keeping trash or recyclables, and that's final." David crosses his arms over his chest, looking every bit as fierce as Poppa can. I almost want to cheer.

But Mum's face crumples. "We can't!" she cries. "He can't bear to lose his things! They comfort him. Haven't you ever watched *Hoarders*?"

"He's had a stroke and isn't capable of working with a therapist to fix this. His recovery is our priority, and this junk is in the way of the real end goal here. Jeez, Sis. Use your brain."

Heather shoots me a look of pure panic. I motion with my chin to come with me, away from the sibling squabble.

"My gosh," Heather whispers once we're alone. "I had no idea that would make her flip!"

"It's okay, you didn't do anything wrong. She's just on edge about Poppa."

We wander up the hall outside the master suite. Like my apartment in New York, it's lined with frames, but instead of photographs, they're paintings. More than a hundred tiny still-lifes in crazy colors fill the wall: bruise-purple pears and blue apples, leopard-print ponies, orange-leafed lilies with green blossoms. Each is signed M.M. Tilman.

"This is my nana's work," I murmur.

"Wow. I guess treasures like this make your mom want to sort everything carefully."

"That's one layer of it." I tweak frames that are out of alignment. "Another is that she's scared to do what she wants. Like, she won't go to Paris unless Poppa's house is fixed up first."

"But she's considering it. That's good news."

I shake my head. "I thought so too, until just now. She's going to make it impossible to go. Today she's clinging to margarine tubs, tomorrow it'll be the fifty thousand jigsaw puzzles. We're never going to leave. I'll be stuck here in the sticks for my senior year watching Mum unravel over the destiny of every cotton ball in Poppa's medicine cabinet."

"Honey, you have a real gift for dreaming up worst-case scenarios. Take a deep breath, okay? I'm gonna pray." She lays a hand on my shoulder and bows her head. "Lord, you know Dani and her family better than they know themselves. You know what's broken and how to fix it. Rescue and help them, Lord, through me and anybody else you care to send their way. Amen."

"Girls!" Mum calls in a bright voice. "How do you like your eggs?"

Heather grins. "Sunny side up for me," she calls back. "Dani wants scrambled."

"What? I like them once over light—" I groan. "Very funny. Food as commentary, like 'this is your brain on stress'?"

"The eggs reminded me of something Granny Ruddle used to say: 'When the heat is on, you sit where the good Lord set you, and your gold will rise right to the tippy top, like a fried egg. But you try to git? You'll end up a skitter-scatter scramble.'"

"Mmm," I grunt. I'm not sure if that's the stupidest thing I've ever heard or the wisest.

* * *

Mum makes the smoothest of apologies to Heather, all traces of her former hysteria locked down and tucked out of sight. As we eat, she explains her sketchy plan to clear out the mess. The worst rooms will be first priority, and while Heather and I may suggest what should be thrown out, recycled or donated, Mum wants final say. I exchange a worried look with my uncle. He pulled her a few inches from the ledge, but not off of it.

Reading the panic in my eyes, David cajoles Mum into a shopping trip for organizing and cleaning supplies, since it's always been her gift to make the house look nice. The praise seems to soften Mum's features from tense to confidently determined. Hmm. I clearly need more flattery in my repertoire if I hope to get Mum on the plane to Paris.

I promise that we'll stick to tidying the bedroom we're sharing. Heather nods her bowed head, looking deeply contrite for her sin of unauthorized recycling.

The moment we hear tires on gravel, I leap up and head to the pantry, Heather following.

"Thank heavens for my uncle." I hand her a box of trash bags "I wasn't sure how we were going to get anything done without Mum having a micromanaging stressfest. Your hangdog look was the *pièce de résistance*. Brilliant. Totally."

She grins. "*Merci*. Fletch says I have a flair for the dramatic."

I'm pretty sure he didn't mean it as a compliment, but I keep the thought to myself.

"If there are any other nasty secrets in the room besides Mum's ruined baby picture, I hope we can deal with them before she gets back."

Heather separates dress shirts from their gift boxes while I sort through a pile of my less-than-stellar childhood crafts. I'm not sure whether to be embarrassed by how pathetic an artist I was in kindergarten, or miffed that my lopsided creations aren't revered simply because I'm the only grandchild. Rhys sniffs out a hand-tooled-leather coin purse I made in sixth grade and wastes no time gnawing it down to slobbery globs of hide that stain his teeth grey.

I snatch the gooey mess away from him and banish him to the back yard, clipping him to the old-school steel-link dog chain David rigged up yesterday.

When I return, Heather is digging through a box of papers, shaking her head in dismay. She shows me some of Mum's school papers and programs, ticket stubs and scrapbooks, which have been roughly crumpled and crammed away like they're trash. While Heather smooths out and stacks individual papers, I thumb through the scrapbooks. They're packed with minimalist, strikingly composed pages from magazines. On each page, Mum jotted words: "serene," "luxurious," "fresh," "bargain." Was she studying advertisements for fun?

Rhys goes berserk barking. His woofs grow louder and more frantic, then taper off. Not like he's gotten bored, but distant.

I leap to my feet. "Uh oh. If anything happens to that dog, Theo will kill me."

"You want help catching him?" Heather asks.

"Nah. I'll manage. What you're doing is more important."

When I check the back patio, the chain tethered to the railing is tightly looped around a nearby tree with no dog attached. What the heck? I jog out to the chain's end and find the clasp bent wide open. Rhys must've seen a squirrel and broken free.

"Rhys? Ree-eess!"

Nothing but chirping birds and the air conditioner's hum.

How could I lose him my second day here? I kick the tree in frustration and a flock of twittering sparrows flees. There's no sign of him in shrubs around the house or the garage, which now has a coffin in a parking bay. The garden shed holds only dusty tools and ancient sacks of peat moss. I search the pine grove behind the house and outbuilding; still no dog.

Rhys must've taken off through the woods. I can do this. It's just trees. Birds. Chirpy crickets. Spiders. Rattlesnakes. Pumas. What chance does Rhys have against a puma? *God, help me.* He could end up disemboweled on a rock, left for vultures to pick apart.

I run back to the garage, grab a splintered baseball bat and dive into the thicket. Brambles scratch my bare arms. Dandelions spill silken seeds that flutter into my face and tickle my nose. Burrs hitch a ride on my shorts and socks as I kick deeper through the undergrowth.

"Rhys! Ree-eess!"

I swat away gnats buzzing around my head. I'd rather roam

89

the Met when it's wall-to-wall sweaty tourists than be out in all this creepy nature.

Tat-dat-dat-dat-dat. Tat-dat-dat-dat-dat.

What was *that*? The rapid tapping repeats. It can't be a rattlesnake, can it?

"Woof!" Rhys's distant bark rings through the trees. I turn in circles trying to guess his direction. If there are poisonous snakes in these woods, we're both dead.

A flash of red catches my eye as a mid-sized bird swoops past. It lands on a dead tree and cocks its head. I stare at its skunk-striped face, funny red hat of a crest and instinctively pat my pockets for a sketch pad and pencil. The bird turns and pecks the tree: Tat-dat-dat-dat-dat.

That's what I've been scared of? A harmless woodpecker?

More distant barks pull my attention to the deep woods. I tighten my grip on the bat, and follow. Past the brambles, the woods are soft and cool. Ferns and moss make a pungent carpet across the forest floor. Light shivers among the breeze-bent branches. I close my eyes, suck in lungfuls of woodsy air, strange as it tastes to my city-girl tongue. Breaths come like prayer.

Behind me, branches swish. A guy on a black horse circles me, the rifle in his right hand pointed at the sky. One false move, though, and he just might turn its sights on me.

Chapter 10

"You blind or just illiterate?" the rider growls, continuing to circle his horse around me. He waves the rifle at my bat. "We've got 'no hunting' signs posted every fifteen feet."

My fear turns to annoyance. Who hunts with a baseball bat? Of all the stupid accusations.

"Then what are you doing with a gun?" I counter. "Stop pointing that thing at me!"

"My land, I get to ask the questions."

"No it's not. It's my grandfather's. Fern Pond to the road and Clayton Farm to the creek."

"Is that so?" He lays the rifle across his lap, the barrel pointed away, then pulls off his velvet riding helmet and smooths his black hair.

This is no man. He's just a kid, my age. And not exactly how I pictured the hick locals, who Mum always describes as "Pennsyltucky cowboys." No, he's in breeches and tall boots, riding with an English saddle, not Western.

"So Old Man Tilman's got a family, huh? Don't look like him. Taller than him, aren't ya?"

I shrug.

"You got a name, Tilman? Or should I just call ya bat hunter?"

"My mother's a Tilman, not me. I'm Dani. Dani Deane."

"I'm Law Flynn." He holds out his hand, but I don't shake it. Frowning, he pops his helmet back on. "Isn't Danny kind of a weird name for a girl?"

"It's short for Danielle. I wouldn't call Law a normal name either."

"Law?" He snorts.

"Didn't you say your name was Law Flynn?"

"No. It's *Lawf*-lyn, L-A-U-G-H-L-I-N."

"Laughlin what?"

He mumbles something I can't make out.

"What was that?"

"O'Donnell, okay?" he barks, making his horse snort and prance with fright. "Yeah, I'm a Mick. I don't drink beer for breakfast, but I do have a short fuse, so don't mess with me."

This guy I thought would shoot me full of holes is so touchy about his name and ethnicity, it cracks me up. Especially because he seems intensely American compared to the guy in Wilkes-Barre who changed Beth's flat tire. As my nervous chuckles dissolve into laughter, he dismounts and strides toward me.

Something cool bumps my ankle. The rifle. All mirth vanishes from my mind, like nothing will ever be funny again. I back away so fast, I trip over a tree root and fall on my butt.

He stands over me with the gun pointed at my feet. "You think I'm funny, Danny Boy?"

I shake my head. "N-no," I stutter, scrambling back farther. For a long, tense minute, I stare at his grip, watching for his finger to stray near the trigger. It doesn't, so maybe I can talk my way out of this. "I just— What did you call yourself? A Mick? Seriously? Is being Irish considered weirdly ethnic here? In New York, you could have earlobes stretched to your shoulders and pierce your whole face with nails and hardly get a passing glance from anyone."

"Oh, in Noo Yourk, eh?" he says in a Monty Python voice. Mocking me. Sheesh.

I stand and dust off my backside. "My dad was British. I guess I say some things a bit like he did."

I expect him to comment on my use of the past tense, but he

turns away, pats his horse's glossy shoulder, then takes up the reins again. "Old Man Tilman still up at North Penn? Heard he had a stroke or something."

"Yeah. What of it?" I can do the surly act too, buster.

Laughlin looks at his boots and mumbles, "Hope he's okay." He mounts the horse in one fluid motion, and circles me once again. "You see any foxes or coyotes out here, gimme a holler. Something made feather dusters of a couple of our hens. I aim to see it doesn't happen again."

Rhys bounds up to me, panting with joy. "There you are, you little Houdini!" I cry.

"Might want to keep your pets tied up till I find the hen killer. Got it?"

"Thanks for the neighborly warning, Law." I flash a syrupy smile and bat my eyelashes.

"Just watch where you wander, Danny Boy."

* * *

When I emerge from the woods, Heather is waving my phone over her head, calling my name. I awkwardly crouch-jog toward her, the bat in one hand, Rhys's collar firmly gripped in the other. I tell her about the dog's escape and the jerk on a horse who prodded me with a gun and accused me of trespassing on my own family's land. She's both appalled and intrigued by my run-in with Laughlin. If she didn't have news of her own to share, I swear she'd run off into the woods to see him for herself.

She hands me my phone and tells me Theo's been trying to reach me. Nothing urgent. He just wanted to check in while he had a few minutes to spare. While Heather pets Rhys and chatters away about our boyfriends' packed schedule at the wedding today, I scan Theo's texts about the hotel, Fletcher's snoring, how he's praying for us and missing me, and when to call him back this evening.

"You didn't tell him about the dog disappearing, did you?" I ask Heather. "I don't want him to think I'm irresponsible and ungrateful."

"I said, 'she stepped out' in my best secretary voice. Happy?"

"Sorry. I know you hate running interference."

"You don't need it, honestly. Theo doesn't expect you to be perfect. Now that Rhys is back, you should tell him about your adventure. I mean, come on. You creeping through the woods with a baseball bat? The guy on horseback, out fox hunting? It's pretty funny."

I force myself to chuckle. I could've been shot. Rhys, too. I doubt Theo would be especially amused to hear about our brush with death.

As we head back inside, Heather says, "You know how I like to roam when I'm on the phone? I discovered something kind of weird while I was talking to the guys." She leads me around the perimeter of the living room, pointing to the framed clippings. Most of them are about Mum — her full-ride college scholarship, academic awards, prize-winning ad campaigns.

"So there is some truth mixed in with the lies," I murmur.

"It got me wondering what your grandpop thinks is worth hanging on his walls, so...I did a quick look around the house."

"And?" I demand, feeling stupid I didn't think of this myself.

"I found artwork by you and your nana all over, but not a single thing your mom made."

Mum and David hobble in, laden with bulging shopping bags. I offer to show Mum the pile of dated clothing I think we could donate, and suggest we run a load over to Goodwill.

"Not now, darling." Mum says. "I need to pack some things for Pop and take him lunch."

"It will only take a minute. It's not like they won't feed him if you aren't there at noon."

She shakes her head. "He won't eat what they give him. He...tossed his supper into the hall outside his room last night, tray and all."

* * *

Mum is frustratingly tight-lipped as we drive to the hospital. I try striking up a conversation in French, just so we can practice, but Mum's frown deepens, so I pull out my sketch pad and draw her instead.

"Must you?" she finally says, annoyed.

"Well, yes actually, because..." I set down my pencil and look out the window. "I kind of have some make-up art to do. See, I, well...I botched my final."

"What? I left you there so you could concentrate! Did you and Theo just goof off?"

"Of course not! We worked really hard, but I was still worried sick. Also, I maybe didn't read the assignment very carefully. Which is totally my fault. Anyway, Ms. Q is giving me a makeup assignment that she'll e-mail on Monday. That's the whole story, I swear."

"I ought to ground you." She brakes for a red light and gives me a hard, sideways look. "But squeezing yourself into that horrid pit of a room seems like punishment enough."

"I'm sorry Poppa has treated your space so badly. But don't worry, we're making great progress."

"It was never really my space. I couldn't even pick my own carpet. David did. A surprise for my ninth birthday."

"That explains a lot. So he was what, five?"

"Mmm. The little prince thought lurid purple was a better

'girl color' than pink." There's a resentful edge to her voice.

"We'll pick better colors this time, Mum, and before you know it, we'll be painting like maniacs beside the Seine."

I grin at her, but she stares straight ahead, focused on finding a parking spot.

"Just you wait. Baguettes and brie, the Musée d'Orsay and Petit Palais, mimes and accordions, cobbled streets and golden light — it's going to be so inspiring, so awesome."

She cuts the engine. I freeze, wondering if she'll snap at me or recite one of her defeated martyr lines. But she simply wipes something off her cheek (a tear?) and gets out of the car.

Once in Poppa's room, Mum sets out the food we brought, nodding as he chatters at her.

"Blue has is ripple leftover pond car hill."

"David's new truck is very nice indeed," Mum answers, as if Poppa had actually said something intelligible. "Want some cinnamon on your applesauce, Pop?"

"Carburetor. Grip gone axel bat."

"Mmm. I imagine the food here isn't what you're used to."

Holy cow, does she understand what he's trying to say?

"Axel bat!" he repeats, slamming his fist on the tray table and making the dishes jump.

Nope. She's just making her best guess. And that time she was wrong.

She tries again. "You're not allowed to have beer in here, Pop. It's against the rules."

"Guh- guh—" he stutters, pointing at Mum. Is he trying to say her name?

"Grace?" I offer.

"Goose," he says, then his face clouds with anger. Once again, his mouth has betrayed him. He roars in frustration and shoves everything off the bedside table.

Mum cringes as his tissue box, empty cups, and get-well plant from Beth crash to the floor. "Pop, relax, I'm right here." She pats his arm, but he slaps her hand away.

"Hey!" I blurt, indignant that he'd strike her.

Mum just raises a hand of warning to me, as if to say, *it's my problem. Leave it.* She signals me to bring her a trash can, then bends to clean up the mess.

With a critical squint, Poppa watches her arrange the unbroken items on the bedside table. "No eye brass!" he accuses.

"No...iris?" I guess.

Poppa glares at me, like I'm the one babbling nonsense. "Dabble goose axel bat!"

"Of course Danielle can understand you," Mum says, nudging me until I smile.

I doubt I can play this game half as well as she does. It's like all her years of accommodating his whims have trained her for this moment of pseudo-mind-reading.

"I, ah, thought I saw an iris bouquet," I lie. "I must be mis-remembering."

Mum beams at me, then tidies up Poppa's lunch tray. "Here, try the chicken salad. It has grapes in it, just like your favorite at Corner Café."

He pokes suspiciously at the sandwich, then takes a bite. And another. "Chartreuse," he says, as if that pronounced it quite good.

* * *

"Hello?" Theo shouts in the phone as raucous bhangra music blares behind him.

"Thebes? Where are you? A Bollywood film festival?"

He laughs, a warm, deep rumble like the school furnace on a

wet morning. "No, I'm at the reception." The music and chatter fade out. "Man does this crowd know how to celebrate. I totally wish you were here. You'd love all the color — the bride's red sari, our orange ties, the bridesmaids' gold dresses. The food's phenomenal, too." He sighs. "How's your day been?"

"Weird in so many ways. Mum and I went to see Poppa this afternoon. He's still talking nonsense, and worse, Mum acts like she can understand him. It's so stressful to watch."

"Sorry, Dee. How's everything else going?"

"If we can get Poppa's house cleaned up, Mum says we'll go to Paris like we planned."

"Cool. Or not cool? How bad is the place? Worse than you expected?"

"No, just...different."

"Yeah? Different how?" His voice lifts with curiosity.

Sweaty heat rises under my arms, at my neck and hairline. What would he think of the faked officer portrait, or worse, what Poppa did to Mum's baby picture? But he didn't ask me to share every psycho detail. I can be more general, right?

"Poppa's obsessed with war stuff. Collects it. Which is weird when he was never in the military."

"He taught history, right? And war memorabilia are valuable, so it doesn't seem so strange. Or is there something else?"

"Nope!" I chirp, then clench my teeth. I shouldn't be so cheerful about shutting him out. "I, um… need to go help with our thank-you supper for the neighbor — my uncle's 'old flame,' according to Mum. I think David wants to rekindle whatever they had, because he gave Poppa's back patio an extreme makeover in like two hours: powerwashing, weeding, hanging lanterns. No one goes to so much trouble just to say 'thanks for driving my father to the hospital.'"

"Well, if he has a reason to stick around Dunn Creek, it will make your Paris trip easier."

"You're right! I should be encouraging this."

"Dani, no! Down, girl. No matchmaking, I beg you."

"Relax. I'll just do my best to make sure Uncle David doesn't scare her off."

"I'll pray for him, and you too. I wish I could zap myself there right now and help you with stuff. You're gonna need serious muscle to clear out decades of junk in two weeks."

My stomach clenches at the thought of him seeing the insanity first hand. "That's...sweet, but what are the chances your mom will let you off the hook from working the file room at her practice?"

"Since no one else hired me, pretty much zero. She wouldn't dream of letting me relax over the summer when I could be building my résumé."

I shouldn't feel as relieved as I do at this news. "Sorry, hon. Just remember, when alphabetizing those files, Mac goes before Mc."

Mick. What rifle-dude called himself. Should I tell Theo about that? Nah. He'd freak if he knew that guy threatened me, and chances are I'll never see the creep again anyway.

"I guess I should let you go," Theo says. *"Je t'adore, Danielle."*

"Me, too," I whisper.

"Ah, ah!" he scolds. *"En français."*

"Je t'adore, Theodore, lumière de ma vie."

"Light of my life?" He laughs. "Now you're just showing off."

* * *

"So what's the verdict?" Heather whispers as we set the

picnic table. She juts her chin toward our guest, Sarah from next door. "Like her? Hate her?"

"Not enough data." As I set silverware at each place, I study the petite, bushy-haired woman in a tie-dyed sundress and Birkenstocks. She sips wine and chats animatedly with Mum like a long-lost sister.

My uncle has eyes for Sarah alone. While staring longingly at her, he absently tosses the salad, pitching most of it onto the table.

"Salad emergency at two o'clock," I hiss to Heather. "Help clean up. I'll distract them."

I carry a bowl of chips over to Mum and Sarah, blocking their view of my idiot uncle.

"Thank you, Danielle," Sarah says, her piercing-blue eyes studying me with kind interest. "I've heard you're an artist, like your grandmother."

I nod. "Mum, too. Did she tell you she has a solo show in New York in September? We're going to Paris in July so she can finish getting ready for it."

Mum clasps her forehead, as if I'd announced she suffered from hemorrhoids.

"She did not. That's fantastic, Grace." Sarah squeezes Mum's arm. "Your Mama would be so proud. And Paris? I just might hide in your suitcase. I've never been anywhere but Dublin."

"Nothing's definite," Mum says. "Pop's so frail, and there's so much to do on the house."

I'm about to protest, but my uncle steps in front of me and tops off Sarah's glass of wine. "Your son coming tonight?" he asks.

"He'll be a bit late," she says. After mowing, he has evening feed at Grouse Hill."

"Busy guy, huh?"

"Savage class lad," she says in an odd accent. "Loves work. Always looking for it."

Looking for work? We have loads. You could use some serious muscle, Theo said.

"Does he do other kinds of odd jobs?" I ask. "Painting? Helping people move?"

"You bet," Sarah says. "You know someone who's hiring?"

"Yeah, us."

Mum's mouth falls open.

"Before you say we can't afford it, Mum, hear me out. Poppa's house is crammed with stuff he doesn't use or need. Let us hold a sale and we'll easily earn enough to pay Sarah's son."

Mum cringes. "Honestly, Danielle. Can't we please discuss this in private?"

"No need for formalities with me, Grace," Sarah says. "You helped me pull out my first wiggly tooth. And Davey and I, well...." She blushes and looks at her hands.

"We had other kinds of firsts," he murmurs.

"Diary-worthy," she breathes.

David clears his throat and gives me a hearty pat on the back. "Well, I agree with Dani. We could use some help with projects around here. Her sale idea's a pretty good one too. But one way or another, we'd pay a fair wage, if you think your son could spare the time."

"Spare the time for what?" A compact, muscular guy in snug jeans ambles onto the patio and stubs out his cigarette on the porch rail. He runs a hand over his glossy, black hair and my heart seizes up. I've seen that gesture, and this guy, before.

This morning. In the woods.

Sarah steps over to him, beaming. "Here he is! This is my son, Laughlin."

Chapter 11

"The neighbors have a job for you, son," Sarah says. "Isn't that great?"

She introduces him around and he greets Uncle David, Mum, and Heather with a "howdy" and a handshake. But when he comes to me, he hitches his thumbs in his pockets and smirks. "How's hunting, Danny Boy?"

Heather looks from him to me with raised eyebrows. I drop my arm and fold my hand into a gun shape that only she can see. She lets out a tiny gasp.

"We got acquainted this morning, didn't we?" Laughlin says. "Found your lost dog."

I blink at him. Is he freaking kidding me?

"So, whaddaya say, Laughlin?" my uncle asks. "You able to work for me next week? We could use a hand with some projects around here."

He folds his arms. "Well, it is a busy time of year for me. Lotta grass to mow. Pets to feed. Horses to wrangle."

"Please?" Heather flashes a nervous smile. "We really need someone strong."

Jeez, Heather, why don't you go drool on his biceps while you're at it?

"Is that so?" he drawls.

I'd love to throw a whole pitcher of iced tea in his arrogant face, but God help me, I really do need this jerk and his muscles or we'll never get to Paris.

"I'd be grateful if you took the job," I say in a low voice.

"Well, golly, how could I say no to that?" His eyes twinkle maliciously.

"The grill ought to be ready," I blurt. "I'll go get the burgers."

I hightail it into the house, Heather at my heels.

"You didn't mention that he's *gorgeous*," she accuses as I dig in the fridge. "You could swim in those eyes, they're *so* blue. And he rode up on a *horse*? How did you not swoon?"

I hand her the plate of hamburger patties. "He pointed a rifle at me. Why does that detail elude you?"

"Was he dressed as yummy as he is tonight?"

If I tell her about the riding breeches and boots, she'll faint dead away. "Heather, you have a boyfriend. One who writes you poems and doesn't smoke or threaten people with guns."

"Oh, I know. But what's the harm in appreciating the scenery around here?"

We head back outside with the burgers. On one side of the patio, Mum and Sarah laugh their heads off, while David and Laughlin sit bent over a list like they're making battle plans. My uncle jumps up when he sees us, waving to Heather to bring the meat over to the grill.

Laughlin ambles toward me, his mouth curved in a defiant sneer. "So, Danny Boy, I guess we'll be seeing a lot of each other this summer. *That* will be fun."

I nearly spout off that I have a boyfriend who'd happily rearrange his pretty face if he gives me any trouble, but I swallow back the words and my pride. Mum needs Paris, I need Paris. It's just two weeks. I've got to make nice and not let him get to me.

"Oh, definitely," I say, struggling to keep the sarcasm out of my voice. "Fun as a basket of puppies." *When you're wearing a suit made of bacon*, I silently add.

* * *

The opening bars of the first hymn blare from the organ at Poppa's Methodist church. As I reach for a hymnal, a calloused hand brushes mine. I flinch, stunned that Laughlin and his mom have slid into the pew with us. Isn't it enough that I have to spend next week working with this chain-smoking, rifle-toting hoodlum? Can't I have a moment's peace in church?

"Ladies first," he murmurs, handing me the hymnal. His dark green polo and khakis remind me of the St. Fabian Catholic guys I often see on the bus. His usual tobacco smell has been subdued by a leather-scented cologne, or else he came straight from his horse-farm job.

Everyone's well into the first verse before I find the page, I'm so flustered. When I offer to share the hymnal, he balances a corner of the cover on his palm and stares into the distance, leaving me to awkwardly manage the weight. Some gentleman.

Mum fidgets and Heather doodles during the sermon, while Laughlin's intently focused. But during the sung parts of the service, he zones out. For the offertory, a middle-aged couple plays a guitar-piano duet, and Laughlin grips his bulletin in odd, curved-finger positions as if playing along on an invisible instrument. I watch, fascinated, until my view's blocked by a large brass circular thing. Metallic coolness bumps my wrist.

The brass thing clatters onto the pew between Laughlin and me, clanging like a bell. Coins plunk onto the wood floor, bills and checks flutter around under the whirring ceiling fans. I realize with horror that the offering plate I was supposed to pass is now sitting next to Laughlin's loafer. He gives me a look like I'm a leper who steals from the blind.

Two ushers dive in to gather up the spill. Shame sears through me as I bend to help.

Squeezing past Laughlin and Sarah, I slink out of the sanctuary, my hot face hung low. Just off the narthex, I find a tiny powder room, painted puce and reeking of Pine-Sol. I duck inside and lock the door behind me. A few violent punches on the towel dispenser bar cools my temper a little. For good measure, I soak the paper towel with icy water and apply it to my burning cheeks. I wish I'd never met that awful boy. He's probably sitting out there basking in delight over humiliating me so utterly.

The doorknob rattles. "Dani?" Heather calls. "Want company?"

"No thanks. I'll be all right." I press the wet paper towel to my sweaty neck.

"See you in a bit, then, I guess." She gives the door a little pat, a reassurance I could've used. My throat tightens and I wish I hadn't sent her away.

If Dad were here, he'd quip that "dignity is overrated" and make a pun so terrible that I'd have to laugh. But he's not here. He's long gone. And he'll never, ever be able to help me again.

I sit on the toilet and hug my knees to hold in a sob that always lurks in a far corner of my gut. Why am I such a baby? My heart should be full of praise that Mum's actually in church for a change, even if it's only for appearances. My mind should be busy contemplating house cleaning strategies and ways to get my grandfather talking normally. Heck, conjugating French verbs would be a better use of my inner life than wallowing in my grief all over again.

There's a gentle tap at the door. "You flush yourself, Danny Boy?" Laughlin calls softly. "If you don't come back, folks will think you pocketed some of the money you dumped."

I dumped? I leap up, yank open the door, and stand toe-to-toe with him. "You rotten jerk!" I hiss, poking his shoulder. "You dropped the plate on purpose, just to embarrass me!"

Laughlin steps back, one eyebrow raised. "Whoa, there, Miss Spitfire. I didn't do —"

"Spare me." I stride away, slip into the sanctuary, and hunch in a back pew.

A moment later, he slides in beside me. "Before you go up for communion, you might want to—" he points at my foot. A long swath of toilet paper is stuck to my shoe. Fantastic.

* * *

As I haul another load of cardboard out to the recycling bin in the garage, a boxy Volvo station wagon clatters up the driveway, engine puttering like Chitty-Chitty Bang-Bang. Its once-navy paint is faded like stonewashed denim and peppered with rust spots. Must be a granny from Poppa's church bringing us dinner, as we were promised this morning. I hope it's one of those epic tuna noodle casseroles with crushed potato chips on top that Mum always jokes about. I bet it's as delicious as it is lowbrow.

I wedge the cardboard into the bulging bin and go to greet our ancient visitor. Before I can even dust the paper fibers off my shirt, a car door slams and someone big rushes at me. The next thing I know, I'm being swept up in strong arms and twirled around to the sound of a deep, bass laugh.

"Theo? What are you —? How did you —?"

He sets me down, touches his forehead to mine, and whispers, "I had to see you. Oh, babe, I have so much to tell you."

"You can *drive*? But you're not eighteen yet."

"Relax. It's completely legal here. I got my permit last summer, and passed the test over Easter break. Sorry I couldn't tell you. Mom swore me to secrecy. Anyway, I only drive here, just Gertie. She's not much to look at, but no one will care if she gets a few dings from my newbie mistakes. I need her to get to my new job from the lake house."

"New job? You won't be filing dental records?

"Nope. I got an e-mail last night from the camp that wait-listed me. They were so impressed with my extra recommendation letters and 'gumption,' they shuffled around some staff so they could hire me. The camp is just up the road, and I get every Saturday off."

"Wait. You'll be *here*? To do things with *me*? Every Saturday?"

"Yes!" He picks me up and twirls me again.

"Wow, that's just...wow." My mind reels. Extra help the next few weekends would sure make the Paris trip easier. But that would mean letting him see, up close, the evidence of how screwed up my family is.

"Anyway," he says, "that's my good news."

"Oh. There's bad news?"

He grimaces. "More like...weird news."

"Theo!" Mum cries in surprise behind me. "What brings you here?"

"I'm your new neighbor," he says. "Well, kind of. Our vacation place is in Pinehaven and on Monday I start work at a camp in Eyrie Falls. Fletch and I were wondering if you could spare the girls this evening. Mom and Jeff thought they might like to come swim and have dinner at the lake house."

"Fletcher's here?" I ask. Is that his weird news?

Theo squints at the car. "The dork is hiding behind the seat, waiting to pop out and surprise Heather. Is she even here right now?"

"She's napping," Mum says, then asks me, "Did you think to pack a swimsuit, darling?"

"What about visiting Poppa?" The question leaps out of my mouth, and seems to physically slam into Theo. "I'd kind of...promised." I add, trying to backpedal.

Theo's frown deepens.

Mum crosses her arms. "I'm perfectly capable of visiting Pop without your help. In fact, I could use a break from your relentless assistance. Take her away, Theo, I beg you."

"Yes ma'am." Taking my arm, he leads me toward the house.

"Why are we going this way? The car's behind us." I swivel toward the driveway.

"Can't we talk alone for a minute?"

"Oh-kay," I agree warily and stand my ground.

"Inside? Come on, Dee, there's a coffin in the garage and cannons on the lawn! I'm dying to see what else you edited out of your story." His eyes shine with excitement.

If he can show me his secret hideout and share the mortifying details of his crybaby period, I can't completely shut him out. Besides, it's not *my* weirdness he's so curious about.

"Brace yourself," I say.

He follows me into the living room. His gaze sweeps across the trophy-laden shelves, then he stops in front of Poppa's portrait, frozen with horror. "He wasn't *in* the Navy?"

"It's an authentic uniform, just not his. Nana's technique is outstanding, though."

Theo swallows. "Uh...sure."

Heather lumbers out of the kids' wing, bundled up in a cardigan, her skin porcelain-pale under the freckles. "I feel kinda weird. Achy and cold." She notices Theo and stares like he's an alien that landed in Poppa's living room.

"He's just half the surprise. There's more outside. I guarantee it will make you feel better. Right, Thebes? Theo? Earth calling Theodore."

"Surprise, right." He rushes over to help me lead her.

When we approach the car, Fletcher leaps up from behind the back seat.

Heather frowns. "Who's that?"

"It's Fletch. Your boyfriend?" Theo motions to his friend to join us.

"Hey, Peaches," Fletcher says in a smarmy, lounge-singer voice.

Heather squints at him. "Fletchie? What happened to your glasses?"

"My glasses!" he cries, indignant. He looks at each of us with outraged disbelief. "You saw me in contacts Thursday *and* Friday. After your numerous critiques of my bespectacled appearance the past year, I at last relented and submitted to the exquisite torture of sticking my finger in my own eye. Now *this* is how you react to my sacrifice?"

Theo and I exchange a look. Three days was all it took for old Fletcher to reappear.

"Oh, Mr. Grumpy." Heather pats his cheek. "Your glasses made you look smart. Like a great, big, giant Einstein brain."

"What have you *done* to her?" Fletcher demands. "Did that addict uncle of yours give her Rohypnol or Ketamine? You know, roofies, Special K?"

"Dude, get a grip," Theo says. "Her uncle has been clean for years."

"Don't worry, Fletchie." Heather snuggles up to his wooden frame like he's a huggable tree. "I'm just a little sleepy."

"She napped for hours," I say. "I think she might be fighting off some kind of bug."

"Maybe the lake isn't the best idea if she's under the weather," Theo offers.

Fletcher slips a possessive arm around Heather. "We drove all this way to see our girlfriends. So I've given up my Sunday for nothing?"

Here we go again. It's all about him.

"I'm not sick," Heather protests. "I just need to wake up more."

"You sure about this, Heather?" Theo asks. "My friend can

be very...persuasive when he wants something. Sometimes he forgets how to properly prioritize the needs of others."

Heather nods, saying in a thin voice, "Don't you dare leave me behind."

Fletcher's posture softens. He studies Heather's wan face and strokes her arm, then flashes Theo a chastened smile. "I'll take good care of her, my man. I promise."

As he leads Heather to the car, Theo and I follow a few paces behind.

"He will completely melt down the minute she starts coughing. Or puking," I observe.

"He's trying so hard not to be that jerky guy who hurts Heather. But change isn't like flipping a switch. Not for anyone." Theo's expression wilts a bit.

"What's wrong? Is it your weird news? You want to talk about it?"

"Maybe later. We need to get to the lake house while they're still getting along. Besides—" he slides a finger down my fore-arm— "I could sure use an hour relaxing with you."

* * *

"*Voilà!*" Heather steps out of the lake house basement bathroom, modeling a flattering turquoise one-piece from the big box of lost swimwear Theo's mom gave us.

"*Très chic.* Much too pretty to get wet. And you really shouldn't. Not if you're sick."

"Honey, Fletch drove hours to see me. Sitting on the sidelines isn't really an option."

"Kind of like modesty isn't for me." I look down at the borrowed blue tankini that doesn't quite cover my middle. I follow Heather outside with my arms crossed over my bare tummy, feeling weirdly exposed and shy.

The guys are anything but shy when we get to the dock. They rush at me; Theo grabs me under the arms, Fletch pulls my feet from under me, and they swing me out over the water and drop me. I yelp when my back hits cool wetness and I plunge into the chilly lake. Kicking up to the surface, I see Fletcher leap off the dock with Heather flung over his shoulder, squealing. As their wicked splash explodes to my left, Theo does a long, shallow dive right over my head.

The moment his head bobs up, I deluge him with full arm splashes. "If you're going to play dirty, I will, too!"

He guards his face, crying, "Okay, okay! I'm sorry! Truce? Please?"

"I don't negotiate with terrorists," I retort, and keep on splashing.

He lunges forward, grabs my hands, and wraps my arms around his neck. "There. Now you can throttle me properly. None of this wussy splashing." He slides his hands around my waist and pulls me so close I could count the droplets on his lashes. "Go ahead," he says. "What are you waiting for?"

Getting back my ability to speak for starters. The strange sensations of being soaking wet and skin-to-skin fill me with a delicious terror that wants to dive into the sun-dappled depths of his hazel eyes, and equally longs for a puffy layer of parka between us.

"Before you kill me," he continues, "You ought to know you look especially gorgeous tonight and I hope you'll remember me fondly as the guy who just wanted to relax with you when we were under a lot of stress. Also, I'd really like to kiss you, but you probably don't fraternize with the enemy any more than you negotiate with terrorists."

"I don't what-ernize?"

"Fraternize. You know, get cozy." His thumbs stroke my ribcage, making me shiver.

"Right. That could be...dangerous." Especially when his tantalizing torso is no longer hidden. I tear my eyes away from his pecs and teasingly pat the tank-shaped stripes of pale skin on his shoulders left by his crew uniform. "Nice tan lines, boat boy."

"Nice abs, *ma chérie*." He tilts his head and leans in. I can feel his breath on my face. His lips nearly brush mine when we're swamped by two huge waves that make us cough and splutter and pull apart. Heather and Fletcher laugh maniacally when they surface, having executed perfectly synchronized cannonball jumps to our left and right.

Theo leaps onto Fletcher's back and the guys wrestle each other for a while. So much for our romantic evening.

Heather and I grow bored and swim out to the floating dock moored a distance from the shore. She discovers a springboard on the far side and calls the guys to come join us. Soon we're taking turns doing silly jumps and dives: Granny Ruddle, Daffy Duck, Rock-Paper-Scissors, the Chickenpox Itch, Pompous Politician (all five kinds), the Electric Macarena.

When Heather gets too tired to haul herself onto the diving dock, Theo shoots his friend a stern look. Fletch gives Heather a piggyback ride to the main dock, then bundles her up in towels. Theo follows, retrieving an inflatable raft and paddling it back out to me. He pats one end of the raft and calls to me, so I swim over to join him.

We tread water side by side as we lean on the raft, chins resting on our arms. The evening sun casts a golden glow on Theo's damp hair, the curve of his ear and jaw, the hollow at the base of his throat. My mental sketchbook fills with warm, shimmering images as buttery as any Parisian croissant.

"The light's so beautiful right now, I could fill ten galleries with trees, ripples on the water, the contours of these muscles." I trace the lines along his upper arm with a fingertip.

His ears turn pink. "Just promise you'll never paint me as a fighter pilot or biker dude or some other whopper of a lie like that creepy portrait your grandma did." He shudders.

"Sure thing." I lean my head on his shoulder, pressing my cheek to his warm, bare arm. "I'm so glad you're here."

"Me, too." He rests his head on mine and breathes out a ragged sigh. "I've had such a weird day."

Finally, his news. "Yeah? What happened?"

"First thing this morning we had a surprise visitor, who hollered and tried to break the door down."

"What? Who was it?"

"The infamous Dr. Ted. You know, my dad."

Chapter 12

Startled, I lose my grip on the raft and scramble to not go under the water. "Your dad? Are you kidding me? What did he want? How'd he get in the building?"

"The next-door neighbors know him from years ago," Theo says, "so they must've buzzed him in. When I opened our door, he pounced on me, all crazy-eyed and smelling like he'd bathed in coffee. He looked about ninety, and as if he'd dumpster-dived in his linen suit. He spewed out this nutty story about being up all night, roaming the city, trying to find Courtney."

"His new wife, the young one?"

"Yeah, number four. She disappeared with all her stuff, closed some bank accounts. It seemed like she'd been planning this for a while."

"What did he expect you guys to do about it?"

"He'd tracked Beth to our place and seemed to think she was in on the whole thing. She and Courtney were friends in college. Roommates, actually."

"No way! I thought you said he met his wife at a boring fundraiser. She's Beth's friend? Beth's *age*?"

He squeezes the bridge of his nose and nods. "Dad raged around accusing Beth of forcing Courtney on him, and using her to destroy his life. It was totally insane. Sure, Dad first met her when Beth brought her to Grandma Wescott's birthday party, but I don't think he and Courtney said more than ten words to each other then. They got together completely apart from Beth."

"So how'd Beth handle his freaking out at her?"

"She fell apart. Started bawling, apologizing — basically for having the nerve to ever have friends. Dad's accusations made no sense, but Beth just took the blame."

"Wow. That sounds an awful lot like Mum."

"I bet Beth would have dropped everything for the next week and helped him if my mom hadn't stepped in. She told Dad we'd had no contact with Courtney in months and that he needed to stop scapegoating his daughter and take responsibility for wrecking his own relationships."

"I think I kind of love your mom. I wish someone would be as direct with Poppa."

"She was fabulous. Well, except when she told Dad to move along, because we had somewhere to be. Suddenly, he got really interested in my camp job. Over-the-moon excited that I'm working at a psychiatric camp. He actually called me 'a chip off the old block.' I seriously wanted to die."

"Oh, Theo. I'm so sorry."

"That's not even the worst part. I stupidly told him the name of the place, and it turns out he knows the director. They did residency together. I got this sinking feeling the director pushed to hire me because he recognized the name Dad and I share. Anyway, Dad bragged that he'd call his old pal and make sure I'm treated right. I begged him not to, but he just said I should never miss a chance to work my connections. Like all that matters is using people to get ahead."

"Will he honestly have time to bug your new boss when his wife has disappeared?"

"I don't know. It seems like he focuses on whatever pumps up his ego. Thinking he could help me follow in his footsteps had him loads more excited than the drama with Courtney. I'm terrified that he'll randomly show up at camp and make a scene."

"You could ask your mom to warn the camp staff about him," I suggest.

"Good idea. Thanks." He laces his fingers with mine. "I used to think Beth had it worse, being the one Dad blamed and picked on, but it's no picnic being on his good side either."

Whoa. So Theo's the favored last-born, like my uncle. But being Poppa's favorite hasn't exactly made David's life better, now that I think about it.

"Is it just embarrassing, or bad in some other way?" I ask.

"There's this weird pressure. Like Dad *needs* me to live his dream. Like his happiness depends on it. What if I'm no good at psych stuff, or I really hate it?"

"What if you're great and love it? That seems more likely to me."

Theo drops his head onto the raft and groans.

"I get it. It's complicated. You want his approval, but not his pressure. Whatever your gifts are, Thebes, even if they're similar to your dad's — God gave them to you for a reason."

He turns his head and peers at me with one eye. "I know, Dee. That's what scares me."

* * *

A harsh buzzing noise yanks me from sleep. I panic and pat my legs, fearing that the minotaur nightmare has come true. Then I see a branch from the overgrown shrub outside fall to the ground. My gosh, someone's out there trimming bushes and it's only quarter to seven. Ugh. My uncle must think I'm staying with Heather on the other side of the house. He was asleep when we got back from the lake house and I decided to camp in Poppa's room rather than with my feverish best friend. Heather's teeth had chattered the whole ride home, despite her constant denials of feeling the least bit sick.

I roll over, cover my ears with a feather pillow and try to sink into memories of my post-dinner walk with Theo. We'd strolled hand-in-hand around the perimeter of the lake, listening to the krr-ik, krr-ok of frogs and watching fireflies twinkle among the shadowy trees. Near the end of our circuit, he led me to a grove of white pines arching over our heads like cathedral vaults. Here, he said, was where he got the coolest wedding idea for Beth.

"Imagine the trees full of white lights and paper lanterns," he said, waving an arm skyward. "Picture rows of folding chairs here." He indicated the area beneath, carpeted in sherbet-orange fallen needles. Then he took my hand and led me to the lake end of the grove, where the trees framed a view of the water.

"This is where the minister says, 'Will you?' and they both say —"

"I do," I whispered.

He tweaked my nose. "No, they say 'I will.' The 'I do' wording went out a long time ago. So whaddaya think? Picturesque, a little rustic, but not gross, right? A place with good memories for Beth, not like some bland banquet hall."

"She'll love it." I turned to face the lake, fighting off a vague sense of disappointment. It's great that he loves his family. Sweet of him to be so thoughtful. So romantic. For his sister.

"What I especially like," he said, "is making Beth my guinea pig, so when my day comes, everything will be perfect."

I spun around. *His* day? Oh. My. Gosh.

A firefly alighted on the V-neck of my tee shirt and sat blinking to every third beat of my galloping heart. I watched Theo watching it, all my nerves quivering.

He touched a finger to my sternum and the little bug crawled onto his hand. "Nothing to be afraid of, *chérie*."

The bug blinked again and flew up between us, making us both startle and laugh.

"Every day with you is a miracle." His eyes shone with hope that we'd have many more miraculous tomorrows. His hands grasped mine, and I realized my face was wet.

"What's wrong, babe?"

"How can I leave for a month? Mum needs to get away — from Poppa, from everything sad that's keeping her from painting. But now you're here, like a dream, and I don't know what to do. If I go, what will happen to us?"

"What are you saying? Of course you're going to Paris. Whatever it takes for you to be okay. Obviously I'll miss you, but we'll Skype like we planned. When your grandpa went in the hospital, I thought I wouldn't see you at all this summer, so the next two Saturdays, and the ones in August are a special gift, right? We'll make it through this, Dani. I know we will."

He wrapped me in his arms and pressed his lips to mine. A symphony sang through every inch of me, scalp to soles. Nothing to be afraid of. Nothing.

A knock on the window makes me jolt up in bed. Laughlin's shock of dark hair and his surly smile are framed in a sunny pane. He salutes me, gives a coy wave, then guns the hedge clipper motor and slices away more branches.

I flop back on the bed and groan. How am I ever going to make it till next Saturday?

* * *

Mum and David head out after breakfast to move Poppa to his new room in the rehabilitation hospital in Elmerton, leaving Heather and me to tackle the rec room mess. I get Poppa's entire inventory of jigsaw puzzles sorted into categories before Heather even crawls out of bed. And I do mean crawl. I nearly trip over her on my way to the bathroom.

She's such a shivering wreck, I wrap her in a blanket from David's room and help her back to bed.

"I'm supposed to be helping you," she protests. "There has to be something I can do besides sit around feeling crummy. How about ads for the yard sale? I could design a flyer."

We toss around ideas until we settle on an event name, hours, and items to feature. With my jotted ad text and the WiFi password my uncle gave us, Heather gets busy on her laptop, hunting for clip art and experimenting with typefaces. I go in search of a printer. Among Poppa's mail towers in the dining room, I find his desktop computer and a fairly new ink jet printer piled high with unopened reams of white, blue, green, and goldenrod paper. Awesome.

Movement outside draws my eye to the window. Laughlin is dragging heaps of branches toward the garage, a lit cigarette dangling from a corner of his mouth.

I race to the side door and holler, "Laughlin O'Donnell, you better not start any fires!"

He blows out a cloud of smoke and yells, "This stuff's too green to burn, city slicker."

I scowl at him, fists on hips. "Don't leave your butts all over the ground, either!"

He drops his branch pile and steps closer, his chin lifted in a defiant tilt. "I thought they'd make you feel right at home. Ah, but I forgot the rusty cans and broken glass."

"Right. Because I obviously grew up in a rat-infested alley among the winos. It's great to know we have *such* an insightful handyman on the job." I shut the door before he can make more snide remarks, or get close enough to see my flaming cheeks. Maybe I do prefer concrete to all this grass that's full of icky bugs and worms. At least trash can't crawl all over you.

When I return to Heather with news about the printer and

paper stockpile, I find her kneeling on the floor, head resting on the nightstand, a book cradled to her chest.

"What are you doing down there? You okay?"

She yawns. "Just sleepy. My low battery warning…had to plug in. Um…." She looks at the book in her grasp, then thrusts it at me. "I found this, uh, diary behind the nightstand when I was looking for an outlet."

The book has a little, heart-shaped padlock holding it snugly closed. Is this Mum's? No, the pebbled, faux-leather cover is embossed with the letters MM in dull gold. I prod the gold-edged pages with a fingernail, but the stiff paper has no give.

Heather clambers back into bed. "Who's MM?"

"My nana, Magdalene Miroux. She must've had this before she married Poppa."

"Only one way to find out. Crrrk." Heather squeezes an imaginary tool in her hand.

"What? Break into it? Isn't that like sacrilege or something?"

"She's not a pharaoh, so I doubt there's an ancient mummy curse on her girlhood diary. Come on, you've gotta be curious."

I trace the gold letters with a fingertip: up, down, up, down like mountain ranges. Part of me fears Mum's wrath — that she'll be even angrier about this than she was about those stupid margarine tubs. But the desire to know Nana as more than a vague blur grows every minute.

"All right. I guess I need wire cutters. If Mum gets back before I do, cover for me."

Outside, I hear the distant scrape of a rake and Laughlin whistling a high, clear, melancholy sort of tune. I duck through a side door of the garage into Poppa's workshop area and squeeze around a rusty cannon he's restoring. Among the paint cans, stirrers, and brushes, I find a pair of cutters like Dad used in his studio to trim picture-hanging wire.

I set the journal on Poppa's workbench and grasp the lock in the clippers. This isn't like desecrating a grave, is it? People usually lock journals so their embarrassing opinions don't become public knowledge. But you can't embarrass the dead.

This is family history I deserve to know. Family history that could open up Mum's world to me so I can help her. I squeeze the clippers and snip through the flimsy lock. My heart thumps as I open the diary and a sweet, citrusy floral scent wafts out. Orange blossom, I think. I flip through decades of time: 1964. 1967. 1971. 1984. 1990. The entries are infrequent, and the whole blasted thing is in French.

I return to the first page. "2 Mai 1961. *Joyeux anniversaire à moi. Pour fêter ça, j'ai peint toute la journée.*" Joyous anniversary to me? Nana wasn't married this early. Wait, *anniversaire* can also mean birthday. I think it says, "Happy birthday to me. To celebrate, I painted all day."

Out in the garage, there's a loud thud.

"Laughlin?" I call. "Are you okay?"

No answer. Clutching the journal, I shimmy around the cannon to go investigate. Poppa's RAV-4 in the first bay is locked up tight. The door in front of the center bay is open, but the recycling bins are just as I left them yesterday. In the third bay, my uncle's coffin project sits steady on a set of sawhorses. At the back wall, the tall bin of fishing equipment looks untouched.

I stoop to examine the two hefty toolboxes Uncle David stowed near the coffin, testing a lid to see if it could have caused the thud. Something whooshes near my face — the top half of the coffin swinging open. I shriek and stumble backwards, knocking over the bin of plastics, which tumble and roll all over the garage.

From inside the coffin comes a low, menacing laugh. I scream again when a dark head of hair rises up out of the hole.

"I vant to dreenk your blood," Laughlin says. He sees me cowering on the floor and laughs so hard the coffin rocks on the sawhorses.

"What are you *doing* in there?" I snarl.

"You shoulda seen your face. It was all *duh-ee*." His features contort like a sideshow freak.

"You are such an idiot. You better not have damaged my uncle's project."

"He built this?" Laughlin strokes the carved trim. "Whoa. Pretty slick work. I figured it was headed for the yard with the cannons and a lawn zombie or something."

"Lawn zombie? You country people are completely mental." I get to my feet and gather up the runaway containers, Nana's journal tucked under my arm. "Wouldn't kill you to help, Drac," I grumble at him.

"Well, Miss High-and-Mighty, maybe I will, maybe I won't." He crosses his arms, defiant.

"You're stuck in there, aren't you?"

"Maybe."

"Give me one good reason why I shouldn't walk away right now and leave you there."

"I'll get fired and you'll have to get your city-girl hands dirty."

"You arrogant, little—" The distant sound of tires on gravel stops me short.

"Sounds like your precious mummy is coming," he taunts.

"Argh. Let's get you out of there before we both get in trouble. Whaddaya need?"

"Just c'mere," he says.

He wraps his beefy arms around my shoulders and writhes like a snake to free his legs. His hot breath on my neck and his evergreen-cigarette-sweat smell make me want to run and hurl behind a bush, but I grit my teeth and let him treat me like a human lifebuoy. He urges me to slowly back up as he gets one foot and then the other on the ground.

I wiggle free of his grasp, shuddering a little. He manages to close the coffin seconds before Mum's Audi comes to a halt outside. We busy ourselves cleaning up containers.

Mum crunches across the gravel, exclaiming, "What happened?"

"I reckon some 'coons got in here, ma'am, looking for scraps."

I hold Nana's journal behind my back and nod along to Laughlin's stupid lie, thankful that at least he didn't blame me.

"Hey guys," Uncle David says, "How about we load the recycling in my truck and I'll haul it out."

"Haven't you done enough damage for one day?" Mum snaps.

"We can't keep trash, Grace. It attracts pests. Those raccoons will be back tonight, and they'll bring friends."

"Do what you like. You always have." Mum turns away and stomps off to the house.

I shake my head in astonishment. I swear I've heard Poppa say the exact same thing to her more than once.

Laughlin frowns and carries away the biggest bin of cardboard.

Once he's out of earshot, I say to David, "I take it things didn't go well at the rehab hospital."

"I couldn't do it, Dani. Couldn't play along that Pop's making any sense. What good is it to keep lying to him? Therapy won't work if he thinks he doesn't need it."

"How'd he respond?"

"Not too well. He's so mad, he won't talk at all now."

Chapter 13

I find my mother in the dining room, sorting papers and smacking them onto piles, her whole body stiff with pent-up exasperation.

"Mum? What happened?"

She blows air out her nose, then in an icy voice says, "As usual, my darling brother won't cooperate. Pop was improving, and now? He might as well be dead."

"Wait, what? I thought he just stopped talking."

"Pop can't work again; he can't even answer the phone."

"Work? He's retired. And if worse comes to worst, I guess he'll learn sign language and get one of those phones for the deaf."

"He could never learn to sign. His language center is *broken*. When he was talking, there was hope that the words would come back, but now?"

"He's mad and can't yell at you for it. Or won't. I'd say that's a huge improvement."

Mum looks like I slapped her. "I'm supposed to be happy that he might be permanently handicapped?"

And Heather says I have a gift for dreaming up worst-case scenarios. I guess I learned from the pro. How does she talk me down when I'm this freaked out? She strips away the crazy.

"Might be?" I say. "That doesn't sound definite. And you've got to admit his being quiet isn't entirely bad. When's the last time he sat and listened to what you had to say?"

"I— He— We talk. All the time. Last week I told him about your junior prom."

"Right. And did you tell him about your classes? Your acrylics in the juried show?"

Mum tips her head, thinking. Tips it again, like she sent a search party deep into her brain. "Well…I guess it never came up. We mostly talk about you. David. The news. Books. What's on the History Channel. Stories from his re-enactment group."

"Maybe this is your chance to talk about yourself for a change."

Mum blinks at me and opens her mouth to protest when our phones chirp simultaneously.

How could I forget? It's Monday. Doomsday. I slowly extract my phone from my pocket, dreading what Ms. Quinlan has assigned for my make-up art final. The way she'd asked if I have the temperament for a career in illustration, I bet she dreamed up something painful and boring, like having me draw machine parts.

Mum's relieved sigh stirs me to action. I open the incoming message and read:

Re: Danielle's art final make-up

Find a mock client and illustrate a document of his or her choice to the client's specifications. Create 10-12 sketches the client must review and approve, and from those, create four colored illustrations. All materials are due August 1. E-mail if you have any questions.

—Christine Quinlan, Rexford Academy

"Wow. This project might actually be fun, if I can find someone good to work with."

"David might like some art for his website," Mum suggests.

"She said 'document,' like a book. You have a favorite from when you were a kid?"

She gets a dreamy, far-away look. "I always loved it when

Mama read me *Madeline*. She named the girls at Madeline's school after her cousins: Clothilde, Mignon, Isabeau, Josette...."

"'In an old house in *Paris* that was covered with vines.' That's perfect!" I clasp her hands and bounce on my toes. "I can work on it on the trip. This is going to be a blast!"

Mum is dazed by my glee. "But Ludwig Bemelmans's illustrations are classic. Are you sure your teacher will allow it?"

"It's *my client's* choice, not Ms. Q's. And I won't be copying the old illustrations, but creating all new art that shows Paris today. I can even draw real French schoolkids, right?"

"In theory," Mum admits. "Summer holidays don't start until the second week of July, so there'll still be some around."

My heart simply soars. How could she possibly say no to our Paris trip when my artistic future depends on it?

* * *

I skip back to tell Heather about my art final and show her the journal, but there's a neon post-it stuck to the door:

> *Hey Dani, I finished our design project from this morning. Show you after my nap.* —*Heather*

Rats. Does this mean I should show the journal to Mum? Not without having some clue what's in here. What if Nana wrote in French mostly to hide her less than glowing thoughts? Did she see how mean Poppa was to Mum, record it all? Mum doesn't need to relive those awful years. She's got plenty of real, present Poppa-induced pain to deal with.

As much as I wish I knew how Nana affected Mum's life, there's too much other work to be done to spend hours translating. I tuck the book into a low shelf of the wraparound bookcases in Poppa's room, among his history books and collection of canteens, ammo cases, gas masks, and assorted military hats and caps. Clearly World War II is his special favorite, probably because he was a kid at the time and it seemed exciting.

Mum continues to be tense and cranky as we work through the afternoon. We argue in circles for ages about the puzzles. I point out that the mostly unopened boxes have such dated typestyles and logos, they have to be older than I am. How much could Poppa miss them if he's never opened the boxes after all these years? If they meant something, he'd keep them in a room he actually visits. More debates spring up about his VHS tape collection and books about beekeeping and origami and a dozen other hobbies he's never going to take up.

Mum's voice gets so shrill I expect Heather to stumble out and ask her to quiet down. Instead, my uncle comes in from the yard to intervene. He points out that making the house handicap-friendly is *her* goal, and she's lucky to have my help. He reminds her that Poppa could land back in the hospital with more broken bones if we can't clear the rooms of extra stuff. Assuming he ever does come home.

This idea stuns Mum to silence. David goes on to tell her that a brand-new nursing home near his workshop in Maine just started taking applications. This sparks a whole new argument.

I slip out of the room, queasy with anxiety. Every few minutes, Mum's voice rises and I catch snatches of her quarrel with David about Maine's awful winters and how such a huge change would kill Poppa. It's all so hard-edged, nothing like the good-natured squabbles between Dad and his big sister, Cecily. He'd call her "cesspool," she'd call him "Graham cracker," then they'd exchange rude gestures, even in their forties.

I slink back to Poppa's room and flop on the bed. All this conflict is the exact opposite of what I expected. Or at least hoped for. Where's my happy montage of dancing with brooms, carrying away preposterous piles of junk, emptying crammed rooms bucket-brigade style while singing show tunes from *Annie* and *Oliver*? If Dad were here, it would be like that, with a bit of closet-raiding dress-up thrown in to make the pictures funnier.

Dear God, I miss funny. Miss Dad's gift for making Mum laugh. Miss Dad, period.

He's still here, Dani, living in you, Mum once told me.

My therapists said something like that, too. *You're bargaining now...angry now...depressed now, but someday soon, you'll wake up and feel your dad there with you, a comforting presence.* It sounded crazy to me, like hoping to be possessed. Maybe that's why it hasn't really happened for me yet. I doubt too much.

Because if he really were living on in me, I'd have some clue how to resolve conflict the way he did — delightfully, unexpectedly. A kind or funny gesture would show everyone how fantastic compromise can be, or better, he'd find a third way that let both fighters win.

So here are the facts: I want to get rid of nearly everything. Mum is scared to get rid of anything. David is on my side, and on Mum's side is Poppa.

Or is he? Has Mum actually talked to him about the house? Tried to gauge how he feels about the mess here? Sure, he has chased away a string of maid services Mum hired, "those infernal women who can't stay out of my business." Is it neatness that he hates, or having his privacy invaded by strangers? I wish I could pop over and have a chat with him. Of course, he would have to be mute at a time like this, wouldn't he? And yet, he can understand us, even if he can't form words himself. Maybe yes and no questions would be feasible. But what to ask?

I wonder if Heather might have some ideas. I'd love to show her Nana's journal, too. The amount of work it will take to learn anything from it is kind of overwhelming. But hey, Heather's stuck in bed, too weak to help with cleaning. Maybe this is why God told her to come — to help me uncover the secrets in here.

With the journal disguised in a towel, I tiptoe past the rec room, where David and Mum now talk in low, somber voices. Gently I rap on the door of Mum's old room. "Heather? Are you awake? Could I see the flyer you designed for me?"

"I sent it to your folder on the school drive," she calls.

"Oh. Okay. I also wanted to talk to you about that, um, book of Nana's." I try to twist the doorknob, but it pulls against me.

"No, Dani. Please stay out," she says in a teary voice. She's close. Just inside the door.

"What's wrong?"

"Trust me, you don't want to be near me right now. If you want to talk, call me. Okay?"

"That's insane. I'm not going anywhere until you tell me what's wrong."

"I think Paulie has wild-type varicella."

What does Paulie have to do with anything? "Your little brother has what?"

"Varicella zoster. Most people get it only once, but I've been researching. There are strains that can re-infect people who've had the virus before. Or the shot."

Wait a second. Paulie. Virus. Pox party.

I step away from the door and slump against the opposite wall. "You have *chickenpox*?"

"I'm sorry!" she cries. "So, so sorry!"

* * *

Tuesday morning, Heather's pox-spattered face watches me from the back window of Mum's Audi. She presses her hand to the glass as they drive away. I stand at the edge of the gravel, waving, and harden my face into a brave mask to keep my tears at bay.

How am I going to cope without her humor, her support, her willingness to do absolutely anything we need? Four days to prepare for the sale and now I won't even have Mum's help until she gets back tomorrow. Every mile she drives to New York, she's being exposed to Heather's horrible, super-contagious virus.

The high-pitched whine of my uncle's router cries from the garage. He'll be in there all day beautifying that creepy coffin and building jewelry boxes. I should have known his client projects would take priority over anything I need. What does he care if we ever get the house cleaned out? He can just run back to Maine and leave us to pick up the pieces.

And Paris? How will we ever get to Paris?

I tip backwards and plop onto the grass, weakened by my clear defeat.

This whole situation is completely hopeless. I can't pull off this yard sale on my own. There's still so much stuff to sort that Mum has to review and approve. A hundred of Heather's beautiful flyers to post and no one to drive me. If only Theo would answer my texts about Heather's sickness and our need for help. Surely they'd give him a few hours off for an emergency.

But maybe he doesn't want to answer. Maybe he met some stunning psych-major college girl with no loony relatives or ink stains on her hands. I bet she rows crew and volunteers with the Psychotic Hobo Rescue Mission and is so perfectly perfect he's forgotten all about me.

Rhys runs to my side and I hug him tight, my frustrated tears wetting his soft, golden fur. A moment later, an acrid, burning smell stings my sore eyes.

Oh no, no, no. Not now. Please not now.

"Sorry to hear about Red," Laughlin says from somewhere behind me. "Chickenpox twice. That sucks." He sits on the other side of Rhys and takes a long drag on his cigarette. I hear him exhale. The smoke tickles my nose.

"If you're here to humiliate me," I choke, "I've saved you the trouble."

"Now why would you say a thing like that?"

Seriously? I sit up and scrub the tears off my face. "The offering plate?"

"That was an accident. I thought you had a grip."

"How about the stunt with the coffin?"

"Pfft. Seems to me I was the one humiliated there. Getting stuck in a place I had no business being? Having to climb this fancy New York girl to get free?"

His reply is so unexpected, I sit there staring. He's right. He was completely ridiculous. Giggles bubble up inside of me.

"Yep," he says, blowing out more smoke, "that's me, the dude with 'laugh' in his name. I think that's why my dad picked it."

"You made him happy."

He tips his head, puzzled. "Ya think? From what Ma said, I was supposed to make him settle down. That's what makes me so funny. Ha." He grinds out his cigarette in the grass. "Dave said you need to hang some signs around town. We can hike over the creek to get my truck, or I can just come getcha in a couple minutes."

So David was paying attention when I told him about the flyers, unlike the half dozen times I've asked about the weird outbuilding behind the pine grove.

Still, I recoil at the thought of riding in a redneck pickup with this chain-smoking rebel without a cause. "Gosh, no, you don't have to do that."

"I don't. I was being polite. You should try it sometime." He jumps to his feet and calls over his shoulder, "I'll be back in ten for the signs."

"Laughlin, wait!" I scramble after him. "Sorry. I was rude. Give me a sec to get the signs from inside, and I'll walk with you. You shouldn't have to make a special trip."

When I return minutes later with my stack of flyers, tape and staple gun, Laughlin is roughhousing with Rhys. Seeing me, he freezes. Rhys takes the opportunity to jump up and lick his face. Laughlin collapses in the grass, squealing in a girly falsetto, "Eeew, dog germs. I'll have to go buy a new face!"

I shake my head. "Is that how you think I actually am?"

He sits up. "Kind of. Aren't you? When I first saw you in the woods, you were spazzing around like butterflies would eat you alive."

"I'm not a fan of bugs and dirt. Big deal. I'd like to see how brave you are in my world, and, say, fend off a stoned pan-handler. Without your rifle."

"I'll take the bugs and dirt, thanks." He gets to his feet, giving Rhys another scratch behind the ears. "Your dog's cool. What kind is he?"

"Australian Shepherd, Husky, and Golden Retriever, we think. I got him for Christmas. He reminds us of my dad who died after a car crash. Dad had red-gold hair and blue eyes — some of the same expressions, too. Rhys was Dad's middle name."

"That was a really nice present."

It was amazing. I'd given up on Christmas being anything but gloomy without Dad when Theo appeared with this puppy he'd found by scouring pet shelter websites for weeks. Because he's that kind of boyfriend.

And here I am, six months later, weirdly unable to mention his name in Laughlin's presence. But why?

Am I that kind of girlfriend?

Chapter 14

Sarah and Laughlin's house is as different from Poppa's as apples are from grenades. The tall, rickety Victorian farmhouse is painted a sunny yellow. Along the sagging front porch, wind chimes made of bamboo, of teapots and cutlery, of laser-engraved tubes merrily jingle and clank in the breeze. Much of the front yard is a lush, disorganized garden of mixed flowers and vegetables. Rust-red chickens wander among the plants, pecking bugs.

"What beautiful birds," I murmur.

"You wanna meet one?" Laughlin scoops up the nearest hen, tucks her under his arm, and strokes the back of her neck. "This here's...April. Yep. Pale patch over her left eye. You can pet her if you want."

I reach toward her tentatively.

"Not like that," he scolds. "They peck if you go near the face. Here." He grabs my wrist and sets my hand on the hen's soft, feathered side.

I flinch away, more from his grasp than the bird. My skin stays weirdly warm where he touched me.

He laughs. "Even chicken about chickens, aren't ya, City Girl?"

I roll my eyes. "Oh yes. Mortally terrified. Watch me shake and sweat."

At my sarcastic response, his mouth curls into an evil grin. He steps toward me and shoves the hen into my arms. "Gotta face your fears or life'll pass you by."

April struggles against me for a moment, but I adjust my grip and she settles in, making a soft clucking sound. When I look up, Laughlin nods approval. Heat flushes through my face.

I look away, asking, "Did you find out what's been killing your hens?"

"Ma thinks it's a weasel. They're sneaky and vicious, and kill for spite, not just food. But I'm building a safer roost in the old dairy. Those varmints can't burrow through cement."

"Do you need to work on that now?"

"Nah. Paying work comes first." He takes April and sets her on the ground. "I'll finish tonight after my school stuff's done."

"Wait, you're still in school? Shouldn't you be there now?

"I'm in cyber school. Less of a hassle. I can squeeze it in around my jobs."

"How many do you have exactly?"

"Not enough for the new roof Ma needs."

I follow Laughlin to a small barn, where he parked his pickup, an older Toyota, shiny with new burgundy paint. He opens my door for me, all gentlemanly. I freeze at the sight of his rifle displayed on a rack in the cab's rear window, but clamber in when he clears his throat.

After hanging signs at every intersection near Poppa's, we head into Dunn Creek. It's like so many little Victorian towns I've seen taking drives with Dad through upstate New York: a steepled church, Greek-temple-style bank, tree-lined rows of mostly-empty storefronts, sprinkled with fake-quaint benches and lampposts. Meanwhile, everyone shops at the strip mall by the highway that looks like every other strip mall in every other tiny town from here to Seattle.

Laughlin and I each pick a side of the street and ask shopkeepers' permission to post signs in their windows. Within fifteen minutes I reach the end of the shopping district, and get stuck waiting for the dry cleaner to wrap up his phone conversation about alterations. A colorful mural in the entry catches my eye. It reminds me of an ad Mum had in her scrapbook with the labels "clean, trusted, reliable." Same layout and color scheme, though that had been for washing machines, or maybe dish soap.

"You like it?" the man calls from behind me. "A local artist painted that. She's off to greener pastures these days. New York, New York. Madison Avenue."

I swivel around. "Grace Tilman?"

His face lights up. "You've heard of her? She's that famous?"

"She's my mother."

He comes out from behind the counter, arms outstretched, like he wants to hug me. I pre-empt the embrace by thrusting a flyer at him. "Help her…us, get the word out? Giant yard sale!"

He takes the flyer, misty eyed. "For dear Grace, anything. This mural is the best advertisement I've ever had. People see it from the street and stop in, even after all these years. She has a real gift, your mother. I hope New York is treating her well."

I nod like an idiot, unsure how else to respond, and thank him as I go. Is New York treating Mum well? Art school doesn't seem to suit her any better than her former job as an ad agency account executive. Gosh, that's an awfully business-y sounding job title now that I think about it. I wonder if she ever got to create anything. Maybe not. Huh.

I find Laughlin outside the hardware store, handing a business card to a guy in paint-spattered clothes.

"So Miz Kuntzler up at Grouse Hill Farm will vouch for ya?" Paint Guy asks.

Laughlin nods. "Yessir. Worked for her since I was twelve. Stable maintenance, horse care, painting inside and out."

"All right. I'll be in touch, L.K." They shake hands, Laughlin suddenly seeming like, well, a grown man. Intriguing.

He reddens when he sees me and retreats toward his truck.

I trot behind him. "So this is why you were so eager to help, huh, L.K.? A chance to line up more work? Why do you use initials? How did you get a paying job so young?"

"Gah! What are you? A snoopy reporter or something?"

"I'm just trying to figure you out. You remind me of the guys at my school trying to get into Harvard. So why do you work so hard? What's your big dream?"

He squints at me. "You're a real weird girl, aren't you?"

"You didn't answer my question."

He busies himself lighting a fresh cigarette. "You wouldn't understand."

"Try me."

"You're from another universe, Danny Boy, tooling around in an Audi, living in a high rise condo, going to private school. Don't look all shocked. Your uncle's a chatty guy."

"And I suppose he told you my life is completely perfect, huh? Because I can just buy my dad back from the dead, right? Or hire wizards to magically make Poppa talk again and stop being a nut-job hoarder."

"I know money doesn't fix everything, but having some doesn't hurt. With Dad out of Ma's life, it's up to me to take care of her."

My hand flies to my mouth. Behind the tobacco smoke and gun and pickup is someone who only wants his mother safe.

Just like me.

* * *

The shopping district in Elmerton, the neighboring college town, is so much larger than Dunn Creek's, it even has a busker. Laughlin stops to chat with the tattooed dude who plucks elaborate tunes on a battered guitar outside the busy coffee shop, his guitar case open to collect donations. There's something familiar about the guy. He probably used to busk in New York but got fed up with the high cost of living or wanted to be closer to family.

I run out of flyers before I run out of shops to hang them in. I hand off my last copy at a florist. On my way out, I pass a tiered display of cut flowers and my arm brushes a leafy branch covered with small star-shaped white flowers, releasing the scent of Nana. Orange blossoms.

And I get the craziest idea. A Dad-worthy one.

I call Uncle David to see if he'll go along with my plan. He hems and haws for a bit, but finally agrees. This plan may flop if Poppa can't or won't answer yes/no questions. But if he can, I won't have to wait for Mum's approval for what we sell. I can find out directly from the source. Better yet, I'll be able to prove I know his opinions; it won't be my word against the silent guy's.

I bring a batch of orange blossoms and white dahlias to the counter. The florist is puzzled by my choice of "wedding flowers" for a get-well bouquet, but she pulls out a simple, teal vase and arranges them. As she works, I practice hands-free video-recording her with my phone. She's patient with my attempts to get the camera position and sound quality right, giving a steady stream of commentary about flowers' meanings until I'm happy with my video technique and the bouquet. I should be able to get quality footage when it matters most — the rehab hospital.

Laughlin reaches for the flowers when I approach. "Aw, you shouldn't have."

I dodge his reach. "I didn't. They're for Poppa."

"You could've picked a more cheerful color than white for a sick dude."

"They're to jog his memory about something. Look, you probably have other work you'd rather do, but if you could take me to the rehab hospital for a visit, I'll buy you lunch."

He frowns. "What, like cab fare?"

"Um...I guess?"

His brows pull even further downward. "For a half hour, pizza. An hour? It's steak."

As we drive across town, I tell him about my hatred of hospitals, the hellish weeks Dad lingered in the ICU after his accident, my naive hope he'd get better, and the grim day of his death. But Laughlin just watches the road, like my tale of woe is as moving as a documentary on sedimentary rock.

He parks the truck and retrieves *The Great Gatsby* from under the seat. "The meter starts running now," he says, "and if I finish this before you're back, you're writing my essay."

"I'll be quick." I snap off a sprig of orange blossoms and lay it on his knee.

Hugging the flowers tight, I march across the parking lot, through the automatic doors, and over to information for Poppa's room number. Stale antiseptic scent hits my nostrils and I have to grip the desk to steady myself. I grab a pen to jot the room number on my hand, joking that I'm bad with numbers. The truth is, hospital anxiety makes me forgetful.

I find Poppa sitting at a small table by the window of his new room, dressed like he's about to go for a jog. He must have just come back from physical therapy, and I bet he'll have more speech therapy soon. He angrily scribbles on the page of a large, softbound book: a beginner phonics workbook, like kinder-garteners use. Oh boy, that's got to be humiliating for someone with as big an ego as Poppa. But it's likely to make him eager to get out of this place to recover privately, at home.

I whisper a quick prayer and force a smile. "Hi, Poppa," I call. "Nice place you have here. Hey, I brought you something."

He takes the flowers, eyes lighting up. His mouth forms the syllables of my name, but he shakes his head, vocalizing nothing.

"That's right. I'm Danielle, named after you. That makes me special, right?"

Poppa ducks his head, a shy smile crossing his face. He cautiously sniffs the flowers.

"I thought you'd like the orange blossoms especially. Nana's favorite flower, right?"

He squints suspiciously at me.

"Um...Mum told me," I lie. Sweat beads on my upper lip. This is going to be a lot harder than I thought. "I, ah...wish I could have known Nana. It's sad she got so sick and left us so young. But you all did so much so she could be at home. We'd, uh, like to do that for you, too."

Poppa's eyes lock on mine and his features brighten with hope. I've apparently said the magic word. *Home.* I can feel the force of it radiating off him like the glow of neon.

Hmm. Forget nostalgia and sweet-talk. It's time to drive a bargain.

"There's just one problem, Poppa. You can't come home without a nurse, and there's no space for one in your house right now."

He prods the tight-petaled center of a dahlia and nods.

"We could fix that problem for you, you know. I'm here to help, and your son and daughter. But we'd need your assistance to do it right."

His face clouds over, confused.

"For your nurse to be comfortable, we'll need to clear out some things, spruce up the place. But we want to make sure you like what we do, so you can always feel at home in your home, you know?"

He shrugs.

Whatever? Of course he doesn't care if the nurse has to trip over his crap. Selfish jerk.

"Well, we don't have to go to all that trouble. You could stay here, or maybe there's a good nursing home nearby."

He grasps my arm and vigorously shakes his head.

"No? You don't like it here? You want to come home?"

His head bobs as he purses his lips trying to form a word. Something with P. Please?

"I don't know, Poppa. You really can't be on your own, and there's no space for a nurse."

"Puh," he sputters, eyes wet. Whether scared or humiliated, I can't tell. But he's in my power now.

"Here's the deal. All the extra stuff in your house has to go, and the kids' wing needs to be spruced up. You let us do that, and I promise we'll bring you home the minute we're done."

He nods and extends his hand to me.

I give him my firmest handshake. "All right. Deal. I'm going to tell you about the projects we have in mind and draw what they'd look like. You can nod yes, or shake your head no as we go." I pull out my phone, click the video icon, and position it on the windowsill so Poppa's centered in the frame. "And this little tool will help us remember exactly what you want."

* * *

Laughlin and I sit in a vinyl-seated booth, saying nothing as we wait for our burgers — my fare for a fifty-minute visit that I hope will set me more firmly on the path to Paris. Laughlin scans the retro diner, looking everywhere but at me, like I'm the delusion he's trying to convince himself isn't real. His stony silence clutches my throat. All I can do is mentally rehearse phrases that might cut the tension. I've offended him somehow and have no idea how to fix it.

A soothing tongue is a tree of life.

Proverbs 15:4. I must have been about six when I got a gold

star for that memory verse. I was all about the gold stars back then. Dutifully parroting words that made the grown-ups smile, earned me extra cookies in Sunday school. The meaning was completely lost on me then. The literal picture of a tongue tree seemed creepy. But the idea that kind, soothing speech could grow something, could make life flourish — well, that's hope-giving.

If God gave me the words to get through to Poppa....

"Laughlin?" I say gently, "I want you to know how grateful I am that you let me see my grandfather alone. You deserve a lot more than lunch for it."

He rearranges packets of sweetener into repeating rainbows: sugar, Equal, Splenda, Sweet-n-Low.

"And I'm sorry for whatever stupid thing I've done to make you mad."

Laughlin continues his sorting project, saying nothing.

Well, I tried. I take a pencil and comment card from the chrome holder, flip to the card's blank side and sketch the waitress who's organizing the pie case.

"*Whoa*," Laughlin whispers.

When I look up, he's staring at my sketch in awed horror. "What?"

"You're like an *artist* artist," he says. "I mean, you can really draw stuff, not just throw paint at a wall and give it a fancy name."

"I'm not a Jackson Pollock fan either." I add meringue swirls to the Key Lime and add shading. "Though I imagine making a big, splattery mess is therapeutic."

He snickers. "You're too tidy for that kind of thing."

"Me? Hardly. I'm just doing what I can to help Mum. She's about three inches away from having a nervous breakdown."

"Because of your grandpop's stroke? Or because your dad died?"

"Both," I whisper, a lump growing in my throat.

The waitress arrives with our drinks and I gulp down half of my Coke. The lump remains, like the words stuck in my throat will suffocate me if I don't say them. So I return to drawing for a while, letting the pencil strokes soothe me. Laughlin fiddles with the sweetener packets again, dealing them into piles like cards, sorting them into new arrangements. *Talk or don't talk,* his motions seem to say. *No pressure.*

When the choked feeling fades, I say, "If Dad were here, he'd know what to do, especially how to keep Poppa from picking on Mum. He always protected her from Poppa's meanness. Without him, it's just me—"

"Trying to keep her safe," he says.

"Yeah."

Our lunch arrives. I bow my head and thank God for the food and for this gruff guy who keeps surprising me. By the time I look up, Laughlin has scarfed most of his burger.

"So," he mumbles as he chews, "Ma says you and your mom are leaving for France in a couple weeks. Some art thing your mom has to do?"

"Mum hasn't been able to paint lately, and she's supposed to have a solo show in the fall for her grad school program. She needs to be away from all this stress, somewhere beautiful and inspiring so she can create again."

"So what happens if you get to France and she still can't paint?"

I choke on my French fry. "That's impossible. Paris is the most inspiring place on earth."

"Wherever you go, there you are," he retorts. "It's something Ma said once about my dad always being on the move, like he'd be happy if he could go try this or that new career or tour with one lame band after another. She meant, you know, happy isn't a place you go to."

"Then what is it, O Wise One?"

"Darned if I know." Laughlin shoves the rest of his burger into his mouth. While straining to chew it, he gulps the last of his soda with an ice-rattling slurp. "I'm going for a smoke. Then this cab," he points his thumb at his chest, "is leaving."

He leaps up and strides toward the door, pausing to point our waitress my direction.

After I pay the bill — less than lunch for one in New York — I head out to Laughlin's truck. The windows are open and he's leaning back in his seat, eyes closed, crooning along to the radio. Or more accurately, harmonizing in a strong, clear tenor.

I open the door as quietly as I can, but he jerks upright and swats off the radio.

"Don't stop," I say. "That was amazing."

"It was nothing."

"Why do you hide your talent, not even singing in church? You have an incredible voice."

"I don't. So just forget about it." He starts up the truck and backs out of the parking spot. "No more side trips today. Dave said he'd train me to use his tools if we got back before two."

"So...you want to be a carpenter?"

"Beats scooping horse manure."

"Or being in a lame band, right?"

He rolls his eyes. "You are such a pain."

I switch the radio back on. I find the oldies station, crank it up, and sing along with Billy Joel in my mediocre soprano.

"Come on, La-La." I poke Laughlin's elbow. "You can at least sing for fun."

"No. And don't call me that stupid nickname."

"LA la-la, LA-la," I tease. "Sing or I keep it up."

"Fine," he huffs, "but this is not gonna be a regular thing. Got it?"

Our voices blend with the music and the air whistling through the windows. He picks up the harmony again. His bell-tone counterpoint sends a shiver down my neck.

By the time we reach Poppa's driveway, Laughlin's taught me a breathing trick so I sound less shrill when I sing. We pull up near the garage, singing along to Lenny Kravitz's "Fly Away," me with my head back and arms thrown high in the air, glorying in the prospect. *Please, God, make this sale a success, make Mum cooperate, and get us on that plane to Paris.*

Laughlin's voice drops out.

I lower my arms, look up, and go quiet, too.

In the garage, Uncle David and Sarah stand staring at each other with one of his intricately inlaid wooden boxes clasped between them. With one deft motion, my uncle sweeps the box out of her grip and holds it at the small of her back as he leans in to kiss her.

BEEEEP. Laughlin leans hard on the truck horn, scowling. "Not gonna happen."

His mother and my uncle pull apart, startled.

"Ma!" Laughlin calls, "You need a lift to work?"

She nervously pats her hair, looks back at David, then walks toward us. Standing on tiptoes, she peers into Laughlin's window. "Hey, honey. I traded shifts. Thought I'd see if I could help while Grace is away."

"Dani needs help IN-side," he says through clenched teeth.

"Uh, yeah. I'd love some help, Ms. O'Donnell," I say. "Thanks."

"Ah, don't be all formal. Just call me Sarah."

"*Aunt* Sarah?" Laughlin murmurs for me alone to hear.

Chapter 15

Sarah slips into the rec room where I'm organizing video tapes. She picks up one of the unsorted boxes, pulls out a tape, and looks confusedly at my sorting system. Her eyes widen as I point out eight different war categories, and finally, "not war" movies.

"You don't think your grandpop will miss these?" she asks.

"His VCR is broken, but the DVD player works fine, so I put every movie on his Netflix queue. He just has to drop the discs in the mail and new ones will come automatically."

She nods and adds *Apocalypse Now* to the Vietnam pile.

We continue working in silence for a while. There's so much I'm dying to ask, but I doubt she'll open up if I interrogate her. As she moves tapes from one box to another, her hands tremble and color flames in her cheeks.

She looks up and her eyes meet mine. "Yes?"

"So...you and my uncle, huh?"

"We aren't— I don't see how...." She licks her lips, shakes her head. "He's a dear, old friend. I admire how he's made something good of himself after slogging through a lot of pain."

"I think he admires you, too. In more ways than one."

Her eyelids slide down. "He shouldn't. I broke his heart, hoping it would get him clean, then went and married a charming drunk in search of a Green Card who broke mine. I'm thankful to reconnect as friends. But as for anything more, that ship sailed a long time ago."

"Not for him."

"I'm part of a past he should never go back to, Dani."

"From the way he looks at you, I'd guess you're the bright

part that kept him from going completely under, and he'd give anything for a second chance."

* * *

Wednesday morning, I finish sorting and pricing the rec room contents, so I treat myself to a tall glass of milk in the sunny kitchen. I find a translation site on my laptop, and open Nana's journal to a random entry from the 1970s, when Mum and David were kids. The curvy, accented script makes me feel like a spy trying to crack code. Phrase by phrase, I translate:

> *You'd think Daniel won the spelling bee rather than Grace. He wielded her little trophy like a scepter and marched her around the crowd, too busy boasting to see how the attention tired her. "She gets her smarts from me." "We Tilmans are naturally gifted with academics." Preening peacock. My suggestion of making her favorite crêpes as a treat was scoffed off. Better to parade her around the ice cream parlor and boast even more. Will the poor child ever have an accomplishment that's truly hers?*

The side door bangs open and Mum calls my name. In a panic I wedge the journal in with the cookbooks, then pull up YouTube on my laptop.

With shaking hands, she lays a flyer on the kitchen table. "Could you please explain what this is?" Her voice quavers.

"An ad for Poppa's sale. I thought Uncle David showed you the design. We hung a hundred of them from here to Elmerton."

She grasps my arm and leans in close. "You've got to take them all down, right now!"

"I'm sorry, Mum, but no. It's what Poppa wants."

She steps back, stunned. "What *he* wants? How could you possibly know?"

"He can communicate more than you think. I'll show you."

It takes some convincing to get her to sit and watch the video I shot during my visit with Poppa. Room by room, I drew the house as it could look cleaned up. I talked Poppa through a list of his belongings we might sell or donate; he nodded approval or shook his head to disapprove. I wrapped up by asking him about the project more generally.

"The money raised from the sale will pay for home-improvement supplies and the wages for a handyman. Any extra beyond that will go into your bank account. Can you trust your children to oversee this?"

Poppa contemplated this a moment, then nodded.

"When this project is finished, you believe David could get you settled in with a nurse?"

At the mention of David, he smiled and nodded again.

"And Grace should take her planned work trip, because it makes you proud when she's a success. Right?"

He rolled his eyes, annoyed, but his head bobbed minutely.

I click off the video.

"Oh, darling," Mum chides, "a work trip?"

"We both have a lot of art to make in Paris, so I think it qualifies."

"I see," she says in a tone that means she doesn't. At all.

"Why are you mad?"

"Why do you feel the need to sneak around and do things behind my back?"

"I'm tired of watching you stress out about making decisions. Uncle David agreed that if we knew Poppa's wishes, the clean-out would be much easier. You've had lots of opportunities to talk to him about his house and what needs to change, but you just won't."

"The poor man has had a stroke!"

"Come on, Mum. You know that isn't the reason you can't talk to him. I've seen how cantankerous and disrespectful he is with you. I was trying to spare you from that. Spare you from feeling worried about his reaction or scared of him flipping out." I reach across the table and rest my hand on hers. "I'm sorry that how I did it feels sneaky to you. I was trying to be helpful."

She purses her lips. "I can't argue with the results though, can I? Video footage. Goodness. Not even your father would have thought of that."

* * *

Over coffee, Mum tells me about taking Heather home. All the Dalys but Heather's dad are now pox-covered, so Mum offered to let Mr. Daly stay at our place so he can escape the germs. As she talks, she digs through her handbag, searching for the art supplies I'd asked her to bring me. She removes bulky items from the top of her bag: a Pantone ink swatch book, paper samples, and a wad of business cards wrapped in a rubber band.

"What's this stuff for?" I wave the swatch book. "You planning to ink Poppa's walls?"

"An emergency cropped up at Deane Studios. The oldest client, Kerrigan-Meade, got into a trade show and they want some new materials designed, but Lisa's still on maternity leave. We don't really have time to find a freelancer, so I was, ah, persuaded to pitch in."

"Ooh, ominous. Did someone threaten to challenge your ownership rights if you didn't come up with the goods?"

Her mouth curves in a bemused smile. "They begged me.

Nate especially. For a minority partner, he's an awfully nosy guy. He got my visual design prof to forward him some of my classwork. The chutzpah!"

"He likes to bring out the best in people. That's why he was Dad's right-hand man, and why you put him in charge, isn't it?"

She shrugs. "I suppose. He offered to take care of the printing end of the project. It's a little...disconcerting to be sought out this way. I'm just a student."

"No, you're a really experienced advertising pro who knows what kinds of designs are effective. Concepts are the hard part of design; the art's easy. Do you have any ideas yet?"

"A few," she admits. "They're pretty rough, though." She shows me her sketched mock-ups of business card layouts and logos. We discuss color choices and negative space and I'm soon in awe of her design mind.

"You're off to a really good start, Mum. And it's nice to see you having some fun."

She stops drumming with her pencil. "Fun..." she says, as if this were the most astonishing word in the universe.

Uncle David saunters in, whistling, his hands clasped behind his back. "Hel-lo, ladies!"

"Back on the happy pills, Dave?" Mum teases.

"No, I rescued a damsel in transport distress who needed a lift to her eleven to seven."

"Laughlin couldn't give Sarah a ride?" I ask.

"He was busy taking a load to the recycling center for me. Sadly, he won't be available to help her this evening either, since he has two lawn mowing jobs. Pity. I suppose she'll need a lift home. Probably dinner, too."

"David! Did you sabotage Sarah's car?" Mum accuses.

He grins. "Just finding creative ways to get around her junior guard. And all I did was vacuum her car for her. A few fuses might have gotten bumped loose. Popping them back in will take seconds. Nothing serious. Not like this peculiar thing that just arrived for Danielle. I didn't think anyone under forty knew how to use this technology." He draws an envelope from behind him, holds it under his nose, and takes a long whiff. "Smells like tent canvas."

"Theo," I say, jumping up.

"Niece o'mine, you best be careful with this," David says, solemnly presenting a letter addressed to me. "There's no love potion in the world quite as powerful."

"You speaking from experience?" I tease.

"You better believe it, kiddo." He winks.

I retreat to Poppa's room and sniff the envelope for myself. The musty scent reminds me of the lake house basement where Heather and I changed into swimsuits surrounded by photos of Theo's maternal grandparents at cocktail parties and polo matches. I open the letter, written in Theo's neat script.

> *Dear Dani,*
>
> *Sorry I haven't responded to your calls or texts. As soon as I got here, they took my phone. We're all on a "technology fast" this week so we can focus on training before the campers get here. For now, they want us to write — letters, journals, poems, whatever helps us feel emotionally healthy. Honestly, our first few training sessions made me feel loads more healthy than I ever have. Compared to what some campers have dealt with — abuse, neglect, parents murdered in front of them — my cheating dad seems incredibly tame.*
>
> *The latest on Dad: he headed to Cape May to look for Courtney at her aunt's beach house, but ran out of gas in*

the Pine Barrens and called Cat in Philly to rescue him. Level-headed chick that my sister is, she called AAA to bring him a can of gas and went back to bed. Cat's text was the last I got before my phone was taken, so I don't know how that story panned out. I'm more than a little worried about Dad's mental state. Why expect Cat to drive an hour at 2 a.m., when he could've called AAA himself? But maybe he's just that stupidly self-centered.

Speaking of family, I'm praying for yours. For you, too. It's a huge relief that Heather's there helping you. Keep her in the loop about how you're feeling, okay?

I'm counting down the hours until I can see you again. Remembering last night keeps me going. The fire in your eyes after I tossed you in the lake. How you tasted of toasted marshmallow when we kissed under the pine trees. I better stop now or I'll never get this in the mail.

Can't wait till Saturday. There are some amazing waterfalls nearby I'm dying to show you. I promise to make the climb worth your while.

For now, I'm with you in dreams.

All my love, Theo

I press the paper to my cheek. He hasn't forgotten me; he's been cut off from the world and locked away. My tragic hero. *Counting down the hours. With you in dreams.*

Saturday. Waterfalls. Could anything be more romantic?

Oh, no. I can't go hiking. We've got the sale Saturday. Theo's letter has turned me into such a puddle of goo, I almost forgot.

David was right to warn me about the swoony side effects.

I've got to write back, pronto. Theo knows nothing about the sale, or Heather's chickenpox, or that Poppa stopped speaking. I grab the nearest paper and pour out the story of my last few days. But when I think of Laughlin's coffin trick, our diner lunch, and truck-ride voice lessons, my pen comes to a halt. How would I feel if Theo got this chummy with some girl with stunningly blue eyes and a give-you-shivers singing voice? Not very happy, that's for sure.

But could any of it be helped? Laughlin and I are just neighbors who've been thrown together a lot. Employer-employee. Or co-workers. Nothing more. No need to make it a bigger deal than it really is.

I pick up my pen again and write:

> It's been lonely without Heather, but I'm managing. Uncle David hired a neighbor to help us. That's been interesting, to say the least. A little hard to describe. I guess you'll see for yourself soon enough.

* * *

The next few days are a flurry of activity as we sort, label, and move Poppa's belongings to staging areas in the living room and garage. Every time I ask my uncle about the weird outbuilding, he suddenly needs something in another room, and my circuits around the place with Rhys don't provide any new clues.

Texts from Heather punctuate the long, busy hours inside. Texting, she says, is the only thing keeping her from scratching her itchy skin raw. Since she returned to New York, Fletcher has been Mr. Wonderful, she tells me. He appeared at her door with flowers, with videos, with books he wants to discuss. He fetched calamine from the pharmacy, fruit from the farmer's market, ginger ale from the corner store. Personally, I'd find the intensity of his attention exhausting. I also wonder how long he can keep his usual bossiness under wraps before he cracks. But Heather seems to be eating it up, certain Fletcher has changed for the better at last.

Laughlin, on the other hand, has changed for the worse. Since Tuesday's truck ride, he seems to be waiting around every corner, ready to prank me. He pops out of a dozen crazy hiding places and scares me. He dumps ice down my shirt, sets up booby traps, and repeatedly trips me. He offers me a cookie that I realize, after taking a bite, is one of Rhys's gourmet dog treats.

On Thursday, I haul a load of recycling out to the garage in the heat of the day, carefully checking possible hiding places before unloading. Distantly, Laughlin's lilting voice sings, "O Danny Boy, the pipes, the pipes are calling." I step out of the garage to listen closer and a massive blast of water drenches me. Laughlin cackles, the garden hose in his grip.

"What is the *matter* with you?" I scream, shaking my soaking arms.

"I warned you that the pipes are calling!" he quips.

I give him a killer scowl.

"Aw, come on, Dani, it's hot as blazes. Here, your turn. Do your worst. All's fair in love and war." He hands me the gun-like hose nozzle, then steps back, striking a crucified pose.

Love and war? Since when is anything like love going on here? This is simply war. His on me. Jerk. I squirt him hard in the face, till he sputters for air. Then I drop the hose and run.

He pursues, grapples me around the ribs and tackles me. We tumble to a stop in the grass. I stare up at him as he pins me to the ground, his soggy shirt clinging to his muscular chest. Oh my. When my gaze drifts up to his face, he grins and shakes his sopping hair like a dog.

"Well, that was fun." He trails a fingertip down my nose,

but I snap my teeth at him. "So you don't want to mud wrestle now, feisty one?"

"Get. Off. Me."

He tilts his head and studies me a moment longer. "Your eyes aren't blue. They're gray."

"OFF!" I repeat.

"On one condition."

I swallow hard. I never should have risen to his bait. Why didn't I just walk away, mad, when I had the chance? If Theo could see me now....

"*What?*" I whisper.

"You've gotta help me with Dave."

My uncle? "Um...okay. Why?"

Laughlin rolls off and lies beside me in the grass. "He seems really cool, but he's not right for Ma. I mean, he has a life somewhere else — a good business, good friends. Ma has roots here, especially our house. She grew up in it, nursed Grandma Keith to her last breath there."

Well, that is unbelievably creepy.

"So," I say, rolling on my side and leaning on my elbow, "does your grandma's spirit linger there? Make lights go on and off? Move the furniture?"

"You bet. We were on *America's Most Haunted* last fall. Seriously, though, Ma doesn't need her heart broken by someone who's just passing through."

"From what she told me, she's not interested in my uncle."

He sits up abruptly. "Really? What'd she say?"

"'That ship sailed a long time ago'."

He beams. "That's right. It totally did." He takes my hand and squeezes it. And not like a handshake.

My stomach plummets. What kind of alliance does he think we've made?

Chapter 16

When we finish loading the last of Poppa's broken electronics into Laughlin's truck, none of us can find my uncle, so Mum asks me to go help unload at the salvage yard. I'm a little leery of being alone with Laughlin so soon after the hose battle. But his mind seems to be somewhere else entirely, barely glancing my direction as he pulls out of Poppa's driveway.

Between aggressive drags on his cigarette, Laughlin mutters, "It's mighty suspicious that Dave disappeared so close to three, when Ma's shift ends."

"Don't worry. He'll get bored with the chase when she keeps rejecting him."

"Yeah, he's kind of ADHD, isn't he? Gets all twitchy every lunch, like he can't sit still."

"Maybe you make him nervous," I tease. "You could totally take him in a fight. Heck, I probably could, he's such a shrimp."

"I would pay serious money to see that. The nasty niece smack-down."

Traffic slows to a crawl just outside Elmerton near Dairy Dell, where the entire county seems to be devouring frozen treats. Laughlin grumbles and edges over the yellow lines to get a better view of the obstacle ahead. Out my window, I notice my uncle at a table in the shade. He's being fed bites of sundae by a woman in scrubs, her frizzy hair in a Gibson Girl bun. Sarah! She slops fudge on his upper lip, then leans across the table and kisses it off of him. So much for her lack of interest. Crap. Laughlin will not be happy about this new development.

Distraction. I need a distraction. I swat the radio on and crank the volume. A cheesy '70s pop song jangles out of the speakers: "Don't Go Breaking My Heart." Over the singing, I shout, "I'd pay serious money to, um, sing this duet with you. Ten bucks for your roof fund. No, twenty." I twist in my seat to block his view out my window.

He flashes an astonished smile, then sings, "So don't ya dare backhand me."

"You put the, uh, fire in my night," I sputter, playing along with his wrong-lyrics game.

He points his cigarette my direction. "Oh, you put a match to my brain."

"I've got good art in my sights." Get your sights on me, not what's outside.

He takes my hand and belts, "Oooh, ooh. No one will show it. When I skipped town…."

"I wore a frown," I add.

"When we're apart."

"An ache in my heart." Eyes on me, buddy. Eyes on me.

The cars behind us honk. Laughlin's gaze darts to the empty road ahead. He drops my hand and hits the gas, still singing, "Don't put ache in my heart."

When I don't immediately jump in, he sings the female part in falsetto, then switches to the male line, the words more silly and sweet as he continues to the end. I applaud, laughing, and offer the promised cash.

"That's okay." He folds my hand closed over the bills. "My pleasure, singing with ya."

I pocket the money, and resume watching the scenery. But amid the muggy wind whistling through the windows, I can hear him humming. When I glance his direction, he has one hand draped over the steering wheel, a contented grin on his lips.

* * *

Unloading at the salvage yard is excruciatingly slow thanks to the human sloth running the place, so I have to tag along with Laughlin to evening feed. Everything about Grouse Hill Farm, from the pristine buildings to the lush grass, says money. Way too much of my summers in England have been spent in places like this, watching my cousin Liza's dorky Pony Club events. I sit on a tack trunk and doodle while Laughlin leads horses in from the fields, schleps water buckets, wrangles hay bales, and heaves massive bags of feed. As he works, a gaggle of sporty teen girls in breeches and boots arrive and busy themselves polishing already-shiny saddles — clearly here to Laughlin-watch.

A blonde plants herself beside me. "Isn't he scrumptious? He's so calm and commanding with the horses. So strong. I saw him *carry* an injured foal a half mile. Is he a good kisser, too?"

"Excuse me?"

"You're his girlfriend, right? I saw you guys singing to each other outside Dairy Dell. It was adorable."

"What? No. We were just joking around. My uncle hired him to help clean out my grandpa's house."

"Yo, Danny Boy," Laughlin calls. He peels off his sweaty shirt for a goggle-eyed audience and tosses it to me, then pulls on a Grouse Hill polo. "Stick that in the truck for me, would ya? Boss doesn't like us out of uniform."

As he strides away, the blonde beside me sighs. "You are so lucky."

I regard the shirt with disgust. "Right. I'm the winner of a toxic mix of B.O., tobacco, and horse manure. So very enviable." I flash her a friendly smile and carry away Laughlin's icky shirt.

On my way out, I meet his boss, Ms. Kuntzler, a lean, leathery lady who seems to know a frightening amount about me.

Apparently she plays Poppa's secretary in their war re-enactment group. We end up in her air-conditioned office, discussing not only the ins and outs of war re-enactment but also Poppa's health and the chances that he'll ever be able to jitterbug again.

Laughlin is sweat-soaked and red-faced when he swings by to get me. As we walk to the truck, he gobbles down a rope of beef jerky. "I need to pop home to get something from the barn, then head back to Elmerton."

I peer into the truck bed at his load of lawn equipment. "Your other lawnmower?"

"Something like that." He gets into the truck and I follow.

"I can walk to Poppa's from your house. No problem."

He flashes a grateful smile and massages the back of his neck, groaning a little. As he pulls the truck onto the road, he flips on the radio.

I switch it off again. "Quiet might be more restful," I tell him. No way are we singing again. Not if it's going to make the whole town gossip about our non-existent relationship.

"I need to get my guitar," he blurts. "For a lesson. You can't tell Ma, okay? She'd freak."

Huh. That explains the weird hand motions he did in church, watching another guitarist play. But Sarah hardly seems like a music hater. "Why do you think she'd do that?"

"Dad's music was always in the middle of my parents' fights. If Ma thinks for a second that I'm anything like him…well, it won't be pretty."

This again? The bad dad's footsteps? "You are *not* destined to be his clone, Thee— er, theoretically speaking. Or metaphorically. You know what I mean. Similar isn't same."

Way to babble like an idiot, way to nearly call him my boyfriend's name.

He nods wearily and smiles. "Thanks. That helps."

When we get to his house, there's an awkward moment when I nearly knock him over with the door he'd come to open for me. I don't take the hand he offers to help me down, but hop to the ground beside him, give him a friendly pat on the shoulder, and head for the woods.

"See ya tomorrow, Danielle!" he calls, stretching out my name in a really weird way.

I wave without looking behind me. I sure hope he reads that as dismissive, not coy.

Entering the delicious coolness of the woods, I shuck off my sneakers and socks and walk right into the stream. There could be piranhas in the water for all I care, I'm so hot. Distant voices, a man and a woman, interrupt my chill-savoring moment. The man laughs, a huff-chuff Uncle David makes when he's nervous. I grab my footwear, creep downstream, and duck under a curved outcropping of rock. I've got to know what's going on with these two.

"You're suffering here, Sar-Bear," David says. Aw, that's a cute nickname. "You know you are. To still be stuck working swing shifts when you're so experienced? That blessed roof that leaks like a sieve? You deserve so much more. I'd be honored to give it to you."

"It's not just me we have to consider, Davey," Sarah says.

"I know. I've been thinking about the abandoned stable on my land. It could bring in income from boarders if only I had someone experienced to run it. I reckon an ambitious young man who's been working at a big operation for years could do real well at it. And one who's also apprentice material? Well, that would be a double blessing from the Lord."

He's trying to convince her to leave — with Laughlin? To move with him to Maine? Whoa. That's a new twist. What will that mean for us and Poppa?

"Davey, it's been a wonderful few days, but what you're suggesting...."

"I've loved you since I was seven years old. If I'd known sooner what Johnny did, I would have been here in a heartbeat. It's just...Pop's old fashioned about divorce. He's likely never heard of marrying for a Green Card. He wouldn't understand all the ways you've been done wrong, how in the eyes of God you're a widow, or as good as. Well, I don't need that proud, old coot's approval."

She gives a mirthless laugh. "Of course you do. And if you're truly serious, I won't have you without it. I want our families on board this time. Okay?"

They roam out of range, so I don't hear my uncle's answer. He won't sweep them away to Maine in days and abandon us, will he? No, getting Poppa's blessing could take a while.

Do I tell Laughlin? It might be better if he heard directly from his mom. It's her news to share, not mine. I'm sure she'll tell him soon.

* * *

Friday morning, Mum realizes we're not really equipped to display all the stuff we're planning to sell. She calls every table rental place in a forty-mile radius (all three of them), only to be told there's no Saturday rentals available until October. So she sends us hunting around the house for furniture that could serve as counter space for the yard sale.

In the pantry, I find a rack of hooks behind the door that hold rings and rings of keys. It's like I'm at a janitor convention. Are these spares of classroom keys? Or did Poppa buy them at flea markets, like the trophy collection? Or...are *some* of them important, but hidden among useless, dummy keys? Like the keys to that padlocked outbuilding.

Anything could be out there — the tables Mum wants, her artwork, or something truly awful. What if it was once my uncle's drug den, full paraphernalia, or a marijuana greenhouse?

I get my opportunity to explore when Mum and David head into town to run errands, and Laughlin's occupied mowing the lawn. I listen for the mower to retreat around the garage, then slip out the side door and jog to the pine grove, keys clanking in my backpack.

As I weave my way through the trees, my toe catches on a hidden hole, and I take a tumble. Something crunches sickeningly under my elbow. I lift my arm to find a crushed animal skull. Eeeew. In the nearby grass are yet more tiny bones and tufts of squirrel-gray fur. I think we've found Laughlin's weasel. Or at least its den.

As I climb to my feet, my knee rolls over a hard lump. Parting the grass, I find a corroded Pac-Man lighter, the initials DJT gouged into it: my uncle's from his pot-smoking days. I pocket the lighter, mark the nearest tree with a Sharpie from my bag, then move on to the outbuilding.

The air grows thick and still as I try key after key on the padlock, knob lock, and deadbolt. The sky clouds over while I move on to the second ring of keys. A distant rumble and the whoosh of wind-swept branches replace the mower's hum. A storm's brewing. I pick up the pace. By the time I get through the third ring and onto the fourth, fat raindrops pelt my skin. I keep on going, though it's growing colder and I can barely see through my dripping hair.

Lightning flashes, an explosion of white light so close I smell metallic burning in the air. I shriek, drop the keys into my backpack, and sprint for the shelter of Poppa's toolshed.

In the eight square feet of standing room among the yard tools and mulch bags and dusty flower pots, I wring out a corner of my soaked tank top and watch the rain fall in hard slabs. Five more minutes — maybe less — and I would've discovered the right keys.

The scritch of a lighter behind me makes me flinch. I whirl around to see a tongue of flame, a flash of face, then glowing embers. A pungent tobacco scent wafts toward me.

Laughlin steps closer, all sculpted lines in the dim light. "Looking for your subway stop, Danny Boy?"

"I wish. You know that little building behind the trees?"

"The one with the deadbolt and chain?"

"Yeah. I found some keys that might work." They clank impressively when I shake my soggy backpack.

He exhales out of the corner of his mouth, a dry cloud that rolls over my shoulder. "I'm sure your collection is real nice and all. But I've seen Dave go in and out of there a couple times. I reckon he's got the keys."

"Are you kidding me? I've asked a thousand times about that place." A cold gust whips through the open door and hits my wet clothes. "I c-can't b-b-b-believe it!"

Laughlin touches my knee and his hot hand slides up to my shorts hem. My goosebumps get goosebumps.

I push his hand away. "W-what are you d-d-doing?"

"You're ice cold, City Girl. Here." Laughlin stubs out his cigarette, pulls off his hoodie and drapes it over my shoulders. It smells of horse and leather and fire. His hands linger on my arms, radiating heat up to my scalp. I half expect steam to rise off me from his molten touch.

He swivels me toward him. "Is that better?"

Lightning flashes, bathing his face in light. For a moment, his eyes are the burning blue of flames on a range. He brushes a strand of wet hair off my cheek. I grasp his wrist and pull his hand away from my face, but can't seem to let go. His pulse thumps against my thumb.

"Laughlin, I—. I— I found a weasel nest in the pine grove."

"Yeah?" A slow smile spreads under his pert little upturned nose.

"I could—" I swallow. "Show you later."

"Mmm. We could have a little...adventure."

He steps closer yet, his mouth now inches from mine. I can almost taste the fire. If I let those full, soft lips touch mine, I'll ignite like a scrap of Kleenex: a flash, then ash.

I can't do this. Won't. It's wrong, all wrong. Nothing between us fits. He's so short. His lazy voice is too high; his strong hands, too square.

"I should go." I abruptly drop his hand, turn on my heel, and run out into the chilly rain.

When I reach shelter under the side door awning, I stop to clutch the stitch in my side. Laughlin stands framed in the shed doorway. He takes a drag from another cigarette and waves.

We stand like that for a long time, just watching.

* * *

At six a.m. on Saturday morning, Mum shakes me awake to tell me Laughlin has arrived with a surprise. My hands tremble as I dress. After that encounter in the shed, I have a very bad feeling about any more surprises coming from him. I pick up his sweatshirt, still damp and horsey smelling, then set it back down. Better that I wash it first — treat it as a neighborly loan, not some strange token of tenderness that passed between us.

Outside, two tiny Latino guys in Grouse Hill polos help Laughlin unload a party tent and a dozen banquet tables from his truck. Oh my gosh. It's exactly what we need to make the sale set-up as nice as a professional flea market. I stumble toward them, giddy with thankfulness.

Laughlin beams at my greeting and introduces me to his buddies, Javier and Arturo. "They used to call us 'Mick and the Spics,'" he jokes. "I like 'The Three Amigos' better, but the skinheads from German Club never gave us any say."

Skinheads? Like racist neo-Nazis? Hmm. Is that why he's in cyber school now?

"So, where'd all this stuff come from?" I ask.

"Compliments of Ms. Kuntzler," he says. "No gymkhanas or garden parties this weekend, so she's happy to help a neighbor in need."

"I could totally kiss her right now."

He smirks and waggles his eyebrows. "I could pass one on for ya."

I feel the color drain from my face. He thinks I want him to keep flirting and making passes. How did things get so weird between us so fast? Why can't I bring myself to say, "Back off, I have a boyfriend"? What will happen when Theo gets here?

Before things can get any stranger, Mum gathers us to get our job assignments for the day. She and Laughlin will be cashiers. Javier and Arturo will help customers carry purchases to their cars. Sarah, David, and I will rotate merchandise and keep the tables tidy. Laughlin flashes a rueful smile at the news that we won't be working closely. I shrug in silent reply and his expression brightens. Oh, crap. He's going to misread my every gesture now, isn't he?

I head inside to hide, but Mum follows and asks for help stocking the change box. As we fish quarters out of Poppa's giant jar of coins, I ask, "What's Theo's job going to be?"

Mum smiles. "Give you a lovely day. You've more than earned a break, sweetheart. We have plenty of help, thanks to Sarah, Laughlin, and his friends."

"I can...leave? Are you kidding me?"

"Is that a problem?"

I shake my head and exhale a relieved laugh. "Not at all. Thank you *so* much!" I dash a text to Theo, silently praying I can keep him and Laughlin from meeting.

> Good news. I can hike today. We got extra help with the sale, so I'm free. Text when you're close and I'll meet you at the end of the driveway.

Seconds later, my phone jangles in my hand — an incoming call, not a text.

"Dani!" Theo says. "Man, I've missed you. Just got your text, but I'm already parked by your mom's car. What should I do about the bulldog?"

"Excuse me?"

"The totally ripped little dude who snarled 'no early sales' at me? I said I was here to meet my girlfriend, and he accused me of being an antique spy. What the heck?"

"Um...just stay put. I'll be right there."

Chapter 17

When I reach to open the side door, it swings open. I back into the kitchen as Laughlin strides toward me, looking pained. He goes to a kitchen window and twitches the curtains aside.

"You know that guy with the beater Volvo?" He points his chin toward Theo. "Says he's here to see his girlfriend. I s'pose that means you." His smoldering eyes dare me to deny it.

I meet his gaze and say, simply, "Yes."

"This a *recent* thing?"

I shake my head. "We've been together since January...last year."

He snorts in disgust. "You are unbelievable. You waltz in here with your 'boo-hoo, my life is so terrible, rescue me,' and make me think you might be worth caring about. Is this all just a game to you, you freaking tease?"

"I didn't— Wasn't— Argh. I never encouraged you and I didn't play with your feelings. Not on purpose, anyway."

"Right. Why would a guy like me *feel* anything? I'm just your work horse here to smooth your path to Paris. Is Volvo boy going with you?"

"No. He's working in Eyrie Falls at a camp for emotionally disturbed kids."

"I guess that makes him perfect for a head case like you."

"Laughlin, please. I never meant to hurt—. I thought we were friends."

When I touch his shoulder, he stares at my hand and croaks, "I *sang* for you."

"Your voice is beautiful. I could listen to it all day."

"No. You don't get to say things like that. Ever." He shoves me aside, then proceeds to knock over every kitchen chair, one by one. "I can't even look at you anymore."

The door slams behind him. I stand there, stunned. A moment later, I hear a gunning engine and the distant squeal of tires.

Mum rushes into the kitchen. "What's going on, darling?"

"Oh, Mum," I wail, "I'm in such a mess."

* * *

When I finally head outside, I find Theo leaning against Gertie's rusty side, texting someone and laughing. It's like mocha, his laugh — rich and warming all the way through.

"Thebes?"

"Hey," he says, not looking up. "Beth says hi." He types a few more words, then pockets his phone and gives me a heart-stopping smile. "Come here, beautiful."

I fall into his arms and hug him tight.

He tips up my chin and kisses me. My body seems to revolt, pulling away when I'd normally linger. I nuzzle against his chest so he can't kiss me again and loosen the awful truth that will only hurt him. But my trembling arms betray me.

"Babe? What's wrong?"

What do I tell him? He doesn't know Laughlin from Adam and wouldn't care that he left in a snit. Mum says it was all just a silly misunderstanding anyway. I've been walking such a fine line with Laughlin, trying to gently fend off his flirtation without directly rejecting him or labeling myself as "taken," scared he'd make my life miserable. And honestly, there's something magnetic about him, so different from the boys I know. Strange and dangerous. When I think how close we were to kissing, my mind glitches.

167

"I— I broke something," I finally say, "and I don't know if it can be fixed."

"Bummer. Maybe you can find a replacement on eBay," he suggests.

Right. I can just picture the ad: Surly, beautiful boy, tobacco-scented, available for odd jobs, practical jokes, and ensuring you stay off your high horse. Sings angelically on occasion.

I shake my head against Theo's chest.

"A one-of-a-kind thing, huh?" He gently pets my hair.

I nod and try to send him a mental image of an antique knickknack that could reasonably stir up such a reaction from me. But all I can imagine is a heart-shaped, smoke-gray music box smashed on the floor, plinking the chorus of "Danny Boy."

"Where's my son?" Sarah calls, jogging toward us. "What happened? Were the Brockmeier brothers here making trouble?" She rakes her hands through her hair. "Wasn't it enough they got him suspended? They won't be happy until he's in jail."

My mouth drops open. Suspended?

"I don't know. Maybe Theo saw something?" I say. "This is Theo Wescott from New York. My boyfriend. Thebes, this is Poppa's neighbor, Sarah O'Donnell."

"Oh?" Sarah looks Theo up and down. "Well. You're very...tall, aren't you? Did you happen to see two big, hammy boys come around? Shaved heads, swastika tattoos?"

"Sorry," Theo says. "I'd definitely remember if I had. Your son has black hair and a maroon truck, right? He came out of the house looking furious and drove away. That's all I saw."

"Really?" Sarah grasps my arm to steady herself. "Oh, Lord, I'm so relieved. When I heard squealing tires, all I could think was that I told him to run if he ever saw those brutes again."

"You have neo-Nazis around here?" I ask.

"Not many, but...they tend to recruit schoolboys. Laughlin

became their target because he befriended Art and Javi. The locals love to blame anyone they can for their lack of jobs, rather than try to get marketable skills themselves. Anyway, they taunted and bullied until Laughlin just snapped. And now there's five grand in damages to be paid."

No wonder the guy is so eager for work. "I'm so sorry."

"Me, too. I wish some things didn't have to be learned the hard way." Sarah stares down the driveway a long moment, then turns to us, eyes narrowed. "He left the house furious, you said? Hmm. Was Dave inside?"

I bite my lip. "I think he might've been."

"I'll try to play peacemaker." She extracts her phone, saying, "nice to meet you, Leo."

"It's Theo," I call after her as she heads back to the house.

Theo chuckles. "Like I've never heard that before. Still better than Teddy, though."

"Speaking of which, how's your dad? Any updates?"

"He's better. Much better. He hired a private investigator to look for Courtney, which seems a lot more sensible."

"Has he made any surprise appearances at camp?"

"Nope. He sent a letter and a care package. Jersey Shore fudge...with walnuts."

"You hate walnuts."

"True, but giving it all away did make me instantly popular. I bet that's what he hoped."

"Seriously? If he only wanted you to share, he would have sent extra of something you actually like. Don't make excuses for him. He doesn't know you at all."

"He's trying, Dani. I have to believe that counts for something. You ready to go hiking?"

I cringe. "I don't know if we should. Not until Laughlin comes back. Is that okay?"

"Sure. That was the plan until half an hour ago. Besides," he rubs his hands together, "I've been dying to look around a bit more."

"We'll be way too busy for that," I say. I'll make sure of it.

* * *

The driveway fills with cars, and soon Javier and Arturo are directing new arrivals to park in the field between the garage and the lower woods near the road. The press of people around the tables feels like coming home. I happily dive into the crowd, making suggestions and keeping the tables orderly. Throw in a half-dozen foreign languages and a busker, and my homesickness would vanish.

Having Theo here doesn't hurt either. He gives me a dazzling smile or a wink every time I glance his way. When a price question arises, he rests a reassuring hand on the small of my back as I haggle with the customer. I stay by his side and tidy the change box while he patiently takes sticky coins from little kids and counts change twice for persnickety grannies. He smells so amazing. And each time his arm brushes mine, I ache to be alone with him. But his line of customers stretches on, unrelenting.

If I can't get out of here, get time with Theo, I'll explode. Laughlin has to come back.

Sarah hasn't stopped watching the driveway since Laughlin left. When I see her struggling to move a tall pile of puzzles, I hurry over to help, asking if we can talk.

She follows me to Poppa's cannon display. "What is it, honey?"

"Laughlin left because of me. We had a fight. Sorry I didn't say anything sooner. I was just really embarrassed. See, he, um…"

"Has feelings for you."

"Yeah. I thought we were getting to be friends, and there never seemed to be a good time to bring up Theo. I don't know what to do. He needs the work, but he said he can't even look at me now. Maybe…if Theo and I left, he'd come back. Could you ask him?"

"He's not answering his phone."

"Could I try texting him?"

Sarah gives me his number and returns to the tent, where she whispers in David's ear. He strokes her upper arm, openly affectionate with her only when Laughlin isn't here to see it.

But maybe he should, since he's so keen to keep them apart. The longer their growing relationship stays secret, the angrier he'll be when he does find out. I text:

> Dani here. Please come back. Your mom's super worried and leaning on David for comfort. T and I will leave at 1, so you won't have to see us, OK?

No way will Laughlin be able to stay away now. I saunter back to the tent, whistling.

* * *

Climbing out of Theo's car, I savor the cool sweetness of the air, mineral-rich and mossy. Somewhere downhill from the parking lot, a river roars. At my feet is a sea of pinkish-purple gravel, a local stone that seems to holds up all the hills from Poppa's to this state park. Above us, evergreens sashay in the breeze and whisper secrets to each other.

Theo shrugs on a backpack and tosses me a canteen. "Come on, Dee! There's lots I want to show you."

He lopes toward the trailhead like a hyper puppy. I catch up with him at a carved wooden map at a fork in the path. Tracing the arc of the falls trail on the map, he says, "This is a magic string of jewels. I hope you brought your sketchpad."

I pat my back pocket. "Always. You have to promise me some good poses."

"Oh yeah? Only if you can keep up with me." He jogs away, laughing.

Let him have his head start. I take a long swig from the canteen, bounce on the balls of my feet and stretch my hamstrings. Then I sprint down the trail behind him. Down a steep slope along a series of switchbacks I go, gravel crunching beneath my feet. Birdsong fills my ears. Any second I'll see him in his purple shirt, pausing to catch his breath.

But as the trail flattens out along a wooded section, I see only a few families with young kids and some gray-haired hippies walking a collection of mutts. Where is he? I pick up the pace, dodging poky kids and curious dogs. This is as romantic as being forced to sub in the hurdles relay last minute. I can almost hear Coach Griggs screaming about my crappy form. Why does she think I need to be a freaking decathlete? My high jump medals ought to be good enough.

"Dani! Wait!" Theo calls. From behind me. I stop in my tracks.

He huffs up beside me. "What the heck? I wasn't trying to ditch you. I ducked behind a tree. As a joke. Man. You must *really* want to draw me."

"And the 'string of jewels' you've been talking up so much."

"Uh huh." He nudges me with his hip. "Admit it. You want to lay me out on a rock and trace every contour of this manly man-ness."

"Shut up, you doofus."

He leans against a tree, arm over his head like a cologne ad model. "Will this do, *chérie*?"

My cheeks burn. "Thebes, please," I beg.

"I'm not moving until you show me a fresh sketch."

"Fine." I sit on a fallen log and lay lines and shapes on the paper to form a romance novel version of my boyfriend. Minutes later, I pass him the page and continue down the trail.

"Hey!" he calls after me. "What happened to my shirt?"

"Just getting into the spirit of things," I say when he catches up with me.

"My arms aren't this big. Not like that guy from next door who's been helping you."

At his surprising mention of Laughlin, I swivel abruptly and nearly lose my balance.

"Hey, take it easy. The trail drops a bit steeply here." He guides me down an uneven stone stairway cut in the hillside.

"I hadn't really noticed. Laughlin's arms, I mean."

Theo leads me around a mucky puddle. "He must be at the gym two hours a day."

"I doubt he has the time, with all his jobs. I'd guess he's gotten so ripped from all the manual labor. Scooping horse manure, carrying huge sacks of oats, that kind of thing."

"Oh, so he's 'ripped' now, huh? I thought you hadn't noticed." Theo totters on a loose step, but I steady him.

I hop over the wobbler and land beside him. "That's *your* word," I retort. "You called him the 'ripped little dude' who barked at you. He happens to be good at moving boxes. There's not much more to say."

"All right." He presses me against a rocky wall so another couple can pass us. My heart hammers at his nearness. "But what I saw for myself about that guy? It wasn't very comforting."

He hikes on, but I stay there clutching the rock face, trying to process his words, his tone. How suspicious he sounds. And jealous. Crap.

I clumsily clomp along to catch up, calling, "Wait!" I hop from a rock to bare dirt, and the earth gives way under me. I fall on my butt and slide down the hill, nearly knocking Theo off his feet. I come to a stop directly under the inseams of his shorts, which are on the loose side. I clamp my eyes shut, but it's too late. Charcoal gray boxer briefs. I did not want to know that.

Theo steps back so I'm no longer getting the blush-worthy view. "You okay, Dee?"

"He's a chain smoker," I say, like it's perfectly normal to continue our conversation flat on my back. "I figured once you saw that, you'd understand what I've been dealing with."

Theo helps me up and dusts dirt off of me. "The Marlboro man. Stupendous."

The memory of that sultry cloud of smoke curling out of Laughlin's soft lips makes my gut twist. So close to betrayal. So close. This conversation has to end. Now.

"That roaring I hear, is that the falls?" I ask. "We almost there?"

"Yeah. Come on." He continues to lead the way down the final steps.

At a particularly big drop, I grip his shoulder for balance and hop down beside him. "About the drawing...I was trying to play along, not hurt you."

His mouth curls, a sad smile. "Sorry for being so touchy. You didn't do anything wrong."

As we continue our descent to the foot of the hill, I slip my hand into his. We reach the riverbank and come around an outcropping of rock. The vista before us is so breathtaking that I halt in my tracks. Water tumbles from a cliff high above and rushes in a ruffling roar over rocks into the sun-speckled river at our feet. Tiny rainbows sparkle among the mist. Ferns on the far banks sway, buffeted by updrafts from the churning waters.

"*Oh*," I breathe. So much beauty. So lavish, excessive.

"Now that we're here..." Theo shyly lowers his eyes. "I was, um, hoping....could I—? Could we—?" He rubs his neck. "Would you come with me somewhere?"

"Okay. Sure."

He leads me across mossy rocks to the far shore, then along the bank toward the waterfall itself. "There's a really cool path, but it can be slippery," he calls over the roaring water and clutches my hand tighter.

We work our way across the wet shale, gripping jutting rocks along the hillside for balance. Soft mist from the waterfall tickles my skin. We then duck under a stony shelf and awkwardly crouch-walk into a high, cavern-like arch. I straighten up, then halt. Before us is the underside of the waterfall, a white curtain shimmering with life and light.

"This is amazing," I whisper, reaching for my sketchpad.

"Not yet." Theo pulls my hand away from my pocket and sets it on his waist. He brushes my cheek with a fingertip, a feathery stroke that makes me shiver. Stepping closer, he leans in and lets out a ragged breath, centimeters from my lips. All my nerve endings crackle with anticipation as he hovers there for an endless moment.

When the kiss comes, it's as hot and sweet as fresh-baked pie filling. We melt into each other, hungry from our six-day fast. I grasp his face with both hands to drink deeper.

My backside tingles, but not because Theo's hands have gone south. It's my blasted phone.

Theo moans when I push him away to fish out my phone.

It's a new text from Mum:

> Laughlin hasn't returned like you said and Sarah is beside herself. Could you two possibly come back?

175

Chapter 18

Theo and I plod up the steep path toward the car, not touching. His disappointment trails us like a stray dog. "I'm so sorry. It was stupid of me to believe Laughlin would come back."

"It's not your fault the dude didn't keep his word."

If only that were true, instead of my moronic assumption that he'd do the predictable thing in the face of certain information.

"Are you mad?" I ask. "Have I wrecked your plan?"

"Well, we did have eight more waterfalls to go."

"Did you expect to make out behind every one of them on this trail?"

His ears turn magenta. "Not...exactly."

"Oh, Thebes, that would've been, well, a really bad idea. By the fourth or fifth fall, kissing wouldn't be enough. We'd be tempted to—"

"That's crazy! It's a public place."

"If we kept going like we were just now, I don't think I'd care."

He jolts to a stop, eyes wide with surprise, then stares at his shoes. "You're right. Didn't really think it through. I just missed you so much."

"Me, too. That's why we have to be careful." I playfully elbow him in the ribs. "Next weekend I'll make it up to you, okay? We can come back, see the rest of the trail."

"No ducking behind the falls, though, huh?"

"Well...." I take his hand. "Maybe two. Or three."

"Oh yeah?" His eyes glint. *"L'espoir fait vivre."*

"Hope gives life?" I guess.

He grins. *"Exactement."* Exactly. "You've been practicing,

haven't you? You and your mom are going to have an amazing time in Paris."

"I hope she'll still go. I've worked my tail off to make it possible, but one word from Poppa and our plans will be in the toilet. I wish I knew why he has so much power over her."

"Well," Theo says, "I have something that might shed some light." He pulls paper out of his back pocket and hands it to me — a pamphlet called "Children of Narcissists."

"Narcissists? Like the pretty boy in the myth who fell in love with his own reflection?"

Theo shrugs. "Maybe? Dr. Hoyt gave that to me after I talked to him about dad. You said your grandpa's similar, so I thought it might help you, too, when you have a minute to read."

I look to the incline ahead, then at the pamphlet again. "I need all the help I can get before I go back to that house. It's just a few pages."

He sits with me on a fallen log as I read about "narcissistic personality disorder," a pattern of self-importance, need for admiration, and lack of empathy. Narcissists inflate accomplishments, expect special treatment, and use charm to get what they want. The next pages spell out how narcissists act as parents, singling out one child for perpetual favor and another for constant blame: the "Golden Child" and the "Scapegoat."

"So the way Poppa treats Mum is the same as your dad treats Beth? And you're…"

"A mini narcissist in the making, just like your uncle. Isn't that great news?"

"What? No, you're not."

"By the grace of God, babe. If my parents had stuck together longer, who knows?"

"And David isn't—"

"Selfish and self-destructive? He used to be, right? Look, I know you're totally embarrassed by this messy stuff with your family, but mine is far from perfect. If we can be real with each other, I think it will help us both."

I get to my feet. "We shouldn't keep Mum waiting. But thanks for this. There's a treatment section, so that's promising."

"Not entirely," Theo says, joining me on the trail, "Dr. Hoyt warned me that narcissists don't tend to change, or even have a clue they need to, until the people around them change."

"Change how?"

"Not letting the narcissist act like they own you or that you're just an extension of them. When they try to bully or manipulate you, you tell them no, they can't do that if they want to have a relationship with you."

I snort. "Are you kidding me?"

"I know, it sounds ridiculously easy."

"No, it sounds completely impossible. Mum's a total doormat with Poppa. I have no idea how to make her grow a backbone."

"It's not all on you to fix this, Dani. Remember, Jesus said, 'things that are impossible for people are possible for God'."

* * *

On the drive back, we pass what looks like a big ball of dryer lint on the roadside. Theo blurts, "Dee, quick! Get my notebook from the glove box and add another opossum to the list."

I find a spiral-bound pad wedged in with ratty maps and flip through the pages. Each lists an animal with tally marks underneath. "What is this? A roadkill journal? That's just ghoulish." I add a fourteenth tally mark under opossum.

"It has pages for live things, too. Driving out here, Fletch got bored and started tracking wildlife. We saw groundhogs and deer out grazing — even some grouse and a pheasant strutting around. Fletch was pretty psyched; he rarely leaves the city."

"Is that why he's being so smothery with Heather? He gets bored easily?"

"Of course not. He's trying to take care of her. Did she tell you she feels smothered?"

"Not in so many words. I just worry, you know?"

"Yeah, me too. I didn't expect him to try to be so radically different from his usual self."

"Can you talk to him?"

"That's the problem. He took my advice, just way too far."

A landscaping crew with a truck full of shrubs blocks our lane. One of the workmen directs us around it and four pickups, including a shiny burgundy Toyota. Could it be Laughlin's? I hike myself up in the seat to peer over the parked trucks but can see only the mansion that's getting some yard pampering. Once Theo pulls back into our lane, I see a dark head bowed over a shovel, and familiar brawny arms straining with labor.

"Stop the car!" I shout. "Pull over! Now, now, now!"

Theo slows and eases Gertie onto the shoulder. "What is it?"

"I saw a species that's not in your journal." I point at the hole-digging runaway. "Behold, the bulldog, in the wild."

"So he got another job. Big deal."

"He hasn't called Sarah all day. That's not normal. I should go see what's up." I toss Theo my phone. "Let Mum know we found him and he's okay. I'll be back in a minute."

"Be careful, babe."

I smile. "Don't worry. His bark is worse than his bite."

Inside, I'm not nearly so confident. I approach Laughlin with mincing steps, as if he were a timid chipmunk and any sudden movement could make him dart into his burrow.

"Hey. Are you okay?" I ask.

"Well, well." Laughlin leans on his shovel with a crooked smile. "You searched and found me. I'd say things are looking up."

"Actually, we were, um, passing through and I happened to see your truck."

"We?" He peers past me, and seeing Gertie, gives a throaty *grrough* of disgust. "You brought Volvo boy *here*?"

"I've been worried about you. When you didn't come back...."

"I'm not at your beck and call." He zealously digs into the side of the hole again.

"So it doesn't concern you that your mother and my uncle have been getting cozy?"

He tosses the dirt with so much force the shovel goes with it. I leap aside, yelping.

"Gah! You didn't help. You never helped. Now it's too late. I caught them making out behind your grandpop's garage this morning, and when I wanted to talk to you, your giant boyfriend was in my face."

"I'm sorry, Laughlin."

"Your little surprise was the last straw on the steaming pile of manure this day has been. You should hear the disgusting messages Ma left on my phone. *Davey* wants to get to know me. *Davey* is taking us out for dinner and mini golf after the yard sale. Seriously, mini golf? Do they think I'm eight?"

"You do seem more like a...shooting range kind of guy."

"I know, right?" He retrieves his shovel and continues digging. "Why should I bother talking to her? She couldn't see the truth about Dave if it walked up and bit her."

"She knows everything there is to know about his past. He put it all out there at the barbeque last week. But he's been clean almost four years. Why can't you give him a chance?"

Laughlin pauses from shoveling to look me in the eye. "You have any idea what he's been doing in that building you tried to bust into yesterday?"

I shake my head. "He's not growing pot, is he? Or making meth?"

He snorts. "I wish. His falling off the wagon would be a heck of a lot less weird. It's no surprise he has that place locked like a vault. It's full of women's clothes and prissy knickknacks and a dress dummy he talks to. Excuse me for not wanting Ma to fall for a freak."

I totter on the crumbly edge of his hole. "That can't be true," I rasp.

"Don't believe me? Go look for yourself."

I take a wobbling backward step. "You're just trying to hurt me back for hurting you."

"Get over yourself." Laughlin's tone is pure acid, but his eyes are clouded with misery.

Suddenly, Theo is clasping my arm to steady me. His voice cracks when he says my name.

"You and me?" Laughlin continues, "We belong together about as much as milk and gasoline."

"What's...going on?" Theo says in a wounded tone.

Great. Now he thinks I'm the pursuer. And a total traitor.

"I don't—" The lie sticks in my throat. Playing dumb will only dig me deeper.

Laughlin crosses his arms over his chest, lifts his chin in a defiant tilt. "Your girl needs to leave me alone. Now if you don't mind, I've got some boxwood to get in the ground." He saunters away, leaving me to clean up this mess.

A monstrous urge surges inside me to grab the shovel and bludgeon him with it. Then I see Theo slinking silently back to the car.

* * *

With trembling hands, I open Gertie's rust-speckled passenger door. I'd rather face those minotaurs from my nightmares than this. I slip into the seat and struggle to close the door with hands now noodle-limp with fear.

Theo is slumped in the driver's seat, the heels of his hands pressed to his temples like he's fighting a migraine. "I've been trying to piece together," he finally says, "why you've constantly changed our plans today. Our coming and going always hinged on the whereabouts of that guy, the neighbor who's so 'interesting' to work with. Why is that, Dani? His big biceps, pretty-boy looks, cowboy attitude, or the fact that he's four inches shorter than you? I feel like an idiot for dreaming about you all week, for believing we have something good. We're apart a few days and you're falling for *that* punk?" His voice cracks.

The weight of his accusation pins me to the seat, and I fight to breathe. How could I have gotten inches away from kissing the ashtray mouth of such a horrible guy? A dozen nasty memories of my week crack wide open. "Of course not! He's done nothing but torment me. Trying to make you jealous is just another of his evil tricks."

Theo cocks his head. "Tormented you how?"

"Let's see." I count off Laughlin's transgressions on my fingers. "He threatened me with a rifle, made me dump the offering plate at church, popped out of Uncle David's coffin project to scare me, fed me dog biscuits, and drenched me with a hose. If you don't believe me, ask Heather. She witnessed most of it."

Theo starts the car. "Why didn't you tell me any of this?"

I watch Laughlin's dark head recede as we pull away. "I thought I had a handle on it. I worked hard to be nice in spite of his obnoxious tricks because we really needed his help. What

182

was I supposed to do? We needed serious muscle. You said so yourself."

"Pay him well, don't prey on his feelings."

"What? I never pranked him back, never encouraged his attention."

"But you never told him about me, did you? This morning, when I said I was looking for my girlfriend, he looked like I'd sucker-punched him."

"Why would I tell him about you? We hired him to help clean out Poppa's house, not share life stories." Laughlin certainly hasn't been quick to reveal anything about himself to me.

"You let him believe you were available. No wonder he peeled out of your grandfather's driveway in such a fury."

"That's ridiculous! He left in a huff because he caught my uncle kissing his mom, and thinks it's my fault."

"Wait, what? Your uncle and his *mom*? That's who you were threatening to play matchmaker for? Because I said it would make your Paris trip easier?"

"I had nothing to do with them getting together. They have a long history."

"Then why bring it up at all, except to derail my argument that you misled this guy?"

"That wasn't the main reason he left," I reply.

"It was *a* reason, wasn't it?" he presses.

I throw up my hands. "Yes. He was also mad that I have a boyfriend, which was the shock of my life. Only middle school boys are so cruel to girls they like."

"Seriously? You've seen Fletcher in action. Some guys play games when they feel insecure, or can't read a girl who gives mixed signals."

"Mixed signals? I didn't give—"

"Fine. Maybe you didn't. Maybe he just misread your niceness. Still, you could've at least *told* me you were having problems with this guy. I would've actually helped you."

"How? By getting into a fist fight with him? I'm not territory for you to squabble over. I'm a person who, believe it or not, is capable of not falling for every pretty face that crosses my path. There's nothing wrong with being friendly and trying to not alienate someone you have to work with. I didn't encourage him, I didn't flirt, and I took off the minute he tried to kiss me!"

Theo hits the brakes so hard, we're thrown against our seatbelts. "He tried to *kiss you*?"

Oh, dear God, me and my self-righteous rambling.

He pulls over to the shoulder and turns off the car. "So you had no clue he was into you while you're practically lip to lip? Nice detail to conveniently forget."

"His pranks were...very confusing. As for the almost kiss — why hurt you with something that didn't actually happen?"

"Stop, Dani, please. At least half this conversation has been cover-ups and lies. How do you think that makes me feel?"

"I never meant to hurt anyone," I whisper, staring at my lap.

Theo touches my cheek. "I know. I get that you're scared and trying to cope. I want to be supportive, to be a team with you, but how can I when you hide stuff and pull these...evasive maneuvers? It feels like there's no trust between us."

I lean into his touch. "I'm sorry, Thebes. Truly. I love you so much."

Theo withdraws his hand and sighs. "We should get back to the sale and help your mom."

As he restarts the car, I search his face, seeking a spark of hope in his hazel eyes. Some sign of tenderness in the soft contour of his mouth. But his expression is as flat as a plank.

For the first time ever, I said "I love you" and he didn't say it back.

Chapter 19

When we return to the sale, Theo keeps a firm grip on my arm, like he's my escort to the principal's office. We pass Arturo and Javier helping a motorcyclist tie his purchases to his bike. They call friendly greetings and I wave back. Theo doesn't. He's a man on a mission.

He marches me to my mother, who's stymied by the five-dollar bill given for a three-dollar purchase. Uh oh. She is beyond exhausted. Theo dives in beside her, retrieving two bucks change for the middle-aged guy who's apparently going to try origami, based on his purchase.

I lead Mum to a chair near a now-empty table and tell her to rest while I get some things from the house. Minutes later, I return with bottled iced tea and a dishpan of warm water. Mum gulps down the tea, not protesting when I remove her shoes and set her feet in the dishpan.

I stand behind her, massaging her shoulders while I watch Theo and my uncle banter with customers. My chest constricts at the sound of Theo's warm, bass laugh. I love that laugh. Love him. All of him. Even his crooked eyebrow and the stark scar across his knuckles from a boat-loading accident. My eyes sting, but I blink away the tears. I can't let him see me fall apart; it will only prove how pathetic I am, the girl he can't trust.

"My angel," Mum murmurs. "Sorry we called you back so soon. You deserve a break."

"It's okay," I say, my voice weirdly reedy. I clear my throat and continue, "Sorry for the mix-up with Laughlin. The one thing I thought would make him come back pushed him farther away. It's...stuff with his mom. He's furious."

"I wondered. Sarah took his absence awfully hard when he's usually quite independent."

"Sarah and David have a history, right? They used to date?"

"They used to be engaged."

"Omigosh," I gasp. "Tell me everything!"

"When Mama got sick, David and I stayed next door with the Keiths while she was in the hospital. David and Sarah did everything together — his best friend and pet rolled into one."

Theo approaches us, rubbing the back of his neck. "Um, Mrs. Deane? This guy in line? He was wondering how much for the cannons."

Mum sighs. "I'll have to ask my father. Take his name and number for now."

"Oh. Okay." He licks his lips, nodding repeatedly like a bobble-head doll. His eyes meet mine for a millisecond, then he drops his gaze and lopes away.

"What's wrong with him?" Mum asks. "Did he find out about Laughlin's crush on you?"

"I'd rather not talk about it."

She squeezes my fingers. "Later, then. Where was I? Right. Mama came home from the hospital and we tried to carry on back at our place. But David unraveled without Sarah. Pop and I caught him huffing airplane glue, and I had to keep quiet about it."

"Wait. Poppa knew from the beginning, and didn't stop it? Didn't get him help?"

"Pop always said 'help is for weaklings.' And I took everything he said as gospel."

"Did Sarah know about David's addiction?"

"Of course. But she's not one to tattle. She's more like me, someone whose help didn't help. We babied David, both of us, and he just got worse."

"What about Nana? What did she think?"

"Poor Mama. She was too exhausted to do much." Mum's tone is resigned. "David wanted connection with her more than anything, but Pop dominated her time and attention. She left David adrift rather than risk Pop's jealousy. In the end, we all enabled my brother, because we thought it was easier."

"So how did David and Sarah end up engaged, with all this in the background?"

"She stuck with him, first as a buddy, later as his steady girlfriend. He gave her a promise ring for her seventeenth birthday."

"So they weren't *engaged* engaged." I shake out my hands, now sore from the lengthy massage session.

"Close enough to scare her parents. They sent her away to live with family in Boston her senior year. She stayed on for nursing school and soon got married. David took the news hard and got loads more reckless once he lost her. So it's bizarre to find her back here, single again."

"Heather would probably call it a God thing."

Mum empties her footbath into the grass. "Well, ignorance is bliss. 'Enabling behavior,' as my old counselor would call it, is easy to slide back into. And so is addiction."

"I pray every day that Uncle David will stay clean."

She gives a derisive snort. "Good luck with that. God never listened when I asked, no matter how hard I begged."

Mum resumes tidying the tables, while I stand frozen, too indignant to respond. What did she expect? God to magically zap David like a fairy godfather? Why can't she see how well her brother is doing now and know that God heard her? Because he relapsed too often in the past. And hope is hard to grasp when God seems so far away, so slow to answer.

David tiptoes up behind Mum and drapes a neon-orange winter scarf around her shoulders. Mum squawks with fright, then rips off the scarf. Her eyes glint with fury, and in an instant she's got the scarf looped around her brother's neck and is choking him with it. "When will you *ever* grow up?" she snarls.

All eyes turn to my enraged mother. Including Theo's. Dread and shame wash over me, cold as lake water. This is it. The nervous breakdown I've feared so long.

David fights to loosen the fabric and gasps, "Sorry, Sis!"

Mum's rage evaporates as quickly as it arrived. She releases the scarf, which hangs down David's back like a professor's hood at graduation. She hunches over, spent. "I don't know why—. Just a silly scarf. I shouldn't have—"

"Hush, Gracie," David interjects. "I know it's not about the scarf."

Mum's neck flushes and her eyes dart left and right, seeking some place of escape. "I should…boxes…pack what's unsold." She power-walks to the house, still blushing.

David rubs his neck and tosses the scarf to me. "Well, that's new. She's never turned her anger on me before."

"She's cracking up, isn't she?"

"Nah. If anything, she's waking up, seeing what's real. I've harmed her a thousand ways and she has every right to be angry."

David returns to helping customers. I aimlessly shuffle around the last merchandise, aching to talk to Theo. He glances my way a few times with that fierce-looking puzzled squint of his that I used to read as scrutiny when I didn't really know him. Back then, Heather said I was imagining him judging me. That might've been true once. But now?

It feels like there's no trust between us.

His words from our argument sink down, down, down into me. No trust. Not just his in me, but mine in him. How could I not trust the boy who pulled me back from the brink when I was fifteen? He has never betrayed me, not once, even in the slightest way.

My eyes drift to him like he's a magnet and I'm a flimsy paperclip. Deftly he sorts the cash, squaring the stacks with his long, tapered fingers. Fingers that stroke and twirl my hair whenever we plop on a park bench. Or trail down my cheek when he wishes me good night.

Theo looks up, and the corner of his mouth quirks when he sees me staring. I turn away, my heart hammering. Was that a mocking smirk? Or, dare I hope, a kind half-smile?

* * *

When the last customers leave, Mum appears with empty boxes and dumps them at my feet. I watch her wearily survey the tables and try to read her mood. Is she back to all-business? On the verge of another temper-flare? Or heading for a strange plane of emoting I've never seen?

She rubs her forehead. "I think this stuff will fit in the garage. David and Sarah offered to get tables at the Elmerton flea market to try to sell these leftovers."

"Is, um, that plan...okay? With you?" I take a small step back in case she blows up.

"Honestly, darling?" She looks left and right to see if anyone can overhear us, then beckons me closer. "I'm so sick of Pop's junk, I'd love to torch the lot of it."

I let out the breath I'd been holding and snigger. "We can tell him it was an act of God. A lightning bolt hit the Daniel Tilman temple of self-worship, consuming all the false images."

Mum laughs. "Temple of self-worship?" She turns toward the house, her expression becoming pensive. "That horrid portrait he made Mama paint — it's just like what Nebuchadnezzar made Shadrach, Meshach, and Abednego bow down before."

"Wait, you know that story? The fiery furnace, from the book of Daniel?"

"Of course. It's Pop's favorite part of the Bible. If I'm remembering correctly, things didn't work out so well for Nebuchadnezzar, did they?"

"Well, he was humble for about five minutes, then went back to boasting about his awesomeness and power. God shut him up by making him go crazy for a while."

"That hits a bit close to home, doesn't it? Though Pop always bragged that he was named after the book's title character — the brave prophet in the lions' den."

"I bet he did, especially when anyone questioned his war hero claims."

Mum tips her head. "You know, it's funny, but he's never made any such claim. He merely filled the stage with all the right props and let people draw their own conclusions."

* * *

David drives off to Grouse Hill with Javier and Arturo to return the tent and tables, leaving Mum, Theo, and me in an awkward trio.

"I suppose we should think about dinner, eh?" Mum says. "Join us, Theo?"

He looks longingly at his car, gnawing his lip. "Sorry. I need to head out. Errands to run."

"Oh." Mum gives us an appraising glance. "Well, I'm beat, so I guess I'll say goodbye. Thank you, Theo. You've been a gem." She opens her arms and embraces him.

Seeing Mum's petite frame engulfed by his bigness reminds me of Dad, and how he sheltered and loved her with tender strength. A sharp pang of missing him makes my chest ache. I stare at my feet and dig the toe of my sneaker into the driveway gravel.

Mum's touch whispers down my arm and then she's gone.

"Hey," Theo says, tapping my toe with his. "Are you upset that I hugged your mom?"

"No, I— It's dumb. You're shorter, your coloring's different, but...you reminded me of Dad for a second. And he's gone, and you're going away and I just feel...sad. Scared." I tuck my teary cheek against my shoulder and wrap my arms around my chest.

"Babe," he says softly, "don't be embarrassed to tell me stuff like that. I want to know how you feel and what you're thinking."

"I feel like I stumbled and I'm supposed to get up, but I don't know how. You always had my back until now. Even when I was five time zones away and refused to answer the phone."

I steel myself to meet his gaze. His eyes are shadowed with fatigue. I worry the silver dove pendant at my throat to keep from reaching to touch his cheek.

"Would it be lame of me to say there was a certain thrill to the chase?"

"No, what's lame is you thinking I'd ever cheat, especially with a short guy from the sticks I have almost nothing in common with."

"*Almost* nothing?"

"We both worry about our single moms. That's all. Honest."

He nods and strokes my forearm. "I miss talking to you about stuff like that. Being cut off has been really hard. Scary. I felt...totally lost and forgotten."

"You have your phone back. Can I text you or call this week?"

"I think so. I might be pretty busy, though. The first campers come tomorrow. How about this: text me a few things each day. Three things? Three true things."

I give a shaky laugh of relief. "Should these three things be on a theme, like the elevator game I used to play with Dad? And you have to guess?"

His expression frosts over. "I'm dead serious, Dani. If you think I'm a joke, that we're a joke...there's nothing more to say." He lumbers toward Gertie, shoulders hunched.

"Thebes, wait. I'm sorry!"

He lifts his hand in a half-hearted wave, but doesn't look back or stop walking.

* * *

My shoulder aches, but I hurl the slobbery tennis ball again. Watching Rhys streak after it doesn't raise my spirits one micrometer. Why isn't this working? When he gallops across an expanse of grass, he's pure joy in action, golden and true. Even after my roughest grief-share sessions, all I had to do was toss a ball and the sight him flying towards his goal never failed to give me a lift. Dad felt closer, like a splinter of his life force had returned to keep me company.

When Rhys returns with the yellow ball triumphantly clenched in his teeth, I drop it into his toy bag, feed him a treat, and clip on his leash. We could head into the cool woods to explore the creekside. Maybe birdsong can do what Rhys at play can't. But Laughlin might be there with his gun, and this time he won't aim it at my feet.

Rhys snuffles through the grass, pulling me toward the pine grove. The carpet of needles reminds me of the cathedral-like arching pines at the lake house. The firefly. Theo's tender touch. His tender words: *Nothing to be afraid of, chérie.*

If only I could believe that. It feels like I have *everything* to be afraid of. If I can't rebuild bridges with Theo, I'll lose him.

Mum's getting wackier by the hour. Poppa may never speak again. My uncle is headed for a fall — or the loony bin, according to Laughlin. Angry Laughlin. If his flip-outs got him kicked out of school, who knows what havoc he could wreak.

Keys rattle over near the outbuilding. The chain jangles and clanks like it's been loosened. I creep closer, carefully crouched behind trees. David's at the door, unlocking the deadbolt and knob lock. He slips inside, but doesn't quite close the door behind him.

Rhys tugs against me, trying to follow a trail of quality smells from root to root in the opposite direction. I resort to making a trail of crumbled dog treats back to my uncle's hideaway.

As we edge closer, I can hear David talking. I strain to catch snatches of words.

"I know," he says with conviction. And then, "things will be different this time."

I tiptoe two steps closer. As I press the door ajar another inch to hear better, I'm overwhelmed by the gamey scent of oil paint and something floral. Orange blossom.

I peek through the gap between the door and frame. David is lying on a green velvet Victorian couch, resting his head on the bosom of someone in a 1970s peasant dress. There's no head on the body. Just a big silver knob where a neck would be. A dressmaker's form?

Holy cow. Laughlin was telling the truth after all.

The shock must make my hands go slack, because Rhys's leash is no longer in my grip. He noses open the door and bounds up to David, tail wagging.

Chapter 20

Uncle David sits up, blushing scarlet. "Hey," he says to me as he pets Rhys.

I stand frozen in the doorway, half afraid that crossing the threshold will involve a painful journey through space and time. How could this little building in Poppa's yard have a century-old Parisian artist's loft wedged inside it?

Below the papered-over windows, stacks of painted canvases line the wall. Nearly all of them are portraits of children, and not just Mum and David. Some kids are in vintage outfits that remind me of Spanky, Alfalfa, and the Little Rascals gang. In one corner is an unfinished canvas with big blocks of underpainting. An abandoned palette sits on the stool in front of it, the paint globs dried out and cracked.

David stays seated in the tight lounge area, looking like he fell into a little girl's dollhouse. Antique end tables that flank the curvy couch are crammed with knickknacks — porcelain figurines of people in poufy costumes and Quimper pottery adorned with Brittany peasants and folk-art flowers in cobalt, goldenrod, and vermillion. To David's right sits a squishy wing chair with bits of lace draped over the arms, and at his feet lies a hand-hooked rug in a stylized Breton floral pattern. In the area behind him, colorful women's outfits hang from the rafters at random intervals. And up above, perched on the rafters, are dozens of cardboard boxes, many labeled in French.

"What…?" is all I can manage to say.

My uncle smiles sheepishly. "Come meet your grandmother." He rests a hand on the dummy and says, "Mama, this is Grace's girl, Danielle, all grown up. Dani, this is your Nana."

"You're completely insane!" I dart through the door to snatch up Rhys's leash.

"Aw, come on, niece o'mine. I was joking. I know it's not *actually* her. My therapist thought it would help if I could role play. You know, say stuff I never said when she was alive."

"Then what's with the…shrine?" I indicate the room around him.

"This was Mama's world apart, where she hid from everyone. She squirreled things away back here out of Pop's sight for years."

"Including her own clothing?"

"Well, that was me. I nabbed a few favorite outfits after she passed."

"Favorite outfits?" My voice hitches with alarm. "What for?"

"My cabaret career, of course."

I drop my head in my hands and groan. Laughlin was absolutely right.

"Sheesh, when did you get to be so gullible? I was kidding. I kept outfits that had good memories. Come on, you know it helps. I've seen you wear your dad's shirts."

"Are you aware that Laughlin got a peek in here when you were having a role-playing session? He now believes you're a cross-dresser. And probably schizophrenic."

David's eyes widen. "No wonder he doesn't want to have dinner with me."

"If he knew the truth, I doubt it would change his opinion about you dating his mom."

David sighs. "I know I look like the poster boy for 'mommy issues' right now. If it weren't for Sarah, I would have handed over the keys to Grace and let you two empty this place. But to build a future with Sarah, I have to work through this part of my past."

"Has Mum seen this place?"

"Not since high school, I bet. Mama added a second lock when Grace left home, and a third after I started at NYU. After she passed, I found the keys in her purse. First time I came in here, it hurt so bad I went on a three week bender that should've killed me."

"You miss her a lot."

His mouth pinches ruefully as he shrugs. "I missed her even when she was alive."

"But what about all these paintings of you as kids?"

"Look at the dates. She painted those when Grace and I were out of the house. Must've worked from memory. They're... different from the portraits in the house that we sat for."

I page through the paintings, studying faces. For all the variety of expressions, the eyes rarely look right. They're bleak, sad, even when the subject is smiling or laughing.

I turn back to David, suddenly teary. "I don't— why am I...?"

"They wreck me, too. It's like she painted the lonely, regret-filled part of herself into us."

I look at the first portrait again. A dark-haired little girl holds a toad in her palm, and looks straight at me with pleading eyes that say, *Won't you please see me? What I have to offer?*

"You can't show these to Mum," I choke. "Promise me you won't. They'll kill her."

"How do you know, Dani? Maybe they'd actually heal her."

Of all the idiotic theories! I stride toward him and use my height to full intimidating advantage. "Would you get a *freaking* clue? She's already falling apart! The last thing she needs is more painful crap stuffed in her face. Paris is what she needs: rest, good food, sunshine, art. I aim to get her there. And you" — I poke his chest — "ought to do the same."

While David blinks and splutters, I whistle for my dog.

"Come on, Rhys. Visiting hours at the nuthouse are over."

I storm away from the outbuilding, pausing to kick a tree with frustration. Pain flares up my leg and I hiss what probably sound like Klingon swearing. Rhys zigzags skittishly behind me as I hobble toward the patio with a stubbed toe.

Sarah approaches, head tilted with concern. "Hey, Dani. Any idea where I might find your uncle?"

"I just saw him...." I indicate the pine grove now blocking our view of Nana's studio.

"Exorcizing his mother's ghost, yes?" Sarah helps me into a patio chair.

"You know about that place? About the dummy he talks to as if it were Nana?"

"Mmm-hmm. I wish he wouldn't role-play without his therapist supervising. It's probably not as helpful as he thinks it is."

"I can't believe he told you about the shrine. I had no clue. I doubt Mum does either."

"Davey and I promised each other total honesty."

"Seriously?" I look at her with new admiration. "How is that even possible?"

"We didn't get here overnight. There was a lot of trial and error — especially error. David's addiction, my mess of a marriage, all fueled by secrets and lies. Hiding things can feel safe, Dani, but secrets end up holding power over you."

"What do you mean?"

"Secrets demand your allegiance and protection. They make you believe that sharing the information with anyone will bring only shame and shunning. Covering up and lying can keep those scared feelings at bay for a little while, but it doesn't really set you free from the fear."

"Not just anyone deserves to know your secrets," I protest.

"True. It's okay to be reserved. But you've got to trust somebody at some point or you'll always be alone with only your fear for company."

I frown. Fear I understand. Fear I have in spades. "So how do you get past being scared? See the Wizard of Oz and ask for some courage?"

She squeezes my upper arm. "No need to tangle with flying monkeys. Just figure out what makes you feel safe, and build from there."

David steps onto the patio and kneels so Rhys can cover him in slobbery kisses. "Love you too, boy," he says, scuffing my dog's head.

My urge to flee makes my legs twitch, but I force myself to sit still and think: what makes me feel safe? Having my uncle's help and support does.

"I'm sorry I flipped out at you," I tell him.

"I understand, kiddo. You're a worrier. Look, I'll leave Mama's studio unlocked. You can have a look around and move whatever you think will upset Grace. Gauge when you think she's ready to see the place and I'll help you show her. I promise not to spring it on her."

"Thanks. That sounds...good."

"So, dinner?" Sarah suggests. "Join us, Dani? Your mother has turned in for the night. I found her asleep on the couch when I was looking for Davey."

"Is, um, Laughlin coming, too?" I ask.

Sarah and David exchange a look I often saw pass between my parents: *you want to handle that?*

"I'm afraid not," Sarah says. "He...wanted a break from us all, so I let him go with the Grouse Hill riders to groom for their show in Virginia all week."

* * *

My ringtone wakes me from a dream of manically painting canvas after canvas of kitschy Eiffel Tower scenes. I'm almost instantly blinded by the sun searing through the windows of Poppa's room. It must be noon or possibly later. I pat around to find my phone.

"Dani?" Heather says, her voice breaking.

"Hey. What's the matter?"

"It's Fletcher. We—" She gulps in a breath like she'd just been sobbing.

"Oh no, not another fight. Jeez. What's he mad about now?"

"It was…me this time. He wouldn't stop bugging me, doing all this crazy-nice stuff I never asked for. He was over here cleaning our bathrooms and ironing Daddy's shirts, and I just snapped. Said horridly mean things. Called him an insufferable show off. Accused him of caring only about one-upping Theo. Of turning everything into a competition."

"Wow. Really? I thought you liked the attention, and how he'd changed."

"I did at first. Kind of. But it got to be too much. I would've been happy with flowers and phone time. If only I'd said so sooner, before it got so deep under my skin. After all the awful things I said, he'll never want to be nice to me again. I actually made him cry."

"So he has a soft side after all. Wow. Still, when his attempts to be nice don't feel nice, he needs to know that. Screaming isn't the optimal way to tell him, of course, but you were honest, Heather. That's healthy. So don't give up. Work it out."

"Okay. I guess I could try," she says, sighing. "You're so lucky. You and Theo never end up screaming at each other."

"My relationship is in a way bigger mess than yours, by a

199

long shot." I tell her about my wacky Saturday, suddenly juggling two guys, both furious I never told either about the other.

"But...do you like Laughlin back?" she asks.

"A little," I admit. "When he isn't pulling pranks, he's...easy to talk to. Helpful. Pretty decent company when you're all alone. After you left, we started hanging out more. Why did I open up, tell him about my problems?"

"You needed someone to talk to, silly. Theo and I abandoned you, even if we didn't mean to. The only thing you're guilty of is being lonely and trying to make a friend."

"He tried to kiss me, Heather."

"'Tried to' means you didn't let him. Are you sad that you didn't?"

I send my mind back to that soggy moment, the scents of peat moss and stale tobacco. Gripping that thick wrist with the strange, square hand attached. Looking down into those bright eyes gazing up at me with a smarmy squint. "Gosh, no," I admit. "It would've been incredibly weird, and probably a bit revolting."

"Okay then. You don't have romantic feelings for him, so stop beating yourself up."

"I accidentally let it slip to Theo about the attempted kiss."

"Uh oh. How'd he take it?"

"Not well. My attempts at damage control made him think I was hiding a torrid affair. He said it feels like there's no trust between us."

"Whoa. Are you two...breaking up?"

"I feel like I'm on probation. He gave me this...challenge before he left: tell him three true things every day. If I screw this up, I guess he's done with me."

"Three true things. Hmm. Sounds like therapy homework. Have you done it yet?"

"I texted him at bedtime yesterday. I haven't heard back. Could you tell me what you think?" I leaf through crumpled drafts until I find the final version I texted. "Here's the first message: 'Hi, Theo. I hate that we fought. That our trust isn't what it should be. So I'm sending the three things you asked for.' Next I wrote, 'One: I worry my family mess will scare you away, because it's so big and strange, but I'm more scared to face it without your support.' After that I wrote, 'Two: that locked outbuilding I told you about was once Nana's studio, but now it's a shrine. I saw my uncle in there, talking to a dressmaker dummy in Nana's clothes.' And finally, 'Three: I'm afraid for Mum to see the shrine to Nana because I think it will destroy her.'"

"A shrine to your nana? A dressmaker dummy?"

"Oh, God help me," I wail. "Why did I tell him that? It's so bizarre, he'll think I just made it up to be funny. What do I do, Heather? I swear it's true. I— I could send you pictures."

"Oh, Dani. If you were spinning tales, you'd make things sound boring and normal, not super strange. You did real good with honesty, okay? Send him pictures if it makes you feel better, but he'd have to be made of marble to not feel the trueness of your heart."

* * *

While I'm waiting for my slice of quiche to reheat, I hear Mum give a loud, exasperated groan from the dining room. When I peek in, I do a double take because the paper piles are completely gone. Mum sits, head in hands, at the dining table, which is clear of all but two packing boxes, a checkbook and a calculator. She groans yet again.

I pad over to her. "It looks amazing in here. Did you do all this today?"

"I've been up since five," she mumbles into her hands. "After twelve hours, I couldn't sleep any more. Unlike you." She gives me a pointed look.

"I've been up a while. I was on the phone with Heather. She's at the tail end of her chickenpox, thank God. No new spots today. Her old ones are almost all scabs now."

Mum nods absently, tapping a fingernail on the checkbook.

"What's up? A money problem?"

Her eyes slide closed in defeat. "There's no way Pop can afford to stay here, with the upkeep costs on top of nursing care. It was different when Mama was sick. They had better insurance, more income. He and my brother could manage the yard and chores."

"So we sell the house."

Mum shakes her head. "I don't know how to get him to agree to it."

"He'll have to. It's the only way."

"It's not the *only* way, darling," she replies, her voice dipping low. When her eyes meet mine, I realize what she's implying.

If Poppa won't move, we'll have to.

Every molecule in me screams *No, no, no!*

"What about David?"

"He has a business to deal with, and employees who count on him."

"So do we!" I counter.

"But I'm not in charge."

"You could be. Dad left Deane Studios to you, after all."

She sits back in the chair, opening and closing her mouth like a goldfish. "I don't— What makes you think…?"

"You were happy dreaming up designs for Dad's old client. Genuinely happy. It's been such a long time, I almost forgot what your happy even looks like. Come on, Mum. Let Uncle

David handle Poppa. He promised he would."

"Oh, sweetheart," Mum says with a pitying voice. "He can't help us with this. Not right now. He's driving his finished projects back to his customers in Maine."

My heart thuds in my chest. I can't believe he'd abandon us, not after that chummy dinner last night, when he and Sarah told hilarious and hair-raising stories from their shared past. "He's gone?"

"Just a few days, he said. He arranged for Arturo to come help us paint tomorrow. His family owns a professional paint sprayer, so it should go quickly."

If David made such detailed arrangements for us, he's more invested in our getting to Paris than Mum's letting on. I bet he has no idea what she's contemplating. He wouldn't have left now if he did. "You haven't told David that Poppa can't afford the house, have you?"

"I didn't know for sure myself until a few minutes ago."

"Call him and tell him. Right now." I pass her cell phone to her. "He deserves to know. You need to stop babying him."

"I know, but his trip home isn't strictly business. Sarah went with him."

* * *

After Mum's long talk with her brother, we head to the rehab hospital to visit Poppa. Mum stops by the nurses' station to drop off a cake from our obscene stockpile of sweets brought daily by the Dunn Creek Methodist hospitality ministry. I check Poppa's room for staff to invite for a bite of cake and see one of the orderlies take a seat in the guest chair.

"How you be, Mr. Tilman?"

"Aye?" Poppa asks.

The orderly smiles. "I'm Moe. Abe's my son. He love history, thanks to you. You was his favorite teacher up the high school. Know what? Abe come to your sale yesterday, got me one of your old books, 'bout Dizzy Gillespie." He shows Poppa the cover.

"No!" Poppa yells. He claws the air trying to grab the book from Moe. "Mine! Give!"

Moe scoots the chair back, out of Poppa's reach, eyes wide with alarm.

"Poppa, stop!" I cry, and wave to Moe to come quickly before Poppa's on his feet.

"What did he just say?" someone asks behind me. I turn to see a ponytailed blonde in a white coat with a stethoscope slung around her neck.

"He say, 'mine' and 'give,' Dr. Sanders," Moe says, coming to the door. "I thought he'd be pleased to know this old book o' his got a good home. He weren't."

Mum rushes to Poppa's side. She tries to coax him to stay seated in bed while he continues snarling, "My Dizzy! Mine!"

"Not anymore, Pop," Mum says. "A former student of yours bought it; be glad he wants to keep learning. Dani talked to you about the box of biographies. You agreed they could go."

Poppa shoots me a poisonous glare and hisses "mine."

"We, uh, brought a cake," I say. "Anyone want some?"

Moe nods and escapes to the nurses' station. The doctor approaches Poppa.

"It's nice to hear your voice, Mr. Tilman." She picks up the chart at the end of his bed, leafs through it, and jots something on the pages. "I see you did almost a mile on the treadmill today, too. Nice work. Nothing will keep a good man down, eh?"

"Dizzy mine," Poppa repeats.

"I'll ask the music therapist to add jazz to your sessions, all right? A nurse will be here in a moment to check your vitals."

Poppa grunts, annoyed, but stops struggling to get out of bed. Maybe they threatened some awful treatment if his blood pressure is too high.

"Perhaps you ladies could come with me?" the doctor says. She points a nurse toward Poppa's room as we follow her to a tiny office.

She closes the door behind us. "Well, wasn't that a treat? You should be extremely proud of your father's progress, Mrs. Deane."

"But what about his aggression?" Mum asks.

"He might have hurt that orderly if I hadn't been there to tell him no," I add.

"With aphasia, some patients struggle more with their frustration," the doctor says. "His refusal to vocalize was a part of that. But his speech today, which clearly made sense in context, is a sign he's turned a corner with his therapy."

Mum shoots me a shocked look. "His neurologist mentioned emotional swings being related to…longer term problems." She shakes her head. "I'm probably worrying unnecessarily."

The doctor tips her head. "We are monitoring him for that, Mrs. Deane. With strokes, every concern deserves consideration. Have you given any thought to next steps in his care? The beds in this unit are in fairly high demand, and I expect he'll be ready to transition to another situation within the next week."

"A *week*? I, ah, need my brother's input on that."

"Your father's social worker can make some inquiries for you, if you'd like. Unless there's someone to be home with him while he gets his speech and occupational therapy on an outpatient basis?"

Chapter 21

When I get in the car in the rehab hospital parking lot, Mum is slumped in her seat, her forehead resting on the steering wheel. "Good God, what do we do now?"

"Well, we have painters coming tomorrow, so maybe we start there?" I suggest.

"I forgot about that. I'd lose my hands right now if they weren't attached to my arms."

"Jesus," I pray, "please keep Mum together. Thanks for all you've done to heal Poppa. Grant us wisdom so we know what to do. And peace, so we can actually do it. Amen."

"Amen," Mum echoes and sits up. "All right, darling. List time."

I whip out my sketchpad and furiously scribble as she dictates a list of phone calls she needs to make, plus a full inventory of painting-prep projects to be tackled ASAP. Thank goodness I slept in so late, because I have a feeling there isn't going to be a bedtime tonight.

When we return to Poppa's, we move furniture into the center of the rooms to be painted, then tackle the time-consuming task of photographing, labeling, and moving each piece of art from its hanging spot to "the trophy room" as we've dubbed it. Mum works with a focus that makes me feel invisible. I try to keep up a conversation so she doesn't vanish into her own little world, but even my heartbreaking boy-problem stories draw only an occasional sympathetic noise from her.

Once we move to her old bedroom, I pluck up the courage to ask, "Why isn't any of your art in the house, Mum?"

She flinches, as if I'd appeared out of nowhere. "My art? Mama hid it all after Pop burned one of my drawings."

"Oh my gosh. Why would he do that?"

"I drew Mama while she was getting chemo. Bald. Bent. Pale as milk. She reminded me of a delicate Indian pipe flower." Mum's mouth twists into a wry frown. "All Pop could see was Mama's suffering. He hated it. Hated me for capturing it."

My throat tightens. How did she endure him always adding insult to injury? "I'm sorry, Mommy," I whisper. "I wish I could see that drawing. More than anything."

"I do, too, so you could know Mama. I did others like it, hid them away in the garage rafters, in a box Mama labeled in French so he'd leave it alone. But after she passed, the box was gone."

A box in the rafters labeled in French. Like one of the dozens stowed in Nana's studio.

I can't tell her.

I have to tell her.

It will break her heart to see that place.

David said it will heal her.

The pro/con list grows and grows in my mind until Mum says, "I wonder if Mama tucked it away in her studio sometime before the end. I'd give anything to get in there again."

"You would?" I rasp, my throat suddenly dry.

"I've tried every key in this house, including a huge collection Pop must have bought in an auction lot with trophies or war memorabilia. I got so frustrated, I bought a glass cutter. To break in like a jewel thief. I just want to see the place again. But I guess it will have to wait."

My head bobs spastically. "Yeah, yeah. No time for that. We have way too much to do before the painters come."

* * *

How goes it with the campers, T? Lots happening here.

One: I wanted to send you photos of Uncle David role playing in Nana's studio (aka the shrine), but he went home to Maine to deal with work stuff. Sarah went with him. It seems like they're getting serious.

Two: Poppa is talking again, so they might release him from rehab earlier than we expected. I hate the idea of him being here, tearing Mum down.

Three: Mum wants to see Nana's studio so bad, she was thinking about cutting open a window. I haven't told her David left it unlocked. We have too much work to do. And I'm terrified. Heather said to read Psalm 31, so I'll try that.

* * *

Arturo and his father are so skilled with their sprayer, Mum and I realize we're in their way more than helping. I'm all for vacating the house for a few hours, because I have a wicked sore throat that the paint fumes only make worse.

"I have the perfect project for us today," Mum says, waggling her eyebrows. "Let's put my glass cutter to use."

I laugh nervously. "Um, yeah. About that…."

"What's wrong, Doodlebug? You *scared*?" she teases.

Of course I am. This version of Mum — the one who's hopeful, brave, and fun — will evaporate as soon as she steps through that door, back into her terrible childhood.

But she's ready to break and enter, she wants to see the place so badly. I might as well come clean about the unlocked door, because she'll see for herself soon enough.

Words from Heather's Psalm roll across my mind: *Keep me free from the trap that is set for me, for you are my refuge. Deliver me, Lord, my faithful God.*

"You don't need to break in, Mum. Uncle David unlocked it. He found the keys in Nana's purse after she died."

"He had keys for over sixteen *years* and never *told* me? What has he *done* to the place?"

"He's kept it like a shrine. Seriously. No pot plants. No used needles or burnt spoons. I swear. Come on, I'll show you."

Mum follows me outside, a kaleidoscope of emotions playing across her face. She mutters to herself as we walk, but I catch only random words, the most repeated being *selfish*. Yikes.

"He wasn't planning to keep this a secret forever, Mum. I think he assumed you'd want to clean the place out, and he's not ready to let Nana go."

Mum narrows her eyes. "What on earth do you mean?"

"He seems to have a lot of unfinished business because...." I frown. "Nana wasn't very motherly to him, was she?"

"Of course she—!" Mum stops herself. Shakes her head. "Mama wasn't one of those mothers who'd sew and keep a full cookie jar. When you fell and scraped your knee, she'd flit about, all kisses and sympathy, so lovely that for a moment you'd forget the sting and the blood. Until she drifted away, leaving you with your pain. That was Mama."

Nana sounds more like an exotic butterfly than the strong parent Mum needed to protect her from Poppa. Yet Mum seems more sad than angry about it.

As we near the studio, she jogs ahead and throws open the door. When I catch up, Mum is wandering around the room in dazed wonder, looking with her hands as much as her eyes. She strokes the silky fabric of Nana's dresses, straightens doilies, and slides her fingers along the contours of the furniture. The figurines she picks up one by one, turning them around in her hands. She then drifts to the easel, first poking the dried paint on the palette, then running her palms across the tops of the brush collection. "Still soft!" she exclaims, eyes alight like a kid on Christmas morning.

"When I was a little girl, I would sit in a playpen right there while Mama worked." She points to a spot under the windows now cluttered with painted canvases. "Mostly I built with blocks, but sometimes she'd give me paper and pencils or paint."

"David told me this was Nana's place away, where she hid from everyone. She let you come in here, but not him?"

"David was a rowdy boy and Mama was sensitive to noise, I suppose because of her brain tumors. It hurt him to be constantly shushed or sent to play catch with Pop. He was too little to understand that Mama wouldn't always be with us. That every moment with her was precious, even if it had to be on her terms. He couldn't stop following me to her studio and misbehaving, so Mama banned me too. I barely spoke to him for months after that."

"Nana wishes things could have been different," I say. "You can see it in her work."

"If you can find any special meaning in Mama's surrealist fruits and flowers, you must've studied some art theory I missed."

"Those still lifes are what she let Poppa see. Her best work is out here, I think."

Mum pages through a stack of canvases, frowning. "Hmm. Is this supposed to be me?" She points to the painting of the girl holding a toad that brought me to tears days ago.

"Your name's on the back. Though Uncle David said you were in college the year she painted it. He feels like there's some of her in there, looking out of your eyes."

"Wishing eyes," Mum murmurs.

"And regretful too, I think. Sorry eyes."

Mum's nostrils flare. She slides the canvas back into the stack and leafs through the other pieces. "These are...really different. I'm not even sure who all these children are."

"Do you think the pieces might be valuable?"

"Perhaps. Mama had a loyal fan base and did quite a few commissions." She lifts a painting out of the pile and turns it over. "Warren...and Daniel? It can't be."

"Can't be what?"

"Pop with his twin brother. It's absolutely unbelievable."

Mum turns over the painting, and there in sepia tones are two filthy, dejected boys in ragged 1940s clothes, standing by a farmyard fence. Besides shades of muddy brown, the only color is vibrant yolk-yellow around the boys' mouths and dotting the fronts of their grubby outfits. Across the bottom of the painting is a wordy title in French: *Nous avions tellement faim, nous avons volé les oeufs du voisin et les avons mangés crus.*

"We were...so hungry," I translate, "we stole...the neighbor's eggs...and ate them raw."

* * *

One: Here are photos of Nana's studio. I finally brought Mum here. She has lots of memories, not all bad.

Two: We found evidence that Poppa grew up dirt poor. Mum had no idea.

Three: I finished the brochure you gave me. It said narcissism can begin from a super shameful experience. To cope, the person creates a "winner" image and protects it at all costs. I wonder if being so poor made Poppa the way he is.

* * *

Mum and I are re-hanging paintings in the master suite Tuesday evening when Rhys goes wild barking, making my already-aching head throb. Hands over my ears, I go to the kitchen window and see David's truck in the driveway, piled high with lumber and tools.

"Hey, Mum, your brother's back!" I call hoarsely.

When I step outside, summer air hits me like a steamy wave that seems to short out my inner thermostat. My hands and feet go achingly cold. Cool sweat prickles my spine.

Rhys sprints past me, and dances around my uncle as he reaches to open the passenger door.

"Hey, furball." Uncle David scuffs Rhys behind the ears and watches me walk unsteadily toward him. "Hey, niece o'mine. What's with the long sleeves? It's nearly ninety."

"Mum cranked up the A/C," I lie.

He nods, then helps Sarah down from the cab of his truck like she's a visiting foreign dignitary. There's nothing pasted on about her smile, though. She's positively glowing.

Mum hugs them both. "You two hungry? Vera Raab sent a ten-pound turkey for dinner."

"People have Christmas in July, so why not Thanksgiving in June?" I quip, my voice sandpapery.

While Mum lays out a spread in the kitchen, I show David and Sarah around the freshly-painted rooms. They marvel at how much we accomplished with a skeleton crew.

I explain that our timeline is tighter than we thought. "Now that Poppa's talking again, they think he won't need such intensive rehab much longer. They want him to transition out of there soon. If we can't find a nursing home with space, he'll have to come home, I guess, and get his therapy as an outpatient."

David exchanges a tense look with Sarah. "Grace and I have *a lot* to discuss."

Dinner is delicious, but swallowing becomes increasingly painful. I put on a kettle and rifle through cabinets for tea bags while David tells us about the goings-on at his shop.

"I'm sorry I didn't take the coffin back north," he says.

"Boy is he ever," Sarah says, giggling.

"The client who ordered it dropped dead while on vacation in Seattle, so the family had him buried out there. I get to keep the deposit, but trying to resell a piece like that? It'll be a major undertaking."

Sarah chortles. "A grave problem that just crypt up on him."

"People are dying for a box like that." Mum jokes. "You have a coroner on the market."

My teakettle whistles. The three of them stop putting the fun in funeral and stare at me.

"Why are you making tea on such a hot day?" David asks.

"The paint fumes." I clear my throat. "Bothering me."

"Aside from the casket fiasco," he continues, "the shop is doing fine. Keegan and Chip have a good handle on the pew installation at First Pres, and I brought materials for a month of projects, so...I'm all set to be here with Pop while you're in Paris."

I stop stirring my tea. "Are you *kidding* me?" I squeak.

"You saw how much I hauled. I never joke about lumber."

"*Paris!*" I hug my steaming mug of tea to my chest.

"Pop's such a handful," Mum says." Are you sure?"

"I know it's not a permanent solution, but there should be one when you get back." David twines his fingers with Sarah's. "That new seniors' facility opening near my place? Spruce View? We put in a couple applications. One for Pop, in assisted living...."

"And one for me," Sarah adds. "For a job in the acute care unit."

David shyly ducks his head. "Because I asked Sarah to be my wife."

"And I said 'yes!'"

Chapter 22

> You okay, Theo? I wish you'd say something. I pray you're just busy and haven't been eaten by a bear, because I have so much to tell you.
>
> One: Uncle David and Poppa's neighbor Sarah returned from Maine ENGAGED. They haven't set a date yet, but it could be as soon as August.
>
> Two: Sarah wants to tell Laughlin in person about the engagement, but he's in Virginia all week working at a horse show. He's gonna flip when he finds out.
>
> Three: My uncle plans to move Poppa to a new nursing home near his place in Maine. But we have to convince Poppa to sell his house. That will be fun.

A few heartbeats after I send my final text, my phone jangles in my hand. When I see Theo on the caller ID, I shiver, and not just because I've been chilly all day.

"Dani!" he crows. "Laughlin's gone *all week*? Why didn't you tell me sooner?"

He's still worried about Laughlin? "That's why I haven't heard from you?"

"When you said nothing about him, I assumed — imagined...." There's a strange edge of despair in his voice.

"Thebes, he knows I'm with you. Once everything came out in the open on Saturday, I never saw or heard from him again."

He grunts, a sound so cynical it's a step away from *yeah, right, liar.*

Coldness wells in my belly. Is this really how it ends with us?

"Even if I had ten witnesses and video footage of my every move the past three days, it wouldn't really matter, would it? I can't make you trust me again." The realization makes my sore throat ache even more. "I've tried so hard to do what you asked. Tried to be real about everything going on here. What more do you want from me?"

"I don't want anything more. I just— I don't know. It was…nice hearing from you."

"Was it? I couldn't guess from all the silence coming back at me."

"Sorry, Dani. I was trying to pull myself together, not—"

"Punish me?"

He gives a startled chuckle. "Well, the quiet's better than what I might have written, honestly. My imagination has not been my friend this week. I hope Dr. Hoyt can help me with that when I see him tomorrow." Splashing and screeching kid voices resound in the background. He must be having evening pool time with some campers.

I think of our swim in the lake two Sundays ago. How good it felt to rest my cheek on his sun-warmed shoulder and just talk. To have him in my life. To be in his.

"How's camp going?" I ask.

"All right, I guess. Hold on a sec." He muffles the mouthpiece, and says something warbled to someone nearby. Gradually, the kid noises fade.

While I wait, I dig through Poppa's medicine cabinet and find vile lemon throat lozenges that soothe my aching throat a little.

"Everyone now calls my cabin 'Yellow Springs,'" he says with a suggestive lift to his voice, like he's telling a punchline. "Eight of our kids are bedwetters at ten, eleven years old. Luckily the head counselor let me pick up some Nite-nites for the cabin — they're big-kid diapers that look like underwear. Oh, and one boy has night terrors. Like thrashing and screaming. So I now have to sleep in a single beside his bunk — not lawsuit close, but near enough that I'll wake up when he starts flailing in his sleep. The *only* thing that calms this kid so he doesn't wake the whole cabin is singing 'Old MacDonald.' Verse after verse. I had to invent new ones for goats and geese and bison and llamas."

"What sound does a llama make?"

"Pfffft. They spray-spit, like camels."

I laugh. "You're doing a good job, Thebes."

"So are you. Helping your family and...being real with me."

His words make something warm flicker inside me for a change. Hope.

"Thanks. I...really, really miss you."

"I do, too." He chuckles wearily. "I mean, I miss you and also normal me, who could sleep through the night without having to sing and do animal impressions every few hours."

"You should probably spend your day off catching up on sleep."

"I'd rather see you," he murmurs shyly. "It's my last chance before your trip, to hang out and see your grandma's studio, and, well, get to know these people joining your family."

"Oh man, I just realized something. If Sarah will be my new aunt, that'll make Laughlin my *cousin*."

"Your first cousin," Theo adds, "which makes it practically illegal for him to put the moves on you ever again."

"Oh-kay. If you say so. I guess we'll see you Saturday."

"Dani, I...owe you some responses. I'll text you back soon. Could you maybe, um, keep doing the Three Things? Hearing from you is— I need it. And it helps me know how to pray."

* * *

With Theo's long silence at last lifted, and David now promising to care for Poppa, my concern cycles back to my botched art final. Four illustrations doesn't sound like much, but Ms. Quinlan expects at least three preliminary sketches for each one. Aside from coming up with a basic concept — updating *Madeline* based on Paris today — all I've done is locate Mum's old copy of the book. I thumb through the dog-eared pages again, pausing to study the full-color images that feature important Paris landmarks.

There's a light rap on the door, then Mum peeks in. "David wants his bedroom back, so I'll have to bunk with you until the new carpet is in and we put the other rooms back together."

"As long as you promise not to wet the bed, scream, or make me sing E-I-E-I-O," I say.

"Excuse me?" She turns from the dresser, where she's deposited her suitcase.

"Inside joke. Something Theo said about a kid in his cabin."

Mum clambers onto the bed beside me, eyes shining. "He finally called you? You're talking again?"

"Who are you? You look like my mother, but sound like Heather."

Mum laughs. "Pardon my excitement. I know you told me you were working things out after the fight Saturday and I shouldn't worry. But you've been a bit off the last few days. Your usual spark seemed...dull."

I stare at Mum's old book resting on my knees. "I thought he'd get over it quicker. He's still only partway there. But he does want to see me Saturday. That's something."

"It is. Be patient and don't lose hope. Relationships that weather some shake ups usually grow stronger in the end."

"I wish I'd never met Laughlin O'Donnell."

Mum smiles wryly. "Without him, we'd still be sitting in a house full of junk. David proposed to Sarah so quickly mostly for his sake — my brother thinks it will be easier for Laughlin to move before the new school year starts."

"How do you feel about their engagement? Do you still think Sarah will bring out the worst in your brother?"

Mum takes out her ponytail elastic and brushes her coffee-colored hair. "They're both far more aware of their issues than I first thought. On this trip, David took Sarah to meet everyone who's anyone in his life — his employees, his church friends, his pastor, his NA sponsor, even his therapist. He has a huge support network that won't let him jump into anything foolish. Still, I'm relieved they're doing couple's counseling that started up there and will continue on Skype."

"How about *our* trip? Are you getting even a teensy bit excited?"

"You clearly are." She points her hairbrush at the book in my lap.

"I thought I'd do some prep for my art final. The update on *Madeline*, remember? Before we fly out on Monday, I think I'll use Internet maps to see which sites aren't too changed from when Bemelmans drew his pictures. You know, I don't remember this book being so dark. Seriously, an appendicitis attack, ambulance ride, huge scar? I only remember these boarding school kids roaming Paris with a nun."

"So many times I wished I could've done that. Gone to boarding school. Oh, I never dwelled on it much. Escaping. They all needed me too much here at home."

I set the book down. "Well, this time you *are* going to escape and put this all behind you. You know why? Because your brother owes you, and because Poppa isn't the only one who needs you. I need you. This trip is our chance to find happiness again."

Her chin trembles.

"Don't worry. David's a lot more responsible now, and Sarah will help him. Besides, Poppa is less ornery with him."

"I know, darling," she whispers hoarsely.

"It's not your fault Poppa plays favorites. Doesn't treat you right. You deserve better."

"Graham used to say that. Over and over. But I…forget. All the things he said about boundaries, standing my ground, it's fading, like the sound of his voice."

"I'll jolly well have to remind you, won't I, love?" I sound more like the GEICO gecko than Dad, but it does the trick. She smiles.

* * *

On Wednesday, I try my best to help Mum and David clear rooms of furniture for the carpet guys. But I'm so tired from days of heavy labor I can't seem to carry anything heavier than a lamp. Mum sends me outside with Rhys for some fresh air, so I kick back on a patio lounge chair with my laptop. Rhys curls up beside me as I look through online street-view maps of Paris, trying to figure out how to recreate an image from *Madeline*'s climax. What archway in a vine-covered wall could an ambulance drive through that gives such an up-close view of the Eiffel Tower? As I scan the virtual streets, the warm sun, hum of bees, and Rhys's soft fur against my leg makes my mind slow and my eyelids heavy.

The Louvre is burning.

Mum and I first think the smell is simply cigarettes as we sit at our easels in the sunny Cour Napoléon. A strolling violinist plays Debussy as we recreate the sparkling panes of the Louvre's glass pyramid and the gracious lines and curves of the palace buildings beyond it. But smoke begins to obscure our view. Soon it billows from windows and visitors flee, screaming. Flames lick the roofline and reach orange fingers toward the sky.

As we pack up, sooty tourists stream by us, weeping.

"Masterpieces, gone! All because a madman was left alone!"

"The only one who could have stopped him walked away."

A figure appears on the rooftop with a torch in his hand. The crowds point and stare at this freakish creature with the body of a man and the head of a vulture.

Poppa screams to the heavens, "No one must see! No one must ever see!"

And the Louvre keeps burning. Masterpieces, burning. Everything beautiful in the world is swallowed in flames.

"Danielle?" Mum's hand on my arm is as cool as lotion. "Why were you yelling 'fire'?"

I blink at her and lick my parched lips. "I dreamed the Louvre was burning."

"Oh sweetheart, that can't happen. They have the most sophisticated fire extinguishing technology in the world there."

She says something about lunch and going to visit Poppa, but my head feels like it's been packed with pillow stuffing. I follow her inside and eat some church-lady entree with noodles and meat and a cream sauce that might be tuna casserole or beef stroganoff or chicken fettuccini alfredo — the texture is all kind of gooey-bumpy in my mouth.

There's a car ride. Trees. Grass. Farms. Trailer park. Trees. Grass. Roadkill: twelfth raccoon. Bicyclists. Shops. Flowers. Parking lot.

Nothing smells right in the rehab hospital. I sniff again and again for the familiar scent of antiseptic, but the air's kind of tissue-bland. Cardboardy.

Poppa smiles when he sees me and returns my wave by waggling his fingers. Itsy bitsy spider. The song runs through my head but it shouldn't be there. Spiders don't belong in hospitals.

Mum gives Poppa a kiss and flatters him to the moon and back. I can't shake the sense that something's off. I check the corners for spider webs as Mum chatters on in soothing tones.

David marrying Sarah. New grandson, Laughlin. Teach him chess, backgammon, Hearts.

Poppa says things back that might or might not be English. Maybe it's his stroke. Maybe my ears are broken.

Then Mum says words, words I know: Firbank, Maine, and Spruce View, all new.

Poppa doesn't like her words. His face gets a scowl-mouth, angry-eyebrow look. "Part...ment? No! Never. Just box, like coffin!"

"It'll be the perfect size. No maintenance. David is under two miles away."

"House ready, I go home. I have shake deal promise!" He rocks the bed, trying to tip it.

"Knock it off, you big baby!" she yells. "The house is *not* ready, and I don't know what kind of deal you think you've struck, and with whom, but you are going to *behave* until David brings you home on Monday. That's what we worked out with your social worker — the only deal that matters. Got it?"

"*Promised*," Poppa hisses, and fixes his glare on me.

I busy myself arranging get-well cards on the window-sill.

* * *

I wake shivering Thursday morning, feeling like I'll never get warm again. The iciness in my hands and feet has traveled up my extremities into my core. I burrow deeper under the covers and groan. I can't recall when I went to bed or if I ever had supper. But one thing I know for sure: this isn't just a bad reaction to paint fumes. I'm genuinely ill.

How could I get the flu now? In just days, Mum and I will drive home to pack for Paris. I can't be sick now, I just can't!

Don't panic. It's just a summer cold. A little medicine and I'll feel fine.

I shrug on Poppa's flannel bathrobe and lumber toward the master bathroom. The door is locked and I can hear the high whine of a hairdryer coming from inside.

I knock and call, "Hey, Mum? Does Poppa have any ibuprofen in there? I feel gross."

"Just a sec!" she calls back. When she opens the door, she yelps and stumbles backward. "Oh darling, I'm so, so sorry."

"Why? What's wrong?"

"You haven't seen yourself, have you? Come." She propels me toward the vanity mirror.

I have to grip the sink to stay upright, because the face looking back at me is covered with little pink spots.

Chapter 23

Mum sends me back to bed, and I'm in no condition to argue with her. But when I close my eyes, my mind fills with images of the Louvre burning, and all of Paris with it.

What do I do now? Without Paris, I can't do a *Madeline* update for my art final. Mum won't be ready for her art show. We'll still be here when Poppa returns, and he'll harass Mum and destroy what little hope she has left. Everything will be ten times worse than before.

Unless…we return to New York.

That's it. We should go home so I can see my own doctor, recover in my own bed. Mum can return to her studio full of supplies and I'll make sure she paints. No excuses. I'll even pose for her in all my speckled glory. And when I'm better, we'll paint the city together.

What if I updated *Madeline* by setting it in NYC? Instead of passing Notre Dame, Madeline and her school pals will pass St. Patrick's cathedral. The Empire State building would be the landmark on the horizon. That would totally work.

The Hudson and East rivers aren't the Seine, but what choice do I have? If I showed up at JFK like this, they'd quarantine me in a prison hospital for attempted germ warfare.

No, home's the only safe place. David can keep his promise and I can keep Mum well away from her father.

Forget about asking the Wizard of Oz for courage. I unsteadily climb out of bed, pull on slippers, click my heels together three times, and chant. "There's no place like home. No place like home. No place like home."

* * *

My attempt to determinedly march to the kitchen to demand we go home is more of a determined stumble. My demands die in my throat when I hear raised voices.

"I can't *believe* you, Grace!" Sarah cries. "You're college educated! How could you fall for a bunch of fear-mongering with no scientific basis?"

"My friends told me vaccines were like injecting your kid with autism serum. Every mother at the park said the same thing."

Remembering playdates in Prospect Park brings itchy thoughts of leaping into leaf piles. I rub my robed back against the wall, which relieves and burns at the same time.

"What other plagues will she be passing along?" Sarah sneers. "Polio? Diphtheria?"

"Of course not. She got those shots eventually. No school would take her without them."

"But not varicella."

I press a rashy cheek against the cool door frame — bliss! — to peek around the corner.

Mum is shaking her head. "It wasn't required if you'd had the infection. So…I wrote that she had chickenpox at two."

"You lied, in other words. Do you realize she's at greater risk for complications at this age: pneumonia, serious skin infections, heart problems?"

"Stop it!" I cry and lurch into the room. The two of them stare at me, horrified. "It's not Mum's fault. Even if I had the shot, I'd still be sick. I caught Heather's mutant chickenpox strain that can reinfect people. And Mum will probably get sick next, because she drove Heather home. We just need to go back to New York. Like now. While Mum is still well enough to drive."

Sarah scoffs at Heather's mutant chickenpox theory, saying it sounds like an Internet hoax. She explains that "wild type varicella" is just the standard virus passed from person to person. Unless we can find someone outside Heather's immediate family who caught the virus twice, we should assume it's a genetic immunity problem.

"Oh. Like a Daly family thing? I guess I could ask Heather."

Mum nods encouragingly and flashes a guilty smile.

"I'll pick up an antiviral drug for you at work," Sarah says. "It should lessen the symptoms and knock a few days off the rash."

"Really? So maybe we could go to Paris a week late?"

She shakes her head. "Meds might shorten the rash to seven or eight days, but you're over twelve, so it's hard to predict how your immune system will cope."

"I wanna go home!" I moan.

"I beg you, Grace, keep her here, where she can't easily infect anyone else. I'm going to get her some meds, and you'd better still be here when I get back." She marches away, closing the side door with a firm thump just shy of a Laughlin slam.

"I wanna go home," I repeat.

* * *

I dial Heather's number, then pull on old mittens Mum gave me so I don't scratch open my pox bumps. The wool only makes my hands itch more. By the time Heather answers, I've found relief by stuffing one mittened hand then the other between my knees, a pressure scratch.

"Hey, Heather? Has anyone outside your family caught chickenpox twice?"

"Hmm. It's the first time for Paulie and Becca. Mama, Ryan, Kev, Shannon, me, all sick twice. Daddy's fine. So's Fletcher, I guess, or he'd be sick by now. Not like he didn't try."

"Well yay for me. I beat Fletcher at something."

"Oh, *no*." Her voice dips low. I expect a rush of apology, of sympathy, but she's silent. After a moment she says, "I

225

wondered if that might happen."

"How could you be so cold? Months of planning for Paris, weeks of labor here, all for nothing! I'll never get out of here now, because you and your stupid germs had to tag along."

"I'm sorry about your trip. Truly. But God told me to come with you."

"Right. God loves me so much, he sent a lovely virus to put me in maximum misery and Mum under maximum stress."

"I never, ever wanted you to get sick, Dani. I've been praying for you nonstop. I know how important you think your Paris trip is for your mom and you. But...maybe there's a reason we don't understand yet that you need to stay."

"Sure," I say with every ounce of dubiousness I can muster.

She sighs. "I get it. You're angry. The timing is really crummy. But the situation makes me think of that unit we did in youth group about Paul."

"That is not a name I want to hear right now." Just thinking about that twerp Paulie and his pox party makes me itch all over.

"I mean the guy in the Bible, not my brother. Apostle Paul went through some rough stuff: shipwrecks and flogging and being chained in dungeons. He went on to say 'God causes all things to work together for good for those who are called according to His purpose.' It wasn't just wishful thinking. In the hardest times, he saw God do amazing things. Saw whole communities change, love each other when they used to hate. Anyway, you being sick, now, like this? It doesn't feel like an accident. I can't help but think that God wants to do something for you, through you, that couldn't happen in Paris."

"Right. Because I have a shining future as Saint Dani, the speckled freak of Dunn Creek whose pox shall ooze a healing balm for the nations. I just need to embrace my inner martyr and all will be well."

She chuckles. "Well, at least my germs haven't damaged your gift for sarcasm. That's hopeful. Antihistamines help with the itching; so do lukewarm baths with a scoop of baking soda."

"I'm still mad at you," I admit, "and at God apparently, too. So, thanks."

"You bet. I'm honored to be in such good company. God and I, of course, love you and believe all things will work together for good. Even if you're mad."

* * *

After I tell Mum that only Heather, her mom, and siblings have been reinfected, I return to bed and find a batch of new texts from Theo on my phone.

No 3 things from you yesterday. Guess it's my turn. Long overdue, really.

One: I've always worried that I'll turn into a cheater like Dad. When I realized I could become like Mom instead, it hit hard. Like an out-of-body rage. Like I wanted to run you over with Gertie. And him. Especially him.

My jealousy was so intense, it scared me. Reading your texts was agony. I couldn't stop picturing you sharing all your worries and dreams with HIM. I was too embarrassed to admit it when we talked Tuesday night. Sorry.

Two: Psalm 31 is awesome; thank Heather for me. The stuff it says about shame and shelter — it was what I needed to hear. God offers safety from all the hurtful crap in my past, from anything new that reminds me of it, too. I'm always loved, I always belong, no matter what.

Three: I keep having the weirdest dream about that place from your pictures, the studio? We found a box there, covered in strange writing I couldn't read. When you opened it, a ghost came out. Weird, huh? Before our hike Saturday, can you show me the place?

I reread the messages, trying to wrap my fevered brain around what Theo said. I had no idea that the mess with Laughlin dragged up all these feelings for him. I didn't know that avoiding becoming his dad's clone included worries about becoming a cheater. And seeing himself like his mom, the one cheated on? Whoa. It's a miracle our fight didn't get uglier, especially since his first urge was to flatten me with his ancient Volvo. As for his wacky dream about a haunted box, it sounds like the lack of sleep is getting to him. Wearily I tap out a response.

Me: I can see you need more time apart. I guess it's a blessing I'm too sick to hike Saturday. Caught chickenpox.

Him: OH NO! That's horrible. I'm happy to just hang out. Or help with whatever.

Me: You should stay away. You could get sick, too.

Him: I got vaccine boosters to apply for camp jobs. Including chickenpox.

Me: But you wanted to run me over with your car.

Him: My parents' divorce really messed with my head. I'll never get better if I can't be real about it.

Me: Okay. But honestly? I don't want you to see me. I look like a freak.

Him: You're my freak. I love you no matter how you look. Rest up. See you soon.

I'm too tired to respond. I rest a tear-wet, itchy cheek against the pillow and read his last text one more time. It's the most bizarrely romantic thing I've ever heard.

* * *

Mum wakes me in the afternoon to feed me turkey soup and medicine from Sarah. New spots have cropped up on my legs and feet, making my misery all the deeper.

She draws me a baking soda bath, like Heather recommended, and leaves me to savor the tepid water. Or so I think. Moments after I pull the rippled, opaque tub door closed, Mum slips back into the room. Her warbled outline paces back and forth outside the tub as she obsesses about our next move.

Do we delay the trip or cancel? If we delay, by how much? Do we cancel our booking with the flat or find someone to take the weeks we can't use? Should we reschedule with the cousins? What should we do? When? What? When?

Her questions are so exhausting, I submerge myself to escape. All the pox on my face and neck quiet their call to be scratched. Heaven. Delicious, cool, wet heaven.

I hear a low rumble, feel a hand grip my arm. Mum hauls me to the surface again. "What are you doing?" she cries in alarm.

I turn my back to her. "How about some privacy? Sheesh. I needed to treat my face. Besides, do we have to decide right this minute?"

"Sorry. You scared me." She slumps on the edge of the tub, facing away from me. "I think we really shouldn't put off a decision too long."

"Well, what do you want to do?"

"I don't know. You've worked so very hard to take this trip. All your planning and dreaming. Even learning a third language. I'd hate for all that effort to go to waste."

Actually, the French has helped me know Nana more deeply than Mum realizes, but I don't say so. "So we delay?" I suggest.

"But what if you end up with pneumonia? It could be well into August until you recover. I don't think our travel insurance would cover both a delay and a cancellation for the same illness. If we cancel up front, though, they'll reimburse for nearly all our expenses."

"What do you want to do?"

Her shoulders rise and fall, a shrug. "I suppose I want to stop living a cursed life. Where every decision doesn't come back to bite me. I mean, look what I've done to you. My beautiful baby. I only wanted to make sure you grew up being able to talk." She buries her face in her hands and heaves a heavy sigh.

Her words pierce me to the core. Cursed. That's an awfully extreme way to think of your life. Yet, how could she not feel that way? A cruel father, sick mother, drug-addict brother, husband snatched away in the prime of life. Our once-broken relationship, now healed, is the only good thing Mum has going for her. Besides her full scholarship and stipend. And the mortgage-free condo and business she inherited. And her brother being clean, running a successful business of his own, and preparing to acquire a wife and stepson. There's nothing cursed about any of that.

Cursed isn't the truth about her story. Cursed is a lie.

The thinnest beam of light cuts through all the fog of my confusion like a laser.

Not an accident. God's doing something. Right here, right now. In the home of Mum's cruel father and sick mother: The most jagged pieces of her life that remain unhealed.

"You're only guilty of loving me, Mum."

"I shouldn't have lied on your school forms."

"Well, I have some problems with telling the truth myself. Just ask my boyfriend. Maybe we can work on that. Together."

* * *

Busy hands can't scratch; busy mind can't feel the itch.

Great theory. Not so easy in practice. Especially when David's screeching table saw drowns out the *Gilmore Girls* reruns I stream on my laptop. After doing seventeen sketches of Rhys and texting every school friend, my mind ranges around for something to occupy it besides imagining how much better I'd feel if I could shuck off my rashy skin like it's dirty laundry.

If Mum weren't gallivanting around on errands, she'd keep me distracted somehow. Probably by riding me about my make-up art final. Madeline's chance at rebirth is looking pretty slim. If we take our Paris trip at all, it'll be weeks from now. Mum hasn't said what the plan is.

David's saw squeals so sharply I have to wrap pillows around my ears. Nana's journal slips out of a pillowcase and plops spread-eagled onto the bedspread. I turn the book over. The entry, from Mum's senior year, begins with an expression of shock: *Ça alors!*

My goodness! I translate. *My lovely girl, going to New York for college!*

Huh. Nana seems surprised by Mum's decision, but why? I open my laptop to help me continue translating.

It's just like I always dreamed. It's nothing like I dreamed. She'll at last leave this provincial backwater that her father can't seem to part from. But advertising school? That such a gifted artist could squander her talent hawking wares — it boggles the mind. And yet, how could it be otherwise? Despite my best intentions, I failed to keep training and encouraging her after she graduated out of my classroom. The shoemaker's children go barefoot. So selfishly I guarded my studio solitude. How could she not see art as an isolating obsession? Instead, she has developed tremendous skill in making us all look far better to the outside world than we truly are. Our family public relations specialist.

So advertising school was Mum's idea? No one forced that on her. Not like this MFA program. My uncle's heroic measures to help her "live her dream" after Dad died were based on a complete misunderstanding. I assumed he was right, because it fit my view of Poppa as completely cruel to Mum. But art school was never her dream. It was Nana's dream for her.

"Darling?" Mum peeks into the room, scaring me so bad, I yelp. "Goodness, you're awfully jumpy for being stuck in bed."

"I didn't hear you come in." I bump a pillow so it falls on top of my translation project.

"It's hard to hear anything when David's working." She picks up the thermometer on the bedside table, shakes it down, then pushes it under my tongue.

"We'b you bim?" I ask.

"Sorry, I'm not fluent in dentist. You're asking where I've been?"

I nod.

"I met with a realtor, and she's quite hopeful about finding us a buyer. My time with Pop? Not so good. The rehab hospital is at capacity, so they'd like to discharge him *tomorrow*. Problem is, you're sleeping in his bed with chickenpox, and he doesn't remember ever having it. His doctor's records only go back a few years because he changed practices a lot — personality conflicts. I finally called Sarah to ask her opinion. She felt we shouldn't risk his catching your chickenpox. It's terrible enough for a teenager. In the elderly, it can be deadly."

"So you daking me 'ome affer all?"

"Sorry. Sarah's right; you could infect people at rest areas and in our building's elevators." She removes the thermometer. "Ah, ninety-nine point four. That's better. Anyway, you need to stay put. So Sarah offered to keep Pop at her place."

Her place? Oh, no. I thought Poppa's last tantrum was bad. This will make him utterly furious. I promised he could come home, and now I'm the reason he can't.

Chapter 24

Sometime in the night, a banging noise wakes me. I stumble across the dark bedroom and open the door, but no one's there. The banging resumes. Behind me. I lumber toward the window, clumsy with fatigue, push it open a crack, and moan, "What?"

"Danny Boy!" Laughlin calls in an agitated stage whisper. "Come outside. I need to talk to you. Now."

"I can't. I'm sick. Goodbye."

"Come on. You said you owed me more than lunch for taking you to see your grandpop."

I sigh. "Will you keep banging on my window until I come out?"

"I could sing instead. 'Fly Away'? I remember you liking that one."

"Don't even—. Give me a minute to get decent."

"Meet you by the garage."

He rustles away and I'm suddenly seized with panic. I don't want to be seen with this nasty rash. And this sort of nighttime rendezvous will look extremely bad if Theo ever finds out. No matter how innocent, he'll call it a tryst, and me, a sneaky, cheating traitor.

Wait a minute. It's not the meeting that's the problem. It's the sneaking.

I dash off a quick text to Theo:

> Laughlin's back, freaked out and wanting to talk. Like now. I think it's safe. My rash will make him keep his distance.

While I wait for Theo's response, I swap pajamas for sweatpants and a hoodie. I consider making a mask out of a floral pillowcase, but realize I'd look like a demented Ku Klux Klan member. Or part of the women's auxiliary. Laughlin would just love *that* after his run-in with skinheads that got him expelled.

My phone chimes: a new text from Theo.

> Him: Not loving this. Ten foot rule, ok? Not just because of the germs.

> Me: Will do. Promise. I'll report in the morning. <3 u, D.

I find Laughlin kicking a stone as he paces in front of Poppa's garage.

"Took you long enough," he snaps. "What's with the hood? I wasn't planning to rob liquor stores with you, just talk."

I can do this. It'll be...like ripping off a Band-Aid. "I didn't want to shock you, but—" I tug the fabric off my head and find the cool night breeze strangely refreshing.

"Shhhiver me timbers," he mutters.

"Great. You're secretly an Irish pirate."

"What? No. Sorry. Didn't want to owe Ma's swear jar for your...." He waves vaguely at my spotted face.

"Chickenpox. And I'm running a fever, so could you cut to the chase?"

He taps his stone into motion again and paces behind it. "How the heck did things get so serious with Ma and your uncle so *fast*? Who gets engaged after a week of dating?"

"They were engaged once before. Your grandparents broke them up and sent your mom away, but she and my uncle wrote each other letters for years."

He gives his worry-stone a hard kick. It flies across the driveway and pings off of a hubcap of my uncle's truck. "How can Ma do this? Turn my whole life upside down the minute my back's turned? Does she seriously expect me to be happy about leaving my home?"

"You did say the roof leaks," I offer.

"But flipping Maine? I'll have to start all over from nothing."

"Well, you might be allowed to go to school again. You could stop hiding your voice and join choir or an *a capella* group, make new friends. And hey, there'd be no more harassment from skinheads. Your mom wants that for you more than anything."

"We don't have to leave the state for that. And why does she have to get *married*?"

"What's your problem exactly, Laughlin? My uncle has loved your mom forever. He wants to give you guys a better life. He has big plans for you especially."

He stares out at the moonlit lawn. "My own boarding stable. Can you believe that? Who would trust their animals to a sixteen-year-old kid who got expelled for busting up a chem lab? Dave lives in La-La Land."

"You're good with animals, you work hard, and you learn fast. That's what David sees. The bad stuff in your past doesn't have to follow you up there. Ms. Kuntzler praises you to the heavens, and her word matters more in the horse world than your school records do."

"I just can't leave, okay? There's this…musician friend who needs my help getting back on his feet. Things have been hard since my— since his wife broke things off."

"Your guitar teacher? Hold on. You said his wife is 'my' something. Your what?"

"Mother," he mutters.

"Your *father* is around here? You're in contact with him?"

Laughlin shrugs. "Sure. Why not? How else am I supposed to get smokes?"

His response is a punch in the gut. "You mean he buys your loyalty with cigarettes?"

"My money. He hooks me up with a carton, I let him keep a pack and, you know, a delivery fee. It's a good system."

There are so many things wrong with this statement, I drop my head in my hands and groan. "Laughlin, how could you give him money? Doesn't he have a drinking problem?"

He pivots toward me, nostrils flaring. "Is that what Ma told you? What does she know about the music business? She's a *nurse*. Of course Dad goes to bars. Where else is he supposed to get gigs? Ma's just mad that he dropped out of medical school and became a musician instead of a doctor." He kicks the ground again, sending gravel spraying.

"A doctor? Seriously? How does he justify giving you cigarettes?"

"It's our thing. Some guys fish or hunt with their dads. At least we chill without killing anything."

"Right, just yourselves. So he got you hooked in the first place?"

"You can't tell Ma. She's always shoving black lung pictures in my face and stuffing my pockets with nicotine gum."

"So what's your plan? Run away to your dad's place? Or just wreck your mom's chance at happiness?"

He rakes his hands through his hair. "I don't know. Dad's been working for months to get established here so he can be close to me. If I leave, who knows when I'll ever see him again?"

"You need to talk to your mom about this, not me. You could probably work out a new custody arrangement. My friend Toshio spends the school year with his mom in New York and school breaks with his dad in Japan."

Laughlin snorts. "What a world you live in, where it's normal to jet halfway around the globe three, four times a year.

We're not that kind of people, Dani. Don't you get it? Dad's not ready to see Ma or take me in. He's patching together what work he can find, same as me. Ma wouldn't like it. She's only interested in success."

"What's that supposed to mean? Are you trying to play *Parent Trap* here? Get them back together?"

"I'm trying to save my family. I thought you of all people would understand." His words are as hard and sharp as tacks.

He stalks away. Once he's beyond the bright circle by the garage, he clicks on a flashlight. I watch the beam bounce over the dark grass and hear, faintly, shuddering breaths of sorrow.

* * *

When Gertie the Volvo comes clattering up Poppa's driveway Saturday morning, I'm torn between the urge to run into Theo's arms and to hide in a closet. My little rash bumps have all become gooey blisters that look even more revolting with the chalky, pink calamine Mum patted onto them. I pull on the cotton gloves Sarah gave me so I don't spread my germs all over Poppa's house, then wince at my reflection. I look like a diseased debutante.

Soon Theo is rapping on the door. I steel myself for his reaction to my altered face. He fills the doorway, seeming bizarrely large after my week among the petite set. He has dark smudges under his eyes and his hands clasped behind his back. He must be so skeeved by my rash that he doesn't want to risk touching anything I might've breathed on.

"Oh, Dee," he says, voice falling, "you look so—"

"Disgusting. I know. I'm sorry."

He shakes his head. "Uncomfortable. That's what I was gonna say. Here." Drawing a hand from behind his back, he produces a bouquet in a riot of pinks and reds. "The florist lady said they all mean something: peonies for healing, geraniums for comfort, cosmos for peace, Gerber daisies for cheer, and roses for...well, you know." He swallows.

Love. Easier to text than to say out loud, especially in the face of, well, my freakish face. My eyes meet his. He squints a little, looking lost. Not quite sure about anything.

"They're gorgeous," I murmur. "Thoughtful. More than I deserve. And so are you."

"Um...thanks? Does that mean I can come in now?"

"Oh! Sorry. Please do. Can I get you anything? Juice? Soda? Tuna Surprise?"

He smiles and steps inside. "Still drowning in casseroles, huh? I'll pass, thanks. So, how was your midnight rendezvous with the bulldog?"

"Pretty much a train wreck. He had a long flip out about his mom's engagement and starting over in Maine. You won't believe why."

"He realized he can't marry you if you're his first cousin."

"Cut it out. It has nothing to do with me, and everything to do with his tobacco supply."

"Hello!" Mum calls, and joins us in the foyer. "Sorry to interrupt, I need to head out soon to help Pop move. Don't forget your acyclovir with lunch. And this needs to be reapplied in another hour or two." She hands me a bottle of calamine. "You two need anything else before I go? What's your plan for today?"

Theo shoots me a fierce look and holds up a fist, which morphs to "I've got your nose," then the number two.

"I'm afraid I don't know Dani's mime game," Mum says. "It was her father's thing."

Dad and I often talked past Mum in sign language. And Theo's motions looked like the letters S, T and U. Why? He's spelling…studio. Duh. "I'd been telling Theo how cool Nana's studio is. Would it be okay if I showed him?"

"I don't like the idea of you two hiding away in the dark by yourselves."

"Right. These oozing sores are so sexy, Theo won't be able to resist ravishing me."

He grimaces.

Mum fights to suppress a smile. "I'd still feel better if the place weren't such a clandestine den. It's time we fix that."

As we follow Mum outside, I ask Theo, "Since when do you know sign language?"

"Since I saw a deaf camper apologize using a motion I'd seen you make. I don't know much, just the alphabet and a few random words. It was your secret language with your dad, wasn't it?"

I bite my lip.

"It's not disloyal to keep using it. It's a way to keep him alive."

I make a W sign, then raise and lower my fingers as my hand moves from right to left.

"It's not weird, Dani. It's just time." He points at his left wrist.

Impressive. I give him a thumbs up. But signing with him is weird. Really weird.

Mum leads us across the back lawn that's grown shaggy since Laughlin last mowed. The hot sun makes me so itchy, I tightly clench the calamine bottle and wish I didn't have to wait an hour to use it. Soon the shade of the pine grove gives some relief. We emerge beside the studio and follow Mum inside.

"David got the ventilation system working, so it shouldn't be quite so stuffy today," she explains. Once she turns on the lights, Theo cranes his neck, trying to look at everything at once.

Mum steps over to one of the huge windows and picks at the stained Kraft paper taped over the glass. Soon we hear the crisp sibilance of tearing paper. The room fills with light. Mum gasps with pleasure and eagerly rips down the remaining window coverings. She peers around the sunny room, and at the wide view beyond it. "Now *that* is more like it. A person could actually paint in here now."

I'm not as sure as Mum that the intense daylight improves the place. The furniture seems shabbier, Nana's paintings more lurid, and the boxes in the rafters suddenly spotlighted. As Mum spells out our lunch options and says her goodbyes, Theo's gaze stays up at the ceiling.

Once we're alone, I say, "Well, that's all there is to see. You wanna go back and watch a movie or something?"

"A movie? Heck, no. What is all *that* stuff?" He points to the rafters, eyes glittering.

"Dusty old junk of Nana's."

He drags a stool over to the opening. "If it is, your mom will want to clear it out, right? Let me help. None of you are tall enough to get up there without a ladder."

My entire trunk seems to flame up with heat. "I, ah, really don't— Uhhh." I reach to grab the stool away from him.

He presses me back. "You have to trust me. Whatever's hidden in those boxes, you should not have to face alone. There's nothing up there that's too much for God to redeem. Not one thing."

I drop my head in defeat. "Okay."

Theo carefully climbs up and passes boxes down to me, one after another, announcing nonsensical labels for each, because he can't read Nana's handwriting. Once we've pulled down about half of the collection, we plop on the couch and each open a box. As we dig through Nana's linoleum prints, sketchbooks, lesson plans for elementary art, I tell Theo about my late-night talk with Laughlin. How he doesn't want his mom to marry my uncle and move them to Maine, because his dad has reappeared on the scene here, wanting to reconnect. I'm certain Laughlin's dad is using tobacco to buy his loyalty. I can't think of any other reason he'd be so eager to stay with this guy who left them years ago.

"You can't? Really? After your dad died, you and your mom had a terrible relationship. But something kept you from giving up on her. Same with me and my dad. Call it the pull of blood — parents made us, they're part of us. Call it one of God's ideas about how people are supposed to live together. You know, number five, honor your father and mother? We want them to be the kind of people who deserve honor. Or to become that way."

He climbs the step-stool again and takes his time shuffling boxes around, leaving me to soak up what he just said. It seems so long ago that Mum was the perfectly controlled, perfectly organized workaholic with perfect hair and clothes and manicure. She found almost nothing funny and almost everything blighted or smudged — me especially — requiring her special touch to fix it. Yet here I am, eighteen months later, fighting tooth and nail for her happiness. Because once the truth came out and I learned how wounded she was, everything changed. The person who deserved honor was in there all along. I just had to find her.

If that seemingly impossible change happened, could things also change between Mum and Poppa if the truth could be found?

"Whoa," Theo says in an awed tone. "You won't believe this, Dee." Cardboard scrapes across wood. As I step closer, he leans to the side, revealing a shoebox covered with crayon scribbles — some little kid's gibberish attempt at letters. "It's the box I dreamed about, with writing on it that I can't read."

"What does Nana's label say? There, where she wrote in black marker."

"La-something...and lions. Wait, I've got it. *La fosse aux lions.* The lions' den."

Chapter 25

"Why 'the lions' den'?" Theo asks, setting the box between us on Nana's velvet couch.

"The Bible story from Daniel. Which is Poppa's name."

"Yours, too. Man. I thought being Theodore the fourth was bad."

Inside the box, I find a jumbled mess of photos, letters, and documents. With my gloved hands, I snatch up a stack and clumsily leaf through in search of photos. Theo peers into the box, not touching anything until I give him the go-ahead. Even then, he takes only one plump envelope.

The photos I find are mostly tattered or stained black-and-white images. A baby sits drooling in a shoddily hand-knit sweater. A grimy toddler clutches a patchwork toy dog. Two skeletal boys wearing only frayed shorts grin beside a swimming hole. The boys, older yet, stand by a farmyard fence in ragged clothes, looking guilty. If the photo were in color, there would be yellow around their mouths and streaking their clothes.

"*The eggs,*" I whisper.

"What eggs?"

I show him the photo. "This is Poppa and his twin brother, Warren. Nana did a painting that looks like this. The title's in French, about being so hungry they stole eggs and ate them raw. I thought she'd painted purely from her imagination, based on Poppa's stories. But here's the reality she worked from. Now I'm not so sure Poppa told her any of this. Maybe his brother did. What did you find?" I ask, pointing to the newspaper articles unfolded in his lap.

He passes me a handwritten envelope, addressed to Maggie

Miroux at Montrose College. "That came with one of the weirdest love letters ever, from some guy your nana jilted. He begs her to take him back, to dump her fiancé, Daniel. He says, 'you have no idea who you're marrying. It's time you know.' He included all these newspaper articles that look like copies made from microfilm. Kind of blurry-edged like the documents I used in my history presentation, remember?"

"Mostly I remember you complaining how hard it is to find things on microfilm. Like looking for a needle in a haystack."

"Newspapers were better cross-referenced then, but yeah, there was nothing like Google in the '60s. The guy must have known there was dirt to be found. I'd guess the family had a reputation."

"What did he find?"

Theo reads the first headline. "'Local Draftee Missing: Presumed Dodger Coward.' The article's about a newlywed named Walter Tilman who never showed up at the Draft Board Office like he was supposed to. There was a local manhunt for him." He turns to the next article in the stack. "There was a second, more intense hunt after eight months passed and it was obvious his wife was pregnant with twins."

"Twins? That was Poppa's dad? He abandoned them?"

"I doubt he knew his wife was pregnant. Still, the reporters say absolutely vicious things about this guy. He was only twenty and probably terrified."

"I want to see. I think." I brush my gloved knuckles over my itchy arms. "If it were your ancestors, wouldn't you? I mean, you said there was nothing God couldn't redeem."

Theo gnaws his lower lip. "I hope you're feeling brave. This may be tough to stomach."

I take the page he passes me, a report on human remains being found. *The body of Walter Tilman has been discovered in an abandoned barn twenty miles east of Dunn Creek. His yellow streak must have been glowing bright to have alerted the hikers to the whereabouts of his remains.... Tilman is survived by the girl gullible enough to marry him and two sons, sure to prove as lily-livered as the craven cur who sired them.*

"How can they hurl insults like this in a news article?" I say. "Aren't journalists supposed to be objective?"

"It's a small town paper, not the *Times*. Besides, scandal sells."

"Why would Poppa choose to stay in this horrible town, to come back here after college?"

"Maybe he's trying to prove he won't run like his father did. It definitely makes sense of his collecting war stuff and doing re-enactments and even that creepy portrait."

"How exactly?"

"He's trying to be who he thinks his father should have been, even if it's all pretend."

* * *

Electronic music jolts me from my dozy state, sacked out on Nana's studio couch while Theo continues sifting through boxes from the rafters.

He picks up my ringing phone and glares at it. "Well, well. It's Laughlin O'Donnell. Your phone knows the number."

"I texted him once, the day of the sale, so we could hike. That's all."

He scowls at me and answers. "Hello? She's resting. Whaddaya want?"

Pause.

Theo's eyes widen. "Oh my gosh. No, we haven't seen him. Mmm. Her grandma's art studio. With the dress dummy, yeah. Of course she told me about it. Well, if your mom had been fighting cancer your whole life, you'd need therapy, too. Listen, I'm gonna check the woods around here. We'll call you back."

"What's going on?" I ask.

"Your grandpa sneaked away when no one was looking."

"Sneaked away? He needs a walker!"

"No, just a cane now. He's stronger than anyone realized. And more angry."

I follow Theo outside, but the heat makes me writhe with itchiness.

"Dee, you're giving me the heebie jeebies. Go back to the studio, put on some calamine and chill, okay? I'll be back in a few minutes."

"But Poppa listens to me. I'm his namesake."

"And that makes you as stubborn as he is. Sheesh. I've been trained to deal with agitated people, Dani. Go back inside."

I heave a sigh of protest and trudge back to the studio. After reapplying calamine, I pull an unopened box over to the couch. It's large and somewhat shallow, labeled in Nana's audacious script *un cœur qui soupire*, a heart that sighs. I pull open the box flaps and there, drawn in cross-hatched graphite, is a shriveled, bald woman with enormous eyes so dark they seem bottomless. The hospital bed, machines, vases of flowers are merely hinted in the background. The focal point is the utter beauty of this face, so like my mother's, and yet so unlike it. Her expression is one I've never seen on Mum's face. Neither determined nor defeated, but simply at peace. Like Saint Stephen in the stained glass window at church, facing death with no fear at all, just acceptance of what is and what will be.

Three more drawings like it sit beneath. So this is the lost box of Mum's art. The rest of the stack is nothing but standard artistic busywork: landscapes, still lifes, and figure drawings. But there's something strangely sorrowful about the work. The trees droop;

the skies are always on the verge of rain. I've never in my life seen such tragic fruit. Where's the passion and dynamism of Mum's logos, typefaces, and poster designs that Heather found in her old room? Those designs make you want things, make you feel a range of emotions, from eager to peaceful, but never sad.

There's a sharp thud against one of the windows. And another and another.

I leap to my feet. Poppa is outside, beating his hands against the glass. "You!" he cries. "Promised home. Lied. What doing? Get out. Out!"

Oh, no. I thought he might be peeved that he had to go to Sarah's, but I never dreamed he'd hunt me down. What do I do? Can he see what I've found? These drawings of cancer-stricken Nana that he hates so much, or worse, the images of his childhood poverty? If he gets in here, really sees, especially the articles about his father…he'll explode, his rage touching all this evidence like a match to a powder keg. I snatch up Mum's drawing of Nana and the stack of old photos and clippings, toss them into the box marked *la fosse aux lions*, and kick it under the sofa.

As I scramble around hiding things, his pounding gets more frantic. "Get out, liar, liar pants-fire. Out, now!" He raises his cane, ready to smash the glass.

Laughlin appears behind him and twists the cane out of Poppa's grasp. He speaks in a calm, commanding voice I can hear faintly through the glass. "You know the rule, Grandpop. No hitting. Why don't we take a walk and you can tell me what's bothering you."

Grandpop? What on earth?

Poppa points at me and demands, "What doing, Flynn?"

Shading his eyes, Laughlin peers in the window and beckons me to come outside. "She's just redding up the place," he tells Poppa.

I whisper a prayer as I rush outside and round the corner of the building. "Hey, Poppa," I say with all the fake cheer I can muster. "It's good to see you up and walking."

Poppa's expression curdles with disgust. "Nasty bad girl. Take my house with lies."

Laughlin's eyes bug out. "Wow, Dani, you look like hell. Why aren't you in bed?"

"Why aren't you keeping a better eye on Poppa?" I snap.

"God smite liars! Spot, spot, spot." Poppa exclaims. He nudges Laughlin in the ribs and barks with laughter. "Spot, Flynn. Spotiddy spotty spot bot!"

"I've done everything I can to keep my promise to you, Poppa. The house is almost ready. My sickness was an accident. Not some plot to hurt you." I rub my tingling calves.

"Lep, lep…uh, leper. Leopard leper!" he adds, pointing and cackling with glee.

Wordplay? Wow, that's a big leap in regaining his speech. Still, his laughter makes my cheeks and neck flare with embarrassment and a wildfire of itchiness. My gloved hands can't scratch fast enough.

Theo jogs up to join us. "Hey. You found him."

Laughlin genuinely smiles. "Yep. Thanks for looking, though. Haven't properly met, have we? I'm Laughlin O'Donnell, Dani's new cousin." He extends his hand to Theo.

So *now* he's my cousin? What's with the change of heart?

Theo shoots me a quizzical look, then he shakes Laughlin's hand. "Theo Wescott."

Poppa's expression instantly hardens. He points an accusing finger at Theo. "You. Tux!"

Theo nods. "I took Dani to our junior prom last month. I guess she sent you pictures."

Poppa's mouth twists, like he finds the idea of my spotted

self at the prom ridiculous, but he manages to not laugh in my face again. Instead, he announces, "Thirsty."

"There's a sink in that place, right?" Laughlin asks, nodding toward the studio.

"Yeah. Some glasses, too," Theo replies. "I could go get—"

"No!" I bark. "Take him to the house for a drink. Please, Theo? I need to talk to my *cousin Flynn* for a minute." I give him a pleading look and circle my open hand over my chest, the sign for "please."

O.K. he spells back to me, but he rolls his eyes, annoyed.

I feel an odd twinge, but not from the strangeness of signing — it's actually pretty useful. What makes me wince is the simmering heat of jealousy in his last backward glance before he leads Poppa away.

* * *

I motion to Laughlin to follow me to the studio. He lingers outside the door, hesitant, taking in the painted canvases, boxes spewing art supplies, and views through the uncovered windows. Scratching an eyebrow, he says, "So, this isn't Dave's hideout? It's…an art place?"

"Nana's studio. And you've got to keep Poppa away. You saw how freaked out he was."

"Sorry. I never dreamed he'd go roaming." Stepping inside, he sits on the doily-festooned chair. "He seemed content on the porch swing, so I went in for my ashtray and a pitcher of ice water. When I got back, he and my best Zippo lighter were gone."

"Was he really roaming, or just looking for me, to give me a piece of his mind? After all, I struck a bargain I couldn't keep: promised we'd bring him home if he let us clear out the extra stuff and do some repairs."

He shakes his head. "Up the creek without a paddle, aren't ya? Good thing I got Grandpop's cane before he brained you."

"Why do you call him 'grandpop' now? And since when are you all smiles about being my cousin?"

"Well, I've been kicking around what you said last night. About making a plan. About Ma. She is happy in a way she never was or likely could be with Dad. They never agreed on much of anything, not like her and Dave, who finish each other's sentences they're so in tune. Anyhow, I figured there had to be another way for me to help Dad without hurting Ma."

I blink at him in surprise. I did not see this coming, not by a mile.

"Oh-kay," I reply, cautious. "I guess I'm glad we had that midnight chat."

"Thanks for hearing me out. I was too freaked out to see straight last night. I needed time to think things through. This morning, Ma went on and on about how excited Mr. Tilman is to have a grandson. Excited. About *me*." His voice rises at the wonder of it all. "Then Dad called out of the blue, and as we talked, we got this genius idea. One that lets everyone win. Ma and Dave. You and your mom. Grandpop. Me and Dad, too."

"Seriously? All of us?"

"Yeah. It's pretty obvious Grandpop wants to be in his own house more than anything. But Dave can't stay with him, and you guys don't want to either. Me and Dad, though? We'd be thrilled to."

"What?" I don't know if it's the chickenpox, but I can't wrap my head around what he seems to be saying. "You and your *dad* want to take care of Poppa? Like live-in care?"

"Well, yeah. It's a huge house. Plenty of space for three guys. Dad is an amazing cook. I could manage the yard. We'd take shifts hanging with Grandpop."

"Have you talked to your mom about this? She has custody, right? I thought she wanted you to be able to go to school away from the skinhead thugs."

"Ma and Dave need time to themselves. And it's not like Dad couldn't have custody — he just didn't fight for it. And Grandpop's a teacher, so our hang-out time could be school."

I frown. Poppa would probably love to tutor Laughlin. It might help his speech improve, too. But his dad doesn't seem like health aide material, from what I know of him. "Why would Mum want a musician to take care of Poppa?"

"He'd be lots cheaper than a homecare worker. And he did some medical school, so he's not totally clueless about health-related stuff. Come on. You know it's the best thing for everyone. You saw how much Grandpop likes me. We joke around. He gave me a nickname."

"I wouldn't be so sure. He ran away from you. He was laughing at how freaky I look, not joking with you. And he probably can't say your name because of his stroke."

"Are you always such a Negative Nancy? You wanna go to Paris or not? Come on, we need to team up."

I sigh. "Mum will want to meet your dad, grill him, check his references, the whole nine yards, like a real job interview. Will he be up for that?"

"I'll take care of that, you get her willing to consider it seriously. Deal?"

"Poppa stays completely away from this studio," I press.

"Absolutely. We're in this together, right, Cuz?"

"I'll see what I can do, Flynn."

Chapter 26

Laughlin and I head through the pine grove toward the house. I point out the predator den I found, but before he can examine the bones littering the grass, his phone rings.

"Uh-oh. It's your mom," he mutters, fumbling to answer. "Howdy, Aunt Grace," he drawls. Then his cheeks flare and he slaps a hand over one eye. "Sorry, Mrs. Deane. Yeah, I'm taking Mr. Tilman on a little walk. Uh huh. Hydrating? I'll see to that. We'll stay clear of Dani." He ends the call and power-walks away.

I jog to catch up with him. "What's wrong?"

"Your mom said...." He takes a ragged breath. "Don't let Grandpop go in his house no matter how much he begs, because your stupid germs are everywhere. If he catches chickenpox, it could kill him. Crap. I've blown it already!"

"Oh. Shoot. Lemme call Theo and tell him."

"It's too late. She's never gonna trust me again. It's all over."

I scroll to Theo's number, and soon hear his totally Emo ringtone chiming nearby.

"Now what?" he snaps, his voice weirdly coming from the phone and around the corner.

"Please don't let Poppa in the house. Mum will freak."

"What kind of idiot do you think I am?"

"None, I just—"

"Forgot you're the poster child for why we need vaccines?"

"I panicked, Thebes. I'm sorry. Look, I'm sending Laughlin right now to get him."

"You do that." Click.

Laughlin disappears around the side of the house. I creep closer and hear Poppa nagging him to get rid of this giant boy so he can go inside.

Laughlin tries to lure Poppa away with the promise of his mother's famous fresh-egg omelet for lunch. Theo offers him another glass of lemonade.

Loud bangs are the response. His cane against patio furniture? "Home, now. Home!"

"Germs in there, germs!" Theo's voice cracks with exasperation.

"Bad girl not take my house!" Poppa retorts.

"She's just sick, Grandpop," Laughlin says, "and we don't want you to catch it."

"I've told him that fifty times!" Theo roars.

Poppa growls, "Tone, young man!"

Help them, Lord. Help!

"Sorry, Mr. Tilman," Theo says. "My anger was out of line. Look, your, um, grandson had a pretty compelling lunch offer."

"Ma doesn't skimp on the fixings either. She uses a special sharp cheese from Heffler's Dairy in Eyrie Falls. Noble, it's called."

"That's top shelf, Mr. Tilman. The best Manhattan shops have Pennsylvania Noble."

"Noble. King. Top shelf."

As Poppa deliberates, I hold my breath. I bet the guys do, too.

"Hungry now. Lunch, Flynn."

"Alrightly, then," Laughlin says. "Follow me."

When I hear Laughlin and Poppa cross the patio, I duck behind a bush and stay hunkered there as they head away from the house toward the wooded pathway back to Sarah's.

Pausing in the middle of the lawn, Poppa calls, "I'll be back." Somehow he sounds more threatening than the Terminator.

"Enjoy your lunch!" Theo responds.

I clamber out of hiding and head to the patio. Theo is slumped in a chair, eyes closed.

"I'm so sorry for foisting Poppa on you. I had no idea—"

"I couldn't handle it, Dee. I thought I could, but I couldn't. No distraction worked, he was so crazy focused. Even with him swinging around that cane, I was scared to lay a hand on him, he's so much smaller than me, so brittle. I did a total crap job of keeping him calm. If anything, I riled him up more."

"All that matters is that you kept him out of the house."

"I did it all wrong. I actually shoved him at one point. And I was such a jerk to you on the phone. Forgive me? Clearly I need way more help from God to keep my cool under pressure."

"Of course. I shouldn't have pushed you into this tough situation without thinking twice. You were so take-charge earlier, I guess I took for granted your instincts, your good heart."

Theo disagrees that he's good hearted and tells me about his ordeal getting Poppa a drink. After pushing past Poppa to get inside, Theo raced around locking doors and windows while Poppa went from window to window, shouting and banging on the glass with his cane. Theo crept through the house like a spy to get back outside unhindered. The lemonade didn't really convince Poppa that Theo isn't part of a conspiracy to steal his house.

"Sorry that was so awful. I really, really appreciate the time it gave me, though."

"So what was your *latest* little chat with Cousin Flynn about?" His tone crackles with annoyance.

"It's weird that he's suddenly calling Poppa 'Grandpop,' when he was so adamant last night that he didn't want his mom marrying into our family."

"I don't trust that guy, Dee. He's kind of…oily. All smooth and full of charm when it suits him. Why's he suddenly flip-flopping about your family?"

I explain Laughlin's change of heart, his plan to kiss up to Poppa, and his dream of moving himself and his dad into Poppa's house, like some kind of bizarre intergenerational bachelor pad.

Laughlin wants me to convince Mum that this is a better idea than moving Poppa to a nursing home near David in Maine. He seems to think Poppa will get belligerent about leaving and make it impossible for the rest of us to have any peace. I could see Laughlin's point, especially after how Poppa just behaved. My big worry now is that Poppa will come back to the studio, break in, and wreck things — especially the evidence of his past.

"Yeah, he's so riled up, there's no telling what he might do." Theo presses a knuckle to his upper lip, thinking. "Wait. I've got an idea. Why don't you pick some stuff you want to keep safe, and I'll take it today to stow at the lake house."

"That's genius, Thebes. I could totally kiss you."

He slides his chair away at record speed. "No offense, but I'll, ah, take a raincheck. I'd actually rather have your promise that you won't keep sneaking around with the cowboy. I want to trust you, but…you two being in cahoots? I just hate it."

I swallow. Theo more than deserves my loyalty, my honesty. Working with Laughlin shouldn't be so clandestine. His Poppa plan needs to be on the up-and-up. Legit.

"Okay," I say. "No sneaking."

* * *

I lay in the soothing bliss of a baking soda bath, my only discomfort the crick in my neck from trying to keep most of my skin submerged. I was only a little sorry that Theo left as early as he did. Once we had lunch, fatigue hung on me like a backpack some trickster was gradually filling with bricks. Theo alternately rubbed his eyes and yawned as I selected key paintings to hide. In the end, we took only what we could carry in one trip. Before we parted, he dropped a long kiss on the top of my head, the only un-rashy part of me.

I reach to touch the spot again, as if he'd somehow imprinted himself there, his longing and confusion and hurt and love resting heavily on me. But even heavier was his parting charge to me: show Mum that wretched box of Poppa's pain, now tucked in a closet.

I'd nodded obediently, too tired to protest. Too weak to beg him to take the box to the lake house. Too scared to refuse him anything he asked, even if it will mean shaking my family to its foundations. Foundations built on hiding, on lies. Built on sand. Like the parable. *When the torrent struck, the house collapsed and its destruction was complete.*

I don't want my family destroyed. Maybe this is the reason I'm here, not home, packing for Paris. Somehow, the thing God wants to do for me, through me, has to do with these secrets that have held power over all of us for so long.

When I return to the bedroom, there's a note from Mum on my bed, reminding me to choke down another dose of acyclovir. On my way to the kitchen, I hear her cell play its dorky xylophone tune and find it on the floor by the side door.

I shout for her, but there's no response as her phone continues ringing. The caller ID says "Deane Studios."

When I answer, Nate is surprised but delighted. "How are ya, kid? Did I miss my chance to shoot your senior pictures?"

"Not yet. That's next spring."

"Seems like yesterday you were a little pink bundle in Graham's arms. Your mother around? I wanted to talk to her about Kerrigan-Meade."

"Is something wrong?"

"Not at all. They loved her business card design. Now they want a new logo, but only if she designs it."

"Oh. Wow. She'd have to hand-draw it; she doesn't know digital design software."

"Well, we could get a freelancer to vectorize a drawing." A digital clock beeps in the background. "Oops, time to move my film to the stop bath. Have Grace call me? Cheers!"

Cheers. The one mannerism of Dad's Nate picked up from years working together.

I carry Mum's phone toward her room. From her bathroom come horrid scraping sounds that set my teeth on edge. I find Mum in the turquoise bathtub, chipping away the old, stained grout. Her clothes and lopsided ponytail are so peppered with grout particles, she looks like a powdered donut attacked her. She doesn't respond when I call to her, but works on with a focused frenzy. When I tap her shoulder, she yelps and drops her tool.

"Didn't mean to scare you. I've been trying to get your attention a while. Your phone?"

"Leave it on the vanity." She takes up her tool and resumes scraping.

"Nate called to say Kerrigan-Meade loved the business cards; now they want a new logo."

"Well, they'll just have to get in line. Because *somebody* told my father he could come home as soon as his house is fixed up. But it's not ready yet because *somebody* brought her sick friend here and proceeded to catch the illness herself. But Pop still expects all the work to be magically done in days and is being a rather terrible nuisance to our generous neighbor. So I'm sorry to say all my time is spoken for."

"Sorry, Mum. I didn't know how else to get Poppa to cooperate. That was the plan at the time, wasn't it? That he'd come home, have a nurse?"

"You had no right to make promises without consulting me. You care about nothing but your precious Paris."

How could she think this is all about me? "*My* precious Paris? I thought this trip was for *us*. You and me, relaxing, connecting, making art together. I'd work on *Madeline*, you'd paint for your show. Don't you want to be with me, Mum?"

She turns away from the tile, her head tilted wearily. "It's not that, darling."

"It's the cost, isn't it? Quebec has French stuff. We could drive there instead."

"Quebec is lovely, I'm sure. It's just.... How do I say this? I—I don't want...to paint."

"What?"

"I don't actually have a show in September, Dani. I asked my prof to postpone. You see, this program...I'm not sure if it's right for me. You and David seemed so excited about my trying it. And I did need a break from the travel at my advertising job. But I'm just not...professional painter material."

"You lied about your solo show, and you're quitting school?"

"I didn't lie, I simply hadn't figured out how to tell you. And nothing's certain about school. I might merely change majors or transfer."

"I could tell you've been unhappy in school, Mum, but I don't quite know why."

Dusting grout flakes off her face, she sits on the edge of the tub. "You know how we take Rhys to the park and I play fetch with him while you draw? It gets dark and the streetlights come on and you and your pencil are still somewhere else."

"Heather calls it 'going deeper in the shadows'."

"Well...I don't have that kind of relationship with paint. Mama did. I wish I did, too. It would be a way to carry on her legacy."

"But you're not her clone."

"I thought that if I tried...." She splays her hands in frustrated defeat. "But passion can't be forced. No one can love with a gun to their head."

My gaze drops to my hand, as if I'd find a smoking revolver there. It's not just art she's talking about. It's me, too. I've pushed and pushed for us to be close like Dad and I were. Tried to force her into his mold. But in so many ways, she doesn't fit.

She doesn't want matching easels on the banks of the Seine. And the pastries and silly hats? Probably not. My magical thinking has only weighed her down with my ridiculous expectations and made her afraid to talk to me.

"No more guns, okay? I...surrender. I hadn't realized how mixed-up you were feeling about art, about life. Dealing with Poppa is stressful enough. We should just cancel the trip. Use the money for something else. A bathroom repair guy, maybe?"

Mum's brows draw together. "You want to cancel Paris?"

"Well, I do need to prepare for the pneumonia, heart palpitations, and flesh-eating bacteria that Sarah promised were coming my way."

My attempt to lighten the moment has the opposite effect. Mum's expression crumples into confused sadness. "How do you do that? Make light? Joke when the world is crumbling?"

What have I done? Is the only part of Dad living on in me the bit that cracks stupid jokes?

"Sorry. I shouldn't joke. It was dumb and tasteless."

"No, it was witty and...humble. You're ready to give up your dream trip for me. And yet you're not angry or hopeless. How come?"

"I guess I'm hoping God has another plan for us that I don't understand yet. I thought Paris would bring us closer together, but now I see it's pushing us farther apart."

"So *God* told you to toss your dreams out the window." Not a question, a cynical statement.

I shake my head. "He told me to love and honor you, like he does."

Chapter 27

God-talk tends to end conversations with Mum. Tonight is no different. She responds to my confession by telling me to go to bed.

I reluctantly comply. She just loves to test my sincerity about the whole "honor your father and mother" commandment. The more I learn about her parents, the more I understand why this part of biblical living rubs her the wrong way. How do you honor a father who uses you as an ego boost, a servant, a scapegoat, or a mother who expects you to follow in her footsteps without bothering to provide hands-on training?

I wish I knew how to help Mum. Had some clue how to show her that faith isn't about following a bunch of crummy rules that make you hurt even more.

I slide into bed and stare at the ceiling. When I was at my wit's end after Dad died, I was just as mad at God as Mum is now. I wanted Dad back more than I wanted anything to do with God. I was ready to throw my sorry life away to be with Dad again.

Dad would have been totally peeved with me if I'd joined him so soon. I can imagine jogging through the pearly gates to embrace him, but he'd shake his head in dismay. "My work is done," he'd say. "Yours was just beginning."

I roll to my side and look out at the dark lawn. I know I should pray, but I have no words. Only desperate need.

That's in a Psalm, I think. If only I could remember which one. I used to have a whole arsenal of verses to aim at my problems. But they've gotten harder and harder to recall. It's not like riding a bike, more like…learning an instrument. The more often you practice, the freer and easier it flows. Neglect it, though, and your skill evaporates.

I grope in the dark for my phone, click over to my Bible app, and search for the words. It returns two results for "desperate need," the first from Psalm 79, verse 8.

Do not hold against us the sins of past generations; may your mercy come quickly to meet us, for we are in desperate need.

I whisper the verse aloud, twice. The third time, I add, "Dear God" and "please."

The night stays quiet.

My heart wrestles on.

* * *

I smell bacon before I hear Mum calling me to open the bedroom door. Quickly, I stuff Nana's journal back under the pillow pile. So far I've had no luck finding any mention of how she got her hands on those photos from Poppa's childhood.

I find Mum balancing a breakfast tray on her laptop. She sets the tray on my bedside table, then sits on the empty side of the bed, fiddling with her laptop. "I thought you might like to stream the church service at St. Stephen's, like Graham did when he was sick." She navigates a menu, then sets the computer in the middle of the bed.

Her mention of Dad doesn't conjure him like usual, and make the room so full of his presence Mum and I can't reach each other. Today it's just us two and this space of possibility.

I swallow. "Stay with me? Please?"

Mum's eyes sweep my face. She bites her lip. Then, with a small shrug, she scoots back and leans against the pillows.

An ensemble of flute, sax, and piano are playing the prelude. The picture shifts, showing the sanctuary from the back.

My heart lifts to see familiar backs of heads. Soon acolytes in monk-like robes process in and light candles — Fletcher and his little sister Melody. He's wearing retro horn-rimmed glasses a few shades darker than his hair, which is wavy on top, but cropped short on the sides. Hmm. Fletch has stayed chic while letting his inner geek re-emerge.

"Aren't those the Reid kids?" Mum asks. "Melody looks over the moon to have her braces off. And Fletcher's changed his hair. He's dating Heather, right?"

"That's the guy, but they're on hiatus." I sip my juice. "How do you know the Reids?"

"Karen — Mrs. Reid — she meets me for lunch sometimes. We got thrown together at one of your school fundraisers and hit it off."

I had no idea Mum was friendly with any of the women her age at my church. "Really?"

"You surprised that I volunteer at your school, or that I'm capable of making friends?"

I stuff a forkful of scrambled eggs in my mouth to avoid answering. As the service proceeds, I mumble the responses as I chew. Thankfully Mum's attention returns to the screen.

Reverend Weatherby's homily focuses on the Gospel reading from Mark 5. Jesus heals the dying daughter of a synagogue leader named Jairus, and an Israelite woman who's basically had her period for twelve years straight. The bleeding woman sneaks up on Jesus while he's headed to the dying girl's house. She desperately wants Jesus to help her, but is too scared to talk to him. She's certain Jesus is way too busy to be bothered with her, but if she could just get close enough to touch the edge of his coat, it would be enough.

But it isn't enough for Jesus to do a hit-and-run healing. He knows the woman is there, knows how fiercely she believes, and knows the exact moment her body is healed. He won't let her be stuck in the shadows any longer. He's determined to make her healing public so that everyone will know she's whole again, no longer an outsider who can't take part in rituals and worship. He restores more than her body. He restores her spiritual and social life, too, and helps the whole community rejoice with her.

I glance over at Mum, looking for any sign this means anything to her. Instead of her usual making-a-list-in-my-head expression, her brows are drawn down, perplexed.

"What's the matter?" I ask.

Her lips tighten across her teeth. She taps the keyboard to mute the sound. "It's a powerful story, and something makes me want it to be for me. But how could it be?"

"You mean, because Jesus isn't walking the earth right now?"

"Exactly. Is it supposed to be a metaphor? I can understand that there are many ways one can bleed. But what does it mean to touch his cloak?"

Wow. That was not a question I expected from her. "Um, why don't we hear what Reverend Wheatherby's application is?" I click the sound back on. But the service has moved on, from the creed to the prayers of the people.

Mum's eyes stay on me. Fear flutters in my gut, a mass of manic moths. She wants to know what *I* think. I ought to be able to answer her question. It's not that complicated. The church — God's people filled with the Holy Spirit — act as Jesus' presence in the world. But that will sound like total gibberish to her. Her rash-speckled kid is divinely gifted to bring her Jesus' healing? Yeah, right. She'll just laugh.

In the midst of my inner freak out, Mum's cell phone rings. She whispers an apology and hurries out of the room.

I've blown it. My one opportunity, like ever, to answer Mum's spiritual questions and I blink at her like an idiot. But what do I know about sharing my faith? I'm only seventeen. I've never gone to seminary or taken a theology class. Theo said it's not all on me to fix things with my family, but with Dad gone, who else is there?

Mum returns, staring at her phone in disbelief. "That was weird. Karen Reid of all people. In the middle of the prayers, she sensed that I was trapped outside, like the sanctuary doors were stuck. When she didn't see me in the narthex, she called."

Hairs on the back of my neck prickle. "That's, um... interesting."

"She asked about Pop and you, said her family is praying for us. And then—" She scratches her temple. "She told me that whatever I'm seeking, I'm going to find it. That I'm very, very close."

My eyes dart to Poppa's closet as if the *la fosse aux lions* box had exploded.

* * *

Mum hugs her knees to her chest and surveys the box contents arrayed on the bed between us. "I suppose Uncle Warren might have given Mama these things."

"Have you ever met him? What happened to him?"

"He visited once, when I was nine or ten, before Mama got really sick. He brought gifts from Montana, I think it was, and told cute stories about the business ventures he and Pop started as kids to earn money. We never saw him again after that. Pop must've been afraid he'd tell us the whole truth. Goodness. Back then, draft dodging was as bad as being a communist."

"I can't imagine growing up with people thinking and saying such awful things about your family. It makes me feel kind of bad for Poppa. How do you feel, knowing this?"

"Pop's reasons for wanting to stay here aren't quite what I

thought. Perhaps I haven't tried hard enough to find a way to let him."

"*What?*" Will she ever stop believing she can win his love by giving in to his whims?

"It's symbolic to him, this house. Proof to the small-minded people in this town that in spite of everything, he's done well for himself."

"How do you figure? His shelves full of trophies were bought, not earned. He has war mementos from other people's fathers and a painting of himself in a dead man's uniform. It seems pretty clear to me that Poppa is haunted by what his father did."

"What are you suggesting, Danielle? Now that we've sighted the ghost, it will disappear and Pop will magically transform?"

I shake my head. "You've seen behind the curtain; Poppa is not the Great and Terrible Oz. At heart, he's a scared kid who grew up with shame instead of a dad. His bragging and putdowns and demands...they're just a way to hide, to cope. You've been on this quest forever to get his approval, but he doesn't have the power to give you courage, smarts, or heart, Mum. You've always had them. So be strong. Don't give in to him."

She leans on one elbow and exhales through her nose. "The thing is, darling, we need a plan B. Spruce View, the place for seniors near David, put Pop on a waiting list. It could be a year before they'll have space in assisted living."

"Well it's not the only senior community in the world. We can find someplace else."

Her frown deepens. "I haven't walked in your spiritual world in a long time. But don't you find it odd that the day I'm in anxious knots wondering what to do about Pop, a friend calls saying what I'm seeking is near? Then the very next moment I learn how much it means for him to stay here? I don't put much stock in signs, darling, but are you *sure* this isn't one?"

I most certainly hope not.

* * *

I must say, God sure has an interesting sense of humor. Here I was, worried that I'd derailed Mum's journey to faith when I couldn't give her profound spiritual answers on the fly, and Fletcher's mom brings us this miraculous message. Suddenly I have the courage to share really difficult stuff with Mum, and she shows astonishing openness to God. But instead of the healing freedom I'd hoped the truth about Poppa would bring, Mum twists this whole chain of events into a divine mandate to hand Poppa her life on a platter. And if I say anything against her new supposed insight, I look like the faithless one, the doubter.

Good one, God. Quite the hilarious twist.

I don't understand what I'm supposed to do, or why my attempts to save Mum from her father constantly backfire. I feel like I'm being forced to face certain death and just roll with it. Like Daniel in the Bible. He steadily did the right thing, only to be thrown to the lions.

Is this *my* lions' den? If it is, when will my guardian angels show up?

The rest I desperately need comes only when my fretful clawing at the doors of heaven exhausts me. I rise from each nightmare-filled nap a little more heartsick than I was before. Several times I stumble to Mum for help reapplying calamine to my back and find her researching yet another possible option that allows Poppa to stay in the house. We could sell off parcels of land and all the silver trophies for more income. Perhaps some graduate students from the university in Elmerton could serve as live-in help in exchange for housing. We could sublet or even sell our New York apartment and move in with Poppa.

My stomach plummets when I see the astronomical sum we could take in each month renting out a place our size in the Upper West Side. That kind of money would go a long way around here. But why should Poppa get all the benefit of my parents' savvy investing that enabled us to buy our apartment in the first place? They were wise enough to buy a wreck of a Brooklyn brownstone, beautifully restore it, and sell it for nearly ten times what they paid. Dad poured over a decade of work into that place to give Mum and me a good life.

Tears spring to my eyes so fast, I scramble to leave the room before Mum sees. Clipping a leash on Rhys, I head out into evening air that's arid as an attic. He snuffles through the grass, crisp from the lack of rain. The soggy sorrow ready to burst out of me could probably revive the whole lawn. Everything I love is in New York: my amazing boyfriend, supportive friends, awesome school, fantastic church. The incredible culture and art. I just can't leave.

Like Laughlin can't leave here. Maybe his plan is the best thing for everyone.

Maybe he's the angel who shuts the lion's mouth.

Rhys stands rigid and alert, ears perked to sounds of movement in the pine grove. I smell smoke, then a funky, skunky aroma. Rhys yanks me into the cover of trees toward the scent.

A sharp crack of gunfire, followed by "What the blazes?" stops us in our tracks.

Rhys creeps to my side, ears pinned back as he barks and barks. I hunker down to quiet him, gripping his muzzle shut and petting flat the raised ridge of fur on his back. Someone's out here with a gun. I do not want to become the next target.

Burning smells and the sound of stomping feet increases Rhys's instinct to flee. He squirms out of my grip and runs. But toward the sound, not away from it. His barks ring in the trees. I follow, ducking behind one trunk and another, fearing I'll hear another shot.

"Rhys! Good grief," Laughlin says. "Whatcha doing out here, boy?" He stoops among burnt grass to pet my dog, a rifle slung over his shoulder and a slender animal pelt in his grip.

He certainly doesn't look much like an angel. Was it like this for Daniel in Babylon?

I step out of my hiding spot. "I was walking him, genius. You could've shot us both!"

"Sorry, Danielle. I forgot about your dog. Grandpop sent me to take care of Hannibal Hen-killer. I had a tight window to catch him in his den."

Danielle and a den. Not Danny Boy and a hole. How much more proof do I need?

I point to the pelt. "What did you do to that poor weasel?"

He shows me the scorched carcass. "It wasn't supposed to be like this. I meant to flush him out of his den, take one quick shot, and his hen-killing days would be over. I lit a gas-soaked rag, dropped it in his back door, then plugged the hole. When he came out his front door, I took a shot but missed, because darned if the loony varmint didn't run back into his burning den. I've never seen anything like it. He'd rather face certain death than take his chances with me."

"That's...pretty nuts," I say, but my mind has latched on tight to his last statement. To avoid certain death, I have to take my chances with him.

He picks up Rhys's leash and hands it to me. We head across the lawn toward the wooded path back to his house. "Sorry I didn't call first about my hunting plans. Didn't really expect to see you roaming, Spotty. Something bugging you? Or are you just too itchy to rest?"

"Can you please refrain from using the word 'itch' in my presence?" Like a reflex, my knuckles skim my arms and neck. "We got some bad news. It's been hard to take it lying down."

"You mean Grandpop getting waitlisted at that place near Dave's?"

He knows. And if he really is my angel, he'll know what needs to happen next.

"Yeah. Mum is making noises about letting him stay here."

"Really?" His eyes flash with hope. "You think she'd be open to my plan with Dad?"

"I sure hope so," I say. "But she doesn't trust just anyone. If we want this to work, it might help if I met your dad first and got a sense of what kind of impression he'd make."

"You bet. We'll come to you. The studio, ten till midnight?"

* * *

Mum is still deep in research mode when I return. I text Theo and head back to the kids' wing to assess what might be needed to make the rooms comfortable for Laughlin and his dad. I'm on page two of a shopping list when Theo calls.

"Hey, Dee. Just back from the pool. What's the matter?"

The details of my dilemma-filled day come out in a gush. Surely I'm the one in the lions' den, I explain, needing an angel to rescue me. Laughlin and his dad staying here and caring for Poppa could be exactly the rescue I need.

Theo grunts skeptically. "How high is your fever right now? You sound delirious."

"This very moment, Mum is researching how to sell our apartment so we can move here. Is that what you want?"

"Of course not. But there has to be another way. The cowboy is bad enough; his dad sounds a lot worse. Seeing his kid in secret, giving him cigarettes? Seems pretty sketchy to me."

"He did some medical school, though."

"So he's a quitter. That's reassuring."

I sigh. "That thought did cross my mind. But come on, Thebes. Can't I give him the courtesy of hearing him out? Maybe he's trying to start over like Uncle David. I know you're annoyed that Laughlin made passes at me, but it's not fair to judge his dad based on that."

"Something is really off about this situation, Dee. I don't trust that kid, and you shouldn't either. You *promised* me you wouldn't sneak around with him."

"I'm not sneaking. I'm telling you absolutely everything. That's what I promised — total honesty."

"I don't like you being around him. At all. Why is that so hard for you to understand?"

"Why are you putting me in this impossible position? I need his help so I can come home and be with *you*. You're acting like I'm a toy you don't want to share."

"Well, you're refusing to hear anything I have to say. So maybe I should stop wasting my breath."

My phone goes silent.

I hurl it onto Mum's bed, flop down beside it, and pummel the mattress until my frustrated, angry sorrow burns down to a bruised ache in my heart.

Chapter 28

Strange noises — chirps, peeps, low croaks — fill the dark night. I pull my sweatshirt tighter. I wish I'd brought Rhys along for company. Or protection, really. Who knows what creepy creatures are groaapping and chee-chee-cheeing in the black grass, black trees, black pond. I grip my flashlight tighter and take the long route — around rather than through the pine grove.

Laughlin said he chose the late hour to meet so I could slip away unnoticed. But I have to wonder how much lying and sneaking is involved on his end. Is Sarah aware that her ex is no longer rocking Boston? She hasn't had exactly complimentary things to say about him. But that might be sour grapes, no more accurate than Theo's distrust of Laughlin, colored by his jealousy.

Lights blaze out of the studio. I stride around to the door on the far side, forcing myself not to peek in the windows. Laughlin meets me at the door, grinning.

A taller man, my height, steps out from behind him, panther-like. My breath hitches in my throat. His beautiful bone structure is like Laughlin's, ripened to maturity; his dark wavy hair and day's growth of beard only intensify his worldly magnetism. His murky green eyes study me like I'm the most fascinating creature he's ever seen. I bet Sarah never considered it "just" a Green Card marriage.

Dark jeans hang from his thin hips. With them he wears a lilac button-down and taupe linen blazer that seems more country club than rock and roll. A Celtic knotwork tattoo peeks from under his right cuff, but he yanks down his sleeve to cover it. The motion sends a whiff of his peppery cologne my direction.

I know that scent, that tattoo. Where have I seen him before?

"Pleased to make yer acquaintance, Miss Deane," he says, hand still clamped over his tattoo. "I'm called Johnny. I hope ye won't be thinkin' me rude to not be shakin' yer hand. Ye've got a right bad dose of it, haven't ye? Appreciate ye meetin' me when yer feelin' poorly."

That accent. *Let me be yer angel.*

"We've met before," I say, realization dawning. "Outside North Penn Hospital. We had a flat tire and you changed it. You gave me a business card, said to call if we needed help with my grandfather. Don't remember what I did with it, though. Sorry."

"Had a fair amount on yer mind that day, I'd imagine." He gives a Laughlin-like crooked smile, but the kindness in his tone reminds me of Dad.

"How about we sit?" Laughlin says.

He and his dad take seats on the couch, leaving the squashy armchair for me. I sink into it, dazed. Maybe it's Johnny's cologne making me woozy and unable to stop staring at him.

He reaches into his breast pocket for a cigarette. "All right if I smoke?"

"Only if you're on fire," I quip, my voice going creaky.

"She's joking," Laughlin says.

A quick glance at Laughlin gets my voice working properly. "No, I'm warning you. Nana's brush-cleaning solvents are super flammable. And the paints have toxic chemicals in them. That's why this is a separate building."

Johnny nods and rolls his cigarette between his fingers, his little tube of comfort. "Artists do need a space apart, and this is a right nice one. That the jacks, behind that door?"

"Bathroom," Laughlin interprets, "or just the toilet."

"Powder room." I drag my knuckles across my itchy forearms.

Johnny continues scanning the room. "A marvelous talent, yer granny was. Such fierce lovely art she's made. People'd pay a pretty penny for it."

"Maybe someday we'll get around to finding buyers. Poppa's our focus right now."

Johnny shifts forward so his knees are practically touching mine. "I know you're worried about his influence o'er yer mother, Dani, how he bullies her. I can shield her from that."

"Oh— uh— kay," I stutter, trying to avoid his piercing look. "That would be...great."

"On a special diet, yer grandpappy, is he? I'd make sure he gets plenty o' calcium to promote healin' in that gammy hip. And of course I'd cook 'im meals that're easy to swallow. Always a concern after a stroke, isn't it?" Roll, roll, roll goes his cigarette in his elegant hand.

"Uh, right." I glance at Laughlin, who watches his dad with admiration.

"Happy to run him to appointments, too. Right, son?" Johnny pats Laughlin's shoulder.

"Yup," Laughlin agrees. "We know all the fastest routes to the doctors around here."

"I believe some home strengthenin' exercises in addition to the PT could get him free of that cane. Also got a full music therapy program, I do. Perfect for him. Improve his mood and speech. I think teachin' him Gaelic pieces might do his brain good. Bit of a mental challenge, keep him sharp." Johnny tucks away the cigarette, extracts a CD from his pocket and passes it to me. "Have a gander. Sample of me work."

I stare at the silver disc, the word Ronan scrawled across it. "This is...great."

"He is, right?" Laughlin gushes. "He knows therapeutic massage, too, but didn't want to brag."

Johnny tips his head, makes a humbly dismissive gesture, his gaze still locked on me.

"You seem to know a lot about elder care, Mr. O'Donnell."

"Just Johnny's fine, m'dear. Might I be able to meet yer lovely mother this week? Surely it would ease her mind tremendous to know her father'd be well looked after in his own home."

"It might be a few days before she's free. And she'll want to see your qualifications in writing. A nice résumé will go a long way with her."

"Wouldn't dream of interviewin' without one." He winks.

"Uh, great. I'll, ah, call Laughlin about a meeting time."

Father and son rise to their feet when I do. Johnny dips his head, looking up through his dark lashes. "I earnestly hope we'll be hearin' from ye soon, Miss Dani Deane. 'Twould be a true pleasure to care for such a fascinatin' man as yer grandfather. Bit of a history buff meself. I'm certain we'd get on like a house on fire."

"Yep," I squeak. "I'll be in touch."

Leaving them, I float across the dark lawn, feeling like I've been in the presence of a magical being. An Irish Merlin. Wait until Mum meets my guardian angel.

* * *

One: Please don't be mad, Thebes. I do appreciate your concern. I'm trying to consider every option that protects Mum. She's my priority here, okay?

Two: Mr. O'Donnell IS a good guy. He's who changed Beth's flat tire when we first got here and cared more about helping us than about catching his bus or keeping his suit clean. He knows loads about strokes and physical therapy and special diets. He has a whole music therapy program that will help Poppa with his speech. We should totally hire him. I hope Mum thinks so, too.

Three: I'm sorry your parents' divorce did you so much harm. I pray you can learn to trust that I'm being true to you.

* * *

I sleep in so late Monday that I miss my chance to talk to Mum before she drives Poppa to his neurology appointment at the hospital in Wilkes-Barre. I take Rhys out for a quick walk, and smell cigarette smoke coming from the pine grove. When I call Laughlin's name, he weirdly doesn't answer. But the longer I'm outside, the worse I feel. My rash has progressed to excruciating new heights of itchiness, like ant armies are practicing marching maneuvers all over my skin. If I don't get my mind occupied, and soon, I'll scratch myself bloody.

If there was ever a time I needed to "go deeper in the shadows" with my pencils, this is it. Since the *Madeline* project is obviously a bust, I need to come up with something new for my art final. Something that'll make Mum smile as much as *Madeline* does.

Because it reminds her of her mother.

And I have something better, even closer to Nana's true self.

I retrieve Nana's journal from its hiding spot and flip to some favorite passages I've bookmarked. Mum's first smile, first steps. Her quick mind, her curiosity. Her tough-minded strength in suffering. Her gentle kindness. Her beauty. Her surprising talents. Nana calls her *mon rayon de soleil*, my ray of sunshine; *ma raison de vivre*, my reason for living.

What are the chances Nana said these things aloud? Mum told me that "Pop dominated her time and attention." And "I missed her even when she was alive," is how David put it.

My gosh, I've been hunting through this journal for deep, dark secrets. But what if the real secrets aren't the darkness, but the light?

I burst into the blue bathroom, where David is recaulking the tile, and spook him with my excitement. He points me to the lone family photo album on a bookstand among the trophies. He watches, confused, as I snap shots of key photos with my phone.

"What's this all about? A secret project?"

"Not a secret. A surprise. I'll tell all soon, okay?"

* * *

By Tuesday, I have a big stack of sketches, but they're all terrible. I'm not skilled enough to work from memory or imagination, and the stilted portraits in the family album don't have any poses or expressions that match Nana's words. I need better photos to work from.

Fortunately, I get an opportunity to hunt around Nana's secret stash of stuff when Mum heads out early to run Poppa to speech therapy in Elmerton, then back to Wilkes-Barre for tests the neurologist ordered. When I get to the studio, I'm hit with the peppery odor of Johnny O'Donnell's cologne, as strong as it had been Sunday night — his magic, surely. A potent reminder that I promised to get him an interview with Mum. I've been afraid to mention him, scared she'll dismiss the idea as a selfish scheme to get to Paris. If Johnny truly is my angel, then God will let the plan come up naturally at just the right time.

Something looks different in here, but I'm not sure what. The boxes we moved down on Saturday are still stacked to one side and piles of paintings line the walls. I could swear the piles were deeper. But Theo did take a bunch to the lake house. I'm probably just misremembering.

Picking through the remaining unopened boxes from Saturday, I find a small batch of candid photos: David and Mum at Halloween and shots from David's sixth birthday party. In one, a sandy-haired woman hunkers down and whispers in her son's ear. The intimacy of the pose seems just right. I can imagine, if Nana had a chance to do it again, she'd use a moment like this to whisper an assurance, call Mum *mon bijou*, my jewel. Maybe I could adapt the faces to make Nana and Mum from people who look a lot like Heather's mom and brother Paulie.

Wait a minute. Mrs. Daly has six kids, ages four to seventeen — enough variety that I could get every pose I need, at least for the preliminary sketches.

Heather loves the idea when I explain it to her. Posing her family will be good "photo styling" practice, a skill she'll need to prepare her college application portfolio for costume design programs. I offer to e-mail her the text I want to illustrate, and leave it to her to pick poses. Imagining what cozy family togetherness looks like is a little tough for me at the moment.

Of course Heather can't let a comment like that go by without wanting to delve deeper. So we talk for a good, long time about my current dilemmas with Poppa and Mum, with Laughlin and his dad, and finally with my angry, jealous boyfriend. Unlike Theo, she doesn't scoff at my theory that I'm in the lions' den. But she does warn me that when you're down a dark hole, it's hard to tell a rescue rope from a snake. She pauses to pray that I'll have the wisdom to know the difference.

"I miss you so much. What's new? Any progress with the Fletcher situation?"

She groans. "You mean my latest disaster? You're gonna love this. I was roaming midtown, bored, and saw him shopping with Melody. So I...followed them. He got a new haircut and glasses, and looks great, more himself. But what really got me was how patient he is with his sister. How sweet and funny. I got all fluttery with hope that maybe he's changing inside, too."

"Stalking the guy was a bit middle school of you, but it's hardly a disaster."

"There's more. I wanted to 'bump into them,' all casual. But when I dodged out of Mel's sight, I ran into Fletch. Literally. Knocked him flat on the floor. When I helped him up, the first thing out of my stupid mouth was, 'I like your glasses.' Then he said, 'that's me, giant Einstein brain, the hopeless nerd.' I told him no, he's Clark Kent. And only I know his secret identity as Super Hottie."

I laugh. "And this is bad how?"

"He was totally embarrassed and took off. He must think I'm so shallow and only care about looks. Really, I just want him to be his best self."

"So that's what you tell him next time."

"I couldn't. Not after how he reacted."

"Suit yourself. But you know what? There's a verse from Proverbs 27 I've been pondering that might help you: 'better is open rebuke than hidden love.'"

The moment she ends the call, I find myself sending yet another text to Theo.

One: I love you. Two: I miss you. Three: Please call me.

* * *

I sleep poorly Tuesday night. Every sound makes me wake and check my phone again for a response from Theo. Still nothing. It seems like no explanation, no apology, no loving words will prove that I only want to get home to him. He still needs time, space, something to get past the whole situation.

I'm feeling more frustrated than hopeful, Lord. I don't know how to fix this, but surely you do. Please heal Theo's hurting heart and help him find his way back to me.

On Wednesday, Heather's photos trickle in, one by one. I pick three favorites to start with, and pop Johnny's CD into my laptop for some background music. His style is an odd rock-folk mashup, shifting from soft acoustic to blaring electronic. The songs tell intricate stories of giants, kings, witches, fairies, and swan children with strange names full of ch and kru and sh sounds that I couldn't spell if my life depended on it. It will definitely be a mental workout for Poppa to learn even the simplest of these songs.

As I work, Mum peeks in and stands riveted by the music, so I quietly tuck my drawings away. She asks for my help packing some of Nana's old art tools to donate to the rehab hospital art therapy room. When we get to the studio, she doesn't seem to notice the strong cologne smell, but she does find a guitar pick on the floor. I blurt a rambling story about Theo learning guitar to lead campfire sing-alongs, all the while wondering why I hadn't noticed it before. I'm not sure if the painting stacks are thinner, but they seem lean compared to last week.

Mum dithers a long time over the tools and supplies, moving things from one box to another and back again. I gently suggest we could jettison the printmaking, ceramics, and weaving stuff, since neither of us have an interest in those media. She agrees, then proceeds to carry a box of kiddie safety scissors with her to the couch and aimlessly jab around in it.

"I guess I should take care of it, then?"

"Good, fine, yes." She waves me away wearily.

I reorganize Nana's stuff by category, glancing up occasionally at Mum. She shifts from the box of scissors to the tabletop figurines, arranging them by height.

"I guess Poppa's been an even bigger handful than usual since the stroke," I say.

"He is what he is. The doctors aren't sure…until the tests…." She studies a ceramic shepherd, then presses it to her chest. "Laughlin's so good with Pop. Could it be a gender thing?"

"Like being more cooperative with men than women?"

"Yes. If we hired help, a homecare person, could we get a male aide? Do they exist?"

I choke with surprise and send up a grateful prayer. "Absolutely. Laughlin knows a guy who's looking for a new position. He could come soon for an interview. Maybe even tomorrow."

Mum's phone alarm chirps, reminding her of Poppa's OT appointment. As we hustle the boxes of art supply donations out to the car, I get a noncommittal response about scheduling an interview with Johnny: Tomorrow *might* work, *maybe* in the afternoon.

When I call Laughlin with the news, he doesn't mind that I can't give a definite time.

"So," I ask, "what does *your* mom think about this plan of yours?"

"Ma? Oh, you know, she's, uh, totally excited to have alone time with Dave. And she'll be able to focus on settling in at the new place and new job without me underfoot."

"Oh, come on. She'll miss you a ton, don't you think?"

"A little, I guess," he mutters, with an overtone of *like I care.*

"Is she sad you'll be back in cyber school? She was so pumped about the extracurriculars you'd finally have a chance to do in Firbank."

"Look, I need to go," he snaps. "We'll swing by tomorrow, a little after three."

He hangs up, leaving me uneasy. Why was he so irritated by my questions?

Chapter 29

Rhys is as keyed up as I am Thursday morning, so I take him for an extra-long walk after breakfast. On the edge of the pine grove near Fern Pond, I find a pile of cigarette butts. Laughlin knows better than to leave these here. Wasn't that our first of many arguments?

Something weird is going on.

I race to the cologne-scented studio and discover that the stacks of Nana's work are now just single paintings — depressing ones of the bony, tattered Tilman twins. Oh my gosh. We've been robbed! Whoever snagged the first few paintings must have panicked when they saw how much stuff we got rid of yesterday.

I'm such an idiot. My secret planning has done ten times more harm than good. I should've said something to Mum or David as soon as I suspected a problem. We could have at least locked the freaking door.

I hunt around to see what else has been stolen. Nana's painting supplies are more crowded, I think. Behind the old cans of turpentine, I find two new ones. That's strange. I open the first and while the liquid is clear, it doesn't smell like piney chemicals, but citrusy cough syrup. Or more accurately, like one of Dad's gin-and-tonics.

In the powder room, the sink is clean, not dusty, and the toilet runs like it was recently flushed. But that can't be. I've been here too long for someone to have done their business, flushed, and left without crossing my path. Something's wrong with the plumbing.

I lift the lid off the tank, and see the flapper is caught on a zipper baggie full of stuff submerged in the water. With shaking hands, I extract it. Inside I find a purple toothbrush, smoker's whitening toothpaste, a razor, and a shaving tonic with the same peppery scent as Johnny O'Donnell.

* * *

My call to Laughlin's cell rings and rings as I pace the side yard. What should I do? Tell Mum? Call off the whole thing? Just because Johnny appears to be squatting in Nana's studio like a hobo, is it fair to assume he's responsible for the missing art? Lots of us have access to the studio. Maybe Uncle David did something with the paintings. He's in quite a few of them.

I leave Laughlin a short message to call me back, then try David's number.

Sarah answers, explaining that my uncle is on the roof at the moment, doing a repair. When I tell her about Nana's missing art, she's as confused and concerned as I am. Especially because she saw a new piece of art at the bank yesterday, hung behind the tellers. She could swear the little boy in the painting looked just like my uncle as a kid.

"I worry Laughlin's involved," Sarah says. "I've seen signs he inherited the shifty gene."

"What do you mean?"

"He's been so secretive the last four or five months. Took up smoking, got into that fight at school, constantly rushes from job to job, or so he says. I can't help worrying he'll turn into his father, who wasn't the most upstanding person. Always seemed to be working some secret scheme or another to support his music."

My whole body goes icy cold. "What kind of schemes?"

"I don't know many details, but he's quite gifted at parting people from their money without his marks being the least aware they're being played. I didn't want Laughlin to grow up around that or honestly even know about it, for fear it would poison him."

Schemes, marks, being played? She makes Johnny sound like a con artist. But he's so thoughtful and smart. So attentive and good at knowing just what you need. And so powerfully charming you don't even consider questioning a thing he says.

"Where's the bank where you saw the painting? Maybe I can find out more there." I jot down the address in my sketchpad and thank her for her help.

Mum appears at the side door, waving. "Ah, there you are! You up for a little outing? You're well past contagious. A dab of makeup would hide the last of your scabs. Please?"

"Where to? How long? The male aide I told you about is coming by to interview for the home care job around three."

"Curtain shopping in Elmerton? Shouldn't take too long."

My hand goes reflexively to my back pocket, where my sketchpad holds that bank address. "Sounds great!" I chirp.

* * *

Escaping Mum for even fifteen seconds to check my phone messages is difficult enough during our shopping expedition in Elmerton. Shaking her long enough to pop into the bank where Sarah saw the painting of David is simply impossible. Mum wants my "expert" opinion on everything from the fabric weight and color to the hardware for the curtain rods.

We lunch at a cutesy café that serves all kinds of crêpes, which I guess is Mum's little act of condolence for the loss of my dream trip. But no amount of Nutella and whipped cream could sweeten the mass of anxiety souring my gut. When someone comes out of the restaurant across the street carrying a painting,

I knock over my *café au lait* straining to see if it's one of Nana's.

Once we're back at Poppa's, Mum asks me to fetch the tools we need to install the new curtain rods, so I take the opportunity to leave Laughlin another message.

What if Theo's right about him? From fairly early on, I figured that Laughlin's tough gruffness was part of his "man of the house" act — his way of pretending he relished being a man already when he's just as much a scared kid as any other teen with a single mom. But maybe that was "the shifty gene" presenting itself, and I'm too darned naive to see a genuine bad boy when he's staring me right in the face.

As I step out of the garage tool room with Poppa's drill and some screwdrivers, Laughlin's maroon truck pulls to a stop where the driveway curves closest to the house. Johnny stays in the passenger seat, giving a little wave, while Laughlin meets me by the garage.

"Hey," he says brightly, "you're looking tons better. Hardly any spots left."

"Why haven't you answered your phone?" I demand.

"I was rushing to finish this at Grouse Hill." He passes me a sheet of thick, cream paper.

"Grouse Hill? You haven't been with Poppa?"

"Ma said your mom picked him up early for some tests in Wilkes-Barre."

"That was Tuesday. Mum and I went shopping for curtains and stuff this morning."

"He must be with Dave. Could you, um, take a look at that before we meet your mom?"

Purely out of curiosity, I glance over the supposed qualifications of John Ronan O'Donnell. Under education he's listed a bachelor's degree in folklore — which explains his obscure song lyrics — plus three years of a doctor of medicine program and a master's degree in music therapy. His work experience includes personal care assistant for the elderly, senior center music therapist, PT assistant, and masseuse. It's a little too perfect a fit for the job.

"Did he invent this all?" I mutter. "MIT doesn't *have* a medical school. And you can't study music therapy at a conservatory. My boyfriend's sister Cat studies at one, and she said they offer degrees only in performance, composing, and conducting."

"But Dad showed me all these old textbooks he had from med school. Maybe MIT closed their program a while ago? I don't know about the conservatory, but he definitely did a lot of work with seniors. I remember four different rich old ladies he took care of. One even sent her car to pick me up from kindergarten when she kept Dad late at work. It was a Bentley. How cool is that?"

So Laughlin is being duped, too. Because I suspect Johnny's real experience with elderly people is swindling them. When I peek over at the truck, he's reading aloud to himself from flashcards, likely rehearsing his lies for Mum.

"Since you seem to have answers for everything, can you explain why I found your dad's belongings in the studio?"

"I asked him to serve as guard, in case Grandpop wandered over there at night."

"You should have talked to *me* first," I whisper through clenched teeth. "There are paintings missing—art he was quite taken with when you brought him to meet me."

He gapes at me. "I don't know anything about that."

"Theo's right. There's something off about this. About him."

Gravel crunches behind me. Johnny says, "Someone's out yonder, walkin' circles. Bald fellow. Your grandpappy, isn't it?" He strides away, tapping a fresh cigarette out of a pack.

"Dad, wait!" Laughlin calls. But Johnny breaks into a run.

I set the résumé on David's coffin project and exchange a confused look with Laughlin. He helps me carry my armload of tools to the house, then we head for the back yard.

* * *

Poppa is out by Fern Pond, climbing through the reeds toward the water. Ignoring our calls and shouts, he kneels on the muddy bank and dunks his arms in the water.

I break into a jog, Laughlin at my heels.

"Where's Dad? I don't see him anywhere," he cries, voice taut.

"Come on. Poppa could drown," I call back.

We find Poppa washing his arms, which are covered with cuts, scrapes, and random spatters of color. He reeks of turpentine and his clothes are dusted with colored powder that intensifies where he's gotten wet. Powdered tempera paint? Nana had cases of it in the studio.

"Why are you such a mess, Poppa? Where have you been? What have you been doing?"

He goes on scrubbing his skin like Lady Macbeth. "Warren and Dan. Dan and Warren. Dannen they called us. Strong together. Don't need no Pa, never did. We had *plenty*."

"He's been saying random stuff like this all week," Laughlin takes one of Poppa's damaged hands and studies it. "Plank of lumber attack you, Grandpop?"

"That wasn't random," I say. "He was answering my questions. He's been with Nana's paintings of him and his twin, doing something…messy, I'd guess."

As Laughlin picks splinters out of Poppa's hands, I hustle back up the bank, shaking with rage. Among the reeds are slivered bits of lumber and slices of fabric. The first scrap I pick up is stiff, paint-caked. A bit of canvas. Once part of a work of art.

286

I march back to Poppa carrying ruined painting pieces. "What have you *done*?"

FU-OHHHM. The air behind us roars. The pond is suddenly orange, reflecting a conflagration. We turn to see flames leap from the studio roof and dark smoke fill the sky.

"Holy shipwreck!" Laughlin exclaims. He clambers up the bank runs straight for the fire, calling his father's name.

Poppa wails, "Maggie?"

"Poppa, can you please stay put for two minutes? Maggie's not in there. She's with Grace. I'm going to get help, but you have to stay here where it's safe. Okay?"

He scowls suspiciously like I'm a random stranger, then bursts out laughing. Great. He's now completely off his rocker. This will be fun.

I scramble after Laughlin, who limps toward me, clutching his shoulder and grimacing in pain. "I tried busting the door, but it wouldn't budge. What if Dad's trapped in there?"

Oh, no. After Poppa's rampage, the place would be full of flammable vapors from turpentine, mineral spirits, paint, and Johnny's booze stash. If he lit that cigarette in his hand....

"I'll go see if Mum has keys. Can you call 911 and keep an eye on Poppa?"

I race to the house, skid into the kitchen, and grab the fire extinguisher from the pantry, yelling for Mum all the while.

She appears, looking puzzled.

"Studio's on fire! You have keys? You have to have the keys."

She shakes her head. "David. I— I'll call him. What happened?"

"Not sure. I gotta see what I can do until the firefighters come." I squeeze her arm as I pass, then sprint out the door toward the unfolding disaster.

The closer I get, the harder it is to breathe. Part of the pine grove is now ablaze, branches crackling and popping above the studio, which is wreathed in dense smoke.

"David has to bring the keys!" I yell to Laughlin as he paces circles around my vacant-faced grandfather.

"Maybe I can bust out the windows," Laughlin hollers back.

I race around the studio's perimeter and extinguish tufts of dry grass that have caught fire. But it's a losing battle. I can't contain a blaze this big alone. Once the whole pine grove goes up, there may be no saving Poppa's house.

I should have brought a shovel. We need to dig a trench like Pa Ingalls in *Little House on the Prairie,* when the brush fire came roaring across the Kansas plains toward their cabin.

"God?" I croak, "I don't know what to do. Please help me."

From the edges of my memory, words come to me: *Do not fear; you are mine. When you walk through the fire, you will not be burned; the flames will not set you ablaze. I will be with you.*

As a cool clarity settles over me, I weave through the smaller fires, spraying them with quick bursts. Mum dashes past me, shrieking "Mama!" She dives into the smoke.

"Dani!" Laughlin jogs up with a load of pond rocks in the pouch of his folded shirt-front. "Help's coming, but Dad's not answering his phone. If he's in there, he needs air. I'm gonna try to bust some vent holes in the glass. Get your mom out of there."

Dropping to my knees, I crawl below the smoke toward the door. I feel Mum's leg and inch close enough to hear her bang her head against the door and whimper, "Mama, Mama."

"We need to get away from here. Chemicals in there. Toxic."

"Mama's work!" She coughs hoarsely. "Everything will be lost!" More coughing.

"Johnny!" I holler, pounding the door with the fire extinguisher. "Open the door or you'll die! Please! We know about the paintings. It's all right. We'll figure it out."

There's no reply; no sounds but the roar and crackle of flame, and rocks pinging glass, but not breaking it.

Maybe Laughlin's wrong. We didn't actually see Johnny go into the studio. He was in the yard, and then he wasn't. Maybe he decided to bail once he saw how kooky Poppa's becoming. In the half minute we were behind him, he could have ducked into the woods and taken the path back to Sarah's. Besides, I don't remember turning on the studio ventilation this morning. With the windows no longer shaded, it probably got really hot inside as the afternoon wore on. That could have been enough to ignite fumes.

My stinging eyes and nose have filled with gooey tears and my throat's a sandy, scorching desert. I try to pull the neck of my t-shirt over my mouth and nose, but my rubbery hands can't grasp the fabric. My cheek hits grass. Cooler here. *He makes me lie down in green pastures. He restores my soul…. And I will dwell in the house of the Lord forever.*

Laughlin's strong grip locks onto my arm. I'm too woozy to fight him as he pulls Mum and me away from the door, the smoke, the flame-licked trees. In the tall grass by Fern Pond, Poppa stands by wringing his hands as Mum and I cough, splutter, and wretch.

Laughlin takes the fire extinguisher I've been hugging and continues my task of putting out smaller fires popping up all over from sparks and airborne bits of burning debris. Every few feet he yells, "Johnny! Where are you?"

Smaller explosions rattle the building, sending out a spray of jingling glass.

Sirens wail in the smoky air.

"Who's Johnny?" asks Mum.

Poppa cries, "Why, Maggie? Why?"

* * *

289

Soon my uncle is directing emergency vehicles into the yard. He and Laughlin talk to the fire chief, who points the ambulance in our direction, and sends a crew with axes into the blaze, while another wrestles out hoses. No need for keys now.

EMTs herd Mum, Poppa, and me over to the ambulance, now parked out of the path of blowing smoke and busy firefighters. When they seat me in a folding chair beside the ambulance, the ladder truck annoyingly blocks my view of the fire. An oxygen mask is strapped to my face. The female EMT flashes a light in my eyes, asks for my name, my age, the name of this place, the date. The answers turn to mush in my mouth.

"Dandy," I slur. "I sen-teen. This Pa's pace. Dunky, Pense-fane. It Thur-say something-ith June, two thousin nine."

She nods as she takes my pulse and blood pressure, then clips a gadget onto my fingertip.

Mum clumsily claws off her mask and slumps over to puke again, causing the male EMT to drop the blood pressure cuff he'd begun strapping to her arm.

"CO poisoning, Suze." Mum's EMT says. "This one needs HBO stat. How's the kid?"

"Mum never...watches TV," I say, my voice breathy but steadying behind the mask.

Suze frowns. "Altered mental state, I'd say."

"I don't think so," Mum's EMT replies. "She heard me say HBO. It's not TV, kid, it's a treatment your mom needs at a hospital."

He steps away from us to radio someone and Suze resumes interrogating me. What's my address and phone number? Who's the current president? Can I count backward from twenty by threes? My answers seem to satisfy her, so she moves on to questioning Poppa.

He bats away the little flashlight she shines in his eyes, and tries to shove her when she reaches for his wrist to check his pulse. "Blamed crow weather," he growls.

"He had a stroke…two weeks ago," I gasp to her. "He wasn't anywhere…near the fire."

"He smells like igniter. He start this thing?"

"Not on purpose. He made a mess…of some art supplies… in that building. But then he left. Another man…a smoker… might've gone…in there afterwards."

She gets on her radio and blathers jargon about stations, county, the PSP that I think was a request for more help to come. Or maybe the cops?

The ladder truck pulls forward and extends its ladder toward the burning trees, once again giving me a view of the smoke-cloaked studio. A huge hole has been hacked through its side and the entire roof is ablaze. Soon a group of masked firefighters emerge carrying a stiff, coal-black, person-shaped form. Someone from the hose truck brings them a big piece of black fabric and unfolds it on the grass. The masked firefighters lay the charred doll on the fabric, then one of them zips the figure inside.

It's not until Laughlin falls to his knees that I realize the black fabric is a body bag.

Chapter 30

I sit alone in an ER bay, oxygen mask still strapped to my face. The pure air makes me both sleepy and hyper-aware. Though I can close my eyes against the intense glare of the fluorescent lights, every voice and machine blip blares, all fabric contact with my pox scabs itches. I grip the dove pendant at my throat, a confirmation gift from Dad, and rub it between my fingers for comfort. All my efforts to save my mother have only left her poisoned, skin graying, too weak to open her eyes. My heart squeezes at the memory of her gurney disappearing into the first ambulance, that awful body bag, and Laughlin, a shuddering curl of grief.

All our sneaking, hiding, covering up have collided, combusted.

Ashes to ashes. We all fall down.

I look longingly at my phone, wishing I could push the right buttons and get answers. Is this God's judgment, or His refining fire, burning away the dross and leaving the pure gold? But my phone's no use in here for the big answers, or even the little ones: where's Mum now? Did Theo get the message I left? The nurse threatened to take my phone if I even turn it on, because it would interfere with the medical equipment.

Please, God, let Mum live. Heal her. Don't make her pay for my impatience, my reckless attempt to be in control.

Footsteps come near and stop. I open my eyes hoping to see a doctor, but it's my uncle with two packed bags. He plops my backpack beside me on the gurney and slumps in the guest chair, still gripping Mum's overnight bag.

"Your doc expects your chest X-ray to be ready soon. If it's clear, and that doohickey on your finger shows your blood oxygen levels are normal, they'll spring ya."

"You're getting pretty…good at being…the responsible one," I rasp through the mask.

He chuckles "Thanks, Lord Vader. Gracie was a good teacher. And she's improving. Don't worry. They've popped her in a glass tube like Snow White for this treatment called hyperbaric oxygen or HBO. Pushes pure air into her lungs to scrub away the carbon monoxide gumming up the places where oxygen needs to be."

"Poppa?"

David looks ceiling-ward, mouth pinched. "He's gonna be here for a while."

"I feel like this…is all my fault."

"It's not, kiddo. You and Laughlin have kind hearts and good intentions, but complete ignorance of the real problem. Sarah blames herself for that. She didn't want to harden Laughlin against his father, so she never told him the whole truth about the terms of the divorce. She offered to let Johnny off the hook for child support if he agreed to no contact with his son."

"Whoa. How come?"

"He broke trust in a lot of big ways. Anyhow, we reckon he fed Laughlin a heap of lies to reconnect with him, and it seems like his intentions weren't good."

"Sarah told you…about Nana's…missing paintings?"

"Saw one myself on the third floor, near where Gracie's being treated. Sarah's been calling around trying to find out how it got here. Best we've pieced together, Johnny used Mama's art to settle some debts with Finbar's Inn. He owed back rent and had run up a huge bar tab. His gigs barely covered his meals. Our silver lining is that he's not leaving behind debt."

It's unbelievable that he could do something so despicable

to people trying to help him. And poor Laughlin had such high hopes for reconnecting with his dad. Hopes now as dead as the unsavable Johnny, so handsome, so gifted, so selfish to the core.

"How's Laughlin?"

"Pretty low. And confused. It's hard to grieve someone who never shared themselves truthfully. You wonder if what you miss is a kernel of something real, or just a fantasy."

A police officer steps into the bay. "Miss Deane? Could I ask a few questions?"

* * *

When my doctor finally releases me, Laughlin's is the first familiar face I see in the ER waiting room. His skin is as pink as his eyes, the teary soot now scrubbed off his cheeks. He waves me over and offers me some of his M&Ms, smiling wearily. Trying for normal.

"You need to leave breathing smoke to the dragons, Cuz. I'm giving it up myself." He lifts his sleeve to show me the tan square of a nicotine patch. "Can't even look at a lighter now without getting the shakes. It could've been me with the cigarette, waltzing into that studio."

"I'm *so* sorry, Laughlin. About your dad. About everything."

"It was all just a con job, Dani. All the crap Dad said about Ma not supporting his music, and that she'd be the same with me — I swallowed it hook, line, and sinker. He had me convinced we were really connecting, when all he wanted was to use me all over again."

"Again? There was a before?"

He nods. "Ma finally told me why Dad wasn't supposed to see me. And it's not because of the other women, or the drinking. He…stole the college fund my grandparents left me."

"No way. Of all the slimy, low-down things."

"I still can't believe he's gone, and how he went. The fire investigator came by to talk to me after the cops. He found damaged paint solvent cans at the site and kept pressing me about the whole timetable, who was out there when, that kind of thing."

"Poppa got left alone for hours, didn't he? While Mum and I were shopping, he must have gone completely mental in there. He clearly tore apart a bunch of Nana's canvases. The turpentine and all — I don't think he was enough in his right mind to know how dangerous the vapors can be in a closed space. Lighting a cigarette would have been enough spark to ignite it. It was an accident, Laughlin. A terrible accident."

"I'm not so sure. Dad knew there was flammable stuff out there. You gave a pretty harsh warning about it. I think when I showed you his résumé, he overheard us talking and knew the jig was up." Laughlin shakes his head. "It's like that crazy weasel all over again."

"No way was this job so important that he'd…give up on life if he didn't get it. He was a smart guy. He would have figured out something else."

"He sought me out when he legally wasn't supposed to. He must've been in bad trouble."

"Or maybe he thought it was worth the risk. He didn't have to teach you guitar, after all. He truly could've been trying to start over with you, but took some shady shortcuts that weren't panning out. Maybe what he couldn't handle was letting you down."

Laughlin sits up tall in his seat and elbows me.

Theo is striding toward us, and I leap to my feet in a panic. After our many fights about Laughlin, here I am hanging out with him yet again.

"Theo, we weren't— I just got released. He was here and I wanted to know what's—"

"Don't," he says. His strong arms wrap me tight in a warm, musky-vanilla hug. Taking a hiccupping breath, he murmurs into my hair, "You're okay. Thank God you're okay."

I feel wetness against my temple. His tears? "Thebes?"

"I've been an idiot," he whispers, "but I'm gonna make it right." He gives me one more squeeze, then steps back, swiping his knuckles across his eyes.

Turning to Laughlin, he offers his hand. "Thanks for saving Dani and her mom."

Laughlin eyes him warily before shaking hands. Then, to my shock, Theo pulls him to his feet and wraps him in a back-thumping bear hug, like he's a crew buddy.

"I'm sorry, man. So sorry for your loss."

When David approaches, I go to his side. We watch the embrace in perplexed silence.

Laughlin takes a choked, phlegmy breath. Wriggling out of Theo's grasp, he puddles into a heap on his seat, head cradled in his arms. At the sight of that posture, my throat tightens. A girl at grief-share used to call it "the black-hole huddle."

"I'll take it from here, guys." David motions for Theo to step aside. Slinging his arm around Laughlin's broad shoulders, he murmurs, "it's okay, son. I'm here."

* * *

Theo takes my backpack and steers me toward the ER exit. "Sarah asked me to bring you to the main lobby and they'll page her to come meet you. Could we maybe talk for a few minutes first? There's a nice park around this side of the building."

"Sure." We follow a path through a park-like strip of land.

My spine tingles under his warm hand and the reassuring strokes from his thumb.

"Hearing the last message you left, with the sirens and your voice so weak…I realized I could have lost you forever, the love of my life. Talk about a wake-up call."

My whole body swivels to face him. Love of his life?

Nervously he gnaws his lower lip, looks up through his tan lashes. "I'm so sorry, babe. I should've had your back while you were going through all this hard stuff. Should've listened, encouraged you, not shut you out. I've been trapped in this cage of messed-up, jealous thoughts and I needed God's help to get free. Can you ever forgive me?"

I nod, tears springing to my eyes. "I've missed you so much."

Theo's fingertips whisper against mine, searching for a welcome there. My hand expands, twines with his, grasps tight.

"Please believe I really meant what I just did back there," he says.

"You mean your bro moment with Laughlin?"

"Yeah. He's your family, not my rival. It was time to make peace. Clear the air."

As we near a bench surrounded by rosebushes heavy with blooms, I sink onto it, pulling Theo with me. "That was… beautiful, but I need your forgiveness, too. I didn't take your feelings into account when it came to Laughlin. I was so scared of being stuck here, I jumped at the first escape plan, even though it was foolish and it hurt you. I ignored your warnings when I should've trusted your instincts. I chalked up your bad opinion to simple jealousy."

"I didn't want him breathing the same air as you. There's nothing simple about jealousy like that. My fear of being hurt like Mom was…. It made me lose sight of everything — who you really are, how good we are together, how God keeps me safe."

"You were right about Laughlin's dad, though. He was shady. A powerful manipulator. I was total putty in his hands. When he changed Beth's flat, he said 'Let me be your angel.' And I wanted to make it fit the story I was telling about myself: Danielle in the lions' den."

"Having the same name as the prophet doesn't mean you're doomed to be his clone."

I give a startled laugh. Nothing like having your own words come back to you, for you. "I still feel stupid for thinking I could force God to follow my script."

"Well, I feel stupider for running away when you needed me most."

"Remember our talk in Linus Land? You said, 'It's not a competition.' Not to be the strong one *or* the weak one. Alone, we're each scared. But you help me and I help you. Together we're both…how did you put it?"

"Stronger. More," he rumbles, his deep voice giving me delicious shivers.

"Right. That's how this works, Theo. Or how it should." When I look up from our clasped hands, I find a golden warmth in his hazel eyes like sunlight on water.

"I want that for us, Dani. More than anything." He presses his lips to mine, a kiss that starts sweet and deepens, filling my lungs with brightness. Light leaks into the darkest rooms inside me, where thick sheets of fear once covered the windows. With one hand, I trace the perfect curve of his ear. The other, I press to his thumping heart. The thrum of his love pulses against my palm.

The moment is broken by his insistent ringtone. He groans and pulls away to answer.

"Hey, Dad. Yep. Danielle's doing well, considering. We were just—." He nuzzles my neck and buries his face in my smoky hair. "I gotta go. Thanks again for helping me get here."

He dives right back into kissing like he's making up for lost time. And oh boy, do I love this kind of make-up work. I'd happily take pages, chapters more. But something he said niggles.

I pull away, press a finger to his lips. "Your *dad* helped you get here? How?"

"I asked him to put in a word with my boss, his old pal? It probably helped that he was having coffee with Courtney at the time."

"Your stepmom is back? How'd he find her?"

"She didn't leave town, just got a sublet. Her Ob-Gyn had called their home phone to confirm an appointment, so Dad went over to the doctor's office to try to talk to her. Turns out she's pregnant, and doesn't want Dad treating her kid the way he treats us."

"Wow. So…you're getting a new brother or sister?"

"If I'm lucky. It won't be easy for Dad to win Courtney back. He has to prove he can become a better father by getting therapy and fixing his relationships with me, Beth, and Cat."

"How's he going to do that?"

"I made it easy with me, needing his help to escape camp to see you. Beth and Cat will be tougher. I gave him some ideas, though. Beth would be happier if she had a different source of funding for her wedding and could make her own decisions about it. And Cat's jazz ensemble would be perfect to hire for the reception. Hey, his wife wants proof he's changing. He needs big gestures, right?"

Chapter 31

Dawn's rays reach into my dream of untangling miles of knotted yarn that hold me prisoner in a damp dungeon. I stretch in the recliner, my neck protesting the cramped position I'd slept in. Despite my discomfort, I'm thankful Sarah was able to get them to bend the rules for us. Usually it's a parent in the guest recliner and the child in the hospital bed.

We were supposed to spend today at the Louvre, Mum and me. It's hard to imagine any work of art as beautiful as she is right now, sleeping peacefully and breathing regular air again.

I dig out my sketchbook as quietly as I can and resume work on my journal project. It's nice to have a stand-in for Nana who looks more like her than Mrs. Daly does. Mum's contented expression will be perfect to work into my sketch of Nana embracing the graduate Grace.

Morning sun stretches across the room as I work, a bright line that slowly moves from Mum's blanketed feet toward her face. Her eyes flutter open when the light reaches chin level.

"Darling? Have you been here all night?"

"Yeah. I didn't want to be at Poppa's without you after what happened. I was afraid Laughlin's father might…haunt me like Dad did."

"That body bag, it was real? Not my smoke-fogged nightmare? They put Laughlin's *father* in it? He's…dead? That's terrible. What was he doing in the studio?"

I confess the whole insane plan I'd tried to help Laughlin pull off, and how Johnny had plans of his own — to turn Nana's art into cash and start a new life at our expense.

Mum blinks with surprise. "You mean it wasn't all destroyed in the fire?"

"No. There were eight paintings in the studio that Poppa chopped to pieces right before the fire. He's furious that Nana let out the secret about his childhood. Last Saturday, Theo took some paintings to the lake house because I was scared Poppa might do this. All the rest, Johnny stole and started selling off. I'm so sorry I didn't tell you everything from the beginning."

"I was sure Mama's best work was gone. Oh darling, it's...a miracle."

"I don't know if we'll be able to get any of the pieces back."

"Where would we put them all, and how would we keep them safe from Pop? Better that her work is out in the world being seen and loved, instead of locked away in the dark."

"I don't think any of her work is really safe from Poppa. Not even the surrealist still lifes that he does like. He's so angry, and honestly seems really, really not right in the head."

She leans back on her pillows. "Vascular dementia. That's the reason for all the tests — diagnosing him. This mess will likely confirm it. It's hard to believe his sharp mind has been snatched from him; he always took such pride in it. Harder still to grasp that this terrible illness opens doors we were sure had closed. Spruce View's dementia ward has plenty of space."

I blink at her, dumbfounded. The lions' hot breath on my neck is gone, just like that.

"That sounds like a miracle, too, Mum."

She doesn't respond, but instead strains to get a glimpse of my drawing in progress. "What're you working on? Can I see?"

"My new art final. I wanted to surprise you when I had a few more sketches done, but I think it's time I stop hiding things from you." I pass her my sketchbook.

"Who am I hugging in the choir robe? Or is it a graduation?

Yours? You're far taller than the girl being embraced here." She squints at the caption I scribbled on the bottom: *un jour de très grande fierté*. My proudest day. She looks up at me, surprised.

She flips back to my sketch of a girl stretched out on the floor, drawing with a crayon while her mother sits at an easel, laying paint on a canvas with equal focus. The collection of tools in the background are just as Nana left that corner of the studio.

"That one's called *mon indispensable*. It means—"

"I know what it means. And this?" She shows me the page with a teen painting a mural in a dry cleaner's shop as her mother looks on, frowning, yet wide-eyed — unexpectedly impressed. I'd had to dig out Mum's old scrapbooks to do that sketch.

"*Le vrai talent ne peut pas se cacher*. True talent—"

"Cannot hide," Mum says, like she knows the French, or heard the phrase before. She glares suspiciously at me. "How could you know these things?"

"Nana hid her diary behind your bedside table, where she hoped you would find it." I pull the journal out of my backpack and pass it to her.

Mum stares at it, awestruck, and whispers something in French. She flips to the pages I've marked with post-it notes, her lips moving as she reads the foreign words of hidden love.

"I have translations of some of the pages if you want them."

Mum shakes her head. "The French, it's coming back to me. She loved me? Was proud? Even of…advertising school?"

"Especially that, because you got there all by yourself. Didn't she ever tell you?"

Mum's eyes slide closed. She hugs the journal to her chest. Her trembling chin drops as she takes a wheezing breath, then sobs. Amid her tears, she chokes, "I hear you now, Mama."

I skootch beside her on the bed, wrap my arms around heaving shoulders, and pray no nurses come in and yell at me for upsetting her. I murmur to her how sorry I am for taking the journal, for hiding it from her. "I was scared it would bring you more pain. I only wanted to understand, so I could help you."

She wipes her face with a hospital sheet. "You learned from my example, and I from Mama's. Living with Pop, being honest wasn't safe. Easier to pretend, to lie, even when you don't need to. I know it frustrated Graham, but he loved away some of the fear. If only I'd known Mama needed that, too. How frightened she must have been, how deeply lonely."

"Remember when Mrs. Reid said what you were looking for was close? The journal was right beside me then, under a pillow. If I hadn't been so obsessed with hiding it from you, it would have been obvious to me that it's what I needed to show you. Instead, I muddled your sign from God. I'm so sorry."

"No, darling. You didn't muddle it. God knew what I needed and when. I got muddled at first because I couldn't get my head around the evidence you'd shown me that Pop's issues started long, long ago. So I fell into my normal mode — make peace at any price. But as the week wore on and I ran him to appointments, listened to his childish jabs, the truth began to sink in: it's not my fault he is the way he is. I feel like someone pulled off my blindfold. Now I can see love in my life that couldn't fully reach me before — Mama's, David's, Graham's, yours, even Pop's, strange as that sounds. Poor, broken man."

"Is it crazy that I want to find Great Uncle Warren? Maybe he could help Poppa put their hard childhood in perspective. Help him feel less ashamed and alone."

"I like that idea. Very much. And I'm learning to stop asking myself 'what have I done to deserve this amazing kid?' and simply accept the gift that you are. I love you with all my heart."

"I love you, too, Mum." I want to do a happy dance, but I just squeeze her hand.

She smiles shyly, picks up my sketchbook again, and leafs through it. "Your work is wonderful. How did you manage this while sick?"

"Heather took photos of her mom and sibs in poses I requested. I need better models for the final illustrations, though."

Mum taps her chin. "Cousin Yvette has four girls. Perhaps they'd pose with me."

"How? Doesn't she live in Rennes?"

"Mmm-hmm. We'll be there in about ten days."

"What? But I told you to cancel the trip!"

"My sweet girl, if there was ever a time we needed a vacation, it's now. We were insured to change travel dates in case of illness, so I did. I was waiting for you to get well to tell you; I didn't want to jinx your recovery. So like it or not, we're going to France."

* * *

In the end, we do right by Johnny O'Donnell, even if he didn't do right by us. Because Mum saw Johnny's sneaky theft the same way "dream-coat" Joseph saw his brothers selling him into slavery: "you intended to harm me, but God intended it for good." It surprised me that Mum knew that Genesis verse, and even more, that she sees God's hand in her own story. Still, there's a lot I have to learn about Mum.

Sunday evening, pools of amber, ruby, emerald light spill from the stained glass onto a rosewood coffin at the front of Dunn Creek Methodist. Its lid now bears a carved Celtic knot, the carpenter's tangible message: *he's your family, not my rival.* Up in the front pew, David's arm stretches to encompass his future bride and stepson as they huddle together, a unit.

The pews behind them fill with parishioners, Laughlin's

lawn clients, Javier and Arturo and their families, Ms. Kuntzler and a row of Grouse Hill riders. Some nurses take seats beside Mum, support for Sarah in this odd place of being Johnny's ex, yet somehow still his widow.

Theo and I take a pew near the back exit for quick access to fellowship hall. With us sit our co-servers for the funeral reception, Heather and Fletcher. Their reconciliation was part of a strange chain, passing person to person, faster than chickenpox. First, Beth got a call from her father, offering to pay for her wedding at the lake house. Learning of Theo's role in it, she was so overcome with gratitude, she begged for a chance to repay him. He, of course, asked her to bring his best friend — and mine — out for the weekend. Stuck together on the long car ride, Heather and Fletcher at last talked honestly about how fear makes her clam up and makes him crazy-anxious to prove himself. Weirdly enough, being insecure together was what they needed most to begin feeling truly secure. Trust is funny that way.

Mid-prelude, musicians arrive bearing instruments — Johnny's former band-mates from assorted rock, punk, and folk groups. They rudely boot out the organist and jam for twenty minutes. Even the handful of hymns get a little raucous, which I suppose is how Johnny would have wanted it. I'll never again hear "Abide with Me" without picturing a green-haired guitarist writhing on the floor. I'm sure Poppa wouldn't approve, were he well enough to be here. But Sarah's pastor takes their antics in stride — even the drum solo in "O Love That Will Not Let Me Go" — seeing a friendship honored as more important than usual funeral etiquette.

When the pastor invites people to say a few words, Laughlin comes forward, guitar in hand. He bows his head a moment, then looks up, scanning the room. "I won't pretend my dad was a perfect guy. He was so good at spinning stories, it was hard to know what was really real about him. But I know he loved the myths and culture of Ireland, even if the real place bored him. And he truly did live to make music. These few months he'd been in my life lately, it was something we shared. Thanks for giving me the best of yourself, Dad. This one's for you."

He plucks arpeggios on the guitar and sings "Danny Boy," his voice clear and sweet as stream water. The final verse leaves us gobsmacked, wet faced.

"But when ye come, and all the flow'rs are dying
If I am dead, as dead I well may be
You'll come and find the place where I am lying
And kneel and say an 'Ave' there for me.
And I shall hear, though soft you tread above me
And all my grave will warmer, sweeter be
For you will bend and tell me that you love me
And I shall sleep in peace until you come to me."

"Your cousin is going places," Theo whispers. "Count on it."

* * *

I hurry out of the pâtisserie with my warm paper sack of provisions. My sandals stutter across cobblestones as I jog back to meet Mum at the spot she staked out for our *al fresco* breakfast, with the view of Notre Dame. I arrive to find her unfolding a second portable easel as she chats on her cheap Euro mobile phone.

"You're sure about this, Nate? The coursework seems legit? Faculty, too? Uh huh." She clips paper to each easel. "All right. I'll do the paperwork. See you in August. Buh-bye."

"What's going on? You promised to stop keeping secrets."

"Not a secret, a surprise. We're taking a plein air painting workshop. Teacher's due any minute." She pulls straw hats from a shopping bag, dons one with a medium brim, then pops the floppy, wide-brimmed one onto my head. "*Parfait. Au revoir* sunburn."

"I thought you didn't want to paint."

She takes a curly palmier from my bag and bites it with relish. "I don't want to paint *for grades*, but for fun. Look at this glorious view. How could you not want to capture it?"

"Okay, sure." I dig for the chocolate croissant, and savor a buttery bite. "So why was Nate calling? Isn't it like four a.m. in New York?"

"Oh my goodness. I didn't even think— I just called." She stares dreamily at the cathedral. "No wonder he sounded so…"

"What? Annoyed?"

"Husky and mmmm…." She turns to me, blushing. "Did I just say that out loud?"

"Yes," I squeak, croissant sticking in my throat. Mum couldn't possibly be into Nate, could she? He's a *business* partner. Her husband's best friend. Okay, late husband. But still, he's five or six years younger. Decent looking, but geeky. Sweet. Smart. And single.

I check Mum's left hand. The gold band is still there on her ring finger. I've gotta stop jumping to conclusions.

"Tomorrow's the application deadline for this certificate program in graphic and digital design. I wanted Nate's opinion — whether it would be adequate training for me to, ah, possibly take on more creative work for Deane Studios."

"That would be…really cool."

"*Bon jour*!" chirps an elderly woman as she approaches with a small wheeled cart of art supplies. "Welcome to plein air painting in Paris, Deane family. Are you ready to see with new eyes? To discover exciting possibilities in the world around you?"

"Oh, yes!" Mum says.

"We sure are," I add, and lick chocolate off my fingertips.

Appendices

Bible references

Chapter 2: I Corinthians 10:13 NIV. **Chapter 3**: Genesis 20:2 NASB. **Chapter 14**: Proverbs 15:4 NIV. **Chapter 18**: Luke 18:27 NASB. **Chapter 19**: Daniel 3-4; Daniel 6. **Chapter 21**: Psalm 31:4-5 NIV. **Chapter 22**: Romans 8:28 NASB. **Chapter 25**: Exodus 20:12 NASB. **Chapter 26**: Luke 6:49 NIV. **Chapter 27**: Psalm 79:8 NIV; Mark 5:21-32. **Chapter 28**: Proverbs 27:5 NIV. **Chapter 29**: Isaiah 43: 1-2 NIV; Psalm 23: 2, 3, 6 NASB. **Chapter 31**: Genesis 50:20 NIV

Acknowledgments

My overflowing thanks to those who helped birth this book:

Milestones Children's Critique Circle — Celia, Doug, Eileen, Jessica, and Michael — for their unflagging encouragement and helpful insights.

My beta-readers, Abby, Angela, Connie, Connor, and Gwen, for insightful comments and suggestions.

Kate Crow, for her eagle-eyed editing and proofreading.

Willemijn Don, for help with translations to French.

Candy Cason, for guidance on speech issues in stroke victims.

Susan Hicks, for insights into firefighting and EMT protocols in north central Pennsylvania.

Joel Garver, who daily shows me true friendship and real love. Together, we are stronger. More.

My Heavenly Father, parent to the parentless, who gathers his children like chicks under his wing.

About the Author

Laurel Garver holds degrees in English and journalism and earns a living as a magazine editor. She enjoys quirky independent films, word games, British television, and Celtic music. She lives in Philadelphia with her husband and daughter. You can visit her online at http://laurelgarver.blogspot.com.

If you enjoyed this novel, please take a moment to post a review on one of the online book retailer sites. This helps new readers discover my work more than anything else. Thank you!

CPSIA information can be obtained at www.ICGtesting.com
Printed in the USA
LVOW10s1651300516

490484LV00057B/1461/P

9 781530 836918